D0202210

LINDA HOWARD

ESCAPE

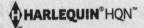
HARLEQUIN® HQN™

ISBN-13: 978-0-373-77840-9

ESCAPE

Copyright © 2014 by Harlequin Books S.A.

The publisher acknowledges the copyright holder of the individual works as follows:

HEARTBREAKER
Copyright © 1987 by Linda Howington

DUNCAN'S BRIDE
Copyright © 1990 by Linda Howington

Recycling programs for this product may not exist in your area.

HARLEQUIN®
www.Harlequin.com

Printed in U.S.A.

CONTENTS

HEARTBREAKER

CHAPTER ONE

SHE FOUND THE paper while she was sorting through the personal things in her father's desk. Michelle Cabot unfolded the single sheet with casual curiosity, just as she had unfolded dozens of others, but she had read only a paragraph when her spine slowly straightened and a tremor began in her fingers. Stunned, she began again, her eyes widening with sick horror at what she read.

Anybody but him. Dear God, anybody but him!

She owed John Rafferty one hundred thousand dollars.

Plus interest, of course. At what percent? She couldn't read any further to find out; instead she dropped the paper onto the littered surface of the desk and sank back in her father's battered old leather chair, her eyes closing against the nausea caused by shock, dread and the particularly sickening feeling of dying hope. She had already been on her knees; this unsuspected debt had smashed her flat.

Why did it have to be John Rafferty? Why not some impersonal bank? The end result would be the same, of course, but the humiliation would be absent. The thought of facing him made her shrivel deep inside, where she protected the tender part of herself. If Rafferty ever even suspected that that tenderness existed, she was lost. A dead duck...or a sitting one, if it made

any difference. A gone goose. A cooked goose. Whatever simile she used, it fit.

Her hands were still shaking when she picked up the
paper to read it again and work out the details of the
financial agreement. John Rafferty had made a personal loan of one hundred thousand dollars to her father,
Langley Cabot, at an interest rate two percent lower
than the market rate…and the loan had been due four
months ago. She felt even sicker. She knew it hadn't
been repaid, because she'd gone over every detail of
her father's books in an effort to salvage something
from the financial disaster he'd been floundering in
when he'd died. She had ruthlessly liquidated almost
everything to pay the outstanding debts, everything except this ranch, which had been her father's dream and
had somehow come to represent a refuge to her. She
hadn't liked Florida ten years ago, when her father had
sold their home and moved her from their well-ordered,
monied existence in Connecticut to the heat and humidity of a cattle ranch in central Florida, but that had been
a decade ago, and things changed. People changed, time
changed…and time changed people. The ranch didn't
represent love or a dream to her; it was, simply, all she
had left. Life had seemed so complicated once, but it
was remarkable how simple things were when it came
down to a matter of survival.

Even now it was hard to just give up and let the inevitable happen. She had known from the beginning
that it would be almost impossible for her to keep the
ranch and put it back on a paying basis, but she'd been
driven to at least *try*. She wouldn't have been able to
live with herself if she'd taken the easy way out and
let the ranch go.

Now she would have to sell the ranch, after all, or at

least the cattle; there was no other way she could repay that hundred thousand dollars. The wonder was that Rafferty hadn't already demanded repayment. But if she sold the cattle, what good was the ranch? She'd been depending on the cattle sales to keep her going, and without that income she'd have to sell the ranch anyway.

It was so hard to think of letting the ranch go; she had almost begun to hope that she might be able to hold on to it. She'd been afraid to hope, had tried not to, but still, that little glimmer of optimism had begun growing. Now she'd failed at this, just as she'd failed at everything else in her life: as daughter, wife, and now rancher. Even if Rafferty gave her an extension on the loan, something she didn't expect to happen, she had no real expectation of being able to pay it off when it came due again. The naked truth was that she had no expectations at all; she was merely hanging on.

Well, she wouldn't gain anything by putting it off. She had to talk to Rafferty, so it might as well be now. The clock on the wall said it wasn't quite nine-thirty; Rafferty would still be up. She looked up his number and dialed it, and the usual reaction set in. Even before the first ring sounded, her fingers were locked so tightly around the receiver that her knuckles were white, and her heart had lurched into a fast, heavy pounding that made her feel as if she'd been running. Tension knotted her stomach. Oh, damn! She wouldn't even be able to talk coherently if she didn't get a grip on herself!

The telephone was answered on the sixth ring, and by then Michelle had braced herself for the ordeal of talking to him. When the housekeeper said, "Rafferty residence," Michelle's voice was perfectly cool and even when she asked to speak to Rafferty.

"I'm sorry, he isn't in. May I take a message?"

It was almost like a reprieve, if it hadn't been for the knowledge that now she'd have to do it all over again. "Please have him call Michelle Cabot," she said, and gave the housekeeper her number. Then she asked, "Do you expect him back soon?"

There was only a slight hesitation before the housekeeper said, "No, I think he'll be quite late, but I'll give him your message first thing in the morning."

"Thank you," Michelle murmured, and hung up. She should have expected him to be out. Rafferty was famous, or perhaps notorious was a better word, for his sexual appetite and escapades. If he'd quieted down over the years, it was only in his hell-raising. According to the gossip she'd heard from time to time, his libido was alive and well; a look from those hard, dark eyes still made a woman's pulse go wild, and he looked at a lot of women, but Michelle wasn't one of them. Hostility had exploded between them at their first meeting, ten years before, and at best their relationship was an armed standoff. Her father had been a buffer between them, but now he was dead, and she expected the worst. Rafferty didn't do things by half measures.

There was nothing she could do about the loan that night, and she'd lost her taste for sorting through the remainder of her father's papers, so she decided to turn in. She took a quick shower; her sore muscles would have liked a longer one, but she was doing everything she could to keep her electricity bill down, and since she got her water from a well, and the water was pumped by an electric pump, small luxuries had to go to make way for the more important ones, like eating.

But as tired as she was, when she was lying in bed she couldn't go to sleep. The thought of talking to Rafferty filled her mind again, and once more her heartbeat speeded up. She tried to take deep, slow breaths. It had always been like this, and it was even worse when she had to see him face-to-face. If only he wasn't so big! But he was six feet three inches and about two hundred pounds of muscled masculinity; he was good at dwarfing other people. Whenever he was close, Michelle felt threatened in some basic way, and even thinking of him made her feel suffocated. No other man in the world made her react the way he did; no one else could make her so angry, so wary—or so excited in a strange, primitive way.

It had been that way from the beginning, from the moment she'd met him ten years before. She had been eighteen then, as spoiled as he'd accused her of being, and as haughty as only a teenager standing on her dignity could be. His reputation had preceded him, and Michelle had been determined to show him that *she* couldn't be lumped with all the women who panted after him. As if he would have been interested in a teenager! she thought wryly, twisting on the bed in search of comfort. What a child she'd been! A silly, spoiled, frightened child.

Because John Rafferty *had* frightened her, even though he'd all but ignored her. Or rather, her own reaction had frightened her. He'd been twenty-six, a *man*, as opposed to the boys she was used to, and a man who had already turned a smallish central Florida cattle ranch into a growing, thriving empire by his own force of will and years of backbreaking work. Her first sight of him, towering over her father while the two men talked cattle, had scared her half to death. Even now she could recall her sudden breathlessness, as if she'd been punched in the stomach.

They'd been standing beside Rafferty's horse, and

he'd had one arm draped across the saddle while his other hand was propped negligently on his hip. He'd been six feet and three inches of sheer power, all hard muscle and intensity, dominating even the big animal with his will. She'd already heard about him; men laughed and called him a "stud" in admiring tones, and women called him the same thing, but always in excited, half-fearful whispers. A woman might be given the benefit of the doubt after going out with him once, but if she went out with him twice it was accepted that she had been to bed with him. At the time Michelle hadn't even considered that his reputation was probably exaggerated. Now that she was older, she still didn't consider it. There was just something about the way Rafferty looked that made a woman believe all the tales about him.

But even his reputation hadn't prepared her for the real man, for the force and energy that radiated from him. Life burned hotter and brighter in some people, and John Rafferty was one of them. He was a dark fire, dominating his surroundings with his height and powerful build, dominating people with his forceful, even ruthless, personality.

Michelle had sucked in her breath at the sight of him, the sun glinting off his coal-black hair, his dark eyes narrowed under prominent black brows, a neat black mustache shadowing the firm line of his upper lip. He'd been darkly tanned, as he always was from hours of working outside in all seasons; even as she'd watched, a trickle of sweat had run down his temple to curve over his high, bronzed cheekbone before tracking down his cheek to finally drip off his square jaw. Patches of sweat had darkened his blue work shirt under his arms and on his chest and back. But even sweat and dirt couldn't detract from the aura of a powerful, intensely sexual male animal; perhaps they had even added to it. The hand on his hip had drawn her gaze downward to his hips and long legs, and the faded tight jeans had outlined his body so faithfully that her mouth had gone dry. Her heart had stopped beating for a moment, then lurched into a heavy rhythm that made her entire body throb. She'd been eighteen, too young to handle what she felt, too young to handle the man, and her own reaction had frightened her. Because of that, she'd been at her snooty best when she'd walked up to her father to be introduced.

They'd gotten off on the wrong foot and had been there ever since. She was probably the only woman in the world at odds with Rafferty, and she wasn't certain, even now, that she wanted it to be any different. Somehow she felt safer knowing that he disliked her; at least he wouldn't be turning that formidable charm of his on her. In that respect, hostility brought with it a certain amount of protection.

A shiver ran over her body as she lay in bed thinking about both him and what she'd admitted only to herself: she was no more immune to Rafferty than the legion of women who had already succumbed. She was safe only as long as he didn't realize how vulnerable she was to his potent masculinity. He would delight in taking advantage of his power over her, making her pay for all the cutting remarks she'd made to him over the years, and for all the other things he disliked about her. To protect herself, she had to hold him at bay with hostility; it was rather ironic that now she needed his goodwill in order to survive financially.

She had almost forgotten how to laugh except for the social sounds that passed for laughter but held no humor, or how to smile except for the false mask of cheerfulness that kept pity away, but in the darkness and privacy of her bedroom she felt a wry grin curving her mouth. If she had to depend on Rafferty's goodwill for survival, she might as well go out to the pasture, dig a hole and pull the dirt in over herself to save him the time and trouble.

The next morning she loitered around the house waiting for him to call for as long as she could, but she had chores to do, and the cattle wouldn't wait. Finally she gave up and trudged out to the barn, her mind already absorbed with the hundred and one problems the ranch presented every day. She had several fields of hay that needed to be cut and baled, but she'd been forced to sell the tractor and hay baler; the only way she could get the hay cut would be to offer someone part of the hay if they'd do the cutting and baling for her. She backed the pickup truck into the barn and climbed into the hayloft, counting the bales she had left. The supply was dwindling; she'd have to do something soon.

There was no way she could lift the heavy bales, but she'd developed her own system for handling them. She had parked the truck just under the door to the hayloft, so all she had to do was push the bales to the open door and tip them through to land in the truck bed. Pushing the hay wasn't easy; they were supposed to be hundred-pound bales, which meant that she outweighed them by maybe seventeen pounds...if she hadn't lost weight, which she suspected she had, and if the bales weighed only a hundred pounds, which she suspected they didn't. Their weight varied, but some of them were so heavy she could barely move them an inch at a time.

She drove the truck across the pasture to where the cattle grazed; heads lifted, dark brown eyes surveyed the familiar truck, and the entire herd began ambling toward her. Michelle stopped the truck and climbed in back. Tossing the bales out was impossible, so she cut the twine there in the back of the truck and loosened the hay with the pitchfork she had brought along, then pitched the hay out in big clumps. She got back in the truck, drove a piece down the pasture, and stopped to repeat the procedure. She did it until the back of the pickup was empty, and by the time she was finished her shoulders were aching so badly the muscles felt as if they were on fire. If the herd hadn't been badly diminished in numbers from what it had been, she couldn't have handled it. But if the herd were larger, she reminded herself, she'd be able to afford help. When she remembered the number of people who used to work on the ranch, the number needed to keep it going properly, a wave of hopelessness hit her. Logic told her there was no way she could do it all herself.

But what did logic have to do with cold reality? She had to do it herself because she had no one else. Sometimes she thought that was the one thing life seemed determined to teach her: that she could depend only on herself, that there was no one she could trust, no one she could rely on, no one strong enough to stand behind her and hold her up when she needed to rest. There had been times when she'd felt a crushing sense of loneliness, especially since her father had died, but there was also a certain perverse comfort in knowing she could rely on no one but herself. She expected nothing of other people, therefore she wasn't disappointed by any failure on their part to live up to her expectations. She simply accepted facts as they were, without any pretty dressing up, did what she had to do, and went on from

there. At least she was free now, and no longer dreaded
waking up each day.

She trudged around the ranch doing the chores, putting her mind in neutral gear and simply letting her
body go through the motions. It was easier that way; she
could pay attention to her aches and bruises when all
the chores were finished, but the best way to get them
done was to ignore the protests of her muscles and the
nicks and bruises she acquired. None of her old friends
would ever have believed that Michelle Cabot was capable of turning her dainty hands to rough, physical
chores. Sometimes it amused her to imagine what their
reactions would be, another mind game that she played
with herself to pass the time. Michelle Cabot had always been ready for a party, or shopping, or a trip to
St. Moritz, or a cruise on someone's yacht. Michelle
Cabot had always been laughing, making wisecracks
with the best of them; she'd looked perfectly *right* with
a glass of champagne in her hand and diamonds in her
ears. The ultimate Golden Girl, that was her.

Well, the ultimate Golden Girl had cattle to feed, hay
to cut, fences that needed repair, and that was only the
tip of the iceberg. She needed to dip the cattle, but that
was something else she hadn't figured out how to manage by herself. There was branding, castrating, breeding.... When she allowed herself to think of everything
that needed doing, she was swamped by hopelessness,
so she usually didn't dwell on it. She just took each day
as it came, slogging along, doing what she could. It was
survival, and she'd become good at it.

By ten o'clock that night, when Rafferty hadn't
called, Michelle braced herself and called him again.
Again the housekeeper answered; Michelle stifled a
sigh, wondering if Rafferty ever spent a night at home.

"This is Michelle Cabot. I'd like to speak to Rafferty, please. Is he home?"

"Yes, he's down at the barn. I'll switch your call to him."

So he had a telephone in the barn. For a moment she thought enviously of the operation he had as she listened to the clicks the receiver made in her ear. Thinking about his ranch took her mind off her suddenly galloping pulse and stifled breathing.

"Rafferty." His deep, impatient voice barked the word in her ear, and she jumped, her hand tightening on the receiver as her eyes closed.

"This is Michelle Cabot." She kept her tone as remote as possible as she identified herself. "I'd like to talk to you, if you have the time."

"Right now I'm damned short of time. I've got a mare in foal, so spit it out and make it fast."

"It'll take more time than that. I'd like to make an appointment, then. Would it be convenient for me to come over tomorrow morning?"

He laughed, a short, humorless bark. "This is a working ranch, sugar, not a social event. I don't have time for you tomorrow morning. Time's up."

"Then when?"

He muttered an impatient curse. "Look, I don't have time for you *now*. I'll drop by tomorrow afternoon on my way to town. About six." He hung up before she could agree or disagree, but as she hung up, too, she thought ruefully that he was calling the shots, so it didn't really matter if she liked the time or not. At least she had the telephone call behind her now, and there were almost twenty hours in which to brace herself for actually seeing him. She would stop work tomorrow in time to shower and wash her hair, and she'd do the whole routine with makeup and perfume, wear her white linen trousers and white silk shirt. Looking at her, Rafferty would never suspect that she was anything other than what he'd always thought her to be, pampered and useless.

IT WAS LATE in the afternoon, the broiling sun had pushed the temperature to a hundred degrees, and the cattle were skittish. Rafferty was hot, sweaty, dusty and ill-tempered, and so were his men. They'd spent too much time chasing after strays instead of getting the branding and inoculating done, and now the deep, threatening rumble of thunder signaled a summer thunderstorm. The men speeded up their work, wanting to get finished before the storm hit.

Dust rose in the air as the anxious bawling increased in volume and the stench of burning hide intensified. Rafferty worked with the men, not disdaining any of the dirty jobs. It was *his* ranch, his life. Ranching was hard, dirty work, but he'd made it profitable when others had gone under, and he'd done it with his own sweat and steely determination. His mother had left rather than tolerate the life; of course, the ranch had been much smaller back then, not like the empire he'd built. His father, and the ranch, hadn't been able to support her in the style she'd wanted. Rafferty sometimes got a grim satisfaction from the knowledge that now his mother regretted having been so hasty to desert her husband and son so long ago. He didn't hate her; he didn't waste that much effort on her. He just didn't have much use for her, or for any of the rich, spoiled, bored, *useless* people she considered her friends.

Nev Luther straightened from the last calf, wiping his sweaty face on his shirtsleeve, then glancing at the sun and the soaring black cloud bank of the approaching storm. "Well, that's it," he grunted. "We'd better get loaded up before that thing hits." Then he glanced at his boss. "Ain't you supposed to see that Cabot gal today?"

Nev had been in the barn with Rafferty when he'd talked to Michelle, so he'd overheard the conversation. After a quick look at his watch, Rafferty swore aloud. He'd forgotten about her, and he wasn't grateful to Nev for reminding him. There were few people walking the earth who irritated him as much as Michelle Cabot.

"Damn it, I guess I'd better go," he said reluctantly. He knew what she wanted. It had surprised him that she had called at all, rather than continuing to ignore the debt. She was probably going to whine about how little money she had left and tell him that she couldn't *possibly* scrape up that amount. Just thinking about her made him want to grab her and shake her, hard. Or better yet, take a belt to her backside. She was exactly what he disliked most: a spoiled, selfish parasite who'd never done a day's work in her life. Her father had bankrupted himself paying for her pleasure jaunts, but Langley Cabot had always been a bit of a fool where his beloved only child had been concerned. Nothing had been too good for darling little Michelle, nothing at all.

Too bad that darling Michelle was a spoiled brat. Damn, she irritated him! She'd irritated him from the first moment he'd seen her, prissing up to where her father had stood talking to him, with her haughty nose in the air as if she'd smelled something bad. Well, maybe she had. Sweat, the product of physical work, was an alien odor to her. She'd looked at him the way she would have looked at a worm, then dismissed him as unimportant and turned her back to him while she coaxed and wheedled something out of her father with that charming Golden Girl act of hers.

"Say, boss, if you don't want to see that fancy little thing, I'd be happy to fill in for you," Nev offered, grinning.

"It's tempting," Rafferty said sourly, checking his watch again. He could go home and clean up, but it would make him late. He wasn't that far from the Cabot ranch now, and he wasn't in the mood to drive all the way back to his house, shower, and then make the drive again just so he wouldn't offend her dainty nose. She could put up with him as he was, dirt, sweat and all; after all, she was the one begging for favors. The mood he was in, he just might call in that debt, knowing good and well she couldn't pay it. He wondered with sardonic amusement if she would offer to pay it in another way. It would serve her right if he played along; it would make her squirm with distaste to think of letting him have her pampered body. After all, he was rough and dirty and worked for a living.

As he strode over to his truck and slid his long length under the steering wheel, he couldn't keep the image from forming in his mind: the image of Michelle Cabot lying beneath him, her slim body naked, her pale gold hair spread out over his pillow as he moved in and out of her. He felt his loins become heavy and full in response to the provocative image, and he swore under his breath. Damn her, and damn himself. He'd spent years watching her, brooding, wanting her and at the same time wanting to teach her in whatever way it took not to be such a spoiled, selfish snob.

Other people hadn't seen her that way; she could be charming when she chose, and she'd chosen to work that charm on the local people, maybe just to amuse herself with their gullibility. The ranchers and farmers in the area were a friendly group, rewarding themselves for their endless hard work with informal get-togethers, parties and barbecues almost every weekend, and Michelle had had them all eating out of her hand. They didn't see the side of her that she'd revealed to him; she was always laughing, dancing…but never with him. She would dance with every other man there, but never with him. He'd watched her, all right, and because he was a healthy male with a healthy libido he hadn't been able to stop himself from responding physically to her lithe, curved body and sparkling smile, even though it made him angry that he responded to her in any way. He didn't want to want her, but just looking at her made him hungry.

Other men had watched her with hungry eyes, too, including Mike Webster. Rafferty didn't think he'd ever forgive her for what she'd done to Mike, whose marriage had been shaky even before Michelle had burst onto the scene with her flirtatious manner and sparkling laughter. Mike hadn't been any match for her; he'd fallen hard and fast, and the Webster marriage had splintered beyond repair. Then Michelle had flitted on to fresher prey, and Mike had been left with nothing but a ruined life. The young rancher had lost everything he'd worked for, forced to sell his ranch because of the divorce settlement. He was just one more man Michelle had ruined with her selfishness, as she'd ruined her father. Even when Langley was deep in financial trouble he'd kept providing money for Michelle's expensive life-style. Her father had been going under, but she'd still insisted on buying her silks and jewels, and skiing vacations in St. Moritz. It would take a rich man to afford Michelle Cabot, and a strong one.

The thought of being the one who provided her with those things, and the one who had certain rights over her because of it, teased his mind with disturbing persistence. No matter how angry, irritated or disgusted he felt toward her, he couldn't control his physical response to her. There was something about her that made him want to reach out and take her. She looked, sounded and smelled expensive; he wanted to know if she tasted expensive, too, if her skin was as silky as it looked. He wanted to bury his hands in her sunlit hair, taste her wide, soft mouth, and trace his fingertips across the chiseled perfection of her cheekbones, inhale the gut-tightening fragrance of her skin. He'd smelled her the day they'd first met, the perfume in her hair and on her skin, and the sweetness of her flesh beneath it. She was expensive all right, too expensive for Mike Webster, and for the poor sap she'd married and then left, certainly too expensive for her father. Rafferty wanted to lose himself in all that richness. It was a pure, primitive male instinct, the reaction of the male to a ready female. Maybe Michelle was a tease, but she gave out all the right signals to bring the men running, like bees to the sweetest flower.

Right now Michelle was between supporters, but he knew it wouldn't be long before she had another man lined up. Why shouldn't he be that man? He was tired of wanting her and watching her turn her snooty little nose up at him. She wouldn't be able to wrap him around her finger as she was used to doing, but that would be the price she had to pay for her expensive tastes. Rafferty narrowed his eyes against the rain that began to splat against the windshield, thinking about the satisfaction of having Michelle dependent on him for everything she ate and wore. It was a hard, primitive satisfaction.

He would use her to satisfy his burning physical hunger for her, but he wouldn't let her get close enough to cloud his mind and judgment.

He'd never paid for a woman before, never been a sugar daddy, but if that was what it took to get Michelle Cabot, he'd do it. He'd never wanted another woman the way he wanted her, so he guessed it evened out.

The threatening storm suddenly broke, sending a sheet of rain sluicing down the windshield to obscure his vision despite the wipers' best efforts. Gusts of wind shoved at the truck, making him fight to hold it steady on the road. Visibility was so bad that he almost missed the turn to the Cabot ranch even though he knew these roads as well as he knew his own face. His features were dark with ill-temper when he drove up to the Cabot house, and his disgust increased as he looked around. Even through the rain, he could tell the place had gone to hell. The yard was full of weeds, the barn and stables had the forlorn look of emptiness and neglect, and the pastures that had once been dotted with prime Brahman cattle were empty now. The little society queen's kingdom had dissolved around her.

Though he'd pulled the truck up close to the house, it was raining so hard that he was drenched to the skin by the time he sprinted to the porch. He slapped his straw hat against his leg to get most of the water off it, but didn't replace it on his head. He raised his hand to knock, but the door opened before he had a chance. Michelle stood there looking at him with the familiar disdain in her cool, green eyes. She hesitated for just a moment, as if reluctant to let him drip water on the carpet; then she pushed the screen door open and said, "Come in." He imagined it ate at her guts to have to be nice to him because she owed him a hundred thousand dollars.

He walked past her, noting the way she moved back so he wouldn't brush against her. Just wait, he thought savagely. Soon he'd do more than just *brush* against her, and he'd make damned certain she liked it. She might turn her nose up at him now, but things would be different when she was naked under him, her legs wrapped around his waist while she writhed in ecstasy. He didn't just want the use of her body; he wanted her to want him in return, to feel as hungry and obsessed as he did. It would be poetic justice, after all the men she'd used. He almost wanted her to say something snide, so he'd have a reason to put his hands on her, even in anger. He wanted to touch her, no matter what the reason; he wanted to feel her warm and soft in his hands; he wanted to make her respond to him.

But she didn't cut at him with her tongue as she usually did. Instead she said, "Let's go into Dad's office," and led the way down the hall with her perfume drifting behind her to tease him. She looked untouchable in crisp white slacks and a white silk shirt that flowed lovingly over her curvy form, but he itched to touch her anyway. Her sunny pale-gold hair was pulled back and held at the nape of her neck with a wide gold clip.

Her fastidious perfection was in direct contrast to his own rough appearance, and he wondered what she'd do if he touched her, if he pulled her against him and got her silk shirt wet and stained. He was dirty and sweaty and smelled of cattle and horses, and now he was wet into the bargain; no, there was no way she'd accept his touch.

"Please sit down," she said, waving her hand at one

of the leather chairs in the office. "I imagine you know why I called."

His expression became even more sardonic. "I imagine I do."

"I found the loan paper when I was going through Daddy's desk the night before last. I don't want you to think that I'm trying to weasel out of paying it, but I don't have the money right now—"

"Don't waste my time," he advised, interrupting.

She stared up at him. He hadn't taken the chair she'd offered; he was standing too close, towering over her, and the look in his black eyes made her shiver.

"What?"

"This song and dance; don't waste my time doing the whole bit. I know what you're going to offer, and I'm willing. I've been wanting to get in your pants for a long time, honey; just don't make the mistake of thinking a few quickies will make us even, because they won't. I believe in getting my money's worth."

CHAPTER TWO

SHOCK FROZE HER in place and leached the color from her upturned face until it was as pale as ivory. She felt disoriented; for a moment his words refused to make sense, rotating in her mind like so many unconnected pieces of a puzzle. He was looming over her, his height and muscularity making her feel as insignificant as always, while the heat and scent of his body overwhelmed her senses, confusing her. He was too close! Then the words realigned themselves, and their meaning slapped her in the face. Panic and fury took the place of shock. Without thinking she drew back from him and snapped, "You must be joking!"

It was the wrong thing to say. She knew it as soon as she'd said it. Now wasn't the time to insult him, not when she needed his cooperation if she wanted to have a prayer of keeping the ranch going, but both pride and habit made her lash back at him. She could feel her stomach tighten even as she lifted her chin to give him a haughty stare, waiting for the reaction that was sure to come after the inadvertent challenge she'd thrown in his teeth. It wasn't safe to challenge Rafferty at all, and now she'd done it in the most elemental way possible.

His face was hard and still, his eyes narrowed and burning as he watched her. Michelle could feel the iron control he exerted to keep himself from moving. "Do I look like I'm joking?" he asked in a soft, dangerous

tone. "You've always had some poor sucker supporting you; why shouldn't it be my turn? You can't lead
me around by the nose the way you have every other
man, but the way I see it, you can't afford to be too
choosy right now."

"What would *you* know about being choosy?" She
went even whiter, retreating from him a few more steps;
she could almost feel his impact on her skin, and he
hadn't even moved. He'd had so many women that she
didn't even want to think about it, because thinking
about it made her hurt deep inside. Had those other
women felt this helpless, this overwhelmed by his heat
and sexuality? She couldn't control her inborn instincts
and responses; she had always sensed her own weakness where he was concerned, and that was what frightened her, what had kept her fighting him all these years.
She simply couldn't face being used by him as casually
as a stallion would service a mare; it would mean too
much to her, and too little to him.

"Don't pull away from me," he said, his voice going
even softer, deeper, stroking her senses like dark velvet.
It was the voice he would use in the night, she thought
dazedly, her mind filled with the image of him covering
a woman with his lean, powerful body while he murmured rawly sexual things in her ear. John wouldn't
be a subtle lover; he would be strong and elemental,
overwhelming a woman's senses. Wildly she blanked
the image from her mind, turning her head away so
she couldn't see him.

Rage lashed at him when she turned away as if she
couldn't bear the sight of him; she couldn't have made
it any plainer that she couldn't bear the idea of sleeping with him, either. With three long strides he circled
the desk and caught her upper arms in his lean, sinewy

hands, pulling her hard against him. Even in his fury he realized that this was the first time he'd touched her, felt her softness and the fragility of her bones. His hands completely encircled her arms, and his fingers wanted to linger, to stroke. Hunger rose again, pushing aside some of the anger. "Don't turn your nose up at me like some Ice Princess," he ordered roughly. "Your little kingdom has gone to hell, honey, in case you haven't noticed. Those fancy playmates of yours don't know you from Adam's housecat now that you can't afford to play. They sure haven't offered to help, have they?"

Michelle pushed against his chest, but it was like trying to move a wall. "I haven't asked them to help!" she cried, goaded. "I haven't asked anyone for help, least of all *you*!"

"Why not me?" He shook her lightly, his eyes narrowed and fierce. "I can afford you, honey."

"I'm not for sale!" She tried to pull back, but the effort was useless; though he wasn't holding her tightly enough to hurt, she was helpless against his steely strength.

"I'm not interested in buying," he murmured as he dipped his head. "Only in renting you for a while." Michelle made an inarticulate sound of protest and tried to turn her head away, but he simply closed his fist in her hair and held her still for his mouth. Just for a moment she saw his black eyes, burning with hunger, then his mouth was on hers, and she quivered in his arms like a frightened animal. Her eyelashes fluttered shut and she sank against him. For years she'd wondered about his mouth, his taste, if his lips would be firm or soft, if his mustache would scratch. Pleasure exploded in her like a fireball, flooding her with heat. Now she knew. Now she knew the warm, heady taste of his mouth, the firm fullness of his lips, the soft prickle of his mustache, the sure way his tongue moved into her mouth as if it were his right to be so intimate. Somehow her arms were around his shoulders, her nails digging through the wet fabric of his shirt to the hard muscle beneath. Somehow she was arched against him, his arms locked tight as he held her and took her mouth so deeply, over and over again. She didn't feel the moisture from his clothing seeping into hers; she felt only his heat and hardness, and dimly she knew that if she didn't stop soon, *he* wouldn't stop at all.

She didn't want to stop. Already she was coming apart inside, because she wanted nothing more than to simply lie against him and feel his hands on her. She'd known it would be like this, and she'd known she couldn't let it happen, couldn't let him get close to her. The feeling was so powerful that it frightened her. *He* frightened her. He would demand too much from her, take so much that there wouldn't be anything left when he moved on. She'd always known instinctively that she couldn't handle him.

It took every bit of inner strength she had to turn her face away from his mouth, to put her hands on his shoulders and push. She knew she wasn't strong enough to move him; when he released her and moved back a scant few inches, she was bitterly aware that it was by his own choice, not hers. He was watching her, waiting for her decision.

Silence filled the room with a thick presence as she struggled to regain her composure under his unwavering gaze. She could feel the situation slipping out of control. For ten years she had carefully cultivated the hostility between them, terrified of letting him discover that just looking at him turned her bones to water. She'd seen too many of his women with stars in their eyes while he gave them his attention, focusing his intense sexual instincts on them, but all too soon he'd moved on to someone else, and the stars had always turned into hunger and pain and emptiness. Now he was looking at her with that penetrating attention, just what she'd always tried to avoid. She hadn't wanted him to notice her as a woman; she hadn't wanted to join the ranks of all those other women he'd used and left. She had enough trouble now, without adding a broken heart, and John Rafferty was a walking heartache. Her back was already to the wall; she couldn't bear anything else, either emotionally or financially.

But his gaze burned her with black fire, sliding slowly over her body as if measuring her breasts for the way they would fit his hands, her hips for the way his would adjust against them, her legs for the way they would wrap around him in the throes of pleasure. He'd never looked at her in that way before, and it shook her down to her marrow. Pure sexual speculation was in his eyes. In his mind he was already inside her, tasting her, feeling her, giving her pleasure. It was a look few women could resist, one of unashamed sexuality, carnal experience and an arrogant confidence that a woman would be ultimately satisfied in his arms. He wanted her; he intended to have her.

And she couldn't let it happen. She'd been wrapped in a silken prison her entire life, stifled first by her father's idealistic adoration, then by Roger Beckman's obsessive jealousy. For the first time in her life she was alone, responsible for herself and finding some sense of worth in the responsibility. Fail or succeed, she needed to do this herself, not run to some man for help. She looked at John with a blank expression; he wanted her, but he didn't like or even respect her, and she wouldn't like or respect herself if she let herself become the parasite he expected her to be.

Slowly, as if her muscles ached, she eased away from him and sat down at the desk, tilting her golden head down so he couldn't see her face. Again, pride and habit came to her aid; her voice was calm and cool when she spoke. "As I said, I don't have the money to repay you right now, and I realize the debt is already delinquent. The solution depends on you—"

"I've already made my offer," he interrupted, his eyes narrowing at her coolness. He hitched one hip up on the desk beside her, his muscled thigh brushing against her arm. Michelle swallowed to alleviate the sudden dryness of her mouth, trying not to look at those powerful, denim-covered muscles. Then he leaned down, propping his bronzed forearm on his thigh, and that was worse, because it brought his torso closer, forcing her to lean back in the chair. "All you have to do is go ahead and accept it, instead of wasting time pretending you didn't like it when I touched you."

Michelle continued doggedly. "If you want repayment immediately, I'll have to sell the cattle to raise the money, and I'd like to avoid that. I'm counting on the sale of the cattle to keep the ranch going. What I have in mind is to sell some of the land to raise the money, but of course that will take longer. I can't even promise to have the money in six months; it just depends on how fast I can find a buyer." She held her breath, waiting for his response. Selling part of the land was the only plan she'd been able to devise, but it all depended on his cooperation.

Slowly he straightened, his dark brows drawing together as he stared down at her. "Whoa, honey, let's backtrack a little. What do you mean, 'keep the ranch going'? The ranch is already dead."

"No, it isn't," she denied, stubbornness creeping into her tone. "I still have some cattle left."

"Where?" His disbelief was evident.

"In the south pasture. The fence on the east side needs repair, and I haven't—" She faltered at the growing anger in his dark face. Why should it matter to him? Their land joined mostly on the north; his cattle weren't in any danger of straying.

"Let's backtrack a little further," he said tightly. "Who's supposed to be working this herd?"

So that was it. He didn't believe her, because he knew there were no cowhands working here any longer. "I'm working the herd," she threw back at him, her face closed and proud. He couldn't have made it any plainer that he didn't consider her either capable or willing when it came to ranch work.

He looked her up and down, his brows lifting as he surveyed her. She knew exactly what he saw, because she'd deliberately created the image. He saw mauve-lacquered toenails, white high-heeled sandals, crisp white linen pants and the white silk shirt, damp now, from contact with his wet clothes. Suddenly Michelle realized that she was damp all along the front, and hectic color rose to burn along her cheekbones, but she lifted her chin just that much higher. Let him look, damn him.

"Nice," he drawled. "Let me see your hands."

Instinctively her hands curled into fists and she glared at him. "Why?"

He moved like a striking rattler, catching her wrist and holding her clenched hand in front of him. She pulled back, twisting in an effort to escape him, but he merely tightened his grip and pried her fingers open, then turned her palm to the light. His face was still and expressionless as he looked down at her hand for a long minute; then he caught her other hand and examined it, too. His grip gentled, and he traced his fingertips over the scratches and half-healed blisters, the forming calluses.

Michelle sat with her lips pressed together in a grim line, her face deliberately blank. She wasn't ashamed of her hands; work inevitably left its mark on human flesh, and she'd found something healing in the hard physical demands the ranch made on her. But no matter how honorable those marks, when John looked at them it was as if he'd stripped her naked and looked at her, as if he'd exposed something private. She didn't want him to know so much about her; she didn't want that intense interest turned on her. She didn't want pity from anyone, but she especially didn't want him to soften toward her.

Then his gaze lifted, those midnight eyes examining every inch of her proud, closed expression, and every instinct in her shrilled an alarm. Too late! Perhaps it had been too late from the moment he'd stepped onto the porch. From the beginning she'd sensed the tension in him, the barely controlled anticipation that she had mistaken for his usual hostility. Rafferty wasn't used to waiting for any woman he wanted, and she'd held him off for ten years. The only time she'd been truly safe from him had been during her brief marriage, when the distance between Philadelphia and central Florida had been more than hundreds of miles; it had been the distance between two totally different life-styles, in both form and substance. But now she was back within reach, and this time she was vulnerable. She was broke, she was alone, and she owed him a hundred thousand dollars. He probably expected it to be easy.

"You didn't have to do it alone," he finally said, his deep voice somehow deeper and quieter. He still held her hands, and his rough thumbs still moved gently, caressingly, over her palms, as he stood and drew her to her feet. She realized that at no time had he hurt her; he'd held her against her will, but he hadn't hurt her. His touch was gentle, but she knew without even trying that she wouldn't be able to pull away from him until he voluntarily let her go.

Her only defense was still the light mockery she'd used against him from the beginning. She gave him a bright, careless smile. "Of course I did. As you so charmingly pointed out, I'm not exactly being trampled by all my friends rushing to my rescue, am I?"

His upper lip curled with contempt for those "friends." He'd never had any patience with the bored and idle rich. "You could've come to me."

Again she gave him that smile, knowing he hated it. "But it would take so *long* to work off a hundred-thousand-dollar debt in that fashion, wouldn't it? You know how I hate being bored. A really good prostitute makes—what?—a hundred dollars a throw? Even if you were up to it three times a day, it would still take about a year—"

Swift, dark fury burned in his eyes, and he finally released her hands, but only to move his grip to her shoulders. He held her still while he raked his gaze down her body again. "Three times a day?" he asked with that deceptive softness, looking at her breasts and hips. "Yeah, I'm up to it. But you forgot about interest, honey. I charge a lot of interest."

She quivered in his hands, wanting to close her eyes

against that look. She'd taunted him rashly, and he'd turned her words back on her. Yes, he was capable of it. His sexual drive was so fierce that he practically burned with it, attracting women like helpless moths. Desperately she dredged up the control to keep smiling, and managed a little shrug despite his hands on her shoulders. "Thanks anyway, but I prefer shoveling manure."

If he'd lost control of his temper then she would have breathed easier, knowing that she still had the upper hand, by however slim a margin. If she could push him away with insults, she'd be safe. But though his hands tightened a little on her shoulders, he kept a tight rein on his temper.

"Don't push too hard, honey," he advised quietly. "It wouldn't take much for me to show you right now what you really like. You'd be better off telling me just how in hell you think you're going to keep this ranch alive by yourself."

For a moment her eyes were clear and bottomless, filled with a desperation he wasn't quite certain he'd seen. Her skin was tight over her chiseled cheekbones; then the familiar cool mockery and defiance were back, her eyes mossy and opaque, her lips curling a little in the way that made him want to shake her. "The ranch is my problem," she said, dismissing the offer of aid implicit in his words. She knew the price he'd demand for his help. "The only way it concerns you is in how you want the debt repaid."

Finally he released her shoulders and propped himself against the desk again, stretching his long legs and crossing his booted feet at the ankle. "A hundred thousand is a lot of money. It wasn't easy to come up with that much cash."

She didn't need to be told that. John might be a mil-

lionaire in assets, but a rancher's money is tied up in
land and stock, with the profits constantly being plowed
back into the ranch. Cash simply wasn't available for
wasting on frivolities. Her jaw tightened. "When do
you want your money?" she demanded. "Now or later?"

His dark brows lifted. "Considering the circumstances, you should be trying to sweeten me up instead of snapping at me. Why haven't you just put the
ranch and cattle up for sale? You can't run the place
anyway, and at least then you'd have money to live on
until you find another meal ticket."

"I *can* run it," she flared, turning pale. She had to;
it was all she had.

"No way, honey."

"Don't call me honey!" The ragged fury of her own
voice startled her. He called every woman "honey."
It was a careless endearment that meant nothing, because so many other women had heard it from him. She
couldn't stand to think of him lying in the dark with
another woman, his voice lazy and dark as they talked
and he called her "honey."

He caught her chin in his big, rough hand, turning
her face up to his while his thumb rubbed over her lower
lip. "I'll call you whatever I want…*honey*, and you'll
keep your mouth shut, because you owe me a lot of
money that you can't repay. I'm going to think awhile
about that debt and what we're going to do about it.
Until I decide, why don't you think about this?"

Too late she tried to draw her head back, but he still
held her chin, and his warm mouth settled over hers before she could jerk free. Her eyes closed as she tried to
ignore the surge of pleasure in her midsection, tried to
ignore the way his lips moved over hers and his tongue
probed for entrance. If anything, this was worse than

before, because now he was kissing her with a slow assurance that beguiled even as he demanded. She tried to turn her head away, but he forestalled the movement, spreading his legs and pulling her inside the cradle of his iron-muscled thighs. Michelle began shaking. Her hands flattened against his chest, but she could feel his heartbeat pulsing strongly against her palm, feel the accelerated rhythm of it, and she wanted to sink herself into him. Slowly he wedged her head back against his shoulder, his fingers woven into her hair as he held her. There was no way she could turn her head away from him now, and slowly she began to give way to his will. Her mouth opened beneath his, accepting the slow thrust of his tongue as he penetrated her in that small way and filled her with his taste.

He kissed her with shattering absorption, as if he couldn't get enough of her. Even the dim thought that he must have practised his technique with hundreds of women didn't lessen its power. She was utterly wrapped around by him, overwhelmed by his touch and scent and taste, her body tingling and aching with both pleasure and the need to have more of him. She wanted him; she'd always wanted him. He'd been an obsession with her from the moment she had seen him, and she'd spent most of the past ten years running from the power of that obsession, only to wind up practically at his mercy anyway—if he had any mercy.

He lifted his head in slow motion, his dark eyes heavy lidded, his mouth moist from kissing her. Blatant satisfaction was written across his hard face as he surveyed her. She was lying limply against him, her face dazed with pure want, her lips red and swollen. Very gently he put her away from him, holding her with his hands on her waist until she was steady on her feet; then he got to his own feet.

As always when he towered over her, Michelle automatically retreated a step. Frantically she searched for control, for something to say to him to deny the response she'd just given him, but what could she say that he'd believe? She couldn't have been more obvious! But then, neither could he. It was useless to try to regain lost ground, and she wasn't going to waste time trying. All she could do was try to put a halt to things now.

Her face was pale as she faced him, her hands twisted together in a tight knot. "I won't sleep with you to pay that debt, no matter what you decide. Did you come here tonight expecting to whisk me straight up to bed, assuming that I'd choose to turn whore for you?"

He eyed her sharply. "The thought crossed my mind. I was willing."

"Well, I'm not!" Breath rushed swiftly in and out of her lungs as she tried to control the outrage that burned in her at the insult. She had to control it; she couldn't afford to fall apart now.

"I'm glad, because I've changed my mind," he said lazily.

"Gosh, that's big of you!" she snapped.

"You'll go to bed with me, all right, but it won't be because of any money you owe me. When the time comes, you'll spread your legs for me because you want me just the way I want you."

The way he was looking at her made her shiver, and the image his rough words provoked shot through her brain like lightning. He would use her up and toss her away, just as he had all those other women, if she let him get too close to her. "Thanks, but no thanks. I've never gone in for group sex, and that's what it would be like with you!"

She wanted to make him angry, but instead he cupped her knotted-up hands in his palm and lightly rubbed his thumb over her knuckles. "Don't worry, I can guarantee there'll just be the two of us between the sheets. Settle down and get used to the idea. I'll be back out tomorrow to look over the ranch and see what needs to be done—"

"No," she interrupted fiercely, jerking her hands from his grip. "The ranch is mine. I can handle it on my own."

"Honey, you've never even handled a checkbook on your own. Don't worry about it; I'll take care of everything."

His amused dismissal set her teeth on edge, more because of her own fear that he was right than anything else. "I don't want you to take care of everything!"

"You don't know what you want," he replied, leaning down to kiss her briefly on the mouth. "I'll see you tomorrow."

Just like that he turned and walked out of the room, and after a moment Michelle realized he was leaving. She ran after him and reached the front door in time to see him sprinting through the downpour to his truck.

He didn't take her seriously. Well, why should he? Michelle thought bitterly. No one else ever had, either. She leaned on the doorframe and watched him drive away; her shaky legs needed the extra support. Why now? For years she'd kept him at a distance with her carefully manufactured hostility, but all of a sudden her protective barrier had shattered. Like a predator, he'd sensed her vulnerability and moved in for the kill.

Quietly she closed the door, shutting out the sound of

rain. The silent house enclosed her, an empty reminder of the shambles of her life.

Her jaw clenched as she ground her teeth together, but she didn't cry. Her eyes remained dry. She couldn't afford to waste her time or strength indulging in useless tears. Somehow she had to hold on to the ranch, repay that debt, and hold off John Rafferty....

The last would be the hardest of all, because she'd be fighting against herself. She didn't want to hold him off; she wanted to creep into his iron-muscled arms and feel them close around her. She wanted to feed her hunger for him, touch him as she'd never allowed herself to do, immerse herself in the man. Guilt arose in her throat, almost choking her. She'd married another man wanting John, loving John, *obsessed* with John; somehow Roger, her ex-husband, had sensed it, and his jealousy had turned their marriage into a nightmare.

Her mind burned with the memories, and to distract herself she walked briskly into the kitchen and prepared dinner for one; in this case, a bowl of cornflakes in milk. It was also what she'd had for breakfast, but her nerves were too raw to permit any serious cooking. She was actually able to eat half of the bowlful of cereal before she suddenly dropped the spoon and buried her face in her hands.

All her life she'd been a princess, the darling, pampered apple of her parents' eyes, born to them when they were both nearing forty and had given up hope of ever having children. Her mother had been a gentle, vague person who had passed straight from her father's keeping into that of her husband, and thought that a woman's role in life was to provide a comfortable, loving home for her husband, who supported her. It wasn't an unusual outlook for her generation, and Michelle didn't fault her mother for it. Langley Cabot had protected and spoiled both his wife and his daughter; that was the way life was supposed to be, and it was a source of pride to him that he supported them very well indeed. When her mother died, Michelle had become the recipient of all that protective devotion. Langley had wanted her to have the best of everything; he had wanted her to be happy, and to his way of thinking he had failed as a father and provider if she weren't.

In those days Michelle had been content to let her father shower her with gifts and luxuries. Her life had been humming along just as she had always expected, until the day Langley had turned her world upside down by selling the Connecticut house where she'd grown up, and moved her down to a cattle ranch in central Florida, not far from the Gulf coast. For the first time in her life, Langley had been unmoved by her pleas. The cattle ranch was his dream come true, the answer to some deeply buried need in him that had been hidden under silk shirts, pin-striped suits and business appointments. Because he'd wanted it so badly, he had ignored Michelle's tears and tantrums and jovially assured her that before long she'd have new friends and would love the ranch as much as he did.

In that, he was partially right. She made new friends, gradually became accustomed to the heat, and even enjoyed life on a working cattle ranch. Langley had completely remodeled the old ranch house when he'd bought it, to ensure that his beloved daughter wasn't deprived in any way of the comfort she was accustomed to. So she'd adjusted, and even gone out of her way to assure him of her contentment. He deserved his dream, and she had felt ashamed that she'd tried to talk him out of it. He did so much to make her happy, the least she could do was return as much of the effort as she could.

Then she'd met John Rafferty. She couldn't believe that she'd spent ten years running from him, but it was true. She'd hated him and feared him and loved him all at once, with a teenager's wildly passionate obsession, but she had always seen one thing very clearly: he was more than she could handle. She had never daydreamed of being the one woman who could tame the rake; she was far too vulnerable to him, and he was too strong. He might take her and use her, but she wasn't woman enough to hold him. She was spoiled and pampered; he didn't even like her. In self-defense, she had devoted herself to making him dislike her even more to make certain he never made a move on her.

She had gone to an exclusive women's college back east, and after graduation had spent a couple of weeks with a friend who lived in Philadelphia. During that visit she'd met Roger Beckman, scion of one of the oldest and richest families in town. He was tall and black haired, and he even had a trim mustache. His resemblance to John was slight, except for those points, and Michelle couldn't say that she had consciously married Roger because he reminded her of John, but she was very much afraid that subconsciously she had done exactly that.

Roger was a lot of fun. He had a lazy manner about him, his eyes wrinkled at the edges from smiling so much, and he loved organized crazy games, like scavenger hunts. In his company Michelle could forget about John and simply have fun. She was genuinely fond of Roger, and came to love him as much as she would ever love any man who wasn't John Rafferty. The best thing she could do was forget about John, put him behind her, and get on with her life. After all, there had never been anything between them except her own fantasies, and Roger absolutely adored her. So she had married him, to the delight of both her father and his parents.

It was a mistake that had almost cost her her life.

At first everything had been fine. Then Roger had begun to show signs of jealousy whenever Michelle was friendly to another man. Had he sensed that she didn't love him as she should? That he owned only the most superficial part of her heart? Guilt ate at her even now, because Roger's jealousy hadn't been groundless. He hadn't been able to find the true target, so he'd lashed out whenever she smiled at any man, danced with any man.

The scenes had gotten worse, and one night he'd actually slapped her during a screaming fight after a party; she'd made the mistake of speaking to the same man twice while they raided the buffet table. Shocked, her face burning, Michelle had stared at her husband's twisted features and realized that his jealousy had driven him out of control. For the first time, she was afraid of him.

His action had shocked Roger, too, and he'd buried his face in her lap, clinging to her as he wept and begged her forgiveness. He'd sworn never to hurt her again; he'd said he would rather cut off his own hands than hurt her. Shaken to the core, Michelle did what thousands of women did when their husbands turned on them: she forgave him.

But it wasn't the last time. Instead, it got worse.

Michelle had been too ashamed and shocked to tell anyone, but finally she couldn't take any more and pressed charges against him. To her horror, his parents quietly bought off everyone involved, and Michelle was left without a legal leg to stand on, all evidence destroyed. Come hell or high water, the Beckmans would protect their son.

Finally she tried to leave him, but she had gotten no further than Baltimore before he caught up with her, his face livid with rage. It was then that Michelle realized he wasn't quite sane; his jealousy had pushed him over the edge. Holding her arm in a grip that left bruises for two weeks, he made the threat that kept her with him for the next two years: if she left him again, he'd have her father killed.

She hadn't doubted him, nor did she doubt that he'd get away with it; he was too well protected by his family's money and prestige, by a network of old family friends in the law business. So she'd stayed, terrified that he might kill her in one of his rages, but not daring to leave. No matter what, she had to protect her father.

But finally she found a way to escape. Roger had beaten her with a belt one night. But his parents had been in Europe on vacation, and by the time they found out about the incident it was too late to use their influence. Michelle had crept out of the house, gone to a hospital where her bruises and lacerations were treated and recorded, and she'd gotten copies of the records. Those records had bought her a divorce.

The princess would carry the scars to her grave.

CHAPTER THREE

THE TELEPHONE RANG as Michelle was nursing her second cup of coffee, watching the sun come up and preparing herself for another day of chores that seemed to take more and more out of her. Dark circles lay under her heavy-lidded eyes, testimony to hours of twisting restlessly in bed while her mind insisted on replaying every word John had said, every sensation his mouth and hands had evoked. His reputation was well earned, she had thought bitterly in the early hours. Lady-killer. His touch was burningly tender, but he was hell on his women anyway.

She didn't want to answer the phone, but she knew John well enough to know he never gave up once he set his mind on something. He'd be back, and she knew it. If that was him on the telephone, he'd come over if she didn't answer. She didn't feel up to dealing with him in person, so she picked up the receiver and muttered a hello.

"Michelle, darling."

She went white, her fingers tightening on the receiver. Had she conjured him up by thinking about him the night before? She tried *not* to think of him, to keep him locked in the past, but sometimes the nightmare memories surfaced, and she felt again the terror of being so alone and helpless, with no one she could trust to come to her aid, not even her father.

"Roger," she said faintly. There was no doubt. No one but her ex-husband said her name in that caressing tone, as if he adored her.

His voice was low, thick. "I need you, darling. Come back to me, please. I'm begging. I promise I'll never hurt you again. I'll treat you like a princess—"

"No," she gasped, groping for a chair to support her shaking legs. Cold horror made her feel sick. How could he even suggest that she come back?

"Don't say that, please," he groaned. "Michelle, Mother and Dad are dead. I need you now more than ever. I thought you'd come for their funeral last week, but you stayed away, and I can't stand it any longer. If you'll just come back I swear everything will be different—"

"We're divorced," she broke in, her voice thin with strain. Cold sweat trickled down her spine.

"We can be remarried. Please, darling—"

"No!" The thought of being remarried to him filled her with so much revulsion that she couldn't even be polite. Fiercely she struggled for control. "I'm sorry about your parents; I didn't know. What happened?"

"Plane crash." Pain still lingered in his hoarse voice. "They were flying up to the lake and got caught in a storm."

"I'm sorry," she said again, but even if she'd known in time to attend the funeral, she never would have gone. She would never willingly be in Roger's presence again.

He was silent a moment, and she could almost see him rub the back of his neck in the unconscious nervous gesture she'd seen so many times. "Michelle, I still love you. Nothing's any good for me without you. I swear, it won't be the same as it was; I'll never hurt you again. I was just so damned jealous, and I know now I didn't have any reason."

But he did! she thought, squeezing her eyes shut as guilt seeped in to mix with the raw terror evoked by simply hearing his voice. Not physically, but had there been any day during the past ten years when she hadn't thought of John Rafferty? When part of her hadn't been locked away from Roger and every other man because they weren't the heartbreaker who'd stolen her heart?

"Roger, don't," she whispered. "It's over. I'll never come back. All I want to do now is work this ranch and make a living for myself."

He made a disgusted sound. "You shouldn't be working that dinky little ranch! You're used to much better than that. I can give you anything you want."

"No," she said softly. "You can't. I'm going to hang up now. Goodbye, and please don't call me again." Very gently she replaced the receiver, then stood by the phone with her face buried in her hands. She couldn't stop trembling, her mind and body reeling with the ramifications of what he'd told her. His parents were dead, and she had been counting on them to control him. That was the deal she'd made with them; if they would keep Roger away from her, she wouldn't release the photos and medical report to the press, who would have a field day with the scandal. Imagine, a Beckman of Philadelphia nothing but a common wife-beater! That evidence had kept her father safe from Roger's insane threats, too, and now he was forever beyond Roger's reach. She had lived in hell to protect her father, knowing that Roger was capable of doing exactly what he'd threatened, and knowing after the first incident that his parents would make certain Roger was protected, no matter what.

She had honestly liked her in-laws until then, but her affection had died an irrevocable death when they had bought Roger out of trouble the first time he'd really hurt her. She had known their weakness then, and she had forced herself to wait. There was no one to help her; she had only herself. Once she had been desperate enough to mention it to her father, but he'd become so upset that she hadn't pushed it, and in only a moment he'd convinced himself that she'd been exaggerating. Marriage was always an adjustment, and Michelle was spoiled, highly strung. Probably it was just an argument over some minor thing, and the young couple would work things out.

The cold feeling of aloneness had spread through her, but she hadn't stopped loving him. He loved her, she knew he did, but he saw her as more of a doll than a human being. His perfect, loving darling. He couldn't accept such ugliness in her life. She had to be happy, or it would mean he'd failed her in some basic way as a father, protector and provider. For his own sake, he had to believe she was happy. That was his weakness, so she had to be strong for both of them. She had to protect him, and she had to protect herself.

There was no way she would ever go back to Roger. She had dealt with the nightmares and put them behind her; she had picked up the pieces of her life and gone on, not letting the memories turn her into a frightened shell. But the memories, and the fear, were still there, and all it took was hearing Roger's voice to make her break out in a cold sweat. The old feeling of vulnerability and isolation swept over her, making her feel sick.

She jerked around, wrenching herself from the spell, and dashed what was left of her coffee down the drain. The best thing was to be active, to busy herself with

whatever came to hand. That was the way she'd handled it when she had finally managed to get away from
Roger, globe-trotting for two years because her father
had thought that would take her mind off the divorce,
and she had let the constant travel distract her. Now she
had real work to do, work that left her exhausted and
aching but was somehow healing, because it was the
first worthwhile work she'd ever done.

IT HAD BEEN eating at him all morning.

He'd been in a bad mood from the moment he'd gotten out of bed, his body aching with frustration, as if
he were some randy teenager with raging hormones.
He was a long way from being a teenager, but his hormones were giving him hell, and he knew exactly why.
He hadn't been able to sleep for remembering the way
she'd felt against him, the sweetness of her taste and the
silky softness of her body. And she wanted him, too; he
was too experienced to be mistaken about something
like that. But he'd pushed too hard, driven by ten years
of having an itch he couldn't scratch, and she'd balked.
He'd put her in the position of paying him with her
body, and she hadn't liked that. What woman would?
Even the ones who were willing usually wanted a pretty
face put on it, and Michelle was haughtier than most.

But she hadn't looked haughty the day before. His
frown grew darker. She had tried, but the old snooty
coldness was missing. She was dead broke and had nowhere to turn. Perhaps she was scared, wondering what
she was going to do without the cushion of money that
had always protected her. She was practically helpless, having no job skills or talents other than social
graces, which weren't worth a hell of a lot on the mar-

ket. She was all alone on that ranch, without the people to work it.

He made a rough sound and pulled his horse's head around. "I'll be back later," he told Nev, nudging the horse's flanks with his boot heels.

Nev watched him ride away. "Good riddance," he muttered. Whatever was chewing on the boss had put him in the worst mood Nev had ever seen; it would be a relief to work without him.

John's horse covered the distance with long, easy strides; it was big and strong, seventeen hands high, and inclined to be a bit stubborn, but they had fought that battle a long time ago. Now the animal accepted the mastery of the iron-muscled legs and strong, steady hands of his rider. The big horse liked a good run, and he settled into a fast, smooth rhythm as they cut across pastures, his pounding hooves sending clods of dirt flying.

The more John thought about it, the less he liked it. She'd been trying to work that ranch by herself. It didn't fit in with what he knew of Michelle, but her fragile hands bore the marks. He had nothing but contempt for someone who disdained good honest work and expected someone else to do it for them, but something deep and primitive inside him was infuriated at the idea of Michelle even trying to manage the backbreaking chores around the ranch. Damn it, why hadn't she asked for help? Work was one thing, but no one expected her to turn into a cowhand. She wasn't strong enough; he'd held her in his arms, felt the delicacy of her bones, the greyhound slenderness of her build. She didn't need to be working cattle any more than an expensive thoroughbred should be used to plow a field. She could get hurt, and it might be days before anyone found her.

He'd always been disgusted with Langley for spoiling and protecting her, and with Michelle for just sitting back and accepting it as her due, but suddenly he knew just how Langley had felt. He gave a disgusted snort at himself, making the horse flick his ears back curiously at the sound, but the hard fact was that he didn't like the idea of Michelle's trying to work that ranch. It was a man's work, and more than one man, at that.

Well, he'd take care of all that for her, whether she liked it or not. He had the feeling she wouldn't, but she'd come around. She was too used to being taken care of, and, as he'd told her, now it was his turn.

Yesterday had changed everything. He'd felt her response to him, felt the way her mouth had softened and shaped itself to his. She wanted him, too, and the knowledge only increased his determination to have her. She had tried to keep him from seeing it; that acid tongue of hers would have made him lose his temper if he hadn't seen the flicker of uncertainty in her eyes. It was so unusual that he'd almost wanted to bring back the haughtiness that aggravated him so much.... Almost, but not quite. She was vulnerable now, vulnerable to him. She might not like it, but she needed him. It was an advantage he intended to use.

There was no answer at the door when he got to the ranch house, and the old truck was missing from its customary parking place in the barn. John put his fists on his hips and looked around, frowning. She had probably driven into town, though it was hard to think that Michelle Cabot was willing to let herself be seen in that kind of vehicle. It was her only means of transportation, though, so she didn't have much choice.

Maybe it was better that she was gone; he could check around the ranch without her spitting and hissing at him like an enraged cat, and he'd look at those cattle in the south pasture. He wanted to know just how many head she was running, and how they looked. She couldn't possibly handle a big herd by herself, but for her sake he hoped they were in good shape, so she could get a fair price for them. He'd handle it himself, make certain she didn't get rooked. The cattle business wasn't a good one for beginners.

He swung into the saddle again. First he checked the east pasture, where she had said the fence was down. Whole sections of it would have to be replaced, and he made mental notes of how much fencing it would take. The entire ranch was run-down, but fencing was critical; it came first. Lush green grass covered the east pasture; the cattle should be in it right now. The south pasture was probably overgrazed, and the cattle would show it, unless the herd was small enough that the south pasture could provide for its needs.

It was a couple of hours before he made it to the south pasture. He reined in the horse as he topped a small rise that gave him a good view. The frown snapped into place again, and he thumbed his hat onto the back of his head. The cattle he could see scattered over the big pasture didn't constitute a big herd, but made for far more than the small one he'd envisioned. The pasture was badly overgrazed, but scattered clumps of hay testified to Michelle's efforts to feed her herd. Slow-rising anger began to churn in him as he thought of her wrestling with heavy bales of hay; some of them probably weighed more than she did.

Then he saw her, and in a flash the anger rose to boiling point. The old truck was parked in a clump of trees, which was why he hadn't noticed it right off, and she was down there struggling to repair a section of fencing

by herself. Putting up fencing was a two-man job; one
person couldn't hold the barbed wire securely enough,
and there was always the danger of the wire backlash-
ing. The little fool! If the wire got wrapped around her,
she wouldn't be able to get out of it without help, and
those barbs could really rip a person up. The thought
of her lying tangled and bleeding in a coil of barbed
wire made him both sick and furious.

He kept the horse at an easy walk down the long
slope to where she was working, deliberately giving
himself time to get control of his temper. She looked up
and saw him, and even from the distance that still separated them he could see her stiffen. Then she turned
back to the task of hammering a staple into the fence
post, her jerky movements betraying her displeasure
at his presence.

He dismounted with a fluid, easy motion, never taking his gaze from her as he tied the reins to a low-hang-
ing tree branch. Without a word he pulled the strand of
wire to the next post and held it taut while Michelle,
equally silent, pounded in another staple to hold it.
Like him, she had on short leather work gloves, but
her gloves were an old pair of men's gloves that had
been left behind and were far too big for her, making it
difficult for her to pick up the staples, so she had pulled
off the left glove. She could handle the staples then,
but the wire had already nicked her unprotected flesh
several times. He saw the angry red scratches; some
of which were deep enough for blood to well, and he
wanted to shake her until her teeth rattled.

"Don't you have any better sense than to try to put
up fencing on your own?" he rasped, pulling another
strand tight.

She hammered in the staple, her expression closed. "It has to be done. I'm doing it."

"Not anymore, you aren't."

His flat statement made her straighten, her hand closing tightly around the hammer. "You want the payment right away," she said tonelessly, her eyes sliding to the cattle. She was a little pale, and tension pulled the skin tight across her high cheekbones.

"If that's what I have to do." He pried the hammer from her grip, then bent to pick up the sack of staples. He walked over to the truck, then reached in the open window and dropped them onto the floorboard. Then he lifted the roll of barbed wire onto the truck bed. "That'll hold until I can get my men out here to do it right. Let's go."

It was a good thing he'd taken the hammer away from her. Her hands balled into fists. "I don't want your men out here doing it right! This is still my land, and I'm not willing to pay the price you want for your help."

"I'm not giving you a choice." He took her arm, and no matter how she tried she couldn't jerk free of those long, strong fingers as he dragged her over to the truck, opened the door and lifted her onto the seat. He released her then, slamming the door and stepping back.

"Drive carefully, honey. I'll be right behind you."

She had to drive carefully; the pasture was too rough for breakneck speed, even if the old relic had been capable of it. She knew he was easily able to keep up with her on his horse, though she didn't check the rearview mirror even once. She didn't want to see him, didn't want to think about selling the cattle to pay her debt. That would be the end of the ranch, because she'd been relying on that money to keep the ranch going.

She'd hoped he wouldn't come back today, though it

had been a fragile hope at best. After talking to Roger that morning, all she wanted was to be left alone. She needed time by herself to regain her control, to push all the ugly memories away again, but John hadn't given her that time. He wanted her, and like any predator he'd sensed her vulnerability and was going to take advantage of it.

She wanted to just keep driving, to turn the old truck down the driveway, hit the road and keep on going. She didn't want to stop and deal with John, not now. The urge to run was so strong that she almost did it, but a glance at the fuel gauge made her mouth twist wryly. If she ran, she'd have to do it on foot, either that or steal John's horse.

She parked the truck in the barn, and as she slid off the high seat John walked the horse inside, ducking his head a little to miss the top of the door frame. "I'm going to cool the horse and give him some water," he said briefly. "Go on in the house. I'll be there in a minute."

Was postponing the bad news for a few minutes supposed to make her feel better? Instead of going straight to the house, she walked down to the end of the driveway and collected the mail. Once the mailbox had been stuffed almost every day with magazines, catalogs, newspapers, letters from friends, business papers, but now all that came was junk mail and bills. It was odd how the mail reflected a person's solvency, as if no one in the world wanted to communicate with someone who was broke. Except for past-due bills, of course. Then the communications became serious. A familiar envelope took her attention, and a feeling of dread welled in her as she trudged up to the house. The electric bill was past due; she'd already had one late notice, and here was another one. She had to come up with the money fast, or the power would be disconnected. Even knowing what it was, she opened the envelope anyway and scanned the notice. She had ten days to bring her account up to date. She checked the date of the notice; it had taken three days to reach her. She had seven days left.

But why worry about the electricity if she wouldn't have a ranch? Tiredness swept over her as she entered the cool, dim house and simply stood for a moment, luxuriating in the relief of being out of the broiling sun. She shoved the bills and junk mail into the same drawer of the entry table where she had put the original bill and the first late notice; she never forgot about them, but at least she could put them out of sight.

She was in the kitchen, having a drink of water, when she heard the screen door slam, then the sharp sound of boot heels on the oak parquet flooring as he came down the hallway. She kept drinking, though she was acutely aware of his progress through the house. He paused to look into the den, then the study. The slow, deliberate sound of those boots as he came closer made her shiver in reaction. She could see him in her mind's eye; he had a walk that any drugstore cowboy would kill for: that loose, long-legged, slim-hipped saunter, tight buttocks moving up and down. It was a walk that came naturally to hell-raisers and heartbreakers, and Rafferty was both.

She knew the exact moment when he entered the kitchen, though her back was to him. Her skin suddenly tingled, as if the air had become charged, and the house no longer seemed so cool.

"Let me see your hand." He was so close behind her that she couldn't turn without pressing against him, so she remained where she was. He took her left hand in his and lifted it.

"They're just scratches," she muttered.

She was right, but admitting it didn't diminish his anger. She shouldn't have any scratches at all; she shouldn't be trying to repair fencing. Her hand lay in his bigger, harder one like a pale, fragile bird, too tired to take flight, and suddenly he knew that the image was exactly right. She was tired.

He reached around her to turn on the water, then thoroughly soaped and rinsed her hand. Michelle hurriedly set the water glass aside, before it slipped from her trembling fingers, then stood motionless, with her head bowed. He was very warm against her back; she felt completely surrounded by him, with his arms around her while he washed her hand with the gentleness a mother would use to wash an infant. That gentleness staggered her senses, and she kept her head bent precisely to prevent herself from letting it drop back against his shoulder to let him support her.

The soap was rinsed off her hand now, but still he held it under the running water, his fingers lightly stroking. She quivered, trying to deny the sensuality of his touch. He was just washing her hand! The water was warm, but his hand was warmer, the rough calluses rasping against her flesh as he stroked her with a lover's touch. His thumb traced circles on her sensitive palm, and Michelle felt her entire body tighten. Her pulse leaped, flooding her with warmth. "Don't," she said thickly, trying unsuccessfully to pull free.

He turned off the water with his right hand, then moved it to her stomach and spread his fingers wide, pressing her back against his body. His hand was wet; she felt the dampness seeping through her shirt in front, and the searing heat of him at her back. The smell of horse and man rose from that seductive heat. Everything about the man was a come-on, luring women to him.

"Turn around and kiss me," he said, his voice low, daring her to do it.

She shook her head and remained silent, her head bent.

He didn't push it, though they both knew that if he had, she wouldn't have been able to resist him. Instead he dried her hand, then led her to the downstairs bathroom and made her sit on the lid of the toilet while he thoroughly cleaned the scratches with antiseptic. Michelle didn't flinch from the stinging; what did a few scratches matter, when she was going to lose the ranch? She had no other home, no other place she wanted to be. After being virtually imprisoned in that plush penthouse in Philadelphia, she needed the feeling of space around her. The thought of living in a city again made her feel stifled and panicky, and she would have to live in some city somewhere to get a job, since she didn't even have a car to commute. The old truck in the barn wouldn't hold up to a long drive on a daily basis.

John watched her face closely; she was distracted about something, or she would never have let him tend her hand the way he had. After all, it was something she could easily have done herself, and he'd done it merely to have an excuse to touch her. He wanted to know what she was thinking, why she insisted on working this ranch when it had to be obvious even to her that it was more than she could handle. It simply wasn't in character for her.

"When do you want the money?" she asked dully.

His mouth tightened as he straightened and pulled her to her feet. "Money isn't what I want," he replied.

Her eyes flashed with green fire as she looked at him. "I'm not turning myself into a whore, even for you! Did you think I'd jump at the chance to sleep with you? Your reputation must be going to your head...*stud*."

He knew people called him that, but when Michelle said it, the word dripped with disdain. He'd always hated that particular tone, so icy and superior, and it made him see red now. He bent down until his face was level with hers, their noses almost touching, and his black eyes were so fiery that she could see gold sparks in them. "When we're in bed, honey, you can decide for yourself about my reputation."

"I'm not going to bed with you," she said through clenched teeth, spacing the words out like dropping stones into water.

"The hell you're not. But it won't be for this damned ranch." Straightening to his full height again, he caught her arm. "Let's get that business settled right now, so it'll be out of the way and you can't keep throwing it in my face."

"You're the one who put it on that basis," she shot back as they returned to the kitchen. He dropped several ice cubes in a glass and filled it with water, then draped his big frame on one of the chairs. She watched his muscular throat working as he drained the glass, and a weak, shivery feeling swept over her. Swiftly she looked away, cursing her own powerful physical response to the mere sight of him.

"I made a mistake," he said tersely, putting the glass down with a thump. "Money has nothing to do with it. We've been circling each other from the day we met, sniffing and fighting like cats in heat. It's time we did something about it. As for the debt, I've decided what I want. Deed that land you were going to sell over to me instead, and we'll be even."

It was just like him to divide her attention like that, so she didn't know how to react or what to say. Part of her wanted to scream at him for being so smugly certain she would sleep with him, and part of her was flooded with relief that the debt had been settled so easily. He could have ruined her by insisting on cash, but he hadn't. He wasn't getting a bad deal, by any means; it was good, rich pastureland he was obtaining, and he knew it.

It was a reprieve, one she hadn't expected, and she didn't know how to deal with it, so she simply sat and stared at him. He waited, but when she didn't say anything he leaned back in his chair, his hard face becoming even more determined. "There's a catch," he drawled.

The high feeling of relief plummeted, leaving her sick and empty. "Let me guess," she said bitterly, shoving her chair back and standing. So it had all come down to the same thing, after all.

His mouth twisted wryly in self-derision. "You're way off, honey. The catch is that you let me help you. My men will do the hard labor from now on, and if I even hear of you trying to put up fencing again, you'll be sitting on a pillow for a month."

"If your men do my work, I'll still be in debt to you."

"I don't consider it a debt; I call it helping a neighbor."

"I call it a move to keep me obligated!"

"Call it what you like, but that's the deal. You're one woman, not ten men; you're not strong enough to take care of the livestock and keep the ranch up, and you don't have the money to afford help. You're mighty short on options, so stop kicking. It's your fault, anyway. If you hadn't liked to ski so much, you wouldn't be in this position."

She drew back, her green eyes locked on him. Her face was pale. "What do you mean?"

John got to his feet, watching her with the old look that said he didn't much like her. "I mean that part of the reason your daddy borrowed the money from me was so he could afford to send you to St. Moritz with your friends last year. He was trying to hold his head above water, but that didn't matter to you as much as living in style, did it?"

She had been pale before, but now she was deathly white. She stared at him as if he'd slapped her, and too late he saw the shattered look in her eyes. Swiftly he rounded the table, reaching for her, but she shrank away from him, folding in on herself like a wounded animal. How ironic that she should now be struggling to repay a debt made to finance a trip she hadn't wanted! All she'd wanted had been time alone in a quiet place, a chance to lick her wounds and finish recovering from a brutal marriage, but her father had thought resuming a life of trips and shopping with her friends would be better, and she'd gone along with him because it had made him happy.

"I didn't even want to go," she said numbly, and to her horror tears began welling in her eyes. She didn't want to cry; she hadn't cried in years, except once when her father died, and she especially didn't want to cry in front of Rafferty. But she was tired and off balance, disturbed by the phone call from Roger that morning, and this just seemed like the last straw. The hot tears slipped silently down her cheeks.

"God, don't," he muttered, wrapping his arms around her and holding her to him, her face pressed against his chest. It was like a knife in him to see those tears on her face, because in all the time he'd known her, he'd never before seen her cry. Michelle Cabot had faced life with either a laugh or a sharp retort, but never with tears. He found he preferred an acid tongue to this soundless weeping.

For just a moment she leaned against him, letting him support her with his hard strength. It was too tempting; when his arms were around her, she wanted to forget everything and shut the world out, as long as he was holding her. That kind of need frightened her, and she stiffened in his arms, then pulled free. She swiped her palms over her cheeks, wiping away the dampness, and stubbornly blinked back the remaining tears.

His voice was quiet. "I thought you knew."

She threw him an incredulous look before turning away. What an opinion he had of her! She didn't mind his thinking she was spoiled; her father had spoiled her, but mostly because he'd enjoyed doing it so much. Evidently John not only considered her a common whore, but a stupid one to boot.

"Well, I didn't. And whether I knew or not doesn't change anything. I still owe you the money."

"We'll see my lawyer tomorrow and have the deed drawn up, and that'll take care of the damned debt. I'll be here at nine sharp, so be ready. A crew of men will be here in the morning to take care of the fencing and get the hay out to the herd."

He wasn't going to give in on that, and he was right; it *was* too much for her, at least right now. She couldn't do it all simply because it was too much for one person to do. After she fattened up the beef cattle and sold them off, she'd have some capital to work with and might be able to hire someone part-time.

"All right. But keep a record of how much I owe you. When I get this place back on its feet, I'll repay every penny." Her chin was high as she turned to face him, her green eyes remote and proud. This didn't solve all her problems, but at least the cattle would be cared for. She still had to get the money to pay the bills, but that problem was hers alone.

"Whatever you say, honey," he drawled, putting his hands on her waist.

She only had time for an indrawn breath before his mouth was on hers, as warm and hard as she remembered, his taste as heady as she remembered. His hands tightened on her waist and drew her to him; then his arms were around her, and the kiss deepened, his tongue sliding into her mouth. Hunger flared, fanned into instant life at his touch. She had always known that once she touched him, she wouldn't be able to get enough of him.

She softened, her body molding itself to him as she instinctively tried to get close enough to him to feed that burning hunger. She was weak where he was concerned, just as all women were. Her arms were clinging around his neck, and in the end it was he who broke the kiss and gently set her away from him.

"I have work to get back to," he growled, but his eyes were hot and held dark promises. "Be ready tomorrow."

"Yes," she whispered.

CHAPTER FOUR

TWO PICKUP TRUCKS came up the drive not long after sunrise, loaded with fencing supplies and five of John's men. Michelle offered them all a cup of fresh coffee, which they politely refused, just as they refused her offer to show them around the ranch. John had probably given them orders that she wasn't to do anything, and they were taking it seriously. People didn't disobey Rafferty's orders if they wanted to continue working for him, so she didn't insist, but for the first time in weeks she found herself with nothing to do.

She tried to think what she'd done with herself before, but years of her life were a blank. What *had* she done? How could she fill the hours now, if working on her own ranch was denied her?

John drove up shortly before nine, but she had been ready for more than an hour and stepped out on the porch to meet him. He stopped on the steps, his dark eyes running over her in heated approval. "Nice," he murmured just loud enough for her to hear. She looked the way she should always look, cool and elegant in a pale yellow silk surplice dress, fastened only by two white buttons at the waist. The shoulders were lightly padded, emphasizing the slimness of her body, and a white enamel peacock was pinned to her lapel. Her sunshine hair was sleeked back into a demure twist; oversized sunglasses shielded her eyes. He caught the tantalizing fragrance of some softly bewitching perfume, and his body began to heat. She was aristocratic and expensive from her head to her daintily shod feet; even her underwear would be silk, and he wanted to strip every stitch of it away from her, then stretch her out naked on his bed. Yes, this was exactly the way she should look.

Michelle tucked her white clutch under her arm and walked with him to the car, immensely grateful for the sunglasses covering her eyes. John was a hardworking rancher, but when the occasion demanded he could dress as well as any Philadelphia lawyer. Any clothing looked good on his broad-shouldered, slim-hipped frame, but the severe gray suit he wore seemed to heighten his masculinity instead of restraining it. All hint of waviness had been brushed from his black hair. Instead of his usual pickup truck he was driving a dark gray two-seater Mercedes, a sleek beauty that made her think of the Porsche she had sold to raise money after her father had died.

"You said your men were going to help me," she said expressionlessly as he turned the car onto the highway several minutes later. "You didn't say they were going to take over."

He'd put on sunglasses, too, because the morning sun was glaring, and the dark lenses hid the probing look he directed at her stiff profile. "They're going to do the heavy work."

"After the fencing is repaired and the cattle are moved to the east pasture, I can handle things from there."

"What about dipping, castrating, branding, all the things that should've been done in the spring? You can't handle that. You don't have any horses, any men, and you sure as hell can't rope and throw a young bull from that old truck you've got."

Her slender hands clenched in her lap. Why did he have to be so right? She couldn't do any of those things, but neither could she be content as a useless ornament. "I know I can't do those things by myself, but I can help."

"I'll think about it," he answered noncommittally, but he knew there was no way in hell he'd let her. What could she do? It was hard, dirty, smelly, bloody work. The only thing she was physically strong enough to do was brand calves, and he didn't think she could stomach the smell or the frantic struggles of the terrified little animals.

"It's my ranch," she reminded him, ice in her tone. "Either I help, or the deal's off."

John didn't say anything. There was no point in arguing. He simply wasn't going to let her do it, and that was that. He'd handle her when the time came, but he didn't expect much of a fight. When she saw what was involved, she wouldn't want any part of it. Besides, she couldn't possibly like the hard work she'd been doing; he figured she was just too proud to back down now.

It was a long drive to Tampa, and half an hour passed without a word between them. Finally she said, "You used to make fun of my expensive little cars."

He knew she was referring to the sleek Mercedes, and he grunted. Personally, he preferred his pickup. When it came down to it, he was a cattle rancher and not much else, but he was damned good at what he did, and his tastes weren't expensive. "Funny thing about bankers," he said by way of explanation. "If they think you don't need the money all that badly, they're eager to loan it to you. Image counts. This thing is part of the image."

"And the members of your rotating harem prefer it, too, I bet," she gibed. "Going out on the town lacks something when you do it in a pickup."

"I don't know about that. Ever done it in a pickup?" he asked softly, and even through the dark glasses she could feel the impact of his glance.

"I'm sure *you* have."

"Not since I was fifteen." He chuckled, ignoring the biting coldness of her comment. "But a pickup never was your style, was it?"

"No," she murmured, leaning her head back. Some of her dates had driven fancy sports cars, some had driven souped-up Fords and Chevys, but it hadn't made any difference what they'd driven, because she hadn't made out with any of them. They had been nice boys, most of them, but none of them had been John Rafferty, so it hadn't mattered. He was the only man she'd ever wanted. Perhaps if she'd been older when she'd met him, or if she'd been secure enough in her own sexuality, things might have been different. What would have happened if she hadn't initiated those long years of hostility in an effort to protect herself from an attraction too strong for her to handle? What if she'd tried to get him interested in her, instead of warding him off?

Nothing, she thought tiredly. John wouldn't have wasted his time with a naive eighteen-year-old. Maybe later, when she'd graduated from college, the situation might have changed, but instead of coming home after graduation she had gone to Philadelphia...and met Roger.

They were out of the lawyer's office by noon; it hadn't been a long meeting. The land would be surveyed, the deed drawn up, and John's ranch would increase by quite a bit, while hers would shrink, but she was grateful that he'd come up with that solution. At least now she still had a chance.

His hand curled warmly around her elbow as they walked out to the car. "Let's have lunch. I'm too hungry to wait until we get home."

She was hungry, too, and the searing heat made her feel lethargic. She murmured in agreement as she fumbled for her sunglasses, missing the satisfied smile that briefly curled his mouth. John opened the car door and held it as she got in, his eyes lingering on the length of silken leg exposed by the movement. She promptly restored her skirt to its proper position and crossed her legs as she settled in the seat, giving him a questioning glance when he continued to stand in the open door. "Is something wrong?"

"No." He closed the door and walked around the car. Not unless she counted the way looking at her made him so hot that a deep ache settled in his loins. She couldn't move without making him think of making love to her. When she crossed her legs, he thought of uncrossing them. When she pulled her skirt down, he thought of pulling it up. When she leaned back the movement thrust her breasts against her lapels, and he wanted to tear the dress open. Damn, what a dress! It wrapped her modestly, but the silk kissed every soft curve just the way he wanted to do, and all morning long it had been teasing at him that the damned thing was fastened with only those two buttons. Two buttons! He had to have her, he thought savagely. He couldn't wait much longer. He'd already waited ten years, and his patience had ended. It was time.

The restaurant he took her to was a posh favorite

of the city's business community, but he didn't worry about needing a reservation. The maître d' knew him, as did most of the people in the room, by sight and reputation if not personally. They were led across the crowded room to a select table by the window.

Michelle had noted the way so many people had watched them. "Well, this is one," she said dryly.

He looked up from the menu. "One what?"

"I've been seen in public with you once. Gossip has it that any woman seen with you twice is automatically assumed to be sleeping with you."

His mustache twitched as he frowned in annoyance. "Gossip has a way of being exaggerated."

"Usually, yes."

"And in this case?"

"You tell me."

He put the menu aside, his eyes never leaving her. "No matter what gossip says, you won't have to worry about being just another member of a harem. While we're together, you'll be the only woman in my bed."

Her hands shook, and Michelle quickly put her menu on the table to hide that betraying quiver. "You're assuming a lot," she said lightly in an effort to counteract the heat she could feel radiating from him.

"I'm not assuming anything. I'm planning on it." His voice was flat, filled with masculine certainty. He had reason to be certain; how many women had ever refused him? He projected a sense of overwhelming virility that was at least as seductive as the most expert technique, and from what she'd heard, he had that, too. Just looking at him made a woman wonder, made her begin dreaming about what it would be like to be in bed with him.

"Michelle, darling!"

Michelle couldn't stop herself from flinching at that particular phrase, even though it was spoken in a lilting female voice rather than a man's deeper tones. Quickly she looked around, grateful for the interruption despite the endearment she hated; when she recognized the speaker, gratefulness turned to mere politeness, but her face was so schooled that the approaching woman didn't catch the faint nuances of expression.

"Hello, Bitsy, how are you?" she asked politely as John got to his feet. "This is John Rafferty, my neighbor. John, this is Bitsy Sumner, from Palm Beach. We went to college together."

Bitsy's eyes gleamed as she looked at John, and she held her hand out to him. "I'm so glad to meet you, Mr. Rafferty."

Michelle knew Bitsy wouldn't pick it up, but she saw the dark amusement in John's eyes as he gently took the woman's faultlessly manicured and bejeweled hand in his. Naturally he'd seen the way Bitsy was looking at *him*. It was a look he'd probably been getting since puberty.

"Mrs. Sumner," he murmured, noting the diamond-studded wedding band on her left hand. "Would you like to join us?"

"Only for a moment," Bitsy sighed, slipping into the chair he held out. "My husband and I are here with some business associates and their wives. He says it's good business to socialize with them occasionally, so we flew in this morning. Michelle, dear, I haven't seen you in so long! What are you doing on this side of the state?"

"I live north of here," Michelle replied.

"You must come visit. Someone mentioned just the other day that it had been forever since we'd seen you!

We had the most fantastic party at Howard Cassa's villa last month; you should have come."

"I have too much work to do, but thank you for the invitation." She managed to smile at Bitsy, but she understood that Bitsy hadn't been inviting her to visit them personally; it was just something that people said, and probably her old acquaintances were curious about why she had left their circle.

Bitsy shrugged elegantly. "Oh, work, schmurk. Let someone else take care of it for a month or so. You need to have some fun! Come to town, and bring Mr. Rafferty with you." Bitsy's gaze slid back to John, and that unconsciously hungry look crawled into her eyes again. "You'd enjoy it, Mr. Rafferty, I promise. Everyone needs a break from work occasionally, don't you think?"

His brows lifted. "Occasionally."

"What sort of business are you in?"

"Cattle. My ranch adjoins Michelle's."

"Oh, a *rancher*!"

Michelle could tell by Bitsy's fatuous smile that the other woman was lost in the romantic images of cowboys and horses that so many people associated with ranching, ignoring or simply not imagining the backbreaking hard work that went into building a successful ranch. Or maybe it was the rancher instead of the ranch that made Bitsy look so enraptured. She was looking at John as if she could eat him alive. Michelle put her hands in her lap to hide them because she had to clench her fists in order to resist slapping Bitsy so hard she'd never even think of looking at John Rafferty again.

Fortunately good manners drove Bitsy back to her own table after a few moments. John watched her sway through the tangle of tables, then looked at Michelle with amusement in his eyes. "Who in hell would call a grown woman *Bitsy*?"

It was hard not to share his amusement. "I think her real name is Elizabeth, so Bitsy is fairly reasonable as a nickname. Of course, she was the ultimate preppy in college, so it fits."

"I thought it might be an indication of her brain power," he said caustically; then the waiter approached to take their orders, and John turned his attention to the menu.

Michelle could only be grateful that Bitsy hadn't been able to remain with them. The woman was one of the worst gossips she'd ever met, and she didn't feel up to hearing the latest dirt on every acquaintance they had in common. Bitsy's particular circle of friends were rootless and a little savage in their pursuit of entertainment, and Michelle had always made an effort to keep her distance from them. It hadn't always been possible, but at least she had never been drawn into the center of the crowd.

After lunch John asked if she would mind waiting while he contacted one of his business associates. She started to protest, then remembered that his men were taking care of the cattle today; she had no reason to hurry back, and, in truth, she could use the day off. The physical strain had been telling on her. Besides, this was the most time she'd ever spent in his company, and she was loathe to see the day end. They weren't arguing, and if she ignored his arrogant certainty that they were going to sleep together, the day had really been rather calm. "I don't have to be back at any certain time," she said, willing to let him decide when they would return.

As it happened, it was after dark before they left Tampa. John's meeting had taken up more time than he'd expected, but Michelle hadn't been bored, because he hadn't left her sitting in the reception area. He'd taken her into the meeting with him, and it had been so interesting that she hadn't been aware of the hours slipping past. It was almost six when they finished, and by then John was hungry again; it was another two hours before they were actually on their way.

Michelle sat beside him, relaxed and a little drowsy. John had stayed with coffee, because he was driving, but she'd had two glasses of wine with her meal, and her bones felt mellow. The car was dark, illuminated only by the dash lights, which gave a satanic cast to his hard-planed face, and the traffic on U.S. 19 was light. She snuggled down into the seat, making a comment only when John said something that required an answer.

Soon they ran into a steady rain, and the rhythmic motion of the windshield wipers added to her drowsiness. The windows began to fog, so John turned the air-conditioning higher. Michelle sat up, hugging her arms as the cooler air banished her drowsiness. Her silk dress didn't offer much warmth. He glanced at her, then pulled to the side of the road.

"Why are we stopping?"

"Because you're cold." He shrugged out of his suit jacket and draped it around her, enveloping her in the transferred heat and the smell of his body. "We're almost two hours from home, so why don't you take a nap? That wine's getting to you, isn't it?"

"Mmm." The sound of agreement was distinctly drowsy. John touched her cheek gently, watching as her eyelids closed, as if her lashes were too heavy for her to hold them open a moment longer. Let her sleep, he thought. She'd be recovered from the wine by the time they got home. His loins tightened. He wanted her awake and responsive when he took her to bed. There was no way he was going to sleep alone tonight. All day long he'd been fighting the need to touch her, to feel her lying against him. For ten years she'd been in his mind, and he wanted her. As difficult and spoiled as she was, he wanted her. Now he understood what made men want to pamper her, probably from the day she'd been placed in her cradle. He'd just taken his place in line, and for his reward he'd have her in his bed, her slim, silky body open for his pleasure. He knew she wanted him; she was resisting him for some reason he couldn't decipher, perhaps only a woman's instinctive hesitance.

Michelle usually didn't sleep well. Her slumber was frequently disturbed by dreams, and she hadn't been able to nap with even her father anywhere nearby. Her subconscious refused to relax if any man was in the vicinity. Roger had once attacked her in the middle of the night, when she'd been soundly asleep, and the trauma of being jerked from a deep, peaceful sleep into a nightmare of violence had in some ways been worse than the pain. Now, just before she slept, she realized with faint surprise that the old uneasiness wasn't there tonight. Perhaps the time had come to heal that particular hurt, too, or perhaps it was that she felt so unutterably safe with John. His coat warmed her; his nearness surrounded her. He had touched her in passion and in anger, but his touch had never brought pain. He tempered his great strength to handle a woman's softness, and she slept, secure in the instinctive knowledge that she was safe.

His deep, dark-velvet voice woke her. "We're home, honey. Put your arms around my neck."

She opened her eyes to see him leaning in the open

door of the car, and she gave him a sleepy smile. "I slept all the way, didn't I?"

"Like a baby." He brushed her mouth with his, a brief, warm caress; then his arms slid behind her neck and under her thighs. She gasped as he lifted her, grabbing him around the neck as he'd instructed. It was still raining, but his coat kept most of the dampness from her as he closed the car door and carried her swiftly through the darkness.

"I'm awake now; I could've walked," she protested, her heart beginning a slow, heavy thumping as she responded to his nearness. He carried her so easily, leaping up the steps to the porch as if she weighed no more than a child.

"I know," he murmured, lifting her a little so he could bury his face in the curve of her neck. Gently he nuzzled her jaw, drinking in the sweet, warm fragrance of her skin. "Mmm, you smell good. Are you clear from the wine yet?"

The caress was so tender that it completely failed to alarm her. Rather, she felt coddled, and the feeling of utter safety persisted. He shifted her in his arms to open the door, then turned sideways to carry her through. Had he thought she was drunk? "I was just sleepy, not tipsy," she clarified.

"Good," he whispered, pushing the door closed and blocking out the sound of the light rain, enveloping them in the dark silence of the house. She couldn't see anything, but he was warm and solid against her, and it didn't matter that she couldn't see. Then his mouth was on hers, greedy and demanding, convincing her lips to open and accept the shape of his, accept the inward thrust of his tongue. He kissed her with burning male hunger, as if he wanted to draw all the sweetness and breath out of her to make it his own, as if the need was riding him so hard that he couldn't get close enough. She couldn't help responding to that need, clinging to him and kissing him back with a sudden wildness, because the very rawness of his male hunger called out to everything in her that was female and ignited her own fires.

He hit the light switch with his elbow, throwing on the foyer light and illuminating the stairs to the right. He lifted his mouth briefly, and she stared up at him in the dim light, her senses jolting at the hard, grim expression on his face, the way his skin had tightened across his cheekbones. "I'm staying here tonight," he muttered harshly, starting up the stairs with her still in his arms. "This has been put off long enough."

He wasn't going to stop; she could see it in his face. She didn't want him to stop. Every pore in her body cried out for him, drowning out the small voice of caution that warned against getting involved with a heartbreaker like John Rafferty. Maybe it had been a useless struggle anyway; it had always been between them, this burning hunger that now flared out of control.

His mouth caught hers again as he carried her up the stairs, his muscle-corded arms holding her weight easily. Michelle yielded to the kiss, sinking against him. Her blood was singing through her veins, heating her, making her breasts harden with the need for his touch. An empty ache made her whimper, because it was an ache that only he could fill.

He'd been in the house a lot over the years, so the location of her room was no mystery to him. He carried her inside and laid her on the bed, following her down to press her into the mattress with his full weight. Michelle almost cried out from the intense pleasure of feeling him cover her with his body. His arm stretched over her head, and he snapped on one of the bedside lamps; he looked at her, and his black eyes filled with masculine satisfaction as he saw the glaze of passion in her slumberous eyes, the trembling of her pouty, kiss-stung lips.

Slowly, deliberately, he levered his knee between hers and spread her legs, then settled his hips into the cradle formed by her thighs. She inhaled sharply as she felt his hardness through the layers of their clothing. Their eyes met, and she knew he'd known before the day even began that he would end it in her bed. He was tired of waiting, and he was going to have her. He'd been patient all day, gentling her by letting her get accustomed to his presence, but now his patience was at an end, and he knew she had no resistance left to offer him. All she had was need.

"You're mine." He stated his possession baldly, his voice rough and low. He raised his weight on one elbow, and with his free hand unbuttoned the two buttons at her waist, spreading the dress open with the deliberate air of a man unwrapping a gift he'd wanted for a long time. The silk caught at her hips, pinned by his own weight. He lifted his hips and pushed the edges of the dress open, baring her legs, then resettled himself against her.

He felt as if his entire body would explode as he looked at her. She had worn neither bra nor slip; the silk dress was lined, hiding from him all day the fact that the only things she had on beneath that wisp of fabric were her panty hose and a minute scrap of lace masquerading as panties. If he'd known that her breasts were bare under her dress, there was no way he could have kept himself from pulling those lapels apart and touching, tasting, nor could he stop himself now. Her breasts were high and round, the skin satiny, her coral-colored nipples small and already tightly beaded. With a rough sound he bent his head and sucked strongly at her, drawing her nipple into his mouth and molding his lips to that creamy, satiny flesh. He cupped her other breast in his hand, gently kneading it and rubbing the nipple with his thumb. A high, gasping cry tore from her throat, and she arched against his mouth, her hands digging into his dark hair to press his head into her. Her breasts were so firm they were almost hard, and the firmness excited him even more. He had to taste the other one, surround himself with the sweet headiness of her scent and skin.

Slowly Michelle twisted beneath him, plucking now at the back of his shirt in an effort to get rid of the fabric between them. She needed to feel the heat and power of his bare skin under her hands, against her body, but his mouth on her breasts was driving her mad with pleasure, and she couldn't control herself enough to strip the shirt away. Every stroke of his tongue sent wildfire running along her nerves, from her nipples to her loins, and she was helpless to do anything but feel.

Then he left her, rising up on his knees to tear at his shirt and throw it aside. His shoes, socks, pants and underwear followed, flung blindly away from the bed, and he knelt naked between her spread thighs. He stripped her panty hose and panties away, leaving her open and vulnerable to his penetration.

For the first time, she felt fear. It had been so long for her, and sex hadn't been good in her marriage anyway. John leaned over her, spreading her legs further, and she felt the first shock of his naked flesh as he positioned himself for entry. He was so big, his muscled body dominating her smaller, softer one completely. She knew from harsh experience how helpless a woman was against a man's much greater strength; John was stronger than most, bigger than most, and he was intent on the sexual act as males have been from the beginning of time. He was quintessentially male, the sum and substance of masculine aggression and sexuality. Panic welled in her, and her slim, delicate hand pressed against him, her fingers sliding into the curling dark hair that covered his chest. The black edges of fear were coming closer.

Her voice was thready, begging for reassurance. "John? Don't hurt me, please."

He froze, braced over her on the threshold of entry. Her warm, sweet body beckoned him, moistly ready for him, but her eyes were pleading. Did she expect pain? Good God, who could have hurt her? The seeds of fury formed deep in his mind, shunted aside for now by the screaming urges of his body. For now, he had to have her. "No, baby," he said gently, his dark voice so warm with tenderness that the fear in her eyes faded. "I won't hurt you."

He slid one arm under her, leaning on that elbow and raising her so her nipples were buried in the hair on his chest. Again he heard that small intake of breath from her, an unconscious sound of pleasure. Their eyes locked, hers misty and soft, his like black fire, as he tightened his buttocks and very slowly, very carefully, began to enter her.

Michelle shuddered as great ripples of pleasure washed through her, and her legs climbed his to wrap around his hips. A soft, wild cry tore from her throat, and she shoved her hand against her mouth to stifle the sound. Still his black eyes burned down at her. "No," he whispered. "Take your hand away. I want to hear you, baby. Let me hear how good it feels to you."

Still there was that slow, burning push deep into her, her flesh quivering as she tried to accommodate him. Panic seized her again. "Stop! John, please, no more! You're…I can't…"

"Shh, shh," he soothed, kissing her mouth, her eyes, nibbling at the velvety lobes of her ears. "It's okay, baby, don't worry. I won't hurt you." He continued soothing her with kisses and soft murmurs, and though every instinct in him screamed to bury himself in her to the hilt, he clamped down on those urges with iron control. There was no way he was going to hurt her, not with the fear he'd seen in the misty green depths of her eyes. She was so delicate and silky, and so tight around him that he could feel the gentle pulsations of adjustment. His eyes closed as pure pleasure shuddered through him.

She was aroused, but not enough. He set about exciting her with all the sensual skill he possessed, holding her mouth with deep kisses while his hands gently stroked her, and he began moving slowly inside her. So slow, holding himself back, keeping his strokes shallow even though every movement wrung new degrees of ecstasy from him. He wanted her mindless with need.

Michelle felt her control slipping away by degrees, and she didn't care. Control didn't matter, nothing mattered but the heat that was consuming her body and mind, building until all sense of self was gone and she was nothing but a female body, twisting and surging beneath the overpowering male. A powerful tension had her in its grip, tightening, combining with the heat as it swept her inexorably along. She was burning alive, writhing helplessly, wild little pleading sobs welling up and escaping. John took them into his own mouth, then put his hand between their bodies, stroking her. She trembled for a moment on the crest of a great wave; then she was submerged in exploding sensation. He held her safely, her heaving body locked in his arms while he thrust deeply, giving her all the pleasure he could.

When it was over she was limp and sobbing, drenched with both her sweat and his. "I didn't know," she said brokenly, and tears tracked down her face. He murmured to her, holding her tightly for a moment, but he was deep inside her now, and he couldn't hold back any longer. Sliding his hands beneath her hips, he lifted her up to receive his deep, powerful thrusts.

Now it was she who held him, cradling him in her body and with her arms tight around him; he cried out, a deep, hoarse sound, blind and insensible to everything but the great, flooding force of his pleasure.

It was quiet for a long time afterward. John lay on top of her, so sated and relaxed that he couldn't tolerate the idea of moving, of separating his flesh from hers. It wasn't until she stirred, gasping a little for breath, that he raised himself on his elbows and looked down at her.

Intense satisfaction, mingled with both gentleness and a certain male arrogance, was written on his face as he leaned above her. He smoothed her tangled hair back from her face, stroking her cheeks with his fingers. She looked pale and exhausted, but it was the sensuous exhaustion of a woman who has been thoroughly satisfied by her lover. He traced the shape of her elegant cheekbones with his lips, his tongue dipping out to sneak tastes that sent little ripples of arousal through him again.

Then he lifted his head again, curiosity burning in his eyes. "You've never enjoyed it before, have you?"

A quick flush burned her cheeks, and she turned her head on the pillow, staring fixedly at the lamp. "I suppose that does wonders for your ego."

She was withdrawing from him, and that was the last thing he wanted. He decided to drop the subject for the time being, but there were still a lot of questions that he intended to have answered. Right now she was in his arms, warm and weak from his lovemaking, just the way he was going to keep her until she became used to his possession and accepted it as fact.

She was his now.

He'd take care of her, even spoil her. Why not? She was made to be pampered and indulged, at least up to a point. She'd been putting up a good fight to work this ranch, and he liked her guts, but she wasn't cut out for that type of life. Once she realized that she didn't have to fight anymore, that he was going to take care of her, she'd settle down and accept it as the natural order of things.

He didn't have money to waste on fancy trips, or to drape her in jewels, but he could keep her in comfort and security. Not only that, he could guarantee that the sheets on their bed would stay hot. Even now, so soon after having her, he felt the hunger and need returning.

Without a word he began again, drawing her down with him into a dark whirlpool of desire and satisfaction. Michelle's eyes drifted shut, her body arching in his arms. She had known instinctively, years ago, that it would be like this, that even her identity would be swamped with the force of his passion. In his arms she lost herself and became only his woman.

CHAPTER FIVE

MICHELLE WOKE EARLY, just as the first gray light of dawn was creeping into the room. The little sleep she'd gotten had been deep and dreamless for a change, but she was used to sleeping alone; the unaccustomed presence of a man in her bed had finally nudged her awake. A stricken look edged into her eyes as she looked over at him, sprawled on his stomach with one arm curled under the pillow and the other arm draped across her naked body.

How easy she'd been for him. The knowledge ate at her as she gingerly slipped from the bed, taking care not to wake him. He might sleep for hours yet; he certainly hadn't had much sleep during the night.

Her legs trembled as she stood, the soreness in her thighs and deep in her body providing yet another reminder of the past night, as if she needed any further confirmation of her memory. Four times. He'd taken her four times, and each time it had seemed as if the pleasure intensified. Even now she couldn't believe how her body had responded to him, soaring wildly out of her control. But he'd controlled himself, and her, holding her to the rhythm he set in order to prolong their lovemaking. Now she knew that all the talk about him hadn't been exaggerated; both his virility and his skill had been, if anything, underrated.

Somehow she had to come to terms with the unpleasant fact that she had allowed herself to become the latest of his one-night stands. The hardest fact to face wasn't that she'd been so easily seduced, but her own piercing regret that such ecstasy wouldn't last. Oh, he might come back...but he wouldn't stay. In time he'd become bored with her and turn his predatory gaze on some other woman just as he always had before.

And she'd go on loving him, just as she had before.

Quietly she got clean underwear from the dresser and her bathrobe from the adjoining bath, but she went to the bathroom down the hall to take a shower. She didn't want the sound of running water to awaken him. Right now she needed time to herself, time to gather her composure before she faced him again. She didn't know what to say, how to act.

The stinging hot water eased some of the soreness from her muscles, though a remaining ache reminded her of John's strength with every step she took. After showering she went down to the kitchen and started brewing a fresh pot of coffee. She was leaning against the cabinets, watching the dark brew drip into the pot, when the sound of motors caught her attention. Turning to look out the window, she saw the two pickup trucks from John's ranch pull into the yard. The same men who had been there the day before got out; one noticed John's car parked in front of the house and poked his buddy in the ribs, pointing. Even from that distance Michelle could hear the muffled male laughter, and she didn't need any help imagining their comments. The boss had scored again. It would be all over the county within twenty-four hours. In the manner of men everywhere, they were both proud and slightly envious of their boss's sexual escapades, and they'd tell the tale over and over again.

Numbly she turned back to watch the coffee dripping; when it finished, she filled a big mug, then wrapped her cold fingers around the mug to warm them. It had to be nerves making her hands so cold. Quietly she went upstairs to look into her bedroom, wondering if he would still be sleeping.

He wasn't, though evidently he'd awoken only seconds before. He propped himself up on one elbow and ran his hand through his tousled black hair, narrowing his eyes as he returned her steady gaze. Her heart lurched painfully. He looked like a ruffian, with his hair tousled, his jaw darkened by the overnight growth of beard, his bare torso brown and roped with the steely muscles that were never found on a businessman. She didn't know what she'd hoped to see in his expression: desire, possibly, even affection. But whatever she'd wanted to see wasn't there. Instead his face was as hard as always, measuring her with that narrowed gaze that made her feel like squirming. She could feel him waiting for her to move, to say something.

Her legs were jerky, but she managed not to spill the coffee as she walked into the room. Her voice was only slightly strained. "Congratulations. All the gossip doesn't give you due credit. My, my, you're really something when you decide to score; I didn't even think of saying no. Now you can go home and put another notch in your bedpost."

His eyes narrowed even more. He sat up, ignoring the way the sheet fell below his waist, and held out his hand for the coffee mug. When she gave it to him, he turned it and drank from the place where she'd been sipping, then returned it to her, his eyes never leaving hers.

"Sit down."

She flinched a little at his hard, raspy, early-morning

voice. He saw the small movement and reached out to take her wrist, making coffee lap alarmingly close to the rim of the mug. Gently but inexorably he drew her down to sit facing him on the edge of the bed.

He kept his hand on her wrist, his callused thumb rubbing over the fine bones and delicate tracery of veins. "Just for the record, I don't notch bedposts. Is that what's got your back up this morning?"

She gave a small defensive shrug, not meeting his eyes.

She'd withdrawn from him again; his face was grim as he watched her, trying to read her expression. He remembered the fear in her last night, and he wondered who'd put it there. White-hot embers of rage began to flicker to life at the thought of some bastard abusing her in bed, hurting her. Women were vulnerable when they made love, and Michelle especially wouldn't have the strength to protect herself. He had to get her to talk, or she'd close up on him completely. "It had been a long time for you, hadn't it?"

Again she gave that little shrug, as if hiding behind the movement. Again he probed, watching her face. "You didn't enjoy sex before." He made it a statement, not a question.

Finally her eyes darted to his, wary and resentful. "What do you want, a recommendation? You know that was the first time I'd…enjoyed it."

"Why didn't you like it before?"

"Maybe I just needed to go to bed with a stud," she said flippantly.

"Hell, don't give me that," he snapped, disgusted. "Who hurt you? Who made you afraid of sex?"

"I'm not afraid," she denied, disturbed by the idea that she might have let Roger warp her to such an extent. "It was just…well, it had been so long, and you're a big man…." Her voice trailed off, and abruptly she flushed, her gaze sliding away from him.

He watched her thoughtfully; considering what he'd learned about her last night and this morning, it was nothing short of a miracle that she hadn't knocked his proposal and half his teeth down his throat when he'd suggested she become his mistress as payment of the debt. It also made him wonder if her part in the breakup of Mike Webster's marriage hadn't been blown out of all proportion; after all, a woman who didn't enjoy making love wasn't likely to be fast and easy.

It was pure possessiveness, but he was glad no other man had pleased her the way he had; it gave him a hold on her, a means of keeping her by his side. He would use any weapon he had, because during the night he had realized that there was no way he could let her go. She could be haughty, bad-tempered and stubborn; she could too easily be spoiled and accept it as her due, though he'd be damned if he hadn't almost decided it *was* her due. She was proud and difficult, trying to build a stone wall around herself to keep him at a distance, like a princess holding herself aloof from the peasants, but he couldn't get enough of her. When they were making love, it wasn't the princess and the peasant any longer; they were a man and his woman, writhing and straining together, moaning with ecstasy. He'd never been so hungry for a woman before, so hot that he'd felt nothing and no one could have kept him away from her.

She seemed to think last night had been a casual thing on his part, that sunrise had somehow ended it. She was in for a surprise. Now that she'd given herself to him, he wasn't going to let her go. He'd learned how to fight for and keep what was his, but his single-minded striving over the years to build the ranch into one of the biggest cattle ranches in Florida was nothing compared to the intense possessiveness he felt for Michelle.

Finally he released her wrist, and she stood immediately, moving away from him. She sipped at the coffee she still held, and her eyes went to the window. "Your men got a big kick out of seeing your car still here this morning. I didn't realize they'd be back, since they put up the fencing yesterday."

Indifferent to his nakedness, he threw the sheet back and got out of bed. "They didn't finish. They'll do the rest of the job today, then move the herd to the east pasture tomorrow." He waited, then said evenly, "It bothers you that they know?"

"Being snickered about over a beer bothers me. It polishes up your image a little more, but all I'll be is the most recent in a long line of one-nighters for you."

"Well, everyone will know differently when you move in with me, won't they?" he asked arrogantly, walking into the bathroom. "How long will it take you to pack?"

Stunned, Michelle whirled to stare at him, but he'd already disappeared into the bathroom. The sound of the shower came on. Move in with him? If there was any limit to his gall, she hadn't seen it yet! She sat down on the edge of the bed, watching the bathroom door and waiting for him to emerge as she fought the uneasy feeling of sliding further and further down a precipitous slope. Control of her own life was slipping from her hands, and she didn't know if she could stop it. It wasn't just that John was so domineering, though he was; the problem was that, despite how much she wished it were different, she was weak where he was concerned. She wanted to be able to simply walk into his arms and let them lock around her, to rest against him and let him handle everything. She was so tired, physically and mentally. But if she let him take over completely, what would happen when he became bored with her? She would be right back where she'd started, but with a broken heart added to her problems.

The shower stopped running. An image of him formed in her mind, powerfully muscled, naked, dripping wet. Drying himself with her towels. Filling her bathroom with his male scent and presence. He wouldn't look diminished or foolish in her very feminine rose-and-white bathroom, nor would it bother him that he'd bathed with perfumed soap. He was so intensely masculine that female surroundings merely accentuated that masculinity.

She began to tremble, thinking of the things he'd done during the night, the way he'd made her feel. She hadn't known her body could take over like that, that she could revel in being possessed, and despite the outdated notion that a man could physically "possess" a woman, that was what had happened. She felt it, instinctively and deeply, the sensation sinking into her bones.

He sauntered from the bathroom wearing only a towel hitched low on his hips, the thick velvety fabric contrasting whitely with the bronzed darkness of his abdomen. His hair and mustache still gleamed wetly; a few drops of moisture glistened on his wide shoulders and in the curls that darkened his broad chest. Her mouth went dry. His body hair followed the tree of life pattern, with the tufts under his arms and curls across his chest, then the narrowing line that ran down his abdomen before spreading again at his groin. He was as superbly built as a triathlete, and she actually ached to touch him, to run her palms all over him.

He gave her a hard, level look. "Stop stalling and get packed."

"I'm not going." She tried to sound strong about it; if her voice lacked the volume she'd wanted, at least it was even.

"You'll be embarrassed if you don't have anything on besides that robe when I carry you into my house," he warned quietly.

"John—" She stopped, then made a frustrated motion with her hand. "I don't want to get involved with you."

"It's a little late to worry about that now," he pointed out.

"I know," she whispered. "Last night shouldn't have happened."

"Damn it to hell, woman, it should've happened a long time ago." Irritated, he dropped the towel to the floor and picked up his briefs. "Moving in with me is the only sensible thing to do. I normally work twelve hours a day, sometimes more. Sometimes I'm up all night. Then there's the paperwork to do in the evenings; hell, you know what it takes to run a ranch. When would I get over to see you? Once a week? I'll be damned if I'll settle for an occasional quickie."

"What about *my* ranch? Who'll take care of it while I make myself convenient to you whenever you get the urge?"

He gave a short bark of laughter. "Baby, if you lay down every time I got the urge, you'd spend the next year on your back. I get hard every time I look at you."

Involuntarily her eyes dropped down his body, and a wave of heat washed over her when she saw the proof of his words swelling against the white fabric of his underwear. She jerked her gaze away, swallowing to relieve the dry tightness of her throat. "I have to take care of my ranch," she repeated stubbornly, as if they were magic words that would keep him at bay.

He pulled on his pants, impatience deepening the lines that bracketed his mouth. "I'll take care of both ranches. Face facts, Michelle. You need help. You can't do it on your own."

"Maybe not, but I need to try. Don't you understand?" Desperation edged into her tone. "I've never had a job, never done anything to support myself, but I'm trying to learn. You're stepping right into Dad's shoes and taking over, handling everything yourself, but what happens to me when you get bored and move on to the next woman? I still won't know how to support myself!"

John paused in the act of zipping his pants, glaring at her. Damn it, what did she think he'd do, toss her out the door with a casual, "It's been fun, but I'm tired of you now?" He'd make certain she was on her feet, that the ranch was functioning on a profitable basis, if the day ever came when he looked at her and *didn't* want her. He couldn't imagine it. The desire for her consumed him like white-burning fire, sometimes banked, but never extinguished, heating his body and mind. He'd wanted her when she was eighteen and too young to handle him, and he wanted her now.

He controlled his anger and merely said, "I'll take care of you."

She gave him a tight little smile. "Sure." In her experience, people looked after themselves. Roger's parents had protected him to keep his slipping sanity from casting scandal on *their* family name. Her own father,

as loving as he'd been, had ignored her plea for help
because he didn't like to think his daughter was un-
happy; it was more comfortable for him to decide she'd
been exaggerating. The complaint she'd filed had disappeared because some judge had thought it would be
advantageous to make friends with the powerful Beckmans. Roger's housekeeper had looked the other way
because she liked her cushy well-paid job. Michelle
didn't blame them, but she'd learned not to expect help,
or to trust her life to others.

John snatched his shirt from the floor, his face dark
with fury. "Do you want a written agreement?"

Tiredly she rubbed her forehead. He wasn't used
to anyone refusing to obey him whenever he barked
out an order. If she said yes, she would be confirming
what he'd thought of her in the beginning, that her body
could be bought. Maybe he even wanted her to say yes;
then she'd be firmly under his control, bought and paid
for. But all she said was, "No, that isn't what I want."

"Then what, damn it?"

Just his love. To spend the rest of her life with him.
That was all.

She might as well wish for the moon.

"I want to do it on my own."

The harshness faded from his face. "You can't."
Knowledge gave the words a finality that lashed at her.

"I can try."

The hell of it was, he had to respect the need to try,
even though nature and logic said she wouldn't succeed. She wasn't physically strong enough to do what
had to be done, and she didn't have the financial resources; she'd started out in a hole so deep that she'd
been doomed to fail from the beginning. She would
wear herself to the bone, maybe even get hurt, but in

the end it would come full circle and she would need someone to take care of her. All he could do was wait, try to watch out for her, and be there to step in when everything caved in around her. By then she'd be glad to lean on a strong shoulder, to take the place in life she'd been born to occupy.

But he wasn't going to step back and let her pretend nothing had happened between them the night before. She was his now, and she had to understand that before he left. The knowledge had to be burned into her flesh the way it was burned into his, and maybe it would take a lesson in broad daylight for her to believe it. He dropped his shirt and slowly unzipped his pants, watching her. When he left, he'd leave his touch on her body and his taste in her mouth, and she'd feel him, taste him, think of him every time she climbed into this bed without him.

Her green eyes widened, and color bloomed on her cheekbones. Nervously she glanced at the bed, then back at him.

His heart began slamming heavily against his rib cage. He wanted to feel the firmness of her breasts in his hands again, feel her nipples harden in his mouth. She whispered his name as he dropped his pants and came toward her, putting his hands on her waist, which was so slender that he felt he might break her in two if he wasn't careful.

As he bent toward her, Michelle's head fell back as if it were too heavy for her neck to support. He instantly took advantage of her vulnerable throat, his mouth burning a path down its length. She had wanted to deny the force of what had happened, but her body was responding feverishly to him, straining against him in search of the mindless ecstasy he'd given her before. She no longer had the protection of ignorance. He was addictive, and she'd already become hooked. As he took her down to the bed, covering her with his heated nakedness, she didn't even think of denying him, or herself.

ARE YOU ON the pill?

No.

Damn. Then, *How long until your next period?*

Soon. Don't worry. The timing isn't right.

Famous last words. You'd better get a prescription.

I can't take the pill. I've tried; it makes me throw up all day long. Just like being pregnant.

Then we'll do something else. Do you want to take care of it, or do you want me to?

The remembered conversation kept replaying in her mind; he couldn't have made it plainer that he considered the relationship to be an ongoing one. He had been so matter-of-fact that it hadn't registered on her until later, but now she realized her acquiescent "I will" had acknowledged and accepted his right to make love to her. It hadn't hit her until he'd kissed her and had driven away that his eyes had been gleaming with satisfaction that had nothing to do with being physically sated.

She had some paperwork to do and forced herself to concentrate on it, but that only brought more problems to mind. The stack of unpaid bills was growing, and she didn't know how much longer she could hold her creditors off. They needed their money, too. She needed to fatten the cattle before selling them, but she didn't have the money for grain. Over and over she tried to estimate how much feed would cost, balanced against how much extra she could expect from the sale of heavier cattle. An experienced rancher would have known, but all she had to go on were the records her father had kept, and she didn't know how accurate they were. Her father had been wildly enthusiastic about his ranch, but he'd relied on his foreman's advice to run it.

She could ask John, but he'd use it as another chance to tell her that she couldn't do it on her own.

The telephone rang, and she answered it absently.

"Michelle, darling."

The hot rush of nausea hit her stomach, and she jabbed the button, disconnecting the call. Her hands were shaking as she replaced the receiver. Why wouldn't he leave her alone? It had been two years! Surely he'd had time to get over his sick obsession; surely his parents had gotten him some sort of treatment!

The telephone rang again, the shrill tone filling her ears over and over. She counted the rings in a kind of frozen agony, wondering when he'd give up, or if her nerves would give out first. What if he just let it keep ringing? She'd have to leave the house or go screaming mad. On the eighteenth ring, she answered.

"Darling, don't hang up on me again, please," Roger whispered. "I love you so much. I have to talk to you or go crazy."

They were the words of a lover, but she was shaking with cold. Roger was already crazy. How many times had he whispered love words to her only moments after a burst of rage, when she was stiff with terror, her body already aching from a blow? But then he'd be sorry that he'd hurt her, and he'd tell her over and over how much he loved her and couldn't live without her.

Her lips were so stiff that she could barely form the words. "Please leave me alone. I don't want to talk to you."

"You don't mean that. You know I love you. No one has ever loved you as much as I do."

"I'm sorry," she managed.

"Why are you sorry?"

"I'm not going to talk to you, Roger. I'm going to hang up."

"Why can't you talk? Is someone there with you?"

Her hand froze, unable to remove the receiver from her ear and drop it onto its cradle. Like a rabbit numbed by a snake's hypnotic stare, she waited without breathing for what she knew was coming.

"Michelle! Is someone there with you?"

"No," she whispered. "I'm alone."

"You're lying! That's why you won't talk to me. Your lover is there with you, listening to every word you're saying."

Helplessly she listened to the rage building in his voice, knowing nothing she said would stop it, but unable to keep herself from trying. "I promise you, I'm alone."

To her surprise he fell silent, though she could hear his quickened breath over the wire as clearly as if he were standing next to her. "All right, I'll believe you. If you'll come back to me, I'll believe you."

"I can't—"

"There's someone else, isn't there? I always knew there was. I couldn't catch you, but I always knew!"

"No. There's no one. I'm here all alone, working in Dad's study." She spoke quickly, closing her eyes at the lie. It was the literal truth, that she was alone, but it was still a lie. There had always been someone else deep in her heart, buried at the back of her mind.

Suddenly his voice was shaking. "I couldn't stand

it if you loved someone else, darling. I just couldn't.
Swear to me that you're alone."

"I swear it." Desperation cut at her. "I'm completely
alone, I swear!"

"I love you," Roger whispered, and hung up.

Wildly she ran for the bathroom, where she retched
until she was empty and her stomach muscles ached
from heaving. She couldn't take this again; she would
have the phone number changed, keep it unlisted. Leaning against the basin, she wiped her face with a wet
cloth and stared at her bloodless reflection in the mirror. She didn't have the money to pay for having her
number changed and taken off the listing.

A shaky bubble of laughter escaped her trembling
lips. The way things were going, the phone service
would be disconnected soon because she couldn't pay
her bill. That would certainly take care of the problem; Roger couldn't call if she didn't have a telephone.
Maybe being broke had some advantages, after all.

She didn't know what she'd do if Roger came down
here personally to take her back to Philadelphia where
she "belonged." If she'd ever "belonged" any one place,
it was here, because John was here. Maybe she couldn't
go to the symphony, or go skiing in Switzerland, or
shopping in Paris. It didn't matter now and hadn't mattered then. All those things were nice, but unimportant.
Paying bills was important. Taking care of the cattle
was important.

Roger was capable of anything. Part of him was so
civilized that it was truly difficult to believe he could
be violent. People who'd known him all his life thought
he was one of the nicest men walking the face of the
earth. And he could be, but there was another part of
him that flew into insanely jealous rages.

If he came down here, if she had to see him again…
if he touched her in even the smallest way…she knew
she couldn't handle it.

The last time had been the worst.

His parents had been in Europe. Roger had accepted
an invitation for them to attend a dinner party with a
few of his business associates and clients. Michelle had
been extremely careful all during the evening not to say
or do anything that could be considered flirtatious, but
it hadn't been enough. On the way home, Roger had
started the familiar catechism: She'd smiled a lot at Mr.
So-and-So; had he propositioned her? He had, hadn't
he? Why didn't she just admit it? He'd seen the looks
passing between them.

By the time they'd arrived home, Michelle had been
braced to run, if necessary, but Roger had settled down
in the den to brood. She'd gone to bed, so worn out from
mingled tension and relief that she'd drifted to sleep almost immediately.

Then, suddenly, the light had gone on and he'd been
there, his face twisted with rage as he yelled at her. Terrified, screaming, stunned by being jerked from a sound
sleep, she'd fought him when he jerked her half off the
bed and began tearing at her nightgown, but she'd been
helpless against him. He'd stripped the gown away and
begun lashing at her with his belt, the buckle biting into
her flesh again and again.

By the time he'd quit, she had been covered with
raw welts and a multitude of small, bleeding cuts from
the buckle, and she'd screamed so much she could no
longer make a sound. Her eyes had been almost swollen shut from crying. She could still remember the silence as he'd stood there by the bed, breathing hard as
he looked down at her. Then he'd fallen on his knees,

burying his face in her tangled hair. "I love you so much," he'd said.

That night, while he'd slept, she had crept out and taken a cab to a hospital emergency room. Two years had passed, but the small white scars were still visible on her back, buttocks and upper thighs. They would fade with time, becoming impossible to see, but the scar left on her mind by the sheer terror of that night hadn't faded at all. The demons she feared all wore Roger's face.

But now she couldn't run from him; she had no other place to go, no other place where she wanted to be. She was legally free of him now, and there was nothing he could do to make her return. Legally she could stop him from calling her. He was harassing her; she could get a court order prohibiting him from contacting her in any way.

But she wouldn't, unless he forced her to it. She opened her eyes and stared at herself again. Oh, it was classic. A counselor at the hospital had even talked with her about it. She didn't want anyone to know her husband had abused her; it would be humiliating, as if it were somehow her fault. She didn't want people to pity her, she didn't want them to talk about her, and she especially didn't want John to know. It was too ugly, and she felt ashamed.

Suddenly she felt the walls closing in on her, stifling her. She had to get out and *do* something, or she might begin crying, and she didn't want that to happen. If she started crying now, she wouldn't be able to stop.

She got in the old truck and drove around the pastures, looking at the new sections of fence John's men had put up. They had finished and returned to their regular chores. Tomorrow they'd ride over on horseback and move the herd to this pasture with its high, thick growth of grass. The cattle could get their fill without walking so much, and they'd gain weight.

As she neared the house again she noticed how high the grass and weeds had gotten in the yard. It was so bad she might need to move the herd to the yard to graze instead of to the pasture. Yard work had come in a poor second to all the other things that had needed doing, but now, thanks to John, she had both the time and energy to do something about it.

She got out the lawn mower and pushed it up and down the yard, struggling to force it through the high grass. Little green mounds piled up in neat rows behind her. When that was finished, she took a knife from the kitchen and hacked down the weeds that had grown up next to the house. The physical activity acted like a sedative, blunting the edge of fear and finally abolishing it altogether. She didn't have any reason to be afraid; Roger wasn't going to do anything.

Subconsciously she dreaded going to bed that night, wondering if she would spend the night dozing, only to jerk awake every few moments, her heart pounding with fear as she waited for her particular demon to leap screaming out of the darkness and drag her out of bed. She didn't want to let Roger have that kind of power over her, but memories of that night still nagged at the edges of her mind. Someday she would be free of him. She swore it; she promised it to herself.

When she finally went reluctantly up the stairs and paused in the doorway to her delicately feminine room, she was overcome by a wave of memories that made her shake. She hadn't expected this reaction; she'd been thinking of Roger, but it was John who dominated this room. Roger had never set foot in here. John had slept sprawled in that bed. John had showered in that bathroom. The room was filled with his presence.

She had lain beneath him on that bed, twisting and straining with a pleasure so intense that she'd been mindless with it. She remembered the taut, savage look on his face, the gentleness of his hands as he restrained his strength which could too easily bruise a woman's soft skin. Her body tingled as she remembered the way he'd touched her, the places he'd touched her.

Then she realized that John had given her more than pleasure. She hadn't been aware of fearing men, but on some deep level of her mind, she had. In the two years since her divorce she hadn't been out on a date, and she'd managed to disguise the truth from herself by being part of a crowd that included men. Because she'd laughed with them, skied and swam with them— as long as it was a group activity, but never *alone* with a man—she'd been able to tell herself that Roger hadn't warped her so badly, after all. She was strong; she could put all that behind her and not blame all men for what one man had done.

She hadn't blamed them, but she'd feared their strength. Though she'd never gone into a panic if a man touched her casually, she hadn't liked it and had always retreated.

Perhaps it would have been that way with John, too, if her long obsession with him hadn't predisposed her to accept his touch. But she'd yearned for him for so long, like a child crying for the moon, that her hunger had overcome her instinctive reluctance.

And he'd been tender, careful, generous in the giving of pleasure. In the future his passion might become rougher, but a bond of physical trust had been forged during the night that would never be broken.

Not once was her sleep disturbed by nightmares of Roger. Even in sleep, she felt John's arms around her.

CHAPTER SIX

SHE HAD HALF expected John to be among the men who rode over the next morning to move the cattle to the east pasture, and a sharp pang of disappointment went through her as she realized he hadn't come. Then enthusiasm overrode her disappointment as she ran out to meet them. She'd never been in on an actual "cattle drive," short as it was, and was as excited as a child, her face glowing when she skidded to a stop in front of the mounted men.

"I want to help," she announced, green eyes sparkling in the early morning sun. The respite from the hard physical work she'd been doing made her feel like doing cartwheels on the lawn. She hadn't realized how tired she'd been until she'd had the opportunity to rest, but now she was bubbling over with energy.

Nev Luther, John's lanky and laconic foreman, looked down at her with consternation written across his weathered face. The boss had been explicit in his instructions that Michelle was not to be allowed to work in any way, which was a damned odd position for him to take. Nev couldn't remember the boss ever wanting anyone *not* to work. But orders were orders, and folks who valued their hides didn't ignore the boss's orders.

Not that he'd expected any trouble doing what he'd been told. Somehow he just hadn't pictured fancy Michelle Cabot doing any ranch work, let alone jumping up and down with joy at the prospect. Now what was he going to do? He cleared his throat, reluctant to do anything that would wipe the glowing smile off her face, but even more reluctant to get in trouble with Rafferty.

Inspiration struck, and he looked around. "You got a horse?" He knew she didn't, so he figured that was a detail she couldn't get around.

Her bright face dimmed, then lit again. "I'll drive the truck," she said, and raced toward the barn. Thunderstruck, Nev watched her go, and the men with him muttered warning comments.

Now what? He couldn't haul her out of the truck and order her to stay here. He didn't think she would take orders too well, and he also had the distinct idea the boss was feeling kinda possessive about her. Nev worked with animals, so he tended to put his thoughts in animal terms. One stallion didn't allow another near his mare, and the possessive mating instinct was still alive and well in humans. Nope, he wasn't going to manhandle that woman and have Rafferty take his head off for touching her. Given the choice, he'd rather have the boss mad about his orders not being followed than in a rage because someone had touched his woman, maybe upset her and made her cry.

The stray thought that she might cry decided him in a hurry. Like most men who didn't have a lot of contact with women, he went into a panic at the thought of tears. Rafferty could just go to hell. As far as Nev was concerned, Michelle could do whatever she wanted.

Having the burden of doing everything lifted off her shoulders made all the difference in the world. Michelle enjoyed the sunshine, the lowing of the cattle as they protested the movement, the tight-knit way the cowboys and their horses worked together. She bumped along the pasture in the old truck, which wasn't much good for rounding up strays but could keep the herd nudging forward. The only problem was, riding—or driving—drag was the dustiest place to be.

It wasn't long before one of the cowboys gallantly offered to drive the truck and give her a break from the dust. She took his horse without a qualm. She loved riding; at first it had been the only thing about ranch life that she'd enjoyed. She quickly found that riding a horse for pleasure was a lot different from riding a trained cutting horse. The horse didn't wait for her to tell it what to do. When a cow broke for freedom, the horse broke with it, and Michelle had to learn to go with the movement. She soon got the hang of it, though, and before long she was almost hoping a stray would bolt, just for the joy of riding the quick-moving animal.

Nev swore long and eloquently under his breath when he saw the big gray coming across the pasture. Damn, the fat was in the fire now.

John was eyeing the truck with muted anger as he rode up, but there was no way the broad-shouldered figure in it was Michelle. Disbelieving, his black gaze swept the riders and lighted unerringly on the wand-slim rider with sunny hair tumbling below a hat. He reined in when he reached Nev, his jaw set as he looked at his foreman. "Well?" he asked in a dead-level voice.

Nev scratched his jaw, turning his head to watch Michelle snatch her hat off her head and wave it at a rambunctious calf. "I tried," he mumbled. He glanced back to meet John's narrowed gaze. Damned if eyes as black as hell couldn't look cold. "Hell, boss, it's her truck and her land. What was I supposed to do? Tie her down?"

"She's not in the truck," John pointed out.

"Well, it was so dusty back there that...ah, *hell*!"

Nev gave up trying to explain himself in disgust and spurred to head off a stray. John let him go, picking his way over to Michelle. He would take it up with Nev later, though already his anger was fading. She wasn't doing anything dangerous, even if he didn't like seeing her covered with dust.

She smiled at him when he rode up, a smile of such pure pleasure that his brows pulled together in a little frown. It was the first time he'd seen that smile since she'd been back, but until now he hadn't realized it had been missing. She looked happy. Faced with a smile like that, no wonder Nev had caved in and let her do what she wanted.

"Having fun?" he asked wryly.

"Yes, I am." Her look dared him to make something of it.

"I had a call from the lawyer this morning. He'll have everything ready for us to sign the day after tomorrow."

"That's good." Her ranch would shrink by a sizable hunk of acreage, but at least it would be clear of any large debt.

He watched her for a minute, leaning his forearms on the saddle horn. "Want to ride back to the house with me?"

"For a quickie?" she asked tartly, her green eyes beginning to spit fire at him.

His gaze drifted to her breasts. "I was thinking more of a slowie."

"So your men would have even more to gossip about?"

He drew a deep, irritated breath. "I suppose you want me to sneak over in the dead of night. We're not teenagers, damn it."

"No, we're not," she agreed. Then she said abruptly, "I'm not pregnant."

He didn't know if he should feel relieved, or irritated that this news meant it would be several days before she'd let him make love to her again. He wanted to curse, already feeling frustrated. Instead he said, "At least we didn't have to wait a couple of weeks, wondering."

"No, we didn't." She had known that the timing made it unlikely she'd conceive, but she'd still felt a small pang of regret that morning. Common sense aside, there was a deeply primitive part of her that wondered what woman wouldn't want to have his baby. He was so intensely masculine that he made other men pale in comparison, like a blooded stallion matched against scrub stock.

The gray shifted restively beneath him, and John controlled the big animal with his legs. "Actually, I don't have time, even for a quickie. I came to give Nev some instructions, then stop by the house to let you know where I'll be. I have to fly to Miami this afternoon, and I may not be back for a couple of days. If I'm not, drive to Tampa by yourself and sign those papers, and I'll detour on my way back to sign them."

Michelle twisted in the saddle to look at the battered, rusting old truck bouncing along behind the cattle. There was no way she would trust that relic to take her any place she couldn't get back from on foot. "I think I'll wait until you're back."

"Use the Mercedes. Just call the ranch and Nev will have a couple of men bring it over. I wouldn't trust that piece of junk you've been driving to get you to the grocery store and back."

It could have been a gesture between friends, a

neighborly loan of a car, even something a lover might do, but Michelle sensed that John intended it to mean more than that. He was maneuvering her into his home as his mistress, and if she accepted the loan of the car, she would be just that much more dependent on him. Yet she was almost cornered into accepting because she had no other way of getting to Tampa, and her own sense of duty insisted that she sign those papers as soon as possible, to clear the debt.

He was waiting for her answer, and finally she couldn't hesitate any longer. "All right." Her surrender was quiet, almost inaudible.

He hadn't realized how tense he'd been until his muscles relaxed. The thought that she might try driving to Tampa in that old wreck had been worrying him since he'd gotten the call from Miami. His mother had gotten herself into financial hot water again, and, distasteful as it was to him, he wouldn't let her starve. No matter what, she was his mother. Loyalty went bone deep with him, a lot deeper than aggravation.

He'd even thought of taking Michelle with him, just to have her near. But Miami was too close to Palm Beach; too many of her old friends were there, bored, and just looking for some lark to spice up their lives. It was possible that some jerk with more money than brains would make an offer she couldn't refuse. He had to credit her with trying to make a go of the place, but she wasn't cut out for the life and must be getting tired of working so hard and getting nowhere. If someone offered to pay her fare, she might turn her back and walk away, back to the jet-set life-style she knew so well. No matter how slim the chance of it happening, any chance at all was too much for him. No way would he risk losing her now.

For the first time in his life he felt insecure about a woman. She wanted him, but was it enough to keep her with him? For the first time in his life, it was important. The hunger he felt for her was so deep that he wouldn't be satisfied until she was living under his roof and sleeping in his bed, where he could take care of her and pamper her as much as he wanted.

Yes, she wanted him. He could please her in bed; he could take care of her. But she didn't want him as much as he wanted her. She kept resisting him, trying to keep a distance between them even now, after they'd shared a night and a bed, and a joining that still shook him with its power. It seemed as if every time he tried to bring her closer, she backed away a little more.

He reached out and touched her cheek, stroking his fingertips across her skin and feeling the patrician bone structure that gave her face such an angular, haughty look. "Miss me while I'm gone," he said, his tone making it a command.

A small wry smile tugged at the corners of her wide mouth. "Okay."

"Damn it," he said mildly. "You're not going to boost my ego, are you?"

"Does it need it?"

"Where you're concerned, yeah."

"That's a little hard to believe. Is missing someone a two-way street, or will you be too busy in Miami to bother?"

"I'll be busy, but I'll bother anyway."

"Be careful." She couldn't stop the words. They were the caring words that always went before a trip, a magic incantation to keep a loved one safe. The thought of not seeing him made her feel cold and empty. Miss him?

He had no idea how much, that the missing was a razor, already slashing at her insides.

He wanted to kiss her, but not with his men watching. Instead he nodded an acknowledgment and turned his horse away to rejoin Nev. The two men rode together for a time, and Michelle could see Nev give an occasional nod as he listened to John's instructions. Then John was gone, kicking the gray into a long ground-eating stride that quickly took horse and rider out of sight.

Despite the small, lost feeling she couldn't shake, Michelle didn't allow herself to brood over the next several days. There was too much going on, and even though John's men had taken over the ranching chores, there were still other chores that, being cowboys, they didn't see. If it didn't concern cattle or horses, then it didn't concern them. Now Michelle found other chores to occupy her time. She painted the porch, put up a new post for the mailbox and spent as much time as she could with the men.

The ranch seemed like a ranch again, with all the activity, dust, smells and curses filling the air. The cattle were dipped, the calves branded, the young bulls clipped. Once Michelle would have wrinkled her nose in distaste, but now she saw the activity as new signs of life, both in the ranch and in herself.

On the second day Nev drove the Mercedes over while one of the other men brought an extra horse for Nev to ride. Michelle couldn't quite look the man in the eye as she took the keys from him, but he didn't seem to see anything unusual about her driving John's car.

After driving the pickup truck for so long, the power and responsiveness of the Mercedes felt odd. She was painfully cautious on the long drive to Tampa. It was hard to imagine that she'd ever been blasé about the ex-

pensive, sporty cars she'd driven over the years, but she could remember her carelessness with the white Porsche her father had given her on her eighteenth birthday. The amount of money represented by the small white machine hadn't made any impression on her.

Everything was relative. Then, the money spent for the Porsche hadn't been much. If she had that much now, she would feel rich.

She signed the papers at the lawyer's office, then immediately made the drive back, not wanting to have the Mercedes out longer than necessary.

The rest of the week was calm, though she wished John would call to let her know when he would be back. The two days had stretched into five, and she couldn't stop the tormenting doubts that popped up in unguarded moments. Was he with another woman? Even though he was down there on business, she knew all too well how women flocked to him, and he wouldn't be working twenty-four hours a day. He hadn't made any commitments to her; he was free to take other women out if he wanted. No matter how often she repeated those words to herself, they still hurt.

But if John didn't call, at least Roger didn't, either. For a while she'd been afraid he would begin calling regularly, but the reassuring silence continued. Maybe something or someone else had taken his attention. Maybe his business concerns were taking all his time. Whatever it was, Michelle was profoundly grateful.

The men didn't come over on Friday morning. The cattle were grazing peacefully in the east pasture; all the fencing had been repaired; everything had been taken care of. Michelle put a load of clothing in the washer, then spent the morning cutting the grass again.

She was soaked with sweat when she went inside at noon to make a sandwich for lunch.

It was oddly silent in the house, or maybe it was just silent in comparison to the roar of the lawn mower. She needed water. Breathing hard, she turned on the faucet to let the water get cold while she got a glass from the cabinet, but only a trickle of water ran out, then stopped altogether. Frowning, Michelle turned the faucet off, then on again. Nothing happened. She tried the hot water. Nothing.

Groaning, she leaned against the sink. That was just what she needed, for the water pump to break down.

It took only a few seconds for the silence of the house to connect with the lack of water, and she slowly straightened. Reluctantly she reached for the light switch and flicked it on. Nothing.

The electricity had been cut off.

That was why it was so quiet. The refrigerator wasn't humming; the clocks weren't ticking; the ceiling fan was still.

Breathing raggedly, she sank into a chair. She had forgotten the last notice. She had put it in a drawer and forgotten it, distracted by John and the sudden activity around the ranch. Not that any excuse was worth a hill of beans, she reminded herself. Not that she'd had the money to pay the bill even if she had remembered it.

She had to be practical. People had lived for thousands of years without electricity, so she could, too. Cooking was out; the range top, built-in oven and microwave were all electric, but she wasn't the world's best cook anyway, so that wasn't critical. She could eat without cooking. The refrigerator was empty except for milk and some odds and ends. Thinking about the milk reminded her how thirsty she was, so she poured a glass of the cold milk and swiftly returned the carton to the refrigerator.

There was a kerosene lamp and a supply of candles in the pantry, so she would have light. The most critical item was water. She had to have water to drink and bathe. At least the cattle could drink from the shallow creek that snaked across the east pasture, so she wouldn't have to worry about them.

There was an old well about a hundred yards behind the house, but she didn't know if it had gone dry or simply been covered when the other well had been drilled. Even if the well was still good, how would she get the water up? There was a rope in the barn, but she didn't have a bucket.

She did have seventeen dollars, though, the last of her cash. If the well had water in it, she'd coax the old truck down to the hardware store and buy a water bucket.

She got a rope from the barn, a pan from the kitchen and trudged the hundred yards to the old well. It was almost overgrown with weeds and vines that she had to clear away while keeping an uneasy eye out for snakes. Then she tugged the heavy wooden cover to the side and dropped the pan into the well, letting the rope slip lightly through her hands. It wasn't a deep well; in only a second or two there was a distinct splash, and she began hauling the pan back up. When she got it to the top, a half cup of clear water was still in the pan despite the banging it had received, and Michelle sighed with relief. Now all she had to do was get the bucket.

By the time dusk fell, she was convinced that the pioneers had all been as muscular as the Incredible Hulk; every muscle in her body ached. She had drawn a bucket of water and walked the distance back to the house so many times she didn't want to think about it. The electricity had been cut off while the washer had been in the middle of its cycle, so she had to rinse the clothes out by hand and hang them to dry. She had to have water to drink. She had to have water to bathe. She had to have water to flush the toilet. Modern conveniences were damned *in*convenient without electricity.

But at least she was too tired to stay up long and waste the candles. She set a candle in a saucer on the bedside table, with matches alongside in case she woke up during the night. She was asleep almost as soon as she stretched out between the sheets.

The next morning she ate a peanut butter and jelly sandwich for breakfast, then cleaned out the refrigerator, so she wouldn't have to smell spoiled food. The house was oddly oppressive, as if the life had gone out of it, so she spent most of the day outdoors, watching the cattle graze, and thinking.

She would have to sell the beef cattle now, rather than wait to fatten them on grain. She wouldn't get as much for them, but she had to have money *now*. It had been foolish of her to let things go this far. Pride had kept her from asking for John's advice and help in arranging the sale; now she had to ask him. He would know who to contact and how to transport the cattle. The money would keep her going, allow her to care for the remainder of the herd until spring, when she would have more beef ready to sell. Pride was one thing, but she had carried it to the point of stupidity.

Still, if this had happened ten days earlier she wouldn't even have considered asking John's advice. She had been so completely isolated from human trust that any overture would have made her back away, rather than entice her closer. But John hadn't let her back away; he'd come after her, taken care of things over her protests, and very gently, thoroughly seduced her. A seed of trust had been sown that was timidly growing, though it frightened her to think of relying on someone else, even for good advice.

It was sultry that night, the air thick with humidity. The heat added by the candles and kerosene lamp made it unbearable inside, and though she bathed in the cool water she had hauled from the well, she immediately felt sticky again. It was too early and too hot to sleep, so finally she went out on the porch in search of a breeze.

She curled up in a wicker chair padded with over-stuffed cushions, sighing in relief as a breath of wind fanned her face. The night sounds of crickets and frogs surrounded her with a hypnotic lullaby, and before long her eyelids were drooping. She never quite dozed, but sank into a peaceful lethargy where time passed unnoticed. It might have been two hours or half an hour later when she was disturbed by the sound of a motor and the crunching of tires on gravel; headlights flashed into her eyes just as she opened them, making her flinch and turn her face from the blinding light. Then the lights were killed and the motor silenced. She sat up straighter, her heart beginning to pound as a tall, broad-shouldered man got out of the truck and slammed the door. The starlight wasn't bright, but she didn't need light to identify him when every cell in her body tingled with awareness.

Despite his boots, he didn't make a lot of noise as he came up the steps. "John," she murmured, her voice only a low whisper of sound, but he felt the vibration and turned toward her chair.

She was completely awake now, and becoming indignant. "Why didn't you call? I waited to hear from you—"

"I don't like telephones," he muttered as he walked toward her. That was only part of the reason. Talking to her on the telephone would only have made him want her more, and his nights had been pure hell as it was.

"That isn't much of an excuse."

"It'll do," he drawled. "What are you doing out here? The house is so dark I thought you must have gone to bed early."

Which wouldn't have stopped him from waking her, she thought wryly. "It's too hot to sleep."

He grunted in agreement, bending down to slide his arms under her legs and shoulders. Startled, Michelle grabbed his neck with both arms as he lifted her, then took her place in the chair and settled her on his lap. An almost painful sense of relief filled her as his nearness eased tension she hadn't even been aware of feeling. She was surrounded by his strength and warmth, and the subtle male scent of his skin reaffirmed the sense of homecoming, of rightness. Bonelessly she melted against him, lifting her mouth to his.

The kiss was long and hot, his lips almost bruising hers in his need, but she didn't mind, because her own need was just as urgent. His hands slipped under the light nightgown that was all she wore, finding her soft and naked, and a shudder racked his body.

He muttered a soft curse. "Sweet hell, woman, you were sitting out here practically naked."

"No one else is around to see." She said the words against his throat, her lips moving over his hard flesh and finding the vibrant hollow where his pulse throbbed.

Heat and desire wrapped around them, sugar-sweet

and mindless. From the moment he touched her, she'd wanted only to lie down with him and sink into the textures and sensations of lovemaking. She twisted in his arms, trying to press her breasts fully against him and whimpering a protest as he prevented her from moving.

"This won't work," he said, securing his hold on her and getting to his feet with her still in his arms. "We'd better find a bed, because this chair won't hold up to what I have in mind."

He carried her inside, and as he had done before, he flipped the switch for the light in the entry, so he would be able to see while going up the stairs. He paused when the light didn't come on. "You've got a blown bulb."

Tension invaded her body again. "The power's off."

He gave a low laugh. "Well, hell. Do you have a flashlight? The last thing I want to do right now is trip on the stairs and break our necks."

"There's a kerosene lamp on the table." She wriggled in his arms, and he slowly let her slide to the floor, reluctant to let her go even for a moment. She fumbled for the matches and struck one, the bright glow guiding her hands as she removed the glass chimney and held the flame to the wick. It caught, and the light grew when she put the chimney back in place.

John took the lamp in his left hand, folding her close to his side with his other arm as they started up the stairs. "Have you called the power company to report it?"

She had to laugh. "They know."

"How long will it take them to get it back on?"

Well, he might as well know now. Sighing, she admitted, "The electricity's been cut off. I couldn't pay the bill."

He stopped, his brows drawing together in increasing temper as he turned. "Damn it to hell! How long has it been off?"

"Since yesterday morning."

He exhaled through his clenched teeth, making a hissing sound. "You've been here without water and lights for a day and a half? Of all the damned stubborn stunts… Why in hell didn't you give the bill to me?" He yelled the last few words at her, his eyes snapping black fury in the yellow light from the lamp.

"I don't want you paying my bills!" she snapped, pulling away from him.

"Well, that's just tough!" Swearing under his breath, he caught her hand and pulled her up the stairs, then into her bedroom. He set the lamp on the bedside table and crossed to the closet, opened the doors and began pulling her suitcases from the top shelf.

"What are you doing?" she cried, wrenching the suitcase from him.

He lifted another case down. "Packing your things," he replied shortly. "If you don't want to help, just sit on the bed and stay out of the way."

"Stop it!" She tried to prevent him from taking an armful of clothes from the closet, but he merely side-stepped her and tossed the clothes onto the bed, then returned to the closet for another armful.

"You're going with me," he said, his voice steely. "This is Saturday; it'll be Monday before I can take care of the bill. There's no way in hell I'm going to leave you here. God Almighty, you don't even have water!"

Michelle pushed her hair from her eyes. "I have water. I've been drawing it from the old well."

He began swearing again and turned from the closet to the dresser. Before she could say anything her underwear was added to the growing pile on the bed.

"I can't stay with you," she said desperately, knowing events were already far out of her control. "You know how it'll look! I can manage another couple of days—"

"I don't give a damn how it looks!" he snapped. "And just so you understand me, I'm going to give it to you in plain English. You're going with me now, and you won't be coming back. This isn't a two-day visit. I'm tired of worrying about you out here all by yourself; this is the last straw. You're too damned proud to tell me when you need help, so I'm going to take over and handle everything, the way I should have in the beginning."

Michelle shivered, staring at him. It was true that she shrank from the gossip she knew would run through the county like wildfire, but that wasn't the main reason for her reluctance. Living with him would destroy the last fragile buffers she had retained against being overwhelmed by him in every respect. She wouldn't be able to keep any emotional distance as a safety precaution, just as physical distance would be impossible. She would be in his home, in his bed, eating his food, totally dependent on him.

It frightened her so much that she found herself backing away from him, as if by increasing the distance between them she could weaken his force and fury. "I've been getting by without you," she whispered.

"Is this what you call 'getting by'?" he shouted, slinging the contents of another drawer onto the bed. "You were working yourself half to death, and you're damned lucky you weren't hurt trying to do a two-man job! You don't have any money. You don't have a safe car to drive. You probably don't have enough to eat— and now you don't have electricity."

"I know what I don't have!"

"Well, I'll tell you something else you don't have: a choice. You're going. Now get dressed."

She stood against the wall on the other side of the room, very still and straight. When she didn't move his head jerked up, but something about her made his mouth soften. She looked defiant and stubborn, but her eyes were frightened, and she looked so frail it was like a punch in the gut, staggering him.

He crossed the room with quick strides and hauled her into his arms, folding her against him as if he couldn't tolerate another minute of not touching her. He buried his face in her hair, wanting to sweep her up and keep her from ever being frightened again. "I won't let you do it," he muttered in a raspy voice. "You're trying to keep me at a distance, and I'll be damned if I'll let you do it. Does it matter so much if people know about us? Are you ashamed because I'm not a member of your jet set?"

She gave a shaky laugh, her fingers digging into his back. "Of course not. *I'm* not one of the jet set." How could any woman ever be ashamed of him?

His lips brushed her forehead, leaving warmth behind. "Then what is it?"

She bit her lip, her mind whirling with images of the past and fears of the future. "The summer I was nineteen…you called me a parasite." She had never forgotten the words or the deep hurt they'd caused, and an echo of it was in her low, drifting voice. "You were right."

"Wrong," he whispered, winding his fingers through the strands of her bright hair. "A parasite doesn't give anything, it only takes. I didn't understand, or maybe I was jealous because I wanted it all. I have it all now, and I won't give it up. I've waited ten years for you, baby; I'm not going to settle for half measures now."

He tilted her head back, and his mouth closed warmly, hungrily, over hers, overwhelming any further protests. With a little sigh Michelle gave in, going up on her tiptoes to press herself against him. Regrets could wait; if this were all she would have of heaven, she was going to grab it with both hands. He would probably decide that she'd given in so she could have an easier life, but maybe that was safer than for him to know she was head over heels in love with him.

She slipped out of his arms and quietly changed into jeans and a silk tunic, then set about restoring order out of the chaos he'd made of her clothes. Traveling had taught her to be a fast, efficient packer. As she finished each case, he carried it out to the truck. Finally only her makeup and toiletries were left.

"We'll come back tomorrow for anything else you want," he promised, holding the lamp for the last trip down the stairs. When she stepped outside he extinguished the lamp and placed it on the table, then followed her and locked the door behind him.

"What will your housekeeper think?" she blurted nervously as she got in the truck. It hurt to be leaving her home. She had hidden herself away here, sinking deep roots into the ranch. She had found peace and healing in the hard work.

"That I should have called to let her know when I'd be home," he said, laughing as relief and anticipation filled him. "I came here straight from the airport. My bag is in back with yours." He couldn't wait to get home, to see Michelle's clothing hanging next to his in the closet, to have her toiletries in his bathroom, to sleep with her every night in his bed. He'd never before wanted to live with a woman, but with Michelle it felt necessary. There was no way he would ever feel content with less than everything she had to give.

CHAPTER SEVEN

IT WAS MIDMORNING when Michelle woke, and she lay there for a moment alone in the big bed, trying to adjust to the change. She was in John's house, in his bed. He had gotten up hours ago, before dawn, and left her with a kiss on the forehead and an order to catch up on her sleep. She stretched, becoming aware of both her nakedness and the ache in her muscles. She didn't want to move, didn't want to leave the comforting cocoon of sheets and pillows that carried John's scent. The memory of shattering pleasure made her body tingle, and she moved restlessly. He hadn't slept much, hadn't let her sleep until he'd finally left the bed to go about his normal day's work.

If only he had taken her with him. She felt awkward with Edie, the housekeeper. What must she be thinking? They had met only briefly, because John had ushered Michelle upstairs with blatantly indecent haste, but her impression had been of height, dignity and cool control. The housekeeper wouldn't say anything if she disapproved, but then, she wouldn't have to; Michelle would know.

Finally she got out of bed and showered, smiling wryly to herself as she realized she wouldn't have to skimp on hot water. Central air-conditioning kept the house comfortably cool, which was another comfort she had given up in an effort to reduce the bills. No matter what her mental state, she would be physically comfortable here. It struck her as odd that she'd never been to John's house before; she'd had no idea what to expect. Perhaps another old ranch house like hers, though her father had remodeled and modernized it completely on the inside before they had moved in, and it was in fact as luxurious as the home she had been used to. But John's house was Spanish in style, and was only eight years old. The cool adobe-colored brick and high ceilings kept the heat at bay, and a colorful array of houseplants brought freshness to the air. She'd been surprised at the greenery, then decided that the plants were Edie's doing. The U-shaped house wrapped around a pool landscaped to the point that it resembled a jungle lagoon more than a pool, and every room had a view of the pool and patio.

She had been surprised at the luxury. John was a long way from poor, but the house had cost a lot of money that he would normally have plowed back into the ranch. She had expected something more utilitarian, but at the same time it was very much his *home*. His presence permeated it, and everything was arranged for his comfort.

Finally she forced herself to stop hesitating and go downstairs; if Edie intended to be hostile, she might as well know now.

The layout of the house was simple, and she found the kitchen without any problem. All she had to do was follow her nose to the coffee. As she entered, Edie looked around, her face expressionless, and Michelle's heart sank. Then the housekeeper planted her hands on her hips and said calmly, "I told John it was about damned time he got a woman in this house."

Relief flooded through Michelle, because something

in her would have shriveled if Edie had looked at her with contempt. She was much more sensitive to what other people thought now than she had been when she was younger and had the natural arrogance of youth. Life had defeated that arrogance and taught her not to expect roses.

Faint color rushed to her cheeks. "John didn't make much of an effort to introduce us last night. I'm Michelle Cabot."

"Edie Ward. Are you ready for breakfast? I'm the cook, too."

"I'll wait until lunch, thank you. Does John come back for lunch?" It embarrassed her to have to ask.

"If he's working close by. How about coffee?"

"I can get it," Michelle said quickly. "Where are the cups?"

Edie opened the cabinet to the left of the sink and got down a cup, handing it to Michelle. "It'll be nice to have company here during the day," she said. "These damn cowhands aren't much for talking."

Whatever Michelle had expected, Edie didn't conform. She had to be fifty; though her hair was still dark, there was something about her that made her look her age. She was tall and broad shouldered, with the erect carriage of a Mother Superior and the same sort of unflappable dignity, but she also had the wise, slightly weary eyes of someone who has been around the block a few times too many. Her quiet acceptance made Michelle relax; Edie didn't pass judgments.

But for all the easing of tension, Edie quietly and firmly discouraged Michelle from helping with any of the household chores. "Rafferty would have both our heads," she said. "Housework is what he pays me to do, and around here we try not to rile him."

So Michelle wandered around the house, poking her head into every room and wondering how long she would be able to stand the boredom and emptiness. Working the ranch by herself had been so hard that she had sometimes wanted nothing more than to collapse where she stood, but there had always been a purpose to the hours. She liked ranching. It wasn't easy, but it suited her far better than the dual roles of ornament and mistress. This lack of purpose made her uneasy. She had hoped living with John would mean doing things with him, sharing the work and the worries with him... just as married couples did.

She sucked in her breath at the thought; she was in his—still *his*—bedroom at the time, standing in front of the open closet staring at his clothes, as if the sight of his personal possessions would bring him closer. Slowly she reached out and fingered a shirtsleeve. Her clothes were in the closet beside his, but she didn't belong. This was his house, his bedroom, his closet, and she was merely another possession, to be enjoyed in bed but forgotten at sunrise. Wryly she admitted that it was better than nothing; no matter what the cost to her pride, she would stay here as long as he wanted her, because she was so sick with love for him that she'd take anything she could get. But what she wanted, what she really wanted more than anything in her life, was to have his love as well as his desire. She wanted to marry him, to be his partner, his friend as well as his lover, to belong here as much as he did.

Part of her was startled that she could think of marriage again, even with John. Roger had destroyed her trust, her optimism about life; at least, she'd thought he had. Trust had already bloomed again, a fragile phoenix poking its head up from the ashes. For the first time she recognized her own resilience; she had been altered by the terror and shame of her marriage, but not destroyed. She was healing, and most of it was because of John. She had loved him for so long that her love seemed like the only continuous thread of her life, always there, somehow giving her something to hold on to even when she'd thought it didn't matter.

At last restlessness drove her from the house. She was reluctant to even ask questions, not wanting to interfere with anyone's work, but she decided to walk around and look at everything. There was a world of difference between John's ranch and hers. Here everything was neat and well-maintained, with fresh paint on the barns and fences, the machinery humming. Healthy, spirited horses pranced in the corral or grazed in the pasture. The supply shed was in better shape than her barn. Her ranch had once looked like this, and determination filled her that it would again.

Who was looking after her cattle? She hadn't asked John, not that she'd been given a chance to ask him anything. He'd had her in bed so fast that she hadn't had time to think; then he'd left while she was still dozing.

By the time John came home at dusk, Michelle was so on edge that she could feel her muscles twitching with tension. As soon as he came in from the kitchen his eyes swept the room, and hard satisfaction crossed his face when he saw her. All day long he'd been fighting the urge to come back to the house, picturing her here, under his roof at last. Even when he'd built the house, eight years before, he'd wondered what *she* would think of it, if she'd like it, how she would look in these rooms. It wasn't a grand mansion like those in Palm Beach, but it had been custom built to his specifications for comfort, beauty and a certain level of luxury.

She looked as fresh and perfect as early-morning sunshine, while he was covered with sweat and dust, his jaw dark with a day's growth of beard. If he touched her now, he'd leave dirty prints on her creamy white dress, and he had to touch her soon or go crazy. "Come on up with me," he growled, his boots ringing on the flagstone floor as he went to the stairs.

Michelle followed him at a slower pace, wondering if he already regretted bringing her here. He hadn't kissed her, or even smiled.

He was stripping off his shirt by the time she entered the bedroom, and he carelessly dropped the dirty, sweat-stained garment on the carpet. She shivered in response at the sight of his broad, hair-covered chest and powerful shoulders, her pulse throbbing as she remembered how it felt when he moved over her and slowly let her take his weight, nestling her breasts into that curly hair.

"What've you been doing today?" he asked as he went into the bathroom.

"Nothing," Michelle answered with rueful truthfulness, shaking away the sensual lethargy that had been stealing over her.

Splashing sounds came from the bathroom, and when he reappeared a few minutes later his face was clean of the dust that had covered it before. Damp strands of black hair curled at his temples. He looked at her, and an impatient scowl darkened his face. Bending down, he pried his boots off, then began unbuckling his belt.

Her heart began pounding again. He was going to take her to bed right now, and she wouldn't have a chance to talk to him if she didn't do it before he reached for her. Nervously she picked up his dirty boots to put them in the closet, wondering how to start. "Wait," she blurted. "I need to talk to you."

He didn't see any reason to wait. "So talk," he said, unzipping his jeans and pushing them down his thighs.

She inhaled deeply. "I've been bored with nothing to do all day—"

John straightened, his eyes hardening as she broke off. Hell, he should have expected it. When you acquired something expensive, you had to pay for its upkeep. "All right," he said in an even tone. "I'll give you the keys to the Mercedes, and tomorrow I'll open a checking account for you."

She froze as the meaning of his words seared through her, and all the color washed out of her face. No. There was no way she'd let him turn her into a pet, a chirpy sexual toy, content with a fancy car and charge accounts. Fury rose in her like an inexorable wave, rushing up and bursting out of control. Fiercely she hurled the boots at him; startled, he dodged the first one, but the second one hit him in the chest. "What the hell—"

"No!" she shouted, her eyes like green fire in a face gone curiously pale. She was standing rigidly, her fists clenched at her sides. "I don't want your money or your damned car! I want to take care of my cattle and my ranch, not be left here every day like some fancy...*sex doll*, waiting for you to get home and play with me!"

He kicked his jeans away, leaving him clad only in his briefs. His own temper was rising, but he clamped it under control. That control was evident in his quiet, level voice. "I don't think of you as a sex doll. What brought that on?"

She was white and shaking. "You brought me straight up here and started undressing."

His brows rose. "Because I was dirty from head to

foot. I couldn't even kiss you without getting you dirty, and I didn't want to ruin your dress."

Her lips trembled as she looked down at the dress. "It's just a dress," she said, turning away. "It'll wash. And I'd rather be dirty myself than just left here every day with nothing to do."

"We've been over this before, and it's settled." He walked up behind her and put his hands on her shoulders, gently squeezing. "You can't handle the work; you'd only hurt yourself. Some women can do it, but you're not strong enough. Look at your wrist," he said, sliding his hand down her arm and grasping her wrist to lift it. "Your bones are too little."

Somehow she found herself leaning against him, her head resting in the hollow of his shoulder. "Stop trying to make me feel so useless!" she cried desperately. "At least let me go with you. I can chase strays—"

He turned her in his arms, crushing her against him and cutting off her words. "God, baby," he muttered. "I'm trying to protect you, not make you feel useless. It made me sick when I saw you putting up that fence, knowing what could happen if the wire lashed back on you. You could be thrown, or gored—"

"So could you."

"Not as easily. Admit it; strength counts out there. I want you safe."

It was a battle they'd already fought more times than she could remember, and nothing budged him. But she couldn't give up, because she couldn't stand many more days like today had been. "Could you stand it if you had nothing to do? If you had to just stand around and watch everybody else? Edie won't even let me help!"

"She'd damned well better not."

"See what I mean? Am I supposed to just sit all day?"

"All right, you've made your point," he said in a low voice. He'd thought she'd enjoy living a life of leisure again, but instead she'd been wound to the breaking point. He rubbed her back soothingly, and gradually she relaxed against him, her arms sliding up to hook around his neck. He'd have to find something to keep her occupied, but right now he was at a loss. It was hard to think when she was lying against him like warm silk, her firm breasts pushing into him and the sweet scent of woman rising to his nostrils. She hadn't been far from his mind all day, the thought of her pulling at him like a magnet. No matter how often he took her, the need came back even stronger than before.

Reluctantly he moved her a few inches away from him. "Dinner will be ready in about ten minutes, and I need a shower. I smell like a horse."

The hot, earthy scents of sweat, sun, leather and man didn't offend her. She found herself drawn back to him; she pressed her face into his chest, her tongue flicking out to lick daintily at his hot skin. He shuddered, all thoughts of a shower gone from his mind. Sliding his fingers into the shiny, pale gold curtain of her hair, he turned her face up and took the kiss he'd been wanting for hours.

She couldn't limit her response to him; whenever he reached for her, she was instantly his, melting into him, opening her mouth for him, ready to give as little or as much as he wanted to take. Loving him went beyond the boundaries she had known before, taking her into emotional and physical territory that was new to her. It was his control, not hers, that prevented him from tumbling her onto the bed right then. "Shower," he muttered, lifting his head. His voice was strained. "Then dinner. Then I have to do some paperwork, damn it, and it can't wait."

Michelle sensed that he expected her to object and demand his company, but more than anyone she understood about chores that couldn't be postponed. She drew back from his arms, giving him a smile. "I'm starving, so hurry up with your shower." An idea was forming in the back of her mind, one she needed to explore.

She was oddly relaxed during dinner; it somehow seemed natural to be here with him, as if the world had suddenly settled into the natural order of things. The awkwardness of the morning was gone, perhaps because of John's presence. Edie ate with them, an informality that Michelle liked. It also gave her a chance to think, because Edie's comments filled the silence and made it less apparent.

After dinner, John gave Michelle a quick kiss and a pat on the bottom. "I'll finish as fast as I can. Can you entertain yourself for a while?"

Swift irritation made up her mind for her. "I'm coming with you."

He sighed, looking down at her. "Baby, I won't get any work done at all if you're in there with me."

She gave him a withering look. "You're the biggest chauvinist walking, John Rafferty. You're going to work, all right, because you're going to show me what you're doing, and then I'm taking over your bookwork."

He looked suddenly wary. "I'm not a chauvinist."

He didn't want her touching his books, either. He might as well have said it out loud, because she read his thoughts in his expression. "You can either give me something to do, or I'm going back to my house right now," she said flatly, facing him with her hands on her hips.

"Just what do you know about keeping books?"

"I minored in business administration." Let him chew on that for a while. Since he obviously wasn't going to willingly let her in his office, she stepped around him and walked down the hall without him.

"Michelle, damn it," he muttered irritably, following her.

"Just what's wrong with my doing the books?" she demanded, taking a seat at the big desk.

"I didn't bring you here to work. I want to take care of you."

"Am I going to get hurt in here? Is a pencil too heavy for me to lift?"

He scowled down at her, itching to lift her out of her chair. But her green eyes were glittering at him, and her chin had that stubborn tilt to it, showing she was ready to fight. If he pushed her, she really might go back to that dark, empty house. He could keep her here by force, but he didn't want it that way. He wanted her sweet and willing, not clawing at him like a wildcat. Hell, at least this was safer than riding herd. He'd double-check the books at night.

"All right," he growled.

Her green eyes mocked him. "You're so gracious."

"You're full of sass tonight," he mused, sitting down. "Maybe I should have made love to you before dinner, after all, worked some of that out."

"Like I said, the world's biggest chauvinist." She gave him her haughty look, the one that had always made him see red before. She was beginning to enjoy baiting him.

His face darkened but he controlled himself, reaching for the pile of invoices, receipts and notes. "Pay attention, and don't screw this up," he snapped. "Taxes are bad enough without an amateur bookkeeper fouling up the records."

"I've been doing the books since Dad died," she snapped in return.

"From the looks of the place, honey, that's not much of a recommendation."

Her face froze, and she looked away from him, making him swear under his breath. Without another word she jerked the papers from him and began sorting them, then put them in order by dates. He settled back in his big chair, his face brooding as he watched her enter the figures swiftly and neatly in the ledger, then run the columns through the adding machine twice to make certain they were correct.

When she was finished, she pushed the ledger across the desk. "Check it so you'll be satisfied I didn't make any mistakes."

He did, thoroughly. Finally he closed the ledger and said, "All right."

Her eyes narrowed. "Is that all you have to say? No wonder you've never been married, if you think women don't have the brains to add two and two!"

"I've been married," he said sharply.

The information stunned her, because she'd never heard anyone mention his being married, nor was marriage something she readily associated with John Rafferty. Then hot jealousy seared her at the thought of some other woman living with him, sharing his name and his bed, having the right to touch him. "Who... when?" she stammered.

"A long time ago. I'd just turned nineteen, and I had more hormones than sense. God only knows why

she married me. It only took her four months to decide ranch life wasn't for her, that she wanted money
to spend and a husband who didn't work twenty hours
a day."

His voice was flat, his eyes filled with contempt.
Michelle felt cold. "Why didn't anyone ever mention
it?" she whispered. "I've known you for ten years, but
I didn't know you'd been married."

He shrugged. "We got divorced seven years before
you moved down here, so it wasn't exactly the hottest
news in the county. It didn't last long enough for folks
to get to know her, anyway. I worked too much to do
any socializing. If she married me thinking a rancher's
wife would live in the lap of luxury, she changed her
mind in a hurry."

"Where is she now?" Michelle fervently hoped the
woman didn't still live in the area.

"I don't know, and I don't care. I heard she married
some old rich guy as soon as our divorce was final. It
didn't matter to me then, and it doesn't matter now."

It was beyond her how any woman could choose another man, no matter how rich, over John. She would
live in a hut and eat rattlesnake meat if it meant staying with him. But she was beginning to understand
why he was so contemptuous of the jet-setters, the idle
rich, why he'd made so many caustic remarks to her
in the past about letting others support her instead of
working to support herself. Considering that, it was
even more confusing that now he didn't want her doing
anything at all, as if he wanted to make her totally dependent on him.

He was watching her from beneath hooded lids, wondering what she was thinking. She'd been shocked to
learn he'd been married before. It had been so long ago

that he never thought about it, and he wouldn't even have mentioned it if her crack about marriage hadn't reminded him. It had happened in another lifetime, to a nineteen-year-old boy busting his guts to make a go of the rundown little ranch he'd inherited. Sometimes he couldn't even remember her name, and it had been years since he'd been able to remember what she looked like. He wouldn't recognize her if they met face-to-face.

It was odd, because even though he hadn't seen Michelle during the years of her marriage, he'd never forgotten her face, the way she moved, the way sunlight looked in her hair. He knew every line of her striking, but too angular face, all high cheekbones, stubborn chin and wide, soft mouth. She had put her mouth to his chest and tasted his salty, sweaty skin, her tongue licking at him. She looked so cool and untouchable now in that spotless white dress, but when he made love to her she turned into liquid heat. He thought of the way her legs wrapped around his waist, and he began to harden as desire heated his body. He leaned back in his chair, shifting restlessly.

Michelle had turned back to the stack of papers on his desk, not wanting to pry any further. She didn't want to know any more about his ex-wife, and she especially didn't want him to take the opportunity to ask about her failed marriage. It would be safer to get back to business; she needed to talk to him about selling her beef cattle, anyway.

"I need your advice on something. I wanted to fatten the cattle up for sale this year, but I need operating capital, so I think I should sell them now. Who do I contact, and how is transportation arranged?"

Right at that moment he didn't give a damn about any cattle. She had crossed her legs, and her skirt had slid up a little, drawing his eyes. He wanted to slide it up more, crumple it around her waist and completely bare her legs. His jeans were under considerable strain, and he had to force himself to answer. "Let the cattle fatten; you'll get a lot more money for them. I'll keep the ranch going until then."

She turned her head with a quick, impatient movement, sending her hair swirling, but whatever she had been about to say died when their eyes met and she read his expression. "Let's go upstairs," he murmured.

It was almost frightening to have that intense sexuality focused on her, but she was helpless to resist him. She found herself standing, shivering as he put his hand on her back and ushered her upstairs. Walking beside him made her feel vulnerable; sometimes his size overwhelmed her, and this was one of those times. He was so tall and powerful, his shoulders so broad, that when she lay beneath him in bed he blocked out the light. Only his own control and tenderness protected her.

He locked the bedroom door behind them, then stood behind her and slowly began unzipping her dress. He felt her shivering. "Don't be afraid, baby. Or is it excitement?"

"Yes," she whispered as he slid his hands inside the open dress and around to cup her bare breasts, molding his fingers over her. She could feel her nipples throb against his palms, and with a little whimper she leaned back against him, trying to sink herself into his hardness and warmth. It felt so good when he touched her.

"Both?" he murmured. "Why are you afraid?"

Her eyes were closed, her breath coming in shallow gulps as he rubbed her nipples to hard little points of fire. "The way you make me feel," she gasped, her head rolling on his shoulder.

"You make me feel the same." His voice was slow and guttural as the hot pressure built in him. "Hot, like I'll explode if I don't get inside you. Then you're so soft and tight around me that I know I'm going to explode anyway."

The words made love to her, turning her shivers into shudders. Her legs were liquid, unable to support her; if it hadn't been for John's muscular body behind her, she would have fallen. She whispered his name, the single word vibrant with longing.

His warm breath puffed around her ear as he nuzzled the lobe. "You're so sexy, baby. This dress has been driving me crazy. I wanted to pull up your skirt…like this…." His hands had left her breasts and gone down to her hips, and now her skirt rose along her thighs as he gathered the material in his fists. Then it was at her waist, and his hands were beneath it, his fingers spread over her bare stomach. "I thought about sliding my hands under your panties…like this. Pulling them down…like this."

She moaned as he slipped her panties down her hips and over her buttocks, overcome by a sense of voluptuous helplessness and exposure. Somehow being only partially undressed made her feel even more naked and vulnerable. His long fingers went between her legs, and she quivered like a wild thing as he stroked and probed, slowly building her tension and pleasure to the breaking point.

"You're so sweet and soft," he whispered. "Are you ready for me?"

She tried to answer, but all she could do was gasp. She was on fire, her entire body throbbing, and still he held her against him, his fingers slowly thrusting into her, when he knew she wanted him and was ready for him. He *knew* it. He was too experienced not to know, but he persisted in that sweet torment as he savored the feel of her.

She felt as sexy as he told her she was; her own sensuality was unfolding like a tender flower under his hands and his low, rough voice. Each time he made love to her, she found a little more self-assurance in her own capacity for giving and receiving pleasure. He was strongly, frankly sexual, so experienced that she wanted to slap him every time she thought about it, but she had discovered that she could satisfy him. Sometimes he trembled with hunger when he touched her; this man, whose raw virility gave him sensual power over any woman he wanted, trembled with the need for *her*. She was twenty-eight years old, and only now, in John's hands, was she discovering her power and pleasure as a woman.

Finally she couldn't take any more and whirled away from his hands, her eyes fierce as she stripped off her dress and reached for him, tearing at his clothes. He laughed deeply, but the sound was of excitement rather than humor, and helped her. Naked, already entwined, they fell together to the bed. He took her with a slow, strong thrust, for the first time not having to enter her by careful degrees, and the inferno roared out of control.

MICHELLE BOUNCED OUT of bed before he did the next morning, her face glowing. "You don't have to get up," he rumbled in his hoarse, early-morning voice. "Why don't you sleep late?" Actually he liked the thought of her dozing in his bed, rosily naked and exhausted after a night of making love.

She pushed her pale, tousled hair out of her eyes,

momentarily riveted by his nudity as he got out of bed. "I'm going with you today," she said, and dashed to beat him to the bathroom.

He joined her in the shower a few minutes later, his black eyes narrowed after her announcement. She waited for him to tell her that she couldn't go, but instead he muttered, "I guess it's okay, if it'll make you happy."

It did. She had decided that John was such an overprotective chauvinist that he would cheerfully keep her wrapped in cotton, so reasoning with him was out of the question. She knew what she could do; she would do it. It was that simple.

Over the next three weeks a deep happiness began forming inside her. She had taken over the paperwork completely, working on it three days out of the week, which gave John more free time at night than he'd ever had before. He gave up checking her work, because he never found an error. On the other days she rode with him, content with his company, and he discovered that he liked having her nearby. There were times when he was so hot, dirty and aggravated that he'd be turning the air blue with savage curses, then he'd look up and catch her smiling at him, and his aggravation would fade away. What did a contrary steer matter when she looked at him that way? She never seemed to mind the dust and heat, or the smells. It wasn't what he'd expected, and sometimes it bothered him. It was as if she were hiding here, burying herself in this self-contained world. The Michelle he'd known before had been a laughing, teasing, social creature, enjoying parties and dancing. This Michelle seldom laughed, though she was so generous with her smiles that it took him a while to notice. One of those smiles made him and all his men a little giddy, but he could remember her sparkling laughter, and he wondered where it had gone.

But it was still so new, having her to himself, that he wasn't anxious to share her with others. They spent the nights tangled together in heated passion, and instead of abating, the hunger only intensified. He spent the days in constant, low-level arousal, and sometimes all he had to do was look at her and he'd be so hard he'd have to find some way of disguising it.

One morning Michelle remained at the house to work in the office; she was alone because Edie had gone grocery shopping. The telephone rang off the hook that morning, interrupting her time and again. She was already irritated with it when it jangled yet again and made her stop what she was doing to answer it. "Rafferty residence."

No one answered, though she could hear slow, deep breathing, as though whoever was on the other end was deliberately controlling his breath. It wasn't a "breather," though; the sound wasn't obscenely exaggerated.

"Hello," she said. "Can you hear me?"

A quiet click sounded in her ear, as if whoever had been calling had put down the receiver with slow, controlled caution, much as he'd been breathing.

He. For some reason she had no doubt it was a man. Common sense said it could be some bored teenager playing a prank, or simply a wrong number, but a sudden chill swept over her.

A sense of menace had filled the silence on the line. For the first time in three weeks she felt isolated and somehow threatened, though there was no tangible reason for it. The chills wouldn't stop running up and down her spine, and suddenly she had to get out of the house, into the hot sunshine. She had to see John, just be able to look at him and hear his deep voice roaring curses, or crooning gently to a horse or a frightened calf. She needed his heat to dispel the coldness of a menace she couldn't define.

Two days later there was another phone call and again, by chance, she answered the phone. "Hello," she said. "Rafferty residence."

Silence.

Her hand began shaking. She strained her ears and heard that quiet, even breathing, then the click as the phone was hung up, and a moment later the dial tone began buzzing in her ear. She felt sick and cold, without knowing why. What was going on? Who was doing this to her?

CHAPTER EIGHT

MICHELLE PACED THE bedroom like a nervous cat, her silky hair swirling around her head as she moved. "I don't feel like going," she blurted. "Why didn't you ask me before you told Addie we'd be there?"

"Because you'd have come up with one excuse after another why you couldn't go, just like you're doing now," he answered calmly. He'd been watching her pace back and forth, her eyes glittering, her usually sinuous movements jerky with agitation. It had been almost a month since he'd moved her to the ranch, and she had yet to stir beyond the boundaries of his property, except to visit her own. He'd given her the keys to the Mercedes and free use of it, but to his knowledge she'd never taken it out. She hadn't been shopping, though he'd made certain she had money. He had received the usual invitations to the neighborhood Saturday night barbecues that had become a county tradition, but she'd always found some excuse not to attend.

He'd wondered fleetingly if she were ashamed of having come down in the world, embarrassed because he didn't measure up financially or in terms of sophistication with the men she'd known before, but he'd dismissed the notion almost before it formed. It wasn't that. He'd come to know her better than that. She came into his arms at night too eagerly, too hungrily, to harbor any feelings that he was socially inferior. A lot of his ideas about her had been wrong. She didn't look down on work, never had. She had simply been sheltered from it her entire life. She was willing to work. Damn it, she insisted on it! He had to watch her to keep her from trying her hand at bulldogging. He was as bad as her father had ever been, willing to do just about anything to keep her happy.

Maybe she was embarrassed because they were living together. This was a rural section, where mores and morality changed slowly. Their arrangement wouldn't so much as raise an eyebrow in Miami or any other large city, but they weren't in a large city. John was too self-assured and arrogant to worry about gossip; he thought of Michelle simply as his woman, with all the fierce possessiveness implied by the term. She was his. He'd held her beneath him and made her his, and the bond was reinforced every time he took her.

Whatever her reason for hiding on the ranch, it was time for it to end. If she were trying to hide their relationship, he wasn't going to let her get away with it any longer. She had to become accustomed to being his woman. He sensed that she was still hiding something of herself from him, carefully preserving a certain distance between them, and it enraged him. It wasn't a physical distance. Sweet Lord, no. She was liquid fire in his arms. The distance was mental; there were times when she was silent and withdrawn, the sparkle gone from her eyes, but whenever he asked her what was wrong she would stonewall, and no amount of probing would induce her to tell him what she'd been thinking.

He was determined to destroy whatever it was that pulled her away from him; he wanted all of her, mind and body. He wanted to hear her laugh, to make her lose her temper as he'd used to do, to hear the haughtiness and petulance in her voice. It was all a part of her, the part she wasn't giving him now, and he wanted it. Damn it, was she tiptoeing around him because she thought she *owed* him?

She hadn't stopped pacing. Now she sat down on the bed and stared at him, her lips set. "I don't want to go."

"I thought you liked Addie." He pulled off his boots and stood to shrug out of his shirt.

"I do," Michelle said.

"Then why don't you want to go to her party? Have you even seen her since you've been back?"

"No, but Dad had just died, and I wasn't in the mood to socialize! Then there was so much work to be done...."

"You don't have that excuse now."

She glared at him. "I decided you were a bully when I was eighteen years old, and nothing you've done over the years has changed my opinion!"

He couldn't stop the grin that spread over his face as he stripped off his jeans. She was something when she got on her high horse. Going over to the bed, he sat beside her and rubbed her back. "Just relax," he soothed. "You know everyone who'll be there, and it's as informal as it always was. You used to have fun at these things, didn't you? They haven't changed."

Michelle let him coax her into lying against his shoulder. She would sound crazy if she told him that she didn't feel safe away from the ranch. He'd want to know why, and what could she tell him? That she'd had two phone calls and the other person wouldn't say anything, just quietly hung up? That happened to people all the time when someone had dialed a wrong number. But she couldn't shake the feeling that something menacing was waiting out there for her if she left the sanctuary of the ranch, where John Rafferty ruled supreme. She sighed, turning her face into his throat. She was overreacting to a simple wrong number; she'd felt safe enough all the time she'd been alone at her house. This was just another little emotional legacy from her marriage.

She gave in. "All right, I'll go. What time does it start?"

"In about two hours." He kissed her slowly, feeling the tension drain out of her, but he could still sense a certain distance in her, as if her mind were on something else, and frustration rose in him. He couldn't pinpoint it, but he knew it was there.

Michelle slipped from his arms, shaking her head as she stood. "You gave me just enough time to get ready, didn't you?"

"We could share a shower," he invited, dropping his last garment at his feet. He stretched, his powerful torso rippling with muscle, and Michelle couldn't take her eyes off him. "I don't mind being late if you don't."

She swallowed. "Thanks, but you go ahead." She was nervous about this party. Even aside from the spooky feeling those phone calls had given her, she wasn't certain how she felt about going. She didn't know how much the ranching crowd knew of her circumstances, but she certainly didn't want anyone pitying her, or making knowing remarks about her position in John's house. On the other hand, she didn't remember anyone as being malicious, and she had always liked Addie Layfield and her husband, Steve. This would be a family oriented group, ranging in age from Frank and Yetta Campbell, in their seventies, to the young children of several families. People would sit around and talk, eat barbecue and drink beer, the children and some of the adults would swim, and the thing would break up of its own accord at about ten o'clock.

John was waiting for her when she came out of the bathroom after showering and dressing. She had opted for cool and comfortable, sleeking her wet hair straight back and twisting it into a knot, which she'd pinned at her nape, and she wore a minimum of makeup. She had on an oversize white cotton T-shirt, with the tail tied in a knot on one hip, and loose white cotton drawstring pants. Her sandals consisted of soles and two straps each. On someone else the same ensemble might have looked sloppy, but on Michelle it looked chic. He decided she could wear a feed sack and make it look good.

"Don't forget your swimsuit," he said, remembering that she had always gone swimming at these parties. She'd loved the water.

Michelle looked away, pretending to check her purse for something. "I'm not swimming tonight."

"Why not?"

"I just don't feel like it."

Her voice had that flat, expressionless sound he'd come to hate, the same tone she used whenever he tried to probe into the reason she sometimes became so quiet and distant. He looked at her sharply, and his brows drew together. He couldn't remember Michelle ever "not feeling" like swimming. Her father had put in a pool for her the first year they'd been in Florida, and she had often spent the entire day lolling in the water. After she'd married, the pool had gone unused and had finally been emptied. He didn't think it had ever been filled again, and now it was badly in need of repairs before it would be usable.

But she'd been with him almost a month, and he didn't think she'd been in his pool even once. He glanced out at the balcony; he could just see a corner of the pool, blue and glittering in the late-afternoon sun. He didn't have much time for swimming, but he'd insisted, eight years ago, on having the big pool and its luxurious landscaping. For her. Damn it, this whole place was for her: the big house, the comforts, that pool, even the damn Mercedes. He'd built it for her, not admitting it to himself then because he couldn't. Why wasn't she using the pool?

Michelle could feel his sharpened gaze on her as they left the room, but he didn't say anything and, relieved, she realized he was going to let it go. Maybe he just accepted that she didn't feel like swimming. If he only knew how much she wanted to swim, how she'd longed for the feel of cool water on her overheated skin, but she just couldn't bring herself to put on a bathing suit, even in the privacy of his house.

She knew that the little white scars were hardly visible now, but she still shrank from the possibility that someone might notice them. She still felt that they were glaringly obvious, even though the mirror told her differently. It had become such a habit to hide them that she couldn't stop. She didn't dress or undress in front of John if she could help it, and if she couldn't, she always remained facing him, so he wouldn't see her back. It was such a reversal of modesty that he hadn't even noticed her reluctance to be nude in front of him. At night, in bed, it didn't matter. If the lights were on, they were dim, and John had other things on his mind. Still she insisted on wearing a nightgown to bed. It might be off most of the night, but it would be on when she got out of bed in the mornings. Everything in her shrank from having to explain those scars.

The party was just as she had expected, with a lot

of food, a lot of talk, a lot of laughter. Addie had once been one of Michelle's best friends, and she was still the warm, talkative person she'd been before. She'd put on a little weight, courtesy of two children, but her pretty face still glowed with good humor. Steve, her husband, sometimes managed to put his own two cents into a conversation by the simple means of putting his hand over her mouth. Addie laughed more than anyone whenever he resorted to that tactic.

"It's an old joke between us," she told Michelle as they put together tacos for the children. "When we were dating, he'd do that so he could kiss me. Holy cow, you look good! Something must be agreeing with you, and I'd say that 'something' is about six-foot-three of pure hunk. God, I used to swoon whenever he spoke to me! Remember? You'd sniff and say he didn't do anything for you. Liar, liar, pants on fire." Addie chanted the childish verse, her eyes sparkling with mirth, and Michelle couldn't help laughing with her.

On the other side of the pool, John's head swiveled at the sound, and he froze, stunned by the way her face lit as she joked with Addie. He felt the hardening in his loins and swore silently to himself, jerking his attention back to the talk of cattle and shifting his position to make his arousal less obvious. Why didn't she laugh like that more often?

Despite Michelle's reservations, she enjoyed the party. She'd missed the relaxed gatherings, so different from the sophisticated dinner parties, yacht parties, divorce parties, fund-raising dinners, et cetera, that had made up the social life John thought she'd enjoyed so much, but had only tolerated. She liked the shrieks of the children as they cannonballed into the pool, splashing any unwary adult in the vicinity, and she liked it that no one got angry over being wet. Probably it felt good in the sweltering heat, which had abated only a little.

True to most of the parties she'd attended, the men tended to group together and the women did the same, with the men talking cattle and weather, and the women talking about people. But the groups were fluid, flowing together and intermingling, and by the time the children had worn down, all the adults were sitting together. John had touched her arm briefly when he sat down beside her, a small, possessive gesture that made her tingle. She tried not to stare at him like an infatuated idiot, but she felt as if everyone there could tell how warm she was getting. Her cheeks flushed, and she darted a glance at him to find him watching her with blatant need.

"Let's go home," he said in a low voice.

"So soon?" Addie protested, but at that moment they all heard the distant rumble of thunder.

As ranchers, they all searched the night sky for signs of a storm that would break the heat, if only for a little while, and fill the slow-moving rivers and streams. Out to the west, over the Gulf, lightning shimmered in a bank of black clouds.

Frank Campbell said, "We sure could use a good rain. Haven't had one in about a month now."

It had stormed the day John had come over to her ranch for the first time, Michelle remembered, and again the night they'd driven back from Tampa…the first time he'd made love to her. His eyes glittered, and she knew he was thinking the same thing.

Wind suddenly kicked up from the west, bringing with it the cool smell of rain and salt, the excitement of a storm. Everyone began gathering up children and food, cleaning up the patio before the rain hit. Soon people were calling out goodbyes and piling into pickup trucks and cars.

"Glad you went?" John asked as he turned onto the highway.

Michelle was watching the lacy patterns the lightning made as it forked across the sky. "Yes, I had fun." She moved closer against him, seeking his warmth.

He held the truck steady against the gusts of wind buffeting it, feeling her breast brush his arm every time he moved. He inhaled sharply at his inevitable response.

"What's wrong?" she asked sleepily.

For answer he took her hand and pressed it to the straining fabric of his jeans. She made a soft sound, and her slender fingers outlined the hard ridge beneath the fabric as her body automatically curled toward him. He felt his jeans open; then her hand slid inside the parted fabric and closed over him, her palm soft and warm. He groaned aloud, his body jerking as he tried to keep his attention on the road. It was the sweetest torture he could imagine, and he ground his teeth as her hand moved further down to gently cup him for a moment before returning to stroke him to the edge of madness.

He wanted her, and he wanted her now. Jerking the steering wheel, he pulled the truck onto the side of the road just as fat raindrops began splattering the windshield. "Why are we stopping?" Michelle murmured.

He killed the lights and reached for her, muttering a graphic explanation.

"John! We're on the highway! Anyone could pass by and see us!"

"It's dark and raining," he said roughly, untying the drawstring at her waist and pulling her pants down. "No one can see in."

She'd been enjoying teasing him, exciting him, exciting herself with the feel of his hardness in her hand, but she'd thought he would wait until they got home. She should have known better. He didn't care if they were in a bedroom or not; his appetites were strong and immediate. She went weak under the onslaught of his mouth and hands, no longer caring about anything else. The rain was a thunderous din, streaming over the windows of the truck as if they were sitting under a waterfall. She could barely hear the rawly sexual things he was saying to her as he slid to the middle of the seat and lifted her over him. She cried out at his penetration, her body arching in his hands, and the world spun away in a whirlwind of sensations.

Later, after the rain had let up, she was limp in his arms as he carried her inside the house. Her hands slid around his neck as he bent to place her gently on the bed, and obeying that light pressure he stretched out on the bed with her. She was exhausted, sated, her body still throbbing with the remnants of pleasure. He kissed her deeply, rubbing his hand over her breasts and stomach. "Do you want me to undress you?" he murmured.

She nuzzled his throat. "No, I'll do it…in a minute. I don't feel like moving right now."

His big hand paused on her stomach, then slipped lower. "We didn't use anything."

"It's okay," she assured him softly. The timing was wrong. She had just finished her cycle, which was one reason he'd exploded out of control.

He rubbed his lips over hers in warm, quick kisses. "I'm sorry, baby. I was so damned ready for you, I thought I was going to go off like a teenager."

"It's okay," she said again. She loved him so much she trembled with it. Sometimes it was all she could do to keep from telling him, from crying the words aloud, but she was terrified that if she did he'd start putting distance between them, wary of too many entanglements. It had to end sometime, but she wanted it to last every possible second.

NOTHING TERRIBLE HAD happened to her because she'd gone to the party; in fact, the trip home had been wonderful. For days afterward, she shivered with delight whenever she thought about it. There hadn't been any other out of the ordinary phone calls, and gradually she relaxed, convinced that there had been nothing to them. She was still far more content remaining on the ranch than she was either socializing or shopping, but at John's urging she began using the Mercedes to run small errands and occasionally visit her friends on those days when she wasn't riding with him or working on the books. She drove over to her house several times to check on things, but the silence depressed her. John had had the electricity turned back on, though he hadn't mentioned it to her, but she didn't say anything about moving back in. She couldn't leave him, not now; she was so helplessly, hopelessly in love with him that she knew she'd stay with him until he told her to leave.

One Monday afternoon she'd been on an errand for John, and on the return trip she detoured by her house to check things again. She walked through the huge rooms, making certain no pipes had sprung a leak or anything else needed repair. It was odd; she hadn't been away that long, but the house felt less and less like her home. It was hard to remember how it had been before John Rafferty had come storming into her life again; his presence was so intense it blocked out lesser details. Her troubled dreams had almost disappeared, and even when she had one, she would wake to find him beside her in the night, strong and warm. It was becoming easier to trust, to accept that she wasn't alone to face whatever happened.

It was growing late, and the shadows lengthened in the house; she carefully locked the door behind her and walked out to the car. Abruptly she shivered, as if something cold had touched her. She looked around, but everything was normal. Birds sang in the trees; insects hummed. But for a moment she'd felt it again, that sense of menace. It was odd.

Logic told her there was nothing to it, but when she was in the car she locked the doors. She laughed a little at herself. First a couple of phone calls had seemed spooky, and now she was "feeling" things in the air.

Because there was so little traffic on the secondary roads between her ranch and John's, she didn't use the rearview mirrors very much. The car was on her rear bumper before she noticed it, and even then she got only a glimpse before it swung to the left to pass. The road was narrow, and she edged to the right to give the other car more room. It pulled even with her, and she gave it a cursory glance just as it suddenly swerved toward her.

"Watch it!" she yelled, jerking the steering wheel to the right, but there was a loud grinding sound as metal rubbed against metal. The Mercedes, smaller than the other car, was pushed violently to the right. Michelle slammed on the brakes as she felt the two right wheels catch in the sandy soil of the shoulder, pulling the car even harder to that side.

She wrestled with the steering wheel, too scared even to swear at the other driver. The other car shot past, and somehow she managed to jerk the Mercedes back onto the road. Shaking, she braked to a stop and leaned her head on the steering wheel, then sat upright as she heard tires squealing. The other car had gone down the road, but now had made a violent U-turn and was coming back. She only hoped whoever it was had insurance.

The car was a big, blue full-size Chevrolet. She could tell that a man was driving, because the silhouette was so large. It was only a silhouette, because he had something black pulled over his head, like a ski mask.

The coldness was back. She acted instinctively, jamming her foot onto the gas pedal, and the sporty little Mercedes leaped forward. The Chevrolet swerved toward her again, and she swung wildly to the side. She almost missed it...almost. The Chevrolet clipped her rear bumper, and the smaller, lighter car spun in a nauseating circle before sliding off the road, across the wide sandy shoulder, and scraping against an enormous pine before it bogged down in the soft dirt and weeds.

She heard herself screaming, but the hard jolt that stopped the car stopped her screams, too. Dazed, her head lolled against the broken side window for a moment before terror drove the fogginess away. She groped for the handle, but couldn't budge the door. The pine tree blocked it. She tried to scramble across the seat to the other door, and only then realized she was still buckled into her seat. Fumbling, looking around wildly for the Chevrolet, she released the buckle and threw herself to the other side of the car. She pushed the door open and tumbled out in the same motion, her breath wheezing in and out of her lungs.

Numbly she crouched by the fender and tried to listen, but she could hear nothing over her tortuous breathing and the thunder of her heart. Old habits took over, and she used a trick she'd often used before to calm herself after one of Roger's insane rages, taking a deep breath and holding it. The maneuver slowed her heartbeat almost immediately, and the roar faded out of her ears.

She couldn't hear anything. Oh, God, had he stopped? Cautiously she peered over the car, but she couldn't see the blue Chevrolet.

Slowly she realized it had gone. He hadn't stopped. She stumbled to the road and looked in both directions, but the road was empty.

She couldn't believe it had happened. He had deliberately run her off the road, not once, but twice. If the small Mercedes had hit one of the huge pines that thickly lined the road head-on, she could easily have been killed. Whoever the man was, he must have figured the heavier Chevrolet could muscle her off the road without any great risk to himself.

He'd tried to kill her.

It was five minutes before another car came down the road; it was blue, and for a horrible moment she panicked, thinking the Chevrolet was returning, but as it came closer she could tell this car was much older and wasn't even a Chevrolet. She stumbled to the middle of the road, waving her arms to flag it down.

All she could think of was John. She wanted John. She wanted him to hold her close and shut the terror away with his strength and possessiveness. Her voice shook as she leaned in the window and told the young boy, "Please—call John Rafferty. Tell him I've been… I've had an accident. Tell him I'm all right."

"Sure, lady," the boy said. "What's your name?"

"Michelle," she said. "My name's Michelle."

The boy looked at the car lodged against the pine.

"You need a wrecker, too. Are you sure you're all right?"

"Yes, I'm not hurt. Just hurry, please."

"Sure thing."

Either John called the sheriff's department or the boy had, because John and a county sheriff's car arrived from opposite directions almost simultaneously. It hadn't been much more than ten minutes since the boy had stopped, but in that short length of time it had grown considerably darker. John threw his door open as the truck ground to a stop and was out of the vehicle before it had settled back on its wheels, striding toward her. She couldn't move toward him; she was shaking too violently. Beneath his mustache his lips were a thin, grim line.

He walked all the way around her, checking her from head to foot. Only when he didn't see any blood on her did he haul her against his chest, his arms so tight they almost crushed her. He buried his hand in her hair and bent his head down until his jaw rested on her temple. "Are you really all right?" he muttered hoarsely.

Her arms locked around his waist in a death grip. "I was wearing my seat belt," she whispered. A single tear slid unnoticed down her cheek.

"God, when I got that phone call—" He broke off, because there was no way he could describe the stark terror he'd felt despite the kid's assurance that she was okay. He'd had to see her for himself, hold her, before he could really let himself believe she wasn't harmed. If he'd seen blood on her, he would have gone berserk. Only now was his heartbeat settling down, and he looked over her head at the car.

The deputy approached them, clipboard in hand. "Can you answer a few questions, ma'am?"

John's arms dropped from around her, but he remained right beside her as she answered the usual questions about name, age and driver's license number. When the deputy asked her how it had happened, she began shaking again.

"A…a car ran me off the road," she stammered. "A blue Chevrolet."

The deputy looked up, his eyes abruptly interested as a routine accident investigation became something more. "Ran you off the road? How?"

"He sideswiped me." Fiercely she clenched her fingers together in an effort to still their trembling. "He pushed me off the road."

"He didn't just come too close, and you panicked and ran off the road?" John asked, his brows drawing together.

"No! He pushed me off the road. I slammed on my brakes and he went on past, then turned around and came back."

"He came back? Did you get his name?" The deputy made a notation on his pad. Leaving the scene of an accident was a crime.

"No, he didn't stop. He…he tried to ram me. He hit my bumper, and I spun off the road, then into that pine tree."

John jerked his head at the deputy and they walked over to the car, bending down to inspect the damage. They talked together in low voices; Michelle couldn't make out what they were saying, but she didn't move closer. She stood by the road, listening to the peaceful sounds of the deepening Florida twilight. It was all so out of place. How could the crickets be chirping so happily when someone had just tried to commit murder? She felt dazed, as if none of this were real. But the damaged car was real. The blue Chevrolet had been real, as had the man wearing the black ski mask.

The two men walked back toward her. John looked at her sharply; her face was deathly white, even in the growing gloom, and she was shaking. She looked terrified. The Mercedes *was* an expensive car; did she expect him to tear a strip off her hide because she'd wrecked it? She'd never had to worry about things like that before, never had to be accountable for anything. If she'd banged a fender, it hadn't been important; her father had simply had the car repaired, or bought her a new one. Hell, he wasn't happy that she'd wrecked the damn car, but he wasn't a fanatic about cars, no matter how much they cost. It would have been different if she'd ruined a good horse. He was just thankful she wasn't hurt.

"It's all right," he said, trying to soothe her as he took her arm and walked her to the truck. "I have insurance on it. You're okay, and that's what matters. Just calm down. I'll take you home as soon as the deputy's finished with his report and the wrecker gets here."

Frantically she clutched his arm. "But what about—"

He kissed her and rubbed her shoulder. "I said it's all right, baby. I'm not mad. You don't have to make excuses."

Frozen, Michelle sat in the truck and watched as he walked back to the deputy. He didn't believe her; neither of them believed her. It was just like before, when no one would believe handsome, charming Roger Beckman was capable of hitting his wife, because it was obvious he adored her. It was just too unbelievable. Even her father had thought she was exaggerating.

She was so cold, even though the temperature was still in the nineties. She had begun to trust, to accept that John stood behind her, as unmoving as a block of granite, his strength available whenever she needed him. For the first time she hadn't felt alone. He'd been there, ready to shoulder her burdens. But suddenly it was just like before, and she was cold and alone again. Her father had given her everything materially, but had been too weak to face an ugly truth. Roger had showered her with gifts, pampering her extravagantly to make up for the bruises and terror. John had given her a place to live, food to eat, mind-shattering physical pleasure…but now he, too, was turning away from a horribly real threat. It was too much effort to believe such a tale. Why would anyone try to kill her?

She didn't know, but someone had. The phone calls… the phone calls were somehow connected. They'd given her the same feeling she'd had just before she got in the car, the same sense of menace. God, had he been watching her at her house? Had he been waiting for her? He could be anywhere. He knew her, but she didn't know him, and she was alone again. She'd always been alone, but she hadn't known it. For a while she'd trusted, hoped, and the contrast with that warm feeling of security made cold reality just that much more piercing.

The wrecker arrived with its yellow lights flashing and backed up to the Mercedes. Michelle watched with detached interest as the car was hauled away from the pine. She didn't even wince at the amount of damage that had been done to the left side. John thought she'd made up a wild tale to keep from having to accept blame for wrecking the car. He didn't believe her. The deputy didn't believe her. There should be blue paint on the car, but evidently the scrapes left by the big pine had obscured it. Maybe dirt covered it. Maybe it was too dark for them to see. For whatever reason, they didn't believe her.

She was utterly silent as John drove home. Edie came to the door, watching anxiously, then hurried forward as Michelle slid out of the truck.

"Are you all right? John left here like a bat out of hell, didn't stop to tell us anything except you'd had an accident."

"I'm fine," Michelle murmured. "I just need a bath. I'm freezing."

Frowning, John touched her arm. It was icy, despite the heat. She wasn't hurt, but she'd had a shock.

"Make some coffee," he instructed Edie as he turned Michelle toward the stairs. "I'll give her a bath."

Slowly Michelle pulled away from him. Her face was calm. "No, I'll do it. I'm all right. Just give me a few minutes by myself."

After a hot but brief shower, she went downstairs and drank coffee, and even managed to eat a few bites of the meal Edie had put back when John tore out of the house.

In bed that night, for the first time she couldn't respond to him. He needed her almost desperately, to reassure himself once again that she was truly all right. He needed to strengthen the bond between them, to draw her even closer with ties as old as time. But though he was gentle and stroked her for a long time, she remained tense under his hands. She was still too quiet, somehow distant from him.

Finally he just held her, stroking her hair until she slept and her soft body relaxed against him. But he lay awake for hours, his body burning, his eyes open. God, how close he'd come to losing her!

CHAPTER NINE

JOHN LISTENED IMPATIENTLY, his hard, dark face angry, his black eyes narrowed. Finally he said, "It hasn't been three months since I straightened all that out. How the hell did you manage to get everything in a mess this fast?"

Michelle looked up from the figures she was posting in, curious to learn the identity of his caller. He hadn't said much more than hello before he'd begun getting angry. Finally he said, "All right. I'll be down tomorrow. And if you're out partying when I get there, the way you were last time, I'll turn around and come home. I don't have time to cool my heels while you're playing." He hung up the phone and muttered a graphic expletive.

"Who was it?" Michelle asked.

"Mother." A wealth of irritation was in the single word.

She was stunned. "*Your* mother?"

He looked at her for a moment; then his mustache twitched a little as he almost smiled. "You don't have to sound so shocked. I got here by the normal method."

"But you've never mentioned... I guess I assumed she was dead, like your father."

"She cut out a long time ago. Ranching wasn't good enough for her; she liked the bright lights of Miami and the money of Palm Beach, so she walked out one fine day and never came back."

"How old were you?"

"Six or seven, something like that. Funny, I don't remember being too upset when she left, or missing her very much. Mostly I remember how she used to complain because the house was small and old, and because there was never much money. I was with Dad every minute I wasn't in school, but I was never close to Mother."

She felt as she had when she'd discovered he had been married. He kept throwing out little tidbits about himself, then dismissing these vital points of his life as if they hadn't affected him much at all. Maybe they hadn't. John was a hard man, made so by a lifetime of backbreaking work and the combination of arrogance and steely determination in his personality. But how could a child not be affected when his mother walked away? How could a young man, little more than a boy, not be affected when his new wife walked out rather than work by his side? To this day John would do anything to help someone who was *trying*, but he wouldn't lift a finger to aid anyone who sat around waiting for help. All his employees were loyal to him down to their last drop of blood. If they hadn't been, they wouldn't still be on his ranch.

"When you went to Miami before, it was to see your mother?"

"Yeah. She makes a mess of her finances at least twice a year and expects me to drop everything, fly down there and straighten it out."

"Which you do."

He shrugged. "We may not be close, but she's still my mother."

"Call me this time," she said distinctly, giving him a hard look that underlined her words.

He grunted, looking irritated, then gave her a wink as he turned to call the airlines. Michelle listened as he booked a flight to Miami for the next morning. Then he glanced at her and said "Wait a minute" into the receiver before putting his hand over the mouthpiece. "Want to come with me?" he asked her.

Panic flared in her eyes before she controlled it and shook her head. "No thanks. I need to catch up on the paperwork."

It was a flimsy excuse, as the accumulated work wouldn't take more than a day, but though John gave her a long, level look, he didn't argue with her. Instead he moved his fingers from the mouthpiece and said, "Just one. That's right. No, not round trip. I don't know what day I'll be coming back. Yeah, thanks."

He scribbled his flight number and time on a notepad as he took the phone from his ear and hung up. Since the accident, Michelle hadn't left the ranch at all, for any reason. He'd picked up the newly repaired Mercedes three days ago, but it hadn't been moved from the garage since. Accidents sometimes made people nervous about driving again, but he sensed that something more was bothering her.

She'd begun totalling the figures she had posted in the ledger. His eyes drifted over her, drinking in her serious, absorbed expression and the way she chewed her bottom lip when she was working. She'd taken over his office so completely that he sometimes had to ask *her* questions about what was going on. He wasn't certain he liked having part of the ranch out of his direct control, but he was damn certain he liked the extra time he had at night.

That thought made him realize he'd be spending the next few nights alone, and he scowled. Once he would have found female companionship in Miami, but now he was distinctly uninterested in any other woman. He wanted Michelle and no one else. No other woman had ever fit in his arms as well as she did, or given him the pleasure she gave just by being there. He liked to tease her until she lost her temper and lashed back at him, just for the joy of watching her get snooty. An even greater joy was taking her to bed and loving her out of her snooty moods. Thanks to his mother, it was a joy he'd have to do without for a few days. He didn't like it worth a damn.

Suddenly he realized it wasn't just the sex. He didn't want to leave her, because she was upset about something. He wanted to hold her and make everything right for her, but she wouldn't tell him about it. He felt uneasy. She insisted nothing was wrong, but he knew better. He just didn't know what it was. A couple of times he'd caught her staring out the window with an expression that was almost...terrified. He had to be wrong, because she had no reason to be scared. And of what?

It had all started with the accident. He'd been trying to reassure her that he wasn't angry about the car, but instead she'd drawn away from him as if he'd slapped her, and he couldn't bridge the distance between them. For just an instant she'd looked shocked, even hurt, then she'd withdrawn in some subtle way he couldn't describe, but felt. The withdrawal wasn't physical; except for the night of the accident, she was as sweet and wild in his arms as she'd ever been. But he wanted all of her, mind and body, and the accident had only made his wanting more intense by taunting him with the knowledge of how quickly she could be taken away.

He reached out and touched his fingertips to her cheekbone, needing to touch her even in so small a way. Her eyes cut up to him with a flash of green, their gazes catching, locking. Without a word she closed the ledger and stood. She didn't look back as she walked out of the room with the fluid grace he'd always admired and sometimes hated because he couldn't have the body that produced it. But now he could, and as he followed her from the room he was already unbuttoning his shirt. His booted feet were deliberately placed on the stairs, his attention on the bedroom at the top and the woman inside it.

SOMETIMES, WHEN the days were hot and slow and the sun was a disc of blinding white, Michelle would feel that it had all been a vivid nightmare and hadn't really happened at all. The phone calls had meant nothing. The danger she'd sensed was merely the product of an overactive imagination. The man in the ski mask hadn't tried to kill her. The accident hadn't been a murder attempt disguised to look like an accident. None of that had happened at all. It was only a dream, while reality was Edie humming as she did housework, the stamping and snorting of the horses, the placid cattle grazing in the pastures, John's daily phone calls from Miami that charted his impatience to be back home.

But it hadn't been a dream. John didn't believe her, but his nearness had nevertheless kept the terror at bay and given her a small pocket of safety. She felt secure here on the ranch, ringed by the wall of his authority, surrounded by his people. Without him beside her in the night, her feeling of safety weakened. She was sleeping badly, and during the days she pushed herself as relentlessly as she had when she'd been working her own ranch alone, trying to exhaust her body so she could sleep.

Nev Luther had received his instructions, as usual, but again he was faced with the dilemma of how to carry them out. If Michelle wanted to do something, how was he supposed to stop her? Call the boss in Miami and tattle? Nev didn't doubt for a minute the boss would spit nails and strip hide if he saw Michelle doing the work she was doing, but she didn't *ask* if she could do it, she simply did it. Not much he could do about that. Besides, she seemed to need the work to occupy her mind. She was quieter than usual, probably missing the boss. The thought made Nev smile. He approved of the current arrangement, and would approve even more if it turned out to be permanent.

After four days of doing as much as she could, Michelle was finally exhausted enough that she thought she could sleep, but she put off going to bed. If she were wrong, she'd spend more hours lying tense and sleepless, or shaking in the aftermath of a dream. She forced herself to stay awake and catch up on the paperwork, the endless stream of orders and invoices that chronicled the prosperity of the ranch. It could have waited, but she wanted everything to be in order when John came home. The thought brought a smile to her strained face; he'd be home tomorrow. His afternoon call had done more to ease her mind than anything. Just one more night to get through without him, then he'd be beside her again in the darkness.

She finished at ten, then climbed the stairs and changed into one of the light cotton shifts she slept in. The night was hot and muggy, too hot for her to tolerate even a sheet over her, but she was tired enough that the heat didn't keep her awake. She turned on her side, almost groaning aloud as her muscles relaxed, and was instantly asleep.

It was almost two in the morning when John silently let himself into the house. He'd planned to take an 8:00 a.m. flight, but after talking to Michelle he'd paced restlessly, impatient with the hours between them. He had to hold her close, feel her slender, too fragile body in his arms before he could be certain she was all right. The worry was even more maddening because he didn't know its cause.

Finally he couldn't stand it. He'd called the airport and gotten a seat on the last flight out that night, then thrown his few clothes into his bag and kissed his mother's forehead. "Take it easy on that damned checkbook," he'd growled, looking down at the elegant, shallow and still pretty woman who had given birth to him.

The black eyes he'd inherited looked back at him, and one corner of her crimson lips lifted in the same one-sided smile that often quirked his mouth. "You haven't told me anything, but I've heard rumors even down here," she'd said smoothly. "Is it true you've got Langley Cabot's daughter living with you? Really, John, he lost everything he owned."

He'd been too intent on getting back to Michelle to feel more than a spark of anger. "Not everything."

"Then it's true? She's living with you?"

"Yes."

She had given him a long, steady look. Since he'd been nineteen he'd had a lot of women, but none of them had lived with him, even briefly, and despite the distance between them, or perhaps because of it, she knew her son well. No one took advantage of him. If Michelle Cabot was in his house, it was because he wanted her there, not due to any seductive maneuvers on her part.

As John climbed the stairs in the dark, silent house, his heart began the slow, heavy rhythm of anticipation. He wouldn't wake her, but he couldn't wait to lie beside her again, just to feel the soft warmth of her body and smell the sweetness of her skin. He was tired; he could use a few hours' sleep. But in the morning... Her skin would be rosy from sleep, and she'd stretch drowsily with that feline grace of hers. He would take her then.

Noiselessly he entered the bedroom, shutting the door behind him. She was small and still in the bed, not stirring at his presence. He set his bag down and went into the bathroom. When he came out a few minutes later he left the bathroom light on so he could see while he undressed.

He looked at the bed again, and every muscle in his body tightened. Sweat beaded on his forehead. He couldn't have torn his eyes away even if a tornado had hit the house at that moment.

She was lying half on her stomach, with all the covers shoved down to the foot of the bed. Her right leg was stretched out straight, her left one drawn up toward the middle of the mattress. She was wearing one of those flimsy cotton shifts she liked, and during the night it had worked its way up to her buttocks. She was exposed to him. His burning gaze slowly, agonizingly moved over the bare curves of her buttocks from beneath the thin cotton garment, to the soft, silky female cleft and folds he loved to touch.

He shuddered convulsively, grinding his teeth to hold back the deep, primal sound rumbling in his chest. He'd gotten so hard, so fast, that his entire body ached and throbbed. She was sound asleep, her breath coming in a deep, slow rhythm. His own breath was billowing in and out of his lungs; sweat was pouring out of him, his muscles shaking like a stallion scenting a mare ready for mounting. Without taking his eyes from her he began unbuttoning his shirt. He had to have her; he couldn't wait. She was moist and vulnerable, warm and female, and…his. He was coming apart just looking at her, his control shredded, his loins surging wildly.

He left his clothes on the bedroom floor and bent over her, forcing his hands to gentleness as he turned her onto her back. She made a small sound that wasn't quite a sigh and adjusted her position, but didn't awaken. His need was so urgent that he didn't take the time to wake her; he pulled the shift to her waist, spread her thighs and positioned himself between them. With his last remnant of control he eased into her, a low, rough groan bursting from his throat as her hot, moist flesh tightly sheathed him.

She whimpered a little, her body arching in his hands, and her arms lifted to twine around his neck. "I love you," she moaned, still more asleep than awake. Her words went through him like lightning, his body jerking in response. Oh God, he didn't even know if she said it to him or to some dream, but everything in him shattered. He wanted to hear the words again, and he wanted her awake, her eyes looking into his when she said them, so he'd know who was in her mind. Desperately he sank deeper into her, trying to absorb her body into his so irrevocably that nothing could separate them.

"Michelle," he whispered in taut agony, burying his open mouth against her warm throat.

Michelle lifted, arching toward him again as her mind swam upward out of a sleep so deep it had bordered on unconsciousness. But even asleep she had known his touch, her body reacting immediately to him, opening for him, welcoming him. She didn't question his presence; he was there, and that was all that mattered. A great burst of love so intense that she almost cried out reduced everything else to insignificance. She was on fire, her senses reeling, her flesh shivering under the slamming thrusts of his loins. She felt him deep inside her, touching her, and she screamed into his mouth like a wild creature as sharp ecstasy detonated her nerves. He locked her to him with iron-muscled thighs and arms, holding her as she strained madly beneath him, and the feel of her soft internal shudders milking him sent him blasting into his own hot, sweet insanity.

He couldn't let her go. Even when it was over, he couldn't let her go. He began thrusting again, needing even more of her to satisfy the hunger that went so deep he didn't think it would ever be satisfied.

She was crying a little, her luminous green eyes wet as she clung to him. She said his name in a raw, shaking voice. He hadn't let her slide down to a calm plateau but kept her body tense with desire. He was slow and tender now, gentling her into ecstasy instead of hurling her into it, but the culmination was no less shattering.

It was almost dawn before she curled up in his arms, both of them exhausted. Just before she went to sleep she said in mild surprise, "You came home early."

His arms tightened around her. "I couldn't stand another night away from you." It was the bald, frightening truth. He would have made it back even if he'd had to walk.

No one bothered them the next morning, and they slept until long after the sun began pouring brightly into the room. Nev Luther, seeing John's truck parked in its normal location, came to the house to ask him a question, but Edie dared the foreman to disturb them with such a fierce expression on her face that he decided the question wasn't important, after all.

John woke shortly after one, disturbed by the heat of the sunlight streaming directly onto the bed. His temples and mustache were already damp with sweat, and he badly needed a cool shower to drive away the sluggishness of heat and exhaustion. He left the bed quietly, taking care not to wake Michelle, though a purely male smile touched his hard lips as he saw her shift lying in the middle of the floor. He didn't even remember pulling it off her, much less throwing it. Nothing had mattered but loving her.

He stood under the shower, feeling utterly sated but somehow uneasy. He kept remembering the sound of her voice when she said "I love you" and it was driving him crazy. Had she been dreaming, or had she known it was him? She'd never said it before, and she hadn't said it again. The uncertainty knifed at him. It had felt so right, but then, they had always fitted together in bed so perfectly that his memories of other women were destroyed. Out of bed... There was always that small distance he couldn't bridge, that part of herself that she wouldn't let him know. Did she love someone else? Was it one of her old crowd? A tanned, sophisticated jet-setter who was out of her reach now that she didn't have money? The thought tormented him, because he knew it was possible to love someone even when they were far away and years passed between meetings. He knew, because he'd loved Michelle that way.

His face was drawn as he cut the water off with a savage movement. *Love.* God, he'd loved her for years, and lied to himself about it by burying it under hostility, then labeling it as lust, want, need, anything to keep from admitting he was as vulnerable as a naked baby when it came to her. He was hard as nails, a sexual outlaw who casually used and left women, but he'd only prowled from woman to woman so restlessly because none of them had been able to satisfy his hunger. None of them had been the one woman he wanted, the one woman he loved. Now he had her physically, but not mentally, not emotionally, and he was scared spitless. His hands were trembling as he rubbed a towel over his body. Somehow he had to make her love him. He'd use any means necessary to keep her with him, loving her and taking care of her until no one existed in her mind except him, and every part of her became his to cherish.

Would she run if he told her he loved her? If he said the words, would she be uncomfortable around him? He remembered how he'd felt whenever some woman had tried to cling to him, whimpering that she loved him, begging him to stay. He'd felt embarrassment, impatience, pity. Pity! He couldn't take it if Michelle pitied him.

He'd never felt uncertain before. He was arrogant, impatient, determined, and he was used to men jumping when he barked out an order. It was unsettling to discover that he couldn't control either his emotions or Michelle's. He'd read before that love made strong men weak, but he hadn't understood it until now. Weak? Hell, he was terrified!

Naked, he returned to the bedroom and pulled on underwear and jeans. She was a magnet, drawing his eyes to her time and again. Lord, she was something to look at, with that pale gold hair gleaming in the bright sunlight, her bare flesh glowing. She lay on her stomach with her arms under the pillow, giving him a view of her supple back, firmly rounded buttocks and long, sleek legs. He admired her graceful lines and feminine curves, the need growing in him to touch her. Was she going to sleep all day?

He crossed to the bed and sat down on the side, stroking his hand over her bare shoulder. "Wake up, lazybones. It's almost two o'clock."

She yawned, snuggling deeper into the pillow. "So?" Her mouth curved into a smile as she refused to open her eyes.

He chuckled. "So get up. I can't even get dressed when you're lying here like this. My attention keeps wander—" He broke off, frowning at the small white scar marring the satiny shoulder under his fingers. She was lying naked under the bright rays of the afternoon sun, or he might not have noticed. Then he saw another one, and he touched it, too. His gaze moved, finding more of them marring the perfection of her skin. They were all down her back, even on her bottom and the backs of her upper thighs. His fingers touched all of them, moving slowly from scar to scar. She was rigid under his hands, not moving or looking at him, not even breathing.

Stunned, he tried to think of what could have made those small, crescent-shaped marks. Accidental cuts, by broken glass for instance, wouldn't all have been the same size and shape. The cuts hadn't been deep; the scarring was too faint, with no raised ridges. That was why he hadn't felt them, though he'd touched every inch of her body. But if they weren't accidental, that meant they had to be deliberate.

His indrawn breath hissed roughly through his teeth. He swore, his voice so quiet and controlled that the explicitly obscene words shattered the air more effectively than if he'd roared. Then he rolled her over, his hands hard on her shoulders, and said only three words. "Who did it?"

Michelle was white, frozen by the look on his face. He looked deadly, his eyes cold and ferocious. He lifted her by the shoulders until she was almost nose to nose with him, and he repeated his question, the words evenly spaced, almost soundless. "Who did it?"

Her lips trembled as she looked helplessly at him. She couldn't talk about it; she just couldn't. "I don't... It's noth—"

"Who did it?" he yelled, his neck corded with rage.

She closed her eyes, burning tears seeping from beneath her lids. Despair and shame ate at her, but she knew he wouldn't let her go until she answered. Her lips were trembling so hard she could barely talk. "John, please!"

"Who?"

Crumpling, she gave in, turning her face away. "Roger Beckman. My ex-husband." It was hard to say the words; she thought they would choke her.

John was swearing again, softly, endlessly. Michelle struggled briefly as he swept her up and sat down in a chair, holding her cradled on his lap, but it was a futile effort, so she abandoned it. Just saying Roger's name had made her feel unclean. She wanted to hide, to scrub herself over and over to be rid of the taint, but John wouldn't let her go. He held her naked on his lap, not saying a word after he'd stopped cursing until he noticed her shivering. The sun was hot, but her skin was cold. He stretched until he could reach the corner of the sheet, then jerked until it came free of the bed, and wrapped it around her.

He held her tight and rocked her, his hands stroking up and down her back. She'd been beaten. The knowledge kept ricocheting inside his skull, and he shook with a black rage he'd never known before. If he'd been able to get his hands on that slimy bastard right then, he'd have killed him with his bare hands and enjoyed every minute of it. He thought of Michelle cowering in fear and pain, her delicate body shuddering under the blows, and red mist colored his vision. No wonder she'd asked him not to hurt her the first time he'd made love to her! After her experience with men, it was something of a miracle that she'd responded at all.

He crooned to her, his rough cheek pressed against her sunny hair, his hard arms locked around her. He didn't know what he said, and neither did she, but the sound of his voice was enough. The gentleness came through, washing over her and warming her on the inside just as the heat of his body warmed her cold skin. Even after her shivering stopped he simply held her, waiting, letting her feel his closeness.

Finally she shifted a little, silently asking him to let her go. He did, reluctantly, his eyes never leaving her white face as she walked into the bathroom and shut the door. He started to go into the bathroom after her, alarmed by her silence and lack of color; his hand was on the doorknob when he reined himself under control. She needed to be alone right now. He heard the sound of the shower, and waited with unprecedented patience until she came out. She was still pale, but not as completely colorless as she'd been. The shower had taken the remaining chill from her skin, and she was wrapped in the terry-cloth robe she kept hanging on the back of the bathroom door.

"Are you all right?" he asked quietly.

"Yes." Her voice was muted.

"We have to talk about it."

"Not now." The look she gave him was shattered. "I can't. Not now."

"All right, baby. Later."

Later was that night, lying in his arms again, with the darkness like a shield around them. He'd made love to her, very gently and for a long time, easing her into rapture. In the lengthening silence afterward she felt his determination to know all the answers, and though she dreaded it, in the darkness she felt able to give them to him. When it came down to it, he didn't even have to ask. She simply started talking.

"He was jealous," she whispered. "Insane with it. I couldn't talk to a man at a party, no matter how ugly or happily married; I couldn't smile at a waiter. The smallest things triggered his rages. At first he'd just scream, accusing me of cheating on him, of loving someone else, and he'd ask me over and over who it was until I couldn't stand it anymore. Then he began slapping me. He was always sorry afterward. He'd tell me how much he loved me, swear he'd never do it again. But of course he did."

John had gone rigid, his muscles shaking with the rage she felt building in him again. In the darkness she stroked his face, giving him what comfort she could and never wondering at the illogic of it.

"I filed charges against him once; his parents bought him out of it and made it plain I wasn't to do such a thing again. Then I tried leaving him, but he found me and carried me back. He…he said he'd have Dad killed if I ever tried to leave him again."

"You believed him?" John asked harshly, the first words he'd spoken. She didn't flinch from the harshness, knowing it wasn't for her.

"Oh, yes, I believed him." She managed a sad little

laugh. "I still do. His family has enough money that he could have it done and it would never be traced back to him."

"But you left him anyway."

"Not until I found a way to control him."

"How?"

She began trembling a little, and her voice wavered out of control. "The...the scars on my back. When he did that, his parents were in Europe; they weren't there to have files destroyed and witnesses bribed until it was too late. I already had a copy of everything, enough to press charges against him. I bought my divorce with it, and I made his parents promise to keep him away from me or I'd use what I had. They were very conscious of their position and family prestige."

"Screw their prestige," he said flatly, trying very hard to keep his rage under control.

"It's academic now; they're dead."

He didn't think it was much of a loss. People who cared more about their family prestige than about a young woman being brutally beaten and terrorized didn't amount to much in his opinion.

Silence stretched, and he realized she wasn't going to add anything else. If he let her, she'd leave it at that highly condensed and edited version, but he needed to know more. It hurt him in ways he'd never thought he could be hurt, but it was vital to him that he know all he could about her, or he would never be able to close the distance between them. He wanted to know where she went in her mind and why she wouldn't let him follow, what she was thinking, what had happened in the two years since her divorce.

He touched her back, caressing her with his fingertips. "Is this why you wouldn't go swimming?"

She stirred against his shoulder, her voice like gossamer wings in the darkness. "Yes. I know the scars aren't bad; they've faded a lot. But in my mind they're still like they were…. I was so scared someone would see them and ask how I got them."

"That's why you always put your nightgown back on after we'd made love."

She was silent, but he felt her nod.

"Why didn't you want *me* to know? I'm not exactly some stranger walking down the street."

No, he was her heart and her heartbreaker, the only man she'd ever loved, and therefore more important to her than anyone else in the world. She hadn't wanted him to know the ugliness that had been in her life.

"I felt dirty," she whispered. "Ashamed."

"Good God!" he exploded, raising up on his elbow to lean over her. "Why? It wasn't your fault. You were the victim, not the villain."

"I know, but sometimes knowledge doesn't help. The feelings were still there."

He kissed her, long and slow and hot, loving her with his tongue and letting her know how much he desired her. He kissed her until she responded, lifting her arms up to his neck and giving him her tongue in return. Then he settled onto the pillow again, cradling her head on his shoulder. She was nude; he had gently but firmly refused to let her put on a gown. That secret wasn't between them any longer, and she was glad. She loved the feel of his warm, hard-muscled body against her bare skin.

He was still brooding, unable to leave it alone. She felt his tension and slowly ran her hand over his chest, feeling the curly hair and small round nipples with their tiny center points. "Relax," she murmured, kissing his shoulder. "It's over."

"You said his parents controlled him, but they're dead. Has he bothered you since?"

She shivered, remembering the phone calls she'd had from Roger. "He called me a couple of times, at the house. I haven't seen him. I hope I never have to see him again." The last sentence was full of desperate sincerity.

"At the house? Your house? How long ago?"

"Before you brought me here."

"I'd like to meet him," John said quietly, menacingly.

"I hope you never do. He's...not sane."

They lay together, the warm, humid night wrapped around them, and she began to feel sleepy. Then he touched her again, and she felt the raw anger in him, the savage need to know. "What did he use?"

She flinched away from him. Swearing softly, he caught her close. "Tell me."

"There's no point in it."

"I want to know."

"You already know." Tears stung her eyes. "It isn't original."

"A belt."

Her breath caught in her throat. "He...he wrapped the leather end around his hand."

John actually snarled, his big body jerking. He thought of a belt buckle cutting into her soft skin, and it made him sick. It made him murderous. More than ever, he wanted to get his hands on Roger Beckman.

He felt her hands on him, clinging. "Please," she whispered. "Let's go to sleep."

He wanted to know one more thing, something that struck him as odd. "Why didn't you tell your dad? He had a lot of contacts; he could have done something. You didn't have to try to protect him."

Her laugh was soft and faintly bitter, not really a laugh at all. "I did tell him. He didn't believe me. It was easier for him to think I'd made it all up than to admit my life had gone so wrong."

She didn't tell him that she'd never loved Roger, that her life had gone wrong because she'd married one man while loving another.

CHAPTER TEN

"Telephone, Michelle!" Edie called from the kitchen.

Michelle had just come in, and she was on her way upstairs to shower; she detoured into the office to take the call there. Her mind was on her cattle; they were in prime condition, and John had arranged the sale. She would soon be leaving the ranks of the officially broke and entering those of the merely needy. John had scowled when she'd told him that.

"Hello," she said absently.

Silence.

The familiar chill went down her spine. "Hello!" she almost yelled, her fingers turning white from pressure.

"Michelle."

Her name was almost whispered, but she heard it, recognized it. "No," she said, swallowing convulsively. "Don't call me again."

"How could you do this to me?"

"Leave me alone!" she screamed, and slammed the phone down. Her legs were shaking, and she leaned on the desk, gulping in air. She was frightened. How had Roger found her here? Dear God, what would John do if he found out Roger was bothering her? He'd be furious.... More than furious. He'd be murderous. But what if Roger called again and John answered? Would Roger ask for her, or would he remain silent?

The initial silence haunted her, reminding her of

the other phone calls she had received. She'd had the same horrible feeling from all of them. Then she knew: Roger had made those other phone calls. She couldn't begin to guess why he hadn't spoken, but suddenly she had no doubt about who her caller had been. Why hadn't she realized it before? He had the resources to track her down, and he was sick and obsessive enough to do so. He knew where she was, knew she was intimately involved with another man. She felt nauseated, thinking of his jealous rages. He was entirely capable of coming down here to snatch her away from the man he would consider his rival and take her back "where she belonged."

More than two years, and she still wasn't free of him.

She thought about getting an injunction against him for harassment, but John would have to know, because the telephone was his. She didn't want him to know; his reaction could be too violent, and she didn't want him to get in any trouble.

She wasn't given the option of keeping it from him. He opened the door to the office, a questioning look on his face as he stepped inside; Edie must have told him Michelle had a call, and that was unusual enough to make him curious. Michelle didn't have time to compose her face. He stopped, eyeing her sharply. She knew she looked pale and distraught. She watched as his eyes went slowly, inevitably, to the telephone. He never missed a detail, damn him; it was almost impossible to hide anything from him. She could have done it if she'd had time to deal with the shock, but now all she could do was stand frozen in her tracks. Why couldn't he have remained in the stable five minutes longer? She would have been in the shower; she would have had time to think of something.

"That was him, wasn't it?" he asked flatly.

Her hand crept toward her throat as she stared at him like a rabbit in a snare. John crossed the room with swift strides, catching her shoulders in his big warm hands.

"What did he say? Did he threaten you?"

Numbly she shook her head. "No. He didn't threaten me. It wasn't what he said; it's just that I can't stand hearing—" Her voice broke, and she tried to turn away, afraid to push her self-control any further.

John caught her more firmly to him, tucking her in the crook of one arm as he picked up the receiver. "What's his number?" he snapped.

Frantically Michelle tried to take the phone from him. "No, don't! That won't solve anything!"

His face grim, he evaded her efforts and pinned her arms to her sides. "He's good at terrorizing a woman, but it's time he knows there's someone else he'll have to deal with if he ever calls you again. Do you still remember his number or not? I can get it, but it'll be easier if you give it to me."

"It's unlisted," she said, stalling.

He gave her a long, level look. "I can get it," he repeated.

She didn't doubt that he could. When he decided to do something, he did it, and lesser people had better get out of his way. Defeated, she gave him the number and watched as he punched the buttons.

As close to him as she was, she could hear the ringing on the other end of the line, then a faint voice as someone answered. "Get Roger Beckman on the line," he ordered in the hard voice that no one disobeyed.

His brows snapped together in a scowl as he listened, then he said "Thanks" and hung up. Still frowning, he held her to him for a minute before telling her,

"The housekeeper said he's on vacation in the south of France, and she doesn't know when he'll be back."

"But I just talked to him!" she said, startled. "He wasn't in France!"

John let her go and walked around to sit behind the desk, the frown turning abstracted. "Go on and take a shower," he said quietly. "I'll be up in a few minutes."

Michelle drew back, feeling cold all over again. Didn't he believe her? She knew Roger wasn't in the south of France; that call certainly hadn't been an overseas call. The connection had been too good, as clear as a local call. No, of course he didn't believe her, just as he hadn't believed her about the blue Chevrolet. She walked away, her back rigid and her eyes burning. Roger wasn't in France, even if the housekeeper had said he was, but why was he trying to keep his location a secret?

AFTER MICHELLE LEFT, John sat in the study, pictures running through his mind, and he didn't like any of them. He saw Michelle's face, so white and pinched, her eyes terrified; he saw the small white scars on her back, remembered the sick look she got when she talked about her ex-husband. She'd worn the same look just now. Something wasn't right. He'd see Roger Beckman in hell before he let the man anywhere near Michelle again.

He needed information, and he was willing to use any means available to him to get it. Michelle meant more to him than anything else in the world.

Something had happened the summer before at his neighbor's house over on Diamond Bay, and his neighbor, Rachel Jones, had been shot. John had seen pure hell then, in the black eyes of the man who had held Rachel's wounded body in his arms. The man had looked as if the pain Rachel had been enduring had been ripping his soul out. At the time John hadn't truly understood the depths of the man's agony; at the time he'd still been hiding the truth of his own vulnerability from himself. Rachel had married her black-eyed warrior this past winter. Now John understood the man's anguish, because now he had Michelle, and his own life would be worthless without her.

He'd like to have Rachel's husband, Sabin, with him now, as well as the big blond man who had been helping them. Those two men had something wild about them, the look of predators, but they would understand his need to protect Michelle. They would gladly have helped him hunt Beckman down like the animal he was.

He frowned. They weren't here, but Andy Phelps was, and Phelps had been involved with that mess at Diamond Bay last summer. He looked up a number and punched the buttons, feeling the anger build in him as he thought of Michelle's terrified face. "Andy Phelps, please."

When the sheriff's deputy answered, John said, "Andy, this is Rafferty. Can you do some quiet investigating?"

Andy was a former D.E.A. agent, and, besides that, he had a few contacts it wasn't safe to know too much about. He said quietly, "What's up?"

John outlined the situation, then waited while Andy thought of the possibilities.

"Okay, Michelle says the guy calling her is her ex-husband, but his housekeeper says he's out of the country, right?"

"Yeah."

"Is she sure it's her ex?"

"Yes. And she said he wasn't in France."

"You don't have a lot to go on. You'd have to prove he was the one doing the calling before you could get an injunction, and it sounds as if he's got a good alibi."

"Can you find out if he's really out of the country? I don't think he is, but why would he pretend, unless he's trying to cover his tracks for some reason?"

"You're a suspicious man, Rafferty."

"I have reason to be," John said in a cold, even tone. "I've seen the marks he left on Michelle. I don't want him anywhere near her."

Andy's voice changed as he digested that information, anger and disgust entering his tone. "Like that, huh? Do you think he's in the area?"

"He's certainly not at his home, and we know he isn't in France. He's calling Michelle, scaring her to death. I'd say it's a possibility."

"I'll start checking. There are a few favors I can call in. You might put a tape on your phone, so if he calls back you'll have proof."

"There's something else," John said, rubbing his forehead. "Michelle had an accident a few weeks ago. She said someone ran her off the road, a guy in a blue Chevrolet. I didn't believe her, damn it, and neither did the deputy. No one saw anything, and we didn't find any paint on the car, so I thought someone might have gotten a little close to her and she panicked. But she said he turned around, came back and tried to hit her again."

"That's not your usual someone-ran-me-off-the-road tale," Andy said sharply. "Has she said anything else?"

"No. She hasn't talked about it at all."

"You're thinking it could be her ex-husband."

"I don't know. It might not have anything at all to

do with the phone calls, but I don't want to take the chance."

"Okay, I'll check around. Keep an eye on her, and hook a tape recorder up to the phone."

John hung up and sat there for a long time, silently using every curse word he knew. Keeping an eye on her would be easy; she hadn't been off the ranch since the accident, hadn't even gone to check her own house. Now he knew why, and he damned himself and Roger Beckman with equal ferocity. If he'd only paid attention the night of the accident, they might have been able to track down the Chevrolet, but so much time had passed now that he doubted it would ever be found. At least Michelle hadn't connected Beckman with the accident, and John didn't intend to mention the possibility to her. She was scared enough as it was.

It infuriated him that he couldn't do anything except wait for Andy to get back to him. Even then, it might be a dead end. But if Beckman was anywhere in the area, John intended to pay him a visit and make damned certain he never contacted Michelle again.

MICHELLE BOLTED UPRIGHT in bed, her eyes wide and her face chalky. Beside her, John stirred restlessly and reached for her, but didn't awaken. She lay back down, taking comfort in his nearness, but both her mind and her heart were racing.

It was Roger.

Roger had been driving the blue Chevrolet. Roger had tried to kill her. He wasn't in France at all, but here in Florida, biding his time and waiting to catch her out alone. She remembered the feeling she had had before the accident, as if someone were watching her with vile malice, the same feeling the phone calls had given her. She should have tied it all together before.

He'd found out about John. Michelle even knew how he'd found out. Bitsy Sumner, the woman she and John had met in Tampa when they'd gone down to have the deed drawn up, was the worst gossip in Palm Beach. It wouldn't have taken long for the news to work its way up to Philadelphia that Michelle Cabot was very snuggly with an absolute *hunk*, a gorgeous, macho rancher with bedroom eyes that made Bitsy feel so *warm*. Michelle could almost hear Bitsy on the telephone, embroidering her tale and laughing wickedly as she speculated about the sexy rancher.

Roger had probably convinced himself that Michelle would come back to him; she could still hear him whispering how much he loved her, that he'd make it up to her and show her how good it could be between them. He would have gone into a jealous rage when he found out about John. At last he had known who the other man was, confirming the suspicions he'd had all along.

His mind must have snapped completely. She remembered what he'd said the last time he had called: "How could you do this to me?"

She felt trapped, panicked by the thought that he was out there somewhere, patiently waiting to catch her alone. She couldn't go to the police; she had no evidence, only her intuition, and people weren't arrested on intuition. Besides, she didn't put a lot of faith in the police. Roger's parents had bought them off in Philadelphia, and now Roger controlled all those enormous assets. He had unlimited funds at his disposal; who knew what he could buy? He might even have hired someone, in which case she had no idea who to be on guard against.

Finally she managed to go to sleep, but the knowledge that Roger was nearby ate at her during the next few days, disturbing her rest and stealing her appetite away. Despite the people around her, she felt horribly alone.

She wanted to talk to John about it, but bitter experience made her remain silent. How could she talk to him when he didn't believe her about the phone calls or the accident? He had hooked a tape recorder up to the telephone, but he hadn't discussed it with her, and she hadn't asked any questions. She didn't want to know about it if he were only humoring her. Things had become stilted between them since the last time Roger had called, and she felt even less able to approach him than she had before. Only in bed were things the same; she had begun to fear that he was tiring of her, but he didn't seem tired of her in bed. His lovemaking was still as hungry and frequent as before.

Abruptly, on a hot, sunny morning, she couldn't stand it any longer. She had been pushed so far that she had reached her limit. Even a rabbit will turn and fight when it's cornered. She was tired of it all, so tired that she sometimes felt she was dragging herself through water. Damn Roger! What did she have to do to get him out of her life? There had to be something. She couldn't spend the rest of her days peering around every corner, too terrified to even go to a grocery store. It made her angry when she thought how she had let him confine her as surely as if he'd locked her in a prison, and beginning today she was going to do something about it.

She still had the file that had won her a divorce; now that his parents were dead the file didn't mean as much, but it still meant something. It was documented proof that Roger had attacked her once before. If he would only call again, she would have his call on tape, and perhaps she could get him to say something damaging. This was Florida, not Philadelphia; that much money would always be influential, but down here he wouldn't have the network of old family friends to protect him.

But the file was in the safe at her house, and she wanted it in her possession, at John's. She didn't feel secure leaving it in an empty house, even though she kept the door locked. The house could easily be broken into, and the safe was a normal household one; she doubted whether it would prove to be all that secure if anyone truly wanted to open it. If Roger somehow got the file, she'd have no proof at all. Those photographs and records couldn't be replaced.

Making up her mind, she told Edie she was going riding and ran out to the stables. It was a pleasant ride across the pastures to her ranch, but she didn't enjoy it as she normally would have, because of the knot of tension forming in her stomach. Roger had seen her the last time she'd been there, and she couldn't forget the terror she'd felt when she'd seen the blue Chevrolet bearing down on her.

She approached the house from the rear, looking around uneasily as she slid off the horse, but everything was normal. The birds in the trees were singing. Quickly she checked all the doors and windows, but they all seemed tight, with no signs of forced entry. Only then did she enter the house and hurry to the office to open the safe. She removed the manila envelope and checked the contents, breathing a sigh of relief that everything was undisturbed, then slid the envelope inside her shirt and relocked the safe.

The house had been closed up for a long time; the air was hot and stuffy. She felt dizzy as she stood up, and her stomach moved queasily. She hurried outside to the back porch, leaning against the wall and gulping fresh air into her lungs until her head cleared and her stomach settled. Her nerves were shot. She didn't know how much longer she could stand it, but she had to wait. He would call again; she knew it. Until then, there was precious little she could do.

Everything was still calm, quiet. The horse nickered a welcome at her as she mounted and turned toward home.

The stableman came out to meet her as she rode up, relief plain on his face. "Thank God you're back," he said feelingly. "The boss is raising pure hell—excuse me, ma'am. Anyway, he's been tearing the place up looking for you. I'll get word to him that you're back."

"Why is he looking for me?" she asked, bewildered. She had told Edie that she was going riding.

"I don't know, ma'am." He took the horse's reins from her hands as she slid to the ground.

Michelle went into the house and sought out Edie. "What has John in such an uproar?" she asked.

Edie lifted her eyebrows. "I didn't get close enough to ask."

"Didn't you tell him I'd gone riding?"

"Yep. That's when he really blew up."

She thought something might have come up and he couldn't find the paperwork he needed on it, but when she checked the office everything looked just as it had when she'd left that morning. Taking the manila envelope from inside her shirt, she locked it inside John's safe, and only then did she feel better. She *was* safe here, surrounded by John's people.

A few minutes later she heard his truck come up the drive, and judging from its speed, his temper hadn't settled any. More curious than alarmed, she walked out to meet him as the truck skidded to a stop, the tires throwing up a spray of sand and gravel. John thrust the door open and got out, his rifle clutched in his hand. His face was tight, and black fire burned in his eyes as he strode toward her. "Where in hell have you been?" he roared.

Michelle looked at the rifle. "I was out riding."

He didn't stop when he reached her, but caught her arm and hauled her inside the house. "Out riding where, damn it? I've had everyone combing the place for you."

"I went over to the house." She was beginning to get a little angry herself at his manner, though she still didn't know what had set him off. She lifted her nose and gave him a cool look. "I didn't realize I had to ask permission to go to my own house."

"Well, honey bunch, you have to do exactly that," he snapped, replacing the rifle in the gun cabinet. "I don't want you going anywhere without asking me first."

"I don't believe I'm your prisoner," she said icily.

"Prisoner, hell!" He whirled on her, unable to forget the raw panic that had filled him when he hadn't been able to find her. Until he knew what was going on and where Roger Beckman was, he'd like to have her locked up in the bedroom for safekeeping. One look at her outraged face, however, told him that he'd gone about it all wrong, and she was digging her heels in.

"I thought something had happened to you," he said more quietly.

"So you went tearing around the ranch looking for something to shoot?" she asked incredulously.

"No. I went tearing around the ranch looking for you, and I carried the rifle in case you were in any danger."

She balled her hands into fists, wanting to slap him. He wouldn't believe her about a real danger, but he was worried that she might sprain an ankle or take a tumble off a horse. "What danger could I possibly be in?" she snapped. "I'm sure there's not a snake on the ranch that would dare bite anything without your permission!"

His expression became rueful as he stared down at her. He lifted his hand and tucked a loose strand of sun-streaked hair behind her ear, but she still glared at him like some outraged queen. He liked her temper a lot better than the distant manner he'd been getting from her lately. "You're pretty when you're mad," he teased, knowing how that would get her.

For a moment she looked ready to spit. Then suddenly she sputtered, "You jackass," and began laughing.

He chuckled. No one could say "jackass" quite like Michelle, all hoity-toity and precise. He loved it. She could call him a jackass any time she wanted. Before she could stop laughing, he put his arms around her and hauled her against him, covering her mouth with his and slowly sliding his tongue between her lips. Her laughter stopped abruptly, her hands coming up to clutch his bulging biceps, and her tongue met his.

"You worried the hell out of me," he murmured when he lifted his mouth.

"Not all of it, I noticed," she purred, making him grin.

"But I wasn't kidding. I want to know whenever you go somewhere, and I don't want you going over to your place alone. It's been empty for quite a while, and a bum could start hanging around."

"What would a bum be doing this far out?" she asked.

"What would a bum be doing anywhere? Crime isn't restricted to cities. Please. For my peace of mind?"

It was so unusual for John Rafferty to plead for anything that she could only stare at him. It struck her that even though he'd said please, he still expected that she would do exactly as he'd said. In fact, she was only being perverse because he'd been his usual autocratic, arrogant self and made her angry. It suited her perfectly to be cautious, for the time being.

The dizziness and nausea she'd felt at the house must have been the beginning symptoms of some sort of bug, because she felt terrible the next day. She spent most of the day in bed, too tired and sick to worry about anything else. Every time she raised her head, the awful dizziness brought on another attack of nausea. She just wanted to be left alone.

She felt marginally better the next morning, and managed to keep something in her stomach. John held her in his arms, worried about her listlessness. "If you aren't a lot better tomorrow, I'm taking you to a doctor," he said firmly.

"It's just a virus," she sighed. "A doctor can't do anything."

"You could get something to settle your stomach."

"I feel better today. What if you catch it?"

"Then you can wait on me hand and foot until I'm better," he said, chuckling at her expression of horror. He wasn't worried about catching it. He couldn't remember the last time he'd even had a cold.

She was much better the next day, and though she still didn't feel like riding around the ranch, she did spend the morning in the office, feeding information into the computer and catching up on the books. It would be easier if they had a bookkeeping program for the computer; she made a note to ask John about it.

Roger still hadn't called.

She balled her fist. She knew he was somewhere

close by! How could she get him to come out of hiding? She could never live a normal life as long as she was afraid to leave the ranch by herself.

But perhaps that was what she would have to do. Obviously Roger had some way of watching the ranch; she simply couldn't believe the blue Chevrolet had been a coincidence, unconnected to Roger. He'd caught her off guard that time, but now she'd be looking for him. She had to draw him out.

When John came to the house for lunch, she had twisted her hair up and put on a bit of makeup, and she knew she looked a lot better. "I thought I'd go to town for a few things," she said casually. "Is there anything you need?"

His head jerked up. She hadn't driven at all since the accident, and now here she was acting as nonchalant about driving as if the accident had never happened at all. Before he had worried that she was so reluctant to go anywhere, but now he wanted her to stay close. "What things?" he asked sharply. "Where exactly are you going?"

Her brows lifted at his tone. "Shampoo, hair conditioner, things like that."

"All right." He made an impatient gesture. "Where are you going? What time will you be back?"

"Really, you missed your calling. You should have been a prison guard."

"Just tell me."

Because she didn't want him to deny her the use of the car, she said in a bored voice, "The drugstore, probably. I'll be back by three."

He looked hard at her, then sighed and thrust his fingers through his thick black hair. "Just be careful."

She got up from the table. "Don't worry. If I wreck

the car again, I'll pay for the damages with the money from the cattle sale."

He swore as he watched her stalk away. Damn, what could he do now? Follow her? He slammed into the office and called Andy Phelps to find out if he had any information on Roger Beckman yet. All Andy had come up with was that no one by the name of Roger Beckman had been on a flight to France in the last month, but he might not have gone there directly. It took time to check everything.

"I'll keep trying, buddy. That's all I can do."

"Thanks. Maybe I'm worried over nothing, but maybe I'm not."

"Yeah, I know. Why take chances? I'll call when I get something."

John hung up, torn by the need to do something, anything. Maybe he should tell Michelle of his suspicions, explain why he didn't want her wandering around by herself. But as Andy had pointed out, he really had nothing to go on, and he didn't want to upset her needlessly. She'd had enough worry in her life. If he had his way, nothing would ever worry her again.

Michelle drove to town and made her purchases, steeling herself every time a car drew near. But nothing happened; she didn't see anything suspicious, not even at the spot where the Chevrolet had forced her off the road. Fiercely she told herself that she wasn't paranoid, she hadn't imagined it all. Roger was there, somewhere. She simply had to find him. But she wasn't brave at all, and she was shaking with nerves by the time she got back to the ranch. She barely made it upstairs to the bathroom before her stomach rebelled and she retched miserably.

She tried it again the next day. And the next. Nothing happened, except that John was in the foulest mood she could imagine. He never came right out and forbade her to go anywhere, but he made it plain he didn't like it. If she hadn't been desperate, she would have thrown the car keys in his face and told him what he could do with them.

Roger had been watching her at her house that day. Could it be that he was watching that road instead of the one leading to town? He wouldn't have seen her when she'd gone over to get the file from the safe because she had ridden in from the back rather than using the road. John had told her not to go to her house alone, but she wouldn't have to go to the house. All she had to do was drive by on the road…and if Roger was there, he would follow her.

CHAPTER ELEVEN

SHE HAD TO be crazy; she knew that. The last thing she wanted was to see Roger, yet here she was trying to find him, even though she suspected he was trying to kill her. No, she wanted to find him *because* of that. She certainly didn't want to die, but she wanted this to be over. Only then could she lead a normal life.

She wanted that life to be with John, but she had never fooled herself that their relationship was permanent, and the mood he was in these days could herald the end of it. Nothing she did seemed to please him, except when they were in bed, but perhaps that was just a reflection of his intense sex drive and any woman would have done.

Her nerves were so raw that she couldn't even think of eating the morning she planned to go to the house, and she paced restlessly, waiting until she saw John get in his pickup and drive across the pastures. She hadn't wanted him to know she was going anywhere; he asked too many questions, and it was hard to hide anything from him. She would only be gone half an hour, anyway, because when it came down to it, she didn't have the courage to leave herself hanging out as bait. All she could manage was one quick drive by; then she would come home.

She listened to the radio in an effort to calm her nerves as she drove slowly down the narrow gravel road. It came as a shock that the third hurricane of the season, Hurricane Carl, had formed in the Atlantic and was meandering toward Cuba. She had completely missed the first two storms. She hadn't even noticed that summer had slid into early autumn, because the weather was still so hot and humid, perfect hurricane weather.

Though she carefully searched both sides of the road for any sign of a car tucked away under the trees, she didn't see anything. The morning was calm and lazy. No one else was on the road. Frustrated, she turned around to drive back to the house.

A sudden wave of nausea hit her, and she had to halt the car. She opened the door and leaned out, her stomach heaving even though it was empty and nothing came out. When the spasm stopped she leaned against the steering wheel, weak and perspiring. This had hung on far too long to be a virus.

She lay there against the steering wheel for a long time, too weak to drive and too sick to care. A faint breeze wafted into the open door, cooling her hot face, and just as lightly the truth eased into her mind.

If this was a virus, it was the nine-month variety.

She let her head fall back against the seat, and a smile played around her pale lips. Pregnant. Of course. She even knew when it had happened: the night John had come home from Miami. He had been making love to her when she woke up, and neither of them had thought of taking precautions. She had been so on edge she hadn't noticed that she was late.

John's baby. It had been growing inside her for almost five weeks. Her hand drifted down to her stomach, a sense of utter contentment filling her despite the miserable way she felt. She knew the problems this would cause, but for the moment those problems were distant, unimportant compared to the blinding joy she felt.

She began to laugh, thinking of how sick she'd been. She remembered reading in some magazine that women who had morning sickness were less likely to miscarry than women who didn't; if that were true, this baby was as secure as Fort Knox. She still felt like death warmed over, but now she was happy to feel that way.

"A baby," she whispered, thinking of a tiny, sweet-smelling bundle with a mop of thick black hair and melting black eyes, though she realized any child of John Rafferty's would likely be a hellion.

But she couldn't continue sitting in the car, which was parked more on the road than off. Shakily, hoping the nausea would hold off until she could get home, she put the car in gear and drove back to the ranch with painstaking caution. Now that she knew what was wrong, she knew what to do to settle her stomach. And she needed to make an appointment with a doctor.

Sure enough, her stomach quieted after she ate a meal of dry toast and weak tea. Then she began to think about the problems.

Telling John was the first problem and, to Michelle, the biggest. She had no idea how he would react, but she had to face the probability that he would not be as thrilled as she was. She feared he was getting tired of her anyway; if so, he'd see the baby as a burden, tying him to a woman he no longer wanted.

She lay on the bed, trying to sort out her tangled thoughts and emotions. John had a right to know about his child, and, like it or not, he had a responsibility to it. On the other hand, she couldn't use the baby to hold him if he wanted to be free. Bleak despair filled her whenever she tried to think of a future without John, but she loved him enough to let him go. Since their first day together she had been subconsciously preparing for the time when he would tell her that he didn't want her any longer. That much was clear in her mind.

But what if he decided that they should marry because of the baby? John took his responsibilities seriously, even to the point of taking a wife he didn't want for the sake of his child. She could be a coward and grab for anything he offered, on the basis that the crumbs of affection that came her way would be better than nothing, or she could somehow find the courage to deny herself the very thing she wanted most. Tears filled her eyes, the tears that came so easily these days. She sniffled and wiped them away.

She couldn't decide anything; her emotions were seesawing wildly between elation and depression. She didn't know how John would react, so any plans she made were a waste of time. This was something they would have to work out together.

She heard someone ride up, followed by raised, excited voices outside, but cowboys were always coming and going at the ranch, and she didn't think anything of it until Edie called upstairs, "Michelle? Someone's hurt. The boys are bringing him in— My God, it's the boss!" She yelled the last few words and Michelle shot off the bed. Afterward she never remembered running down the stairs; all she could remember was Edie catching her at the front door as Nev and another man helped John down from a horse. John was holding a towel to his face, and blood covered his hands and arms, and soaked his shirt.

Michelle's face twisted, and a thin cry burst from her throat. Edie was a big, strong woman, but somehow Michelle tore free of her clutching arms and got to

John. He shrugged away from Nev and caught Michelle with his free arm, hugging her to him. "I'm all right," he said gruffly. "It looks worse than it is."

"You'd better get to a doc, boss," Nev warned. "Some of those cuts need stitches."

"I will. Get on back to the men and take care of things." John gave Nev a warning look over Michelle's head, and though one eye was covered with the bloody towel, Nev got the message. He glanced quickly at Michelle, then nodded.

"What happened?" Michelle cried frantically as she helped John into the kitchen. His arm was heavy around her shoulders, which told her more than anything that he was hurt worse than he wanted her to know. He sank onto one of the kitchen chairs.

"I lost control of the truck and ran into a tree," he muttered. "My face hit the steering wheel."

She put her hand on the towel to keep it in place, feeling him wince even under her light touch, and lifted his hand away. She could see thin shards of glass shining in the black depths of his hair.

"Let me see," she coaxed, and eased the towel away from his face.

She had to bite her lip to keep from moaning. His left eye was already swollen shut, and the skin on his cheekbone was broken open in a jagged wound. His cheekbone and brow ridge were already purple and turning darker as they swelled almost visibly, huge knots distorting his face. A long cut slanted across his forehead, and he was bleeding from a dozen other smaller cuts. She took a deep breath and schooled her voice to evenness. "Edie, crush some ice to go on his eye. Maybe we can keep the swelling from getting any worse. I'll get my purse and the car keys."

"Wait a minute," John ordered. "I want to clean up a little; I've got blood and glass all over me."

"That isn't important—"

"I'm not hurt that badly," he interrupted. "Help me out of this shirt."

When he used that tone of voice, he couldn't be budged. Michelle unbuttoned the shirt and helped him out of it, noticing that he moved with extreme caution. When the shirt was off, she saw the big red welt across his ribs and knew why he was moving so carefully. In a few hours he would be too sore to move at all. Easing out of the chair, he went to the sink and washed off the blood that stained his hands and arms, then stood patiently while Michelle took a wet cloth and gently cleaned his chest and throat, even his back. His hair was matted with blood on the left side, but she didn't want to try washing his head until he'd seen a doctor.

She ran upstairs to get a clean shirt for him and helped him put it on. Edie had crushed a good amount of ice and folded it into a clean towel to make a cold pad. John winced as Michelle carefully placed the ice over his eye, but he didn't argue about holding it in place.

Her face was tense as she drove him to the local emergency care clinic. He was hurt. It staggered her, because somehow she had never imagined John as being vulnerable to anything. He was as unyielding as granite, somehow seeming impervious to fatigue, illness or injury. His battered, bloody face was testimony that he was all too human, though, being John, he wasn't giving in to his injuries. He was still in control.

He was whisked into a treatment room at the clinic, where a doctor carefully cleaned the wounds and stitched the cut on his forehead. The other cuts weren't severe enough to need stitches, though they were all cleaned and bandaged. Then the doctor spent a long time examining the swelling around John's left eye. "I'm going to have you admitted to a hospital in Tampa so an eye specialist can take a look at this," he told John.

"I don't have time for a lot of poking," John snapped, sitting up on the table.

"It's your sight," the doctor said evenly. "You took a hell of a blow, hard enough to fracture your cheekbone. Of course, if you're too busy to save your eyesight—"

"He'll go," Michelle interrupted.

John looked at her with one furious black eye, but she glared back at him just as ferociously. There was something oddly magnificent about her, a difference he couldn't describe because it was so subtle. But even as pale and strained as she was, she looked good. She always looked good to him, and he'd be able to see her a lot better with two eyes than just one.

He thought fast, then growled, "All right." Let her think what she wanted about why he was giving in; the hard truth was that he didn't want her anywhere near the ranch right now. If he went to Tampa, he could insist that she stay with him, which would keep her out of harm's way while Andy Phelps tracked down whoever had shot out his windshield. What had been a suspicion was now a certainty as far as John was concerned; Beckman's threat went far beyond harassing telephone calls. Beckman had tried to make it look like an accident when he had run Michelle off the road, but now he had gone beyond that; a bullet wasn't accidental.

Thank God Michelle hadn't been with him as she usually was. At first he'd thought the bullet was intended for him, but now he wasn't so certain. The bullet had been too far to the right. Damn it, if only he hadn't lost control of the truck when the windshield shattered! He'd jerked the wheel instinctively, and the truck had started sliding on the dewy grass, hitting a big oak head-on. The impact had thrown him forward, and his cheekbone had hit the steering wheel with such force that he'd been unconscious for a few minutes. By the time he'd recovered consciousness and his head had cleared, there had been no point in sending any of his men to investigate where the shot had come from. Beckman would have been long gone, and they would only have destroyed any signs he might have left. Andy Phelps could take over now.

"I'll arrange for an ambulance," the doctor said, turning to leave the room.

"No ambulance. Michelle can take me down there."

The doctor sighed. "Mr. Rafferty, you have a concussion; you should be lying down. And in case of damage to your eye, you shouldn't strain, bend over, or be jostled. An ambulance is the safest way to get you to Tampa."

John scowled as much as he could, but the left side of his face was so swollen that he couldn't make the muscles obey. No way was he going to let Michelle drive around by herself in the Mercedes; the car would instantly identify her to Beckman. If he had to go to Tampa, she was going to be beside him every second. "Only if Michelle rides in the ambulance with me."

"I'll be right behind," she said. "No, wait. I need to go back home first, to pick up some clothes for both of us."

"No. Doc, give me an hour. I'll have clothes brought out to us and arrange for the car to be driven back to the house." To Michelle he said, "You either ride with me, or I don't go at all."

Michelle stared at him in frustration, but she sensed he wasn't going to back down on this. He'd given in surprisingly easy about going to the hospital, only to turn oddly stubborn about keeping her beside him. If someone drove the car back to the ranch, they would be stranded in Tampa, so it didn't make sense. This entire episode seemed strange, but she didn't know just why and didn't have time to figure it out. If she had to ride in an ambulance to get John to Tampa, she'd do it. She was still so scared and shocked by his accident that she would do anything to have him well again.

He took her acquiescence for granted, telling her what he wanted and instructing her to have Nev bring the clothes, along with another man to drive the car home. Mentally she threw her hands up and left the room to make the phone call. John waited a few seconds after the door had closed behind her, then said, "Doc, is there another phone I can use?"

"Not in here, and you shouldn't be walking around. You shouldn't even be sitting up. If the call is so urgent it won't wait, let your wife make it for you."

"I don't want her to know about it." He didn't bother to correct the doctor's assumption that Michelle was his wife. The good doctor was a little premature, that was all. "Do me a favor. Call the sheriff's department, tell Andy Phelps where I am and that I need to talk to him. Don't speak to anyone except Phelps."

The doctor's eyes sharpened, and he looked at the big man for a moment. Anyone else would have been flat on his back. Rafferty should have been, but his system must be like iron. He was still steady, and giving orders with a steely authority that made it almost impossible not to do as he said.

"All right, I'll make the call if you'll lie down. You're

risking your eyesight, Mr. Rafferty. Think about being blind in that eye for the rest of your life."

John's lips drew back in a feral grin that lifted the corners of his mustache. "Then the damage has probably already been done, Doctor." Losing the sight in his left eye didn't matter much when stacked against Michelle's life. Nothing was more important than keeping her safe.

"Not necessarily. You may not even have any damage to your eye, but with a blow that forceful it's better to have it checked. You may have what's called a blowout fracture, where the shock is transmitted to the wall of the orbital bone, the eye socket. The bone is thin, and it gives under the pressure, taking it away from the eyeball itself. A blowout fracture can save your eyesight, but if you have one you'll need surgery to repair it. Or you can have nerve damage, a dislocated lens, or a detached retina. I'm not an eye specialist, so I can't say. All I can tell you is to stay as quiet as possible or you can do even greater damage."

Impatiently John lay down, putting his hands behind his head, which was throbbing. He ignored the pain, just as he ignored the numbness of his face. Whatever damage had been done, was done. So he'd broken his cheekbone and maybe shattered his eye socket; he could live with a battered face or with just one good eye, but he couldn't live without Michelle.

He went over the incident again and again in his mind, trying to pull details out of his subconscious. In that split second before the bullet had shattered the windshield, had he seen a flash that might pinpoint Beckman's location? Had Beckman been walking? Not likely. The ranch was too big for a man to cover on foot. Nor was it likely he would have been on horseback;

riding horses were harder to come by than cars, which
could easily be rented. Going on the assumption that
Beckman had been driving, what route could he have
taken that would have kept him out of sight?

Andy Phelps arrived just moments before Nev. For
Michelle's benefit, the deputy joked about John messing
up his pretty face, then waited while John gave Nev de-
tailed instructions. Nev nodded, asking few questions.
Then John glanced at Michelle. "Why don't you check
the things Nev brought; if you need anything else, he
can bring it to Tampa."

Michelle hesitated for a fraction of a second, feeling
both vaguely alarmed and in the way. John wanted her
out of the room for some reason. She looked at the tall,
quiet deputy, then back at John, before quietly leaving
the room with Nev. Something was wrong; she knew it.

Even Nev was acting strangely, not quite looking
her in the eye. Something had happened that no one
wanted her to know, and it involved John.

He had given in too easily about going to the hospital, though the threat of losing his eyesight was certainly enough to give even John pause; then he had
been so illogical about the car. John was never illogical. Nev was uneasy about something, and now John
wanted to talk privately to a deputy. She was suddenly
certain the deputy wasn't there just because he'd heard
a friend was hurt.

Too many things didn't fit. Even the fact that John
had had an accident at all didn't fit. He'd been driving
across rough pastures since boyhood, long before he'd
been old enough to have a driver's license. He was also
one of the surest drivers she had ever seen, with quick
reflexes and eagle-eyed attention to every other driver
on the road. It just didn't make sense that he would lose

control of his truck and hit a tree. It was too unlikely, too pat, too identical to her own accident.

Roger.

What a fool she had been! She had considered him as a danger only to herself, not to John. She should have expected his insane jealousy to spill over onto the man he thought had taken her away from him. While she had been trying to draw him out, he had been stalking John. Fiercely her hands knotted into fists. Roger wouldn't stand a chance against John in an open fight, but he would sneak around like the coward he was, never taking the chance of a face-to-face confrontation.

She looked down at the two carry-ons Edie had packed for them and put her hand to her head. "I feel a little sick, Nev," she whispered. "Excuse me, I have to get to the restroom."

Nev looked around, worry etched on his face. "Do you want me to get a nurse? You do look kinda green."

"No, I'll be all right." She managed a weak smile as she lied, "I never have been able to stand the sight of blood, and it just caught up with me."

She patted his arm and went around the partition to the public restrooms, but didn't enter. Instead she waited a moment, sneaking peeks around the edge of the partition; as soon as Nev turned to sit down while waiting for her, she darted across the open space to the corridor where the examining rooms were. The door to John's room was closed, but not far enough for the latch to catch. When she cautiously nudged it, the door opened a crack. It was on the left side of the room, so John wouldn't be able to see it. Phelps should be on John's right side, facing him; with luck, he wouldn't notice the slight movement of the door, either.

Their voices filtered through the crack.

"—think the bullet came from a little rise just to the left of me," John said. "Nev can show you."

"Is there any chance the bullet could be in the upholstery?"

"Probably not. The trajectory wasn't angled enough."

"Maybe I can find the cartridge. I'm coming up with a big zero from the airlines, but I have another angle I can check. If he flew in, he'd have come in at Tampa, which means he'd have gotten his rental car at the airport. If I can get a match on his description, we'll have his license plate number."

"A blue Chevrolet. That should narrow it down," John said grimly.

"I don't even want to think about how many blue Chevrolets there are in this state. It was a good idea to keep Michelle with you in Tampa; it'll give me a few days to get a lead on this guy. I can get a buddy in Tampa to put surveillance on the hospital, if you think you'll need it."

"He won't be able to find her if the doctor here keeps quiet and if my file is a little hard to find."

"I can arrange that." Andy chuckled.

Michelle didn't wait to hear more. Quietly she walked back down the corridor and rejoined Nev. He was reading a magazine and didn't look up until she sat down beside him. "Feeling better?" he asked sympathetically.

She gave some answer, and it must have made sense, because it satisfied him. She sat rigidly in the chair, more than a little stunned. What she had overheard had verified her suspicion that Roger was behind John's "accident," but it was hard for her to take in the rest of it. John not only believed her about the phone calls, he had tied them in to the blue Chevrolet and had been quietly trying to track Roger down. That explained why he had suddenly become so insistent that she tell him exactly where she was going and how long she would be there, why he didn't want her going anywhere at all. He had been trying to protect her, while she had been trying to bait Roger into the open.

She hadn't told him what she was doing because she hadn't thought he would believe her; she had learned well the bitter lesson that she could depend only on herself, perhaps learned it too well. Right from the beginning John had helped her, sometimes against her will. He had stepped in and taken over the ranch chores that were too much for her; he was literally carrying her ranch until she could rebuild it into a profitable enterprise. He had given her love, comfort, care and concern, and now a child, but still she hadn't trusted him. He hadn't been tiring of her; he'd been under considerable strain to protect her.

Being John, he hadn't told her of his suspicions or what he was doing because he hadn't wanted to "worry" her. It was just like him. That protective, possessive streak of his was bone deep and body wide, defying logical argument. There were few things or people in his life that he cared about, but when he did care, he went full measure. He had claimed her as his, and what was his, he kept.

Deputy Phelps stopped by to chat; Michelle decided to give him an opportunity to talk to Nev, and she walked back to John's room. The ambulance had just arrived, so she knew they would be leaving soon.

When the door opened, he rolled his head until he could see her with his right eye. "Is everything okay?"

She had to grit her teeth against the rage that filled her when she saw his battered, discolored face. It made her want to destroy Roger in any way she could. The primitive, protective anger filled her, pumping into every cell in her body. It took every bit of control she had to calmly walk over to him as if she weren't in a killing rage and take his hand. "If you're all right, then I don't care what Edie packed or didn't pack."

"I'll be all right." His deep voice was confident. He might or might not lose the sight in his eye, but he'd be all right. John Rafferty was made of the purest, hardest steel.

She sat beside him in the ambulance and held his hand all the way to Tampa, her eyes seldom leaving his face. Perhaps he dozed; perhaps it was simply less painful if he kept his right eye closed, too. For whatever reason, little was said during the long ride.

It wasn't until they reached the hospital that he opened his eye and looked at her, frowning when he saw how drawn she looked. She needed the bed rest more than he did; if it hadn't been for his damned eye, and the opportunity to keep Michelle away from the ranch, he would already have been back at work.

He should have gotten her away when he'd first suspected Beckman was behind her accident, but he'd been too reluctant to let her out of his sight. He wasn't certain about her or how much she needed him, so he'd kept her close at hand. But the way she had looked when she saw he was hurt…a woman didn't look like that unless she cared. He didn't know how much she cared, but for now he was content with the fact that she did. He had her now, and he wasn't inclined to let go. As soon as this business with Beckman was settled, he'd marry her so fast she wouldn't know what was happening.

Michelle went through the process of having him admitted to the hospital while he was whisked off, with

three—*three!*—nurses right beside him. Even as battered as he was, he exuded a masculinity that drew
women like a magnet.

She didn't see him again for three hours. Fretting,
she wandered the halls until a bout of nausea drove
her to find the cafeteria, where she slowly munched
on stale crackers. Her stomach gradually settled. John
would probably be here for at least two days, maybe longer; how could she hide her condition from him when
she would be with him practically every hour of the
day? Nothing escaped his attention for long, whether
he had one good eye or two. Breeding wasn't anything
new to him; it was his business. Cows calved; mares
foaled. On the ranch, everything mated and reproduced.
It wouldn't take long for him to discard the virus tale
she'd told him and come up with the real reason for her
upset stomach.

What would he say if she told him? She closed her
eyes, her heart pounding wildly at the thought. He deserved to know. She wanted him to know; she wanted
to share every moment of this pregnancy with him. But
what if it drove him to do something foolish, knowing that Roger not only threatened her but their child
as well?

She forced herself to think clearly. They were safe
here in the hospital; this was bought time. He wouldn't
leave the hospital when staying here meant that she was
also protected. She suspected that was the only reason
he'd agreed to come at all. He was giving Deputy Phelps
time to find Roger, if he could.

But what if Phelps hadn't found Roger by the time
John left the hospital? What evidence did they have
against him, anyway? He had had time to have any
damage to the Chevrolet repaired, and no one had seen

him shoot at John. He hadn't threatened her during any of those phone calls. He hadn't had to; she knew him, and that was enough.

She couldn't run, not any longer. She had run for two years, fleeing emotionally long after she had stopped physically running. John had brought her alive with his fierce, white-hot passion, forcing her out of her protective reserve. She couldn't leave him, especially now that she carried his child. She had to face Roger, face all the old nightmares and conquer them, or she would never be rid of this crippling fear. She could fight him, something she had always been too terrified to do before. She could fight him for John, for their baby, and she could damn well fight him for herself.

Finally she went back to the room that had been assigned to John to wait. It was thirty minutes more before he was wheeled into the room and transferred very carefully to the bed. When the door closed behind the orderlies he said, from between clenched teeth, "If anyone else comes through that door to do anything to me, I'm going to throw them out the window." Gingerly he eased into a more upright position against the pillow, then punched the button that raised the head of the bed.

She ignored his bad temper. "Have you seen the eye specialist yet?"

"Three of them. Come here."

There was no misreading that low demanding voice or the glint in his right eye as he looked at her. He held his hand out to her and said again, "Come here."

"John Patrick Rafferty, you aren't in any shape to begin carrying on like that."

"Aren't I?"

She refused to look at his lap. "You shouldn't be jostled."

"I don't want to be jostled. I just want a kiss." He gave her a slow, wicked grin despite the swelling in his face. "The spirit's willing, but the body's tired as hell."

She bent to kiss him, loving his lips gently with her own. When she tried to lift her head he thrust his fingers into her hair and held her down while his mouth molded to hers, his tongue making teasing little forays to touch hers. He gave a sigh of pleasure and let her up, but shifted his hand to her bottom to hold her beside him. "What've you been doing while I've been lying in cold halls in between bouts of being stuck, prodded, x-rayed and prodded some more?"

"Oh, I've been really entertained. You don't realize what an art mopping is until you've seen a master do it. There's also a four-star cafeteria here, specializing in the best stale crackers I've ever eaten." She grinned, thinking he'd never realize the truth of that last statement.

He returned the grin, thinking that once he would have accused her of being spoiled. He knew better now, because he'd been trying his damnedest to spoil her, and she persisted in being satisfied with far less than he would gladly have given her any day of the week. Her tastes didn't run to caviar or mink, and she'd been content to drive that old truck of hers instead of a Porsche. She liked silk and had beautiful clothes, but she was equally content wearing a cotton shirt and jeans. It wasn't easy to spoil a woman who was happy with whatever she had.

"Arrange to have a bed moved in here for you," he ordered. "Unless you want to sleep up here with me?"

"I don't think the nurses would allow that."

"Is there a lock on the door?"

She laughed. "No. You're out of luck."

His hand moved over her bottom, the slow, intimate touch of a lover. "We need to talk. Will it bother you if I lose this eye?"

Until then she hadn't realized that he might lose the eye as well as his sight. She sucked in a shocked breath, reaching blindly for his hand. He continued to watch her steadily, and slowly she relaxed, knowing what was important.

"It would bother me for your sake, but as for me... You can be one-eyed, totally blind, crippled, whatever, and I'll still love you."

There. She'd said it. She hadn't meant to, but the words had come so naturally that even if she could take them back, she wouldn't.

His right eye was blazing black fire at her. She had never seen anyone else with eyes as dark as his, night-black eyes that had haunted her from the first time she'd met him. She looked down at him and managed a tiny smile that was only a little hesitant as she waited for him to speak.

"Say that again."

She didn't pretend not to know what he meant, but she had to take another deep breath. Her heart was pounding. "I love you. I'm not saying that to try to trap you into anything. It's just the way I feel, and I don't expect you to—"

He put his fingers over her mouth. "It's about damn time," he said.

CHAPTER TWELVE

"YOU'RE VERY lucky, Mr. Rafferty," Dr. Norris said, looking over his glasses. "Your cheekbone seems to have absorbed most of the impact. It's fractured, of course, but the orbital bone is intact. Nor does there seem to be any damage to the eye itself, or any loss of sight. In other words, you have a hell of a shiner."

Michelle drew a deep breath of relief, squeezing John's hand. He winked at her with his right eye, then drawled, "So I've spent four days in a hospital because I have a black eye?"

Dr. Norris grinned. "Call it a vacation."

"Well, vacation's over, and I'm checking out of the resort."

"Just take it easy for the next few days. Remember that you have stitches in your head, your cheekbone is fractured, and you had a mild concussion."

"I'll keep an eye on him," Michelle said with a note of warning in her voice, looking at John very hard. He was probably planning to get on a horse as soon as he got home.

When they were alone again John put his hands behind his head, watching her with a distinct glitter in his eyes. After four days the swelling around his eye had subsided enough that he could open it a tiny slit, enough for him to see with it again. His face was still a mess, discolored in varying shades of black and purple, with a hint of green creeping in, but none of that mattered beside the fact that his eye was all right. "This has been a long four days," he murmured. "When we get home, I'm taking you straight to bed."

Her blood started running wild through her veins again, and she wondered briefly if she would always have this uncontrolled response to him. She'd been completely vulnerable to him from the start, and her reaction now was even stronger. Her body was changing as his baby grew within her, invisible changes as yet, but her skin seemed to be more sensitive, more responsive to his lightest touch. Her breasts throbbed slightly, aching for the feel of his hands and mouth.

She had decided not to tell him about the baby just yet, especially not while his eyesight was still in doubt, and had been at pains during the past four days to keep her uneasy stomach under control. She munched on crackers almost constantly, and had stopped drinking coffee because it made the nausea worse.

She could still see the hard satisfaction that had filled his face when she'd told him she loved him, but he hadn't returned the words. For a horrible moment she'd wondered if he was gloating, but he'd kissed her so hard and hungrily that she had dismissed the notion even though she'd felt a lingering pain. That night, after the lights were out and she was lying on the cot that had been brought in, he had said, "Michelle."

His voice was low, and he hadn't moved. She'd lifted her head to stare through the darkness at him. "Yes?"

"I love you," he had said quietly.

Tremors shook her, and tears leaped to her eyes, but they were happy tears. "I'm glad," she had managed to say.

He'd laughed in the darkness. "You little tease, just wait until I get my hands on you again."

"I can't wait."

Now he was all right, and they were going home. She called Nev to come pick them up, then hung up the phone with hands that had become damp. She wiped them on her slacks and lifted her chin. "Have you heard if Deputy Phelps has found a lead on Roger yet?"

John had been dressing, but at her words his head snapped around and his good eye narrowed on her. Slowly he zipped his jeans and fastened them, then walked around the bed to tower over her threateningly. Michelle's gaze didn't waver, nor did she lower her chin, even though she abruptly felt very small and helpless.

He didn't say anything, but simply waited, his mouth a hard line beneath his mustache. "I eavesdropped," she said calmly. "I had already made the connection between the phone calls and the guy who forced me off the road, but how did you tie everything together?"

"Just an uneasy feeling and a lot of suspicions," he said. "After that last call, I wanted to make certain I knew where he was. There were too many loose ends, and Andy couldn't find him on any airline's overseas passenger list. The harder Beckman was to find, the more suspicious it looked."

"You didn't believe me at first, about the blue Chevrolet."

He sighed. "No, I didn't. Not at first. I'm sorry. It was hard for me to face the fact that anyone would want to hurt you. But something was bothering you. You didn't want to drive, you didn't want to leave the ranch at all, but you wouldn't talk about it. That's when I began to realize you were scared."

Her green eyes went dark. "Terrified is a better

word," she whispered, looking out the window. "Have you heard from Phelps?"

"No. He wouldn't call here unless he'd found Beckman."

She shivered, the strained look coming back into her face. "He tried to kill you. I should have known, I should have done something."

"What could you have done?" he asked roughly. "If you'd been with me that day, the bullet would have hit you, instead of just shattering the windshield."

"He's so jealous he's insane." Thinking of Roger made her feel sick, and she pressed her hand to her stomach. "He's truly insane. He probably went wild when I moved in with you. The first couple of phone calls, he didn't say anything at all. Maybe he had just been calling to see if I answered the phone at your house. He couldn't stand for me to even talk to any other man, and when he found out that you and I—" She broke off, a fine sheen of perspiration on her face.

Gently John pulled her to him, pressing her head against his shoulder while he soothingly stroked her hair. "I wonder how he found out."

"Bitsy Sumner," Michelle said shakily.

"The airhead we met in the restaurant?"

"That airhead is the biggest gossip I know."

"If he's that far off his rocker, he probably thinks he's finally found the 'other man' after all these years."

She jumped, then gave a tight little laugh. "He has."

"What?" His voice was startled.

She eased away from him and pushed her hair back from her face with a nervous gesture. "It's always been you," she said in a low voice, looking anywhere except at him. "I couldn't love him the way I should have, and somehow he...seemed to know it."

He put his hand on her chin and forced her head around. "You acted like you hated me, damn it."

"I had to have some protection from you." Her green eyes regarded him with a little bitterness. "You had women falling all over you, women with a lot more experience, and who were a lot prettier. I was only eighteen, and you scared me to death. People called you 'Stud!' I knew I couldn't handle a man like you, even if you'd ever looked at me twice."

"I looked," he said harshly. "More than twice. But you turned your nose up at me as if you didn't like my smell, so I left you alone, even though I wanted you so much my guts were tied in knots. I built that house for you, because you were used to a lot better than the old house I was living in. I built the swimming pool because you liked to swim. Then you married some fancy-pants rich guy, damn you, and I felt like tearing the place down stone by stone."

Her lips trembled. "If I couldn't have you, it didn't matter who I married."

"You could have had me."

"As a temporary bed partner? I was so young I thought I had to have it all or nothing. I wanted forever after, for better or worse, and your track record isn't that of a marrying man. Now…" She shrugged, then managed a faint smile. "Now all that doesn't matter."

Hard anger crossed his face, then he said, "That's what you think," and covered her mouth with his. She opened her lips to him, letting him take all he wanted. The time was long past when she could deny him anything, any part of herself. Even their kisses had been restrained for the past four days, and the hunger was so strong in him that it overwhelmed his anger; he kissed her as if he wanted to devour her, his strong

hands kneading her flesh with barely controlled ferocity, and she reveled in it. She didn't fear his strength or
his roughness, because they sprang from passion and
aroused an answering need inside her.

Her nails dug into his bare shoulders as her head fell
back, baring her throat for his mouth. His hips moved
rhythmically, rubbing the hard ridge of his manhood
against her as his self-control slipped. Only the knowledge that a nurse could interrupt them at any moment
gave him the strength to finally ease away from her,
his breath coming hard and fast. The way he felt now
was too private, too intense, for him to allow even the
chance of anyone walking in on them.

"Nev had better hurry," he said roughly, unable to
resist one more kiss. Her lips were pouty and swollen
from his kisses, her eyes half-closed and drugged with
desire; that look aroused him even more, because he
had put it there.

MICHELLE SLIPPED OUT of the bedroom, her clothes in
her hand. She didn't want to take a chance on waking
John by dressing in the bedroom; he had been sleeping heavily since the accident, but she didn't want to
push her luck. She had to find Roger. He had missed
killing John once; he might not miss the second time.
And she knew John; if he made even a pretense of following the doctor's order to take it easy, she'd be surprised. No, he would be working as normal, out in the
open and vulnerable.

He had talked to Deputy Phelps the night before,
but all Andy had come up with was that a blue Chevrolet had been rented to a man generally matching
Roger's physical description, and calling himself Edward Walsh. The familiar cold chill had gone down

Michelle's spine. "Edward is Roger's middle name," she had whispered. "Walsh was his mother's maiden name." John had stared at her for a long moment before relaying the information to Andy.

She wouldn't allow Roger another opportunity to hurt John. Oddly, she wasn't afraid for herself. She had already been through so much at Roger's hands that she simply couldn't be afraid any longer, but she was deathly afraid for John, and for this new life she carried. She couldn't let this go on.

Lying awake in the darkness, she had suddenly known how to find him. She didn't know exactly where he was, but she knew the general vicinity; all she had to do was bait the trap, and he would walk into it. The only problem was that she was the bait, and she would be in the trap with him.

She left a note for John on the kitchen table and ate a cracker to settle her stomach. To be on the safe side, she carried a pack of crackers with her as she slipped silently out the back door. If her hunch was right, she should be fairly safe until someone could get there. Her hand strayed to her stomach. She had to be right.

The Mercedes started with one turn of the ignition key, its engine smooth and quiet. She put it in gear and eased it down the driveway without putting on the lights, hoping she wouldn't wake Edie or any of the men.

Her ranch was quiet, the old house sitting silent and abandoned under the canopy of big oak trees. She unlocked the door and let herself in, her ears straining to hear every noise in the darkness. It would be dawn within half an hour; she didn't have much time to bait the trap and lure Roger in before Edie would find the note on the table and wake John.

Her hand shook as she flipped on the light in the foyer. The interior of the house jumped into focus, light and shadow rearranging themselves into things she knew as well as she knew her own face. Methodically she walked around, turning on the lights in the living room, then moving into her father's office, then the dining room, then the kitchen. She pulled the curtains back from the windows to let the lights shine through like beacons, which she meant them to be.

She turned on the lights in the laundry room, and in the small downstairs apartment used by the housekeeper a long time ago, when there had been a housekeeper. She went upstairs and turned on the lights in her bedroom, where John had taken her for the first time and made it impossible for her to ever be anything but his. Every light went on, both upstairs and downstairs, piercing the predawn darkness. Then she sat down on the bottom step of the stairs and waited. Soon someone would come. It might be John, in which case he would be furious, but she suspected it would be Roger.

The seconds slipped past, becoming minutes. Just as the sky began to take on the first gray tinge of daylight, the door opened and he walked in.

She hadn't heard a car, which meant she had been right in thinking he was close by. Nor had she heard his steps as he crossed the porch. She had no warning until he walked through the door, but, oddly, she wasn't startled. She had known he would be there.

"Hello, Roger," she said calmly. She had to remain calm.

He had put on a little weight in the two years since she had seen him, and his hair was a tad thinner, but other than that he looked the same. Even his eyes still looked the same, too sincere and slightly mad. The sincerity masked the fact that his mind had slipped, not far enough that he couldn't still function in society, but enough that he could conceive of murder and be perfectly logical about it, as if it were the only thing to do.

He carried a pistol in his right hand, but he held it loosely by the side of his leg. "Michelle," he said, a little confused by her manner, as if she were greeting a guest. "You're looking well." It was a comment dictated by a lifetime of having the importance of good manners drilled into him.

She nodded gravely. "Thank you. Would you like a cup of coffee?" She didn't know if there was any coffee in the house, and even if there were, it would be horribly stale, but the longer she could keep him off balance, the better. If Edie wasn't in the kitchen now, she would be in a few minutes, and she would wake John. Michelle hoped John would call Andy, but he might not take the time. She figured he would be here in fifteen minutes. Surely she could handle Roger for fifteen minutes. She thought the brightly lit house would alert John that something was wrong, so he wouldn't come bursting in, startling Roger into shooting. It was a chance, but so far the chances she had taken had paid off.

Roger was staring at her with a feverish glitter in his eyes, as if he couldn't look at her enough. Her question startled him again. "Coffee?"

"Yes. I think I'd like a cup, wouldn't you?" The very thought of coffee made her stomach roll, but making it would take time. And Roger was very civilized; he would see nothing wrong with sharing a cup of coffee with her.

"Why, yes. That would be nice, thank you."

She smiled at him as she got up from the stairs. "Why don't you chat with me while the coffee's brewing? I'm certain we have a lot of gossip to catch up on. I only hope I have coffee; I may have forgotten to buy any. It's been so hot this summer, hasn't it? I've become an iced-tea fanatic."

"Yes, it's been very hot," he agreed, following her into the kitchen. "I thought I might spend some time at the chalet in Colorado. It should be pleasant this time of year."

She found a half-empty pack of coffee in the cabinet; it was probably so stale it would be undrinkable, but she carefully filled the pot with water and poured it into the coffeemaker, then measured out the coffee into the paper filter. Her coffeemaker was slow; it took almost ten minutes to make a pot. The perking, hissing sounds it made were very soothing.

"Please sit down," she invited, indicating the chairs at the kitchen table.

Slowly he took a chair, then placed the pistol on the table. Michelle didn't let herself look at it as she turned to take two mugs from the cabinet. Then she sat down and took another cracker from the pack she had brought with her; she had left it on the table earlier, when she was going around the house turning on all the lights. Her stomach was rolling again, perhaps from tension as much as the effects of pregnancy.

"Would you like a cracker?" she asked politely.

He was watching her again, his eyes both sad and wild. "I love you," he whispered. "How could you leave me when I need you so much? I wanted you to come back to me. Everything would have been all right. I promised you it would be all right. Why did you move in with that brute rancher? *Why did you have to cheat on me like that?*"

Michelle jumped at the sudden lash of fury in his

voice. His remarkably pleasant face was twisting in the hideous way she remembered in her nightmares. Her heart began thudding against her ribs so painfully that she thought she might be sick, after all, but somehow she managed to say with creditable surprise, "But, Roger, the electricity had been disconnected. You didn't expect me to live here without lights or water, did you?"

Again he looked confused by the unexpected change of subject, but only momentarily. He shook his head. "You can't lie to me anymore, darling. You're still living with him. I just don't understand. I offered you so much more: all the luxury you could want, jewelry, shopping trips in Paris, but instead you ran away from me to live with a sweaty rancher who smells of cows."

She couldn't stop the coldness that spread over her when he called her "darling." She swallowed, trying to force back the panic welling in her. If she panicked, she wouldn't be able to control him. How many minutes did she have left? Seven? Eight?

"I wasn't certain you wanted me back," she managed to say, though her mouth was so dry she could barely form the words.

Slowly he shook his head. "You had to know. You just didn't want to come back. You *like* what that sweaty rancher can give you, when you could have lived like a queen. Michelle, darling, it's so sick for you to let someone like him touch you, but you enjoy it, don't you? It's *unnatural!*"

She knew all the signs. He was working himself into a frenzy, the rage and jealousy building in him until he lashed out violently. How could even Roger miss seeing why she would prefer John's strong, clean masculinity and earthy passions to his own twisted parody of love? How much longer would it be? Six minutes?

"I called your house," she lied, desperately trying to defuse his temper. "Your housekeeper said you were in France. I wanted you to come get me. I wanted to come back to you."

He looked startled, the rage draining abruptly from his face as if it had never been. He didn't even look like the same man. "You…you wanted…"

She nodded, noting that he seemed to have forgotten about the pistol. "I missed you. We had so much fun together, didn't we?" It was sad, but in the beginning they *had* had fun. Roger had been full of laughter and gentle teasing, and she had hoped he could make her forget about John.

Some of that fun was suddenly echoed in his eyes, in the smile that touched his mouth. "I thought you were the most wonderful thing I'd ever seen," he said softly. "Your hair was so bright and soft, and when you smiled at me, I felt ten feet tall. I would have given you the world. I would have killed for you." Still smiling, his hand moved toward the pistol.

Five minutes?

The ghost of the man he had been faded, and suddenly pity moved her. It wasn't until that moment that she understood Roger was truly ill; something in his mind had gone very wrong, and she didn't think all the psychiatrists or drugs in the world would be able to help him.

"We were so young," she murmured, wishing things could have been different for the laughing young man he had known. Little of him remained now, only moments of remembered fun to lighten his eyes. "Do you remember June Bailey, the little redhead who fell out Wes Conlan's boat? We were all trying to help her in, and somehow we all wound up in the water except for Toni. She didn't know a thing about sailing, so there she was on the boat, screaming, and we were swimming like mad, trying to catch up to her."

Four minutes.

He laughed, his mind sliding back to those sunny, goofy days.

"I think the coffee's about finished," she murmured, getting up. Carefully she poured two cups and carried them back to the table. "I hope you can drink it. I'm not much of a coffee-maker." That was better than telling him the coffee was stale because she had been living with John.

He was still smiling, but his eyes were sad. As she watched, a sheen of tears began to brighten his eyes, and he picked up the pistol. "I do love you so much," he said. "You never should have let that man touch you." Slowly the barrel came around toward her.

A lot of things happened simultaneously. The back door exploded inward, propelled by a kick that took it off the hinges. Roger jerked toward the sound and the pistol fired, the shot deafening in the confines of the house. She screamed and ducked as two other men leaped from the inside doorway, the biggest one taking Roger down with a tackle that sent him crashing into the table. Curses and shouts filled the air, along with the sound of wood splintering; then another shot assaulted her ears and strengthened the stench of cordite. She was screaming John's name over and over, knowing he was the one rolling across the floor with Roger as they both struggled for the gun. Then suddenly the pistol skidded across the floor and John was straddling Roger as he drove his fist into the other man's face.

The sickening thud made her scream again, and she kicked a shattered chair out of her way, scrambling for the two men. Andy Phelps and another deputy reached them at the same time, grabbing John and trying to wrestle him away, but his face was a mask of killing fury at the man who had tried to murder his woman. He slung their hands away with a roar. Sobbing, Michelle threw her arms around his neck from behind, her shaking body against his back. "John, don't, please," she begged, weeping so hard that the words were almost unintelligible. "He's very sick."

He froze, her words reaching him as no one else's could. Slowly he let his fists drop and got to his feet, hauling her against him and holding her so tightly that she could barely breathe. But breathing wasn't important right then; nothing was as important as holding him and having him hold her, his head bent down to hers as he whispered a choked mixture of curses and love words.

The deputies had pulled Roger to his feet and cuffed his hands behind his back, while the pistol was put in a plastic bag and sealed. Roger's nose and mouth were bloody, and he was dazed, looking at them as if he didn't know who they were, or where he was. Perhaps he didn't.

John held Michelle's head pressed to his chest as he watched the deputies take Beckman out. God, how could she have been so cool, sitting across the kitchen table from that maniac and calmly serving him coffee? The man made John's blood run cold.

But she was safe in his arms now, the most precious part of his world. She had said a lot about his tomcatting reputation and the women in his checkered past; she had even called him a heartbreaker. But she was the true heartbreaker, with her sunlight hair and summergreen eyes, a golden woman who he never would have forgotten, even if she'd never come back into his life. Beckman had been obsessed with her, had gone mad when he lost her, and for the first time John thought he might understand. He wouldn't have a life, either, if he lost Michelle.

"I lost twenty years off my life when I found that note," he growled into her hair.

She clung to him, not loosening her grip. "You got here faster than I'd expected," she gasped, still crying a little. "Edie must've gotten up early."

"No, I got up early. You weren't in bed with me, so I started hunting you. As it was, we barely got here in time. Edie would have been too late."

Andy Phelps sighed, looking around the wrecked kitchen. Then he found another cup in the cabinet and poured himself some coffee. He made a face as he sipped it. "This stuff is rank. It tastes just like what we get at work. Anyway, I think I have my pajama bottoms on under my pants. When John called I took the time to dress, but I don't think I took the time to undress first."

They both looked at him. He still looked a little sleepy, and he certainly wasn't in uniform. He had on jeans, a T-shirt, and running shoes with no socks. He could have worn an ape suit for all she cared.

"I need both of you to make statements," he said. "But I don't think this will ever come to trial. From what I saw, he won't be judged mentally competent."

"No," Michelle agreed huskily. "He isn't."

"Do we have to make the statements right now?" John asked. "I want to take Michelle home for a while."

Andy looked at both of them. Michelle was utterly white, and John looked the worse for wear, too. He had to still be feeling the effects of hitting a steering wheel with his face. "No, go on. Come in sometime this afternoon."

John nodded and walked Michelle out of the house. He'd commandeered Nev's truck, and now he led her to it. Someone else could get the car later.

It was a short, silent drive back to the ranch. She climbed numbly out of the truck, unable to believe it was all over. John swung her up in his arms and carried her into the house, his hard arms tight around her. Without a word to anyone, even Edie, who watched them with lifted brows, he took her straight upstairs to their bedroom and kicked the door shut behind him.

He placed her on the bed as if she might shatter, then suddenly snatched her up against him again. "I could kill you for scaring me like that," he muttered, even though he knew he'd never be able to hurt her. She must have known it, too, because she cuddled closer against him.

"We're getting married right away," he ordered in a voice made harsh with need. "I heard part of what he said, and maybe he's right that I can't give you all the luxuries you deserve, but I swear to God I'll try to make you happy. I love you too much to let you go."

"I've never said anything about going," Michelle protested. Married? He wanted to get married? Abruptly she lifted her head and gave him a glowing smile, one that almost stopped his breathing.

"You never said anything about staying, either."

"How could I? This is your house. It was up to you."

"Good manners be damned," he snapped. "I was going crazy, wondering if you were happy."

"Happy? I've been sick with it. You've given me something that doesn't have a price on it." She lifted her nose at him. "I've heard that mingling red blood with blue makes very healthy babies."

He looked down at her with hungry fire in his eyes. "Well, I hope you like babies, honey, because I plan on about four."

"I like them very much," she said as she touched her stomach. "Even though this is making me feel really ghastly."

For a moment he looked puzzled, then his gaze drifted downward. His expression changed to one of stunned surprise, and he actually paled a little. "You're pregnant?"

"Yes. Since the night you came back from your last trip to Miami."

His right brow lifted as he remembered that night; the left side of his face was still too swollen for him to be able to move it much. Then a slow grin began to widen his mouth, lifting the corners of his mustache. "I was careless one time too many," he said with visible satisfaction.

She laughed. "Yes, you were. Were you trying to be?"

"Who knows?" he asked, shrugging. "Maybe. God knows I like the idea. How about you?"

She reached for him, and he pulled her onto his lap, holding her in his arms and loving the feel of her. She rubbed her face against his chest. "All I've ever wanted is for you to love me. I don't need all that expensive stuff; I like working on the ranch, and I want to build my own ranch up again, even after we're married. Having your baby is…just more of heaven."

He laid his cheek on her golden hair, thinking of the terror he'd felt when he'd read her note. But now she was safe, she was his, and he would never let her go.

She'd never seen any man as married as he planned to be. He'd spend the rest of his life trying to pamper her, and she'd continue to calmly ignore his orders whenever the mood took her, just as she did now. It would be a long, peaceful life, anchored in hard work and happily shrieking kids.

It would be good.

THEIR WEDDING DAY dawned clear and sunny, though the day before Michelle had resigned herself to having the wedding inside. But Hurricane Carl, after days of meandering around like a lost bee, had finally decided to head west and the clouds had vanished, leaving behind a pure, deep blue sky unmarred by even a wisp of cloud.

Michelle couldn't stop smiling as she dressed. If there were any truth in the superstition that it was bad luck for the groom to see the bride on their wedding day, she and John were in for a miserable life, but somehow she just couldn't believe it. He had not only refused to let her sleep in another room the night before, he'd lost his temper over the subject. She was damn well going to sleep with him where she belonged, and that was that. Tradition could just go to hell as far as he was concerned, if it meant they had to sleep apart. She had noticed that he hadn't willingly let her out of his sight since the morning they had caught Roger, so she understood.

His rather calm acceptance of his impending fatherhood had been a false calm, one shock too many after a nerve-racking morning. The reality of it had hit him during the night, and Michelle had awakened to find herself clutched tightly to his chest, his face buried in her hair and his muscled body shaking, while he muttered over and over, "A baby. My God, a baby." His hand had been stroking her stomach as if he couldn't quite imagine his child growing inside her slim body. It had become even more real to him the next morning when even crackers couldn't keep her stomach settled, and he had held her while she was sick.

Some mornings weren't bad at all, while some were wretched. This morning John had put a cracker in her mouth before she was awake enough to even open her eyes, so she had lain in his arms with her eyes closed, chewing on her "breakfast." When it became evident that this was going to be a good morning, the bridegroom had made love to the bride, tenderly, thoroughly, and at length.

They were even dressing together for their wedding. She watched as he fastened his cuff links, his hard mouth curved in a very male, very satisfied way. He had found her lace teddy and garter belt extremely erotic, so much so that now they risked being late to their own wedding.

"I need help with my zipper when you've finished with that," she said.

He looked up, and a slow smile touched his lips, then lit his black eyes. "You look good enough to eat."

She couldn't help laughing. "Does this mean we'll have to reschedule the wedding for tomorrow?"

The smile became a grin. "No, we'll make this one." He finished his cuff links. "Turn around."

She turned, and his warm fingers touched her bare back, making her catch her breath and shiver in an echo of delight. He kissed her exposed nape, holding her as the shiver became a sensuous undulation. He wouldn't have traded being with her on this particular morning for all the tradition in the world.

Her dress was a pale, icy yellow, as was the garden

hat she had chosen to wear. The color brought out the bright sunniness of her hair and made her glow, though maybe it wasn't responsible for the color in her cheeks or the sparkle in her eyes. That could be due to early pregnancy, or to heated lovemaking. Or maybe it was sheer happiness.

He worked the zipper up without snagging any of the delicate fabric, then bent to straighten and smooth her skirt. He shrugged into his jacket as she applied lipstick and carefully set the hat on her head. The yellow streamers flowed gracefully down her back. "Are we ready?" she asked, and for the first time he heard a hint of nervousness in her voice.

"We're ready," he said firmly, taking her hand. Their friends were all waiting on the patio; even his mother had flown up from Miami, a gesture that had surprised him but, on reflection, was appreciated.

Without the shadow of Roger Beckman hanging over her, Michelle had flowered in just these few days. Until she had made the effort to confront Roger, to do something about him once and for all, she hadn't realized the burden she'd been carrying around with her. Those black memories had stifled her spirit, made her wary and defensive, unwilling to give too much of herself. But she had faced him, and in doing so she had faced the past. She wasn't helpless any longer, a victim of threats and violence.

Poor Roger. She couldn't help feeling pity for him, even though he had made her life hell. At her insistence, John and Andy had arranged for Roger to have medical tests immediately, and it hadn't taken the doctors long to make a diagnosis. Roger had a slow but relentlessly degenerative brain disease. He would never be any better, and would slowly become worse until he finally died an early death, no longer knowing anyone or anything. She couldn't help feeling grief for him, because at one time he'd been a good, kind young man. She wished there were some help for him, but the doctors didn't hold out any hope.

John put his arm around her, seeing the shadows that had come into her eyes. He didn't share her sympathy for Beckman, though perhaps in time he would be able to forget the moment when that pistol had swung toward her. Maybe in a few centuries.

He tilted her head up and kissed her, taking care not to smear her lipstick. "I love you," he murmured.

The sun came back out in her eyes. "I love you, too."

He tucked her hand into the crook of his arm. "Let's go get married."

Together they walked down the stairs and out to the patio, where their friends waited and the sun shone down brightly, as if to apologize for the threat of a storm the day before. Michelle looked at the tall man by her side; she wasn't naive enough to think there wouldn't be storms in their future, because John's arrogance would always make her dig in her heels, but she found herself looking forward to the battles they would have. The worst was behind them, and if the future held rough weather and sudden squalls…well, what future didn't? If she could handle John, she could handle anything.

* * * * *

DUNCAN'S BRIDE

CHAPTER ONE

IT WAS TIME he looked for a wife, but this time around he wasn't looking for "love" as part of the bargain. He was older and infinitely wiser, and he knew that "love" wasn't necessary, or even desirable.

Reese Duncan had made a fool of himself once and nearly lost everything. It wouldn't happen again. This time he'd choose a wife with his brain instead of the contents of his jeans, and he'd pick a woman who would be content to live on an isolated ranch, who was willing to work hard and be a good mother to their kids, one who cared more about family than fashion. He'd fallen for a pretty face once, but good looks wasn't on his list of requirements now. He was a normal man with a healthy sex drive; that would be enough to get the kids he wanted. He didn't want passion. Passion had led him into the worst mistake of his life. Now he wanted a reliable, commonsense woman.

The problem was, he didn't have time to find her. He worked twelve to sixteen hours a day, trying to keep his head above water. It had taken him seven years, but it looked like this year would put him in the black, finally. He had lost half his land, a loss that ate at his soul every day of his life, but there was no way in hell he would lose what remained. He had lost most of his cattle; the huge herds were gone, and he worked like a slave taking care of the remaining heads of beef. The ranch hands were gone, too; he hadn't been able to afford their wages. He hadn't bought a new pair of jeans in three years. The barns and house hadn't been painted in eight.

But April, his ex-wife, had her outstanding debts, incurred before their marriage, paid. She had her lump-sum settlement. She had her Manhattan apartment, her expensive wardrobe. What did it matter to her that he'd had to beggar himself and sell his land, his herds, wipe out his bank accounts, to give her the half of his assets to which she felt "entitled"? After all, hadn't she been married to him for two whole years? Hadn't she lived through two hellish Montana winters, entirely cut off from civilization? So what if the ranch had been in his family for a hundred years; two years of marriage "entitled" her to half of it, or its equivalent in cold, hard cash. Of course, she had been more than happy to settle for the cash. If he didn't have that much, he could sell a little land. After all, he had oodles of it; he wouldn't miss a few thousand acres. It helped that her father was a business magnate who had a lot of connections in Montana as well as the other western states, which explained why the judge hadn't been swayed by Reese's arguments that the amount April was demanding would bankrupt him.

That was another mistake he wouldn't make. The woman he married this time would have to sign a prenuptial agreement that would protect the ranch in case of divorce. He wouldn't risk so much as one square foot of the dirt of his children's heritage, or the money it would take to run it. No woman was going to take him to the cleaners again; she might leave, but she wouldn't leave with anything of his.

Given the way he felt, he would have been just as

happy to remain single for the rest of his life if there hadn't been the question of children. He wanted kids. He wanted to teach them to love the land as he had been taught, to leave that land to them, to pass on the legacy that had been passed on to him. More than that, he wanted the life that children would bring to the empty old ranch house, the laughter and tears and anger, the pain of childish fears and the shouts of joy. He wanted heirs of his bone and blood. To have those children, he needed a wife.

A wife would be convenient, too. There was a lot to be said for available sex, especially since he didn't have the time to waste trying to find it. All he needed was a solid, steady, undemanding woman in his bed every night, and his hormones would take care of the rest of it.

But unmarried, marriageable women were scarce in that part of the country; they were all packing up and moving to the cities. Ranch life was hard, and they wanted some excitement in their lives, some luxuries. Reese didn't have the time, money or inclination to go courting, anyway. There was a more efficient way to find a woman than that.

He'd read a magazine article about how many farmers in the Midwest were advertising for wives, and he'd also seen a television program about men in Alaska who were doing the same. Part of him didn't like the idea of advertising, because he was naturally a private man and had become even more so after his disastrous marriage. On the other hand, he wouldn't have to spend a lot of money just to put a few ads in the personal sections of some newspapers, and money meant a lot to him these days. He wouldn't have to meet the women who didn't appeal to him, wouldn't have to waste time driving here and there, taking them out, getting to know them. He didn't particularly want to get to know them, not even the one he would eventually choose to be his wife. There was a hard layer of ice encasing him, and he liked it that way. Vision was much clearer when it was unclouded by emotion. The impersonality of an ad appealed to that part of him, even though the private part of him disliked the public nature of it.

But he'd decided that was the way to go, and Reese Duncan didn't waste time once he'd made a decision. He would put the ad in several of the larger newspapers in the West and Midwest. Drawing a pad of paper toward him to begin framing how he wanted the ad to read, he wrote in bold, slashing strokes: WANTED: A WIFE...

MADELYN SANGER PATTERSON sauntered back into the office after lunch. You never got the sense that Madelyn had hurried over anything, her friend Christine mused as Madelyn strolled toward her. Nor did you ever think that Madelyn sweated. It was ninety-five degrees outside, but no dampness or wrinkles marred her perfect oyster-white dress, set off by the periwinkle silk scarf draped artfully over one shoulder. Madelyn was a clotheshorse; everything looked good on her, but her own sense of style and color added a panache that stirred women to envy and men to lust.

"You're a disgusting person," Christine announced, leaning back in her chair to better appraise Madelyn's approach. "It's unhealthy not to sweat, unnatural not to wrinkle, and ungodly for your hair not to get mussed."

"I sweat," Madelyn said with idle amusement.

"When?"

"Every Tuesday and Thursday at 7:00 p.m."

"I don't believe it. You give your sweat glands an appointment?"

"No, I play racquetball."

Christine held up her fingers in the sign of the cross to ward off the mention of exercise, which in her opinion was the eighth deadly sin. "That doesn't count. Normal people sweat without exertion in weather like this. And do your clothes wrinkle? Does your hair ever hang in your face?"

"Of course."

"In front of witnesses?" Satisfied she had won that exchange, Christine looked pleased with herself.

Madelyn propped herself against the edge of Christine's desk and crossed her legs at the ankle. It was an angular, almost masculine pose that looked graceful when Madelyn did it. She tilted her head to study the newspaper Christine had been reading. "Anything interesting?"

Christine's mother always mailed her the Sunday edition of their newspaper from Omaha, so Christine could stay up-to-date on local news. "My best friend from high school is getting married. Her engagement announcement is here. A distant acquaintance has died, an old boyfriend has made his first million, the drought is driving feed prices sky-high. Usual stuff."

"Does she hold the old boyfriend against you?"

"Nah. She couldn't stand his guts when we were dating. He was a know-it-all."

"And it turns out he did know it all?"

"Evidently. It's disconcerting when things turn out to be exactly as they seemed."

"I know," Madelyn sympathized. "It's hard on your natural skepticism."

Christine folded the paper and handed it to Mad-

elyn, who enjoyed newspapers from different cities.
"There's a good article in here about relocating to a
different part of the country for a job. I wish I'd read it
before I left Omaha."

"You've been here two years. It's too late for culture shock."

"Homesickness is on a different timetable."

"But are you really? Or are you just in a blue mood
because you broke up with the Wall Street Wonder last
week and haven't found a replacement yet?"

Christine sighed dramatically. "I have a bad case
of heartbent."

"What's a dent to a Sherman tank?"

"Bent, not dent!"

"Then shouldn't it be 'heartbend'?"

"That sounds like something you get from diving
too deep, too fast."

"Surfacing."

"Whatever."

They grinned, content with the exchange, and Madelyn returned to her own office with the newspaper in
hand. She and Christine honed their wits on each other
with mutual enjoyment while still maintaining a totally
amicable relationship. Madelyn had learned early that
not everyone enjoyed that kind of conversation. Several teenage boyfriends had been, in various degrees,
insulted, angered, or intimidated, which had promptly
ended her fledgling relationships with them. Boys were
too caught up in their hormonal urges and too wildly
protective of their newfound masculinity to tolerate
what they saw as the faintest slight to that masculinity,
and unfortunately, Madelyn's lazy wit often seemed to
offend. She sighed, thinking about it, because somehow it didn't seem that things were much different now.

She stared at her desk. It was disgustingly and disgracefully clear. She could either stay at the office for the rest of the day or go home, and it wouldn't make a bit of difference either way. Odds were, no one would even know she had left, unless she stopped on the way out and made a point of telling someone. That was how often her phone rang.

There were advantages to being the stepsister of the owner. Boredom, however, wasn't one of them. Being idle was excruciating for her. The time was swiftly approaching when she would have to kiss Robert's cheek, thank him for the thought, but politely decline to continue with this "job."

Maybe she should even consider moving away. The West Coast, maybe. Or Fiji. Robert didn't have any business concerns in Fiji. Yet.

She unfolded the newspaper and leaned back in her chair with her feet propped on top of the desk and her ankles crossed. The decision would wait; she had been working on the problem for some time now, so it would still be there when she finished reading the paper.

She loved out-of-town newspapers, especially the smaller ones, the weekly editions that were more folksy gossip-columns than anything else. The Omaha newspaper was too large for that kind of coziness, but it still had a midwestern flavor to remind her that there was, indeed, a life outside New York City. The city was so large and complex that those who lived in it tended to be absorbed by it. She was constantly looking for windows on other ways of life, not because she disliked New York, but because she was so curious about everything.

She skipped over World Affairs—they were the same in Omaha as in New York—read Midwestern and local news, learning how the drought was affecting farmers and ranchers but creating a booming business for the slaughterhouses, and who had married or was intending to. She read the sale ads, compared the price of real estate in Omaha to that in New York, and was, as always, amazed at the difference. She was skipping around through the want ads when an ad in the personals caught her attention.

"Wanted: a wife for able-bodied rancher. Must be of steady character, want children, and be able to work on ranch. Age 25 to 35 preferable."

Those interested should contact said able-bodied rancher at a box number in Billings, Montana.

Madelyn was instantly diverted, her imagination caught by the ad, though she wasn't certain if she should be amused or outraged. The man was practically advertising for a combination broodmare and ranch hand! On the other hand, he had been brutally honest about his expectations, which was oddly refreshing after some of the personal ads she'd seen in the New York newspapers and magazines. There had been none of that slick "Sensitive Aquarian needs a New-Age Nineties woman to explore the meaning of the universe with him" hypersell that told one nothing except that the writer had no concept of clarity in the written word.

What could be learned about the rancher from that ad, other than his honesty? His age could be anywhere from fifty on down, but since he wanted children she thought he would be younger—probably in his thirties or early forties. Also, that bit about children probably meant one could take the able-bodied part literally. If he wanted a wife of steady character, he probably wasn't a party animal, either. He sounded like a sober, hard-working rancher who wanted a wife but didn't have the time to look for one.

She had read an article several months ago about mail-order brides, and though she'd found it interesting, she had been put off by the impersonality of it all. It was evidently a big business, matching Oriental women with men in Western nations, but it wasn't limited to that; farmers and ranchers in the less-populated states had started advertising, simply because there were so few women in their areas. There was even an entire magazine devoted to it.

Really, this ad was the same in intent as the slick ads: someone was looking for companionship. The need was the same the world over, though it was often couched in more amusing or romantic terms.

And answering the ad was doing nothing more than agreeing to meet someone, like a blind date. It was a way of making contact. All relationships began with a first date, blind or otherwise.

She folded the paper and wished she had something to do other than ponder the issue of social advertising.

She could go upstairs and pound on Robert's desk, but that wouldn't accomplish anything. Robert didn't respond well to force; he wouldn't disturb the smooth running of his offices just to give her something to do. He had offered her the job as a means of giving her a focus in life after losing both her mother and grandmother within a short length of time, but both of them knew that the job had outlived its purpose. Only an incurable optimism had kept her at it this long, hoping it would turn into something legitimate. If she pounded on Robert's desk, he would lean back in his chair and smile at her with his wickedly amused eyes, though his mouth seldom actually joined his eyes in celebration, and say, "The ball's in your court, babe. Serve it or go home."

Yes, it was time to go on to something new. The shock of grief had led to inertia, and inertia was even harder to handle, otherwise she would have left over two years ago.

Wanted: a wife.

She picked up the newspaper and read the ad again.

Naw. She wasn't that desperate. Was she? She needed a new job, a change of scenery, not a husband.

On the other hand, she was twenty-eight, old enough to know that the swinging life wasn't for her. Nor was city living, really, though she had lived in cities most of her life. As a child in Richmond, she had dearly loved the weekends when she had visited her grandmother in the country. Though it had been only a rural house, not an actual farm, she had still reveled in the peace and quiet, and longed for it when her mother had remarried and they had moved to New York.

No, she wasn't desperate at all, but she was curious by nature and badly needed a diversion while she decided what sort of job she should look for, and where. It was like a first date. If it clicked, then it clicked. She had nothing against Montana, and wouldn't that be a wild tale to tell her grandchildren, that she'd been a mail-order bride? If, as was far more likely, nothing came of it, then no harm had been done. She felt far safer answering an ad from a Montana rancher than she would one from a freestyle urbanite.

Feeling a bit exhilarated from the daring of it, she quickly rolled a sheet of paper into her top-of-the-line electronic typewriter, wrote a reply to the ad, addressed an envelope, put a stamp on it and dropped it down the mail chute. As soon as the silver metal flap swallowed the envelope, she felt a peculiar, hollow feeling in her stomach, as though she had done something incredibly stupid. On the other hand, she had had this same feeling the first time she'd gotten behind the wheel of a car. And when she'd ridden one of the super roller coasters. *And* when she'd gone to college, flown for the first time, and gone on her first date. This same feeling had accompanied almost every first in her life, but it had never been a forerunner of disaster. Instead she had thoroughly enjoyed all those firsts. Maybe that was a good sign.

On the other hand…a mail-order bride? *Her?*

Then she shrugged. It was nothing to worry about. The odds were that she would never hear from this Montana rancher. After all, what could they have in common?

REESE DUNCAN FROWNED at the New York return address on the envelope as he slit it open and removed the single sheet of typewritten paper inside. What would anyone in New York know about life on a ranch? He was tempted to toss the letter into the trash; it would be a waste of his time to read it, just as this trip into Billings to pick up the mail had been a waste of time. Today there had been only this one response to his ad, and from New York, of all places.

But the overall response to the ad hadn't been exactly overwhelming, so he might as well read it. In fact, this was just the third answer he'd gotten. Guess there weren't too many women in the world anxious for life on a Montana ranch.

The letter was short, and remarkable in the information it *didn't* give. Her name was Madelyn S. Patterson. She was twenty-eight, had never been married, and was healthy, strong and willing to work. She hadn't sent a picture. She was the only one who hadn't.

She was younger than the other two women who had responded; they were both in their thirties. The schoolteacher was his age, and not bad to look at. The other woman was thirty-six, two years his senior, and had never worked at a paying job; she had remained at home to care for her invalid mother, who had recently died. She was plain, but not homely. Both of them would have far more realistic expectations of the vast, empty spaces and hard life on a ranch than this Madelyn S. Patterson.

On the other hand, she might be some small-town girl who had moved to the big city and found she didn't like it. She must have read his ad in a hometown newspaper that had been mailed to her, because he sure as hell hadn't wasted his money placing it in the *New York Times*. And he hadn't had so many responses that he could afford to ignore one. He would make the same arrangements with her that he'd made with the others, if she were still interested when he wrote to her.

He tapped the folded letter against his thigh as he left the post office and walked to his pickup truck. This was taking up more time than he could truly afford. He wanted to have everything settled by July, and it was already the middle of May. Six weeks. He wanted to find a wife within the next six weeks.

MADELYN ALMOST DROPPED her mail when she saw the Montana address on the plain white envelope. Only nine days had passed since she had answered the ad, so he must have replied almost by return mail. In those nine days she had convinced herself that he wouldn't answer at all.

She sat down at her small dining table and ripped open the envelope. There was only one sheet inside.

Miss Patterson,

My name is Reese Duncan. I'm thirty-four years old, divorced, no children. I own a ranch in central Montana.

If you're still interested, I can see you two weeks from Saturday. Let me know by return mail. I'll send you a bus ticket to Billings.

There was no closing salutation, only his signature, *G. R. Duncan*. What did the *G* stand for? His handwriting was heavy, angular and perfectly legible, and there were no misspellings.

Now she knew his name, age and that he was divorced. He hadn't been real before; he had been only an anonymous someone who had placed an ad for a wife. Now he was a person.

And a busy one, too, if he could only spare the time to see her on a Saturday over two weeks away! Madelyn couldn't help smiling at the thought. He certainly didn't give the impression of being so desperate for a wife that he had been forced to advertise. Once again she had the distinct impression that he was simply too busy to look for one. He was divorced, the letter said, so perhaps he had lost his first wife precisely because he was so busy.

She tapped the letter with her fingernails, studying the handwriting. She was intrigued, and becoming more so. She wanted to meet this man.

MADELYN S. Patterson had answered promptly, which the other two hadn't; he had yet to hear from them. Reese opened her letter.

> Mr. Duncan, I will arrive in Billings on the designated date. However, I can't allow you to pay for my travel expenses, as we are strangers and nothing may come of our meeting.
> My flight arrives at 10:39 a.m. I trust that is convenient. Enclosed is a copy of my flight schedule. Please contact me if your plans change.

His eyebrows rose. Well, well. So she preferred to fly instead of taking the bus. A cynical smile twisted his mouth. Actually, so did he. He had even owned his own plane, but that had been B.A.: before April. His ex-wife had seen to it that it had been years since he'd been able to afford even an airline ticket, let alone his own plane.

Part of him appreciated the fact that Ms. Patterson was sparing him the expense, but his hard, proud core resented the fact that he wasn't able to afford to send her an airline ticket himself. Hell, come to that, even the bus ticket would have put him in a bind this week. Probably when she found out how broke he was, she'd leave so fast her feet would roll back the pavement. There was no way this woman would work out, but he might as well go through the motions to make certain. It wasn't as if applicants were beating down his door.

MADELYN INVITED ROBERT to dinner the Thursday before her Saturday flight to Montana, knowing that he would have a date on Friday night, and she wanted to talk to him alone.

He arrived promptly at eight and walked to her small liquor cabinet, where he poured himself a hefty Scotch and water. He lifted the glass to her, and as always his eyes smiled without his mouth joining in. Madelyn lifted her wineglass in return. "To an enigma," she said.

He arched his elegant dark brows. "Yourself?"

"Not me, I'm an open book."

"Written in an unknown language."

"And if your covers were *ever* opened, what language would be there?"

He shrugged, his eyes still smiling, but he couldn't refute the charge that he held himself off from people. Madelyn was closer to him than anyone; his father had married her mother when she was ten and he sixteen, which should have been too great an age difference for any real closeness, but Robert had unaccountably taken the time to make her feel welcome in her new home, to talk to her and listen in return. Together they had weathered first the death of his father, then, five years later, that of her mother; most stepsiblings probably would have drifted apart after that, but they hadn't, because they truly liked each other as friends as well as brother and sister.

Robert was a true enigma: elegant, handsome, almost frighteningly intelligent, but with a huge private core that no one was ever allowed to touch. Madelyn was unique in that she even knew that core existed. No one else had ever seen that much of him. In the years since he had inherited the Cannon Companies, he had reshaped the various enterprises and made them even larger and richer than before. An enormous amount of power rested in his lean hands, but not even the Cannon empire seemed to reach that private center of him. The inner man was a citadel, inviolate.

It was as if he kept himself leashed, his fires banked. Women flocked around him, of course, but he was particular in his bed partners and preferred monogamy to musical beds. When he chose a particular woman friend, they were usually together for at least a year, and he was entirely faithful to her for as long as the affair lasted. One of his ex-amours had gotten drunk and cried on Madelyn's shoulder at a party shortly after Robert had ended their affair, sobbing that she would never be able to love another man because how could anyone compare to Robert? The woman's drunken confession had, so far, been pathetically accurate; she had drifted into a couple of affairs, but both of them had been short-lived, and since then she had stopped dating entirely.

Now he was watching Madelyn with his amused eyes, and after a minute she answered her own question. "Your language would be an obscure one, dead, of course, and translated into a cipher of your own invention. To paraphrase Winston Churchill, you're an enigma inside a puzzle wrapped in a riddle, or some such complicated drivel."

He almost smiled; his lips twitched, and he dipped his head to acknowledge the accuracy of her assessment. He tasted the Scotch, savoring the smoky bite of it. "What's for dinner?"

"Conversation."

"A true case of eating our words."

"And spaghetti."

He gave the Scotch a pained look and set the glass down; he didn't think it would go well with pasta. Madelyn gave him an angelic look that deepened the amused expression in his eyes. "So what are we conversing about?"

"The fact that I'll be looking for a new job, at the very least," she said as she went into the kitchen. He followed her, and without hesitation began helping her carry the food to the table.

"So it's time, is it?" he asked shrewdly. "What made you decide?"

She shrugged. "Several things. Basically, as you said, it's time."

"You said, 'at the very least.' And at the most?"

Trust Robert to see the implication of every little word. She smiled as she poured wine into their glasses. "I'm flying to Montana this Saturday."

His eyes flickered just a little, signaling his intense interest. "What's in Montana?"

"Not what. Who."

"Who, then?"

"A man named Reese Duncan. There's a possibility of matrimony."

There were times when a look from Robert's pale green eyes could slice like a razor, and now was one of those times. "That sounds like a weather report," he said in an even tone. "Care to give me a percentage? Forty percent chance of matrimony? Fifty?"

"I don't know. I won't know until I meet the man."

He had been forking the pasta onto his plate, but now he carefully laid the utensils down and took a deep breath. Madelyn watched him with interest. It was one of the very few times when she could say she had seen Robert actually surprised.

He said, very carefully, "Do you mean you haven't met him yet?"

"No. We've corresponded, but we've never actually met. And we might not like each other in person.

There's only a very small chance of matrimony, actually. In weather terms, no accumulation expected."

"But it's possible."

"Yes. I wanted you to know."

"How did you get to know him?"

"I don't know him. I know a little about him, but not much."

"So how did you start corresponding?"

"He advertised for a wife."

He looked stunned, really stunned. Madelyn took pity on him and ladled the thick, spicy sauce over his pasta before it grew cold, since it looked as if he had totally forgotten about it.

"You answered a personal ad?" he finally asked in a strained voice.

She nodded and turned her attention to her own plate. "Yes."

"Good God, do you know how risky that is?" he roared, half rising from his chair.

"Yes, I know." She reached over to pat his hand. "Please sit down and eat. You wouldn't panic if I'd told you I'd met someone at a singles bar in Manhattan, and that's a lot riskier than meeting a rancher from Montana."

"From a health viewpoint, yes, but there are other things to consider. What if this man is abusive? What if he has a criminal record, or is a con man? Just how much *do* you know about him?"

"He's your age, thirty-four. He owns a ranch in central Montana, and he's divorced, no children. I've been writing to a box number in Billings."

From the sharp look in Robert's eyes, Madelyn knew that he had made a mental note of everything she'd told him and wouldn't forget a single detail. She also knew that he would have Reese Duncan thoroughly investigated; she thought of protesting, but decided that it wouldn't make any difference. By the time Robert had his report, she would already have met Mr. Duncan and formed her own opinion. She could even see why Robert felt alarmed and protective, though she didn't agree that there was any need for it. Mr. Duncan's blunt correspondence had reassured her that this was a man who dealt in the unvarnished truth and didn't give a damn how it looked or sounded. It was relaxing not to have to gauge the sincerity of a come-on line.

"Can I talk you out of going?" Robert asked. "Or at least into delaying your meeting?"

"No." She smiled, her gray eyes aglow with anticipation. "I'm so curious I can hardly stand it."

He sighed. Madelyn was as curious as a cat, in her own lazy way. She didn't scurry around poking her nose into every new detail that came her way, but she would eventually get around to investigating any subject or situation that intrigued her. He could see where an ad for a wife would have been irresistible to her; once she had read it, it would have been a foregone conclusion that she had to meet the man for herself. If there was no way he could talk her out of going, he could make certain she wouldn't be in danger. Before she got on that plane, he would know if this Reese Duncan had any sort of criminal record, even so much as a parking ticket. If there was any indication that Madelyn wouldn't be perfectly safe, he would keep her off the flight if he had to sit on her.

As if she'd read his mind, she leaned forward. She had that angelic expression again, the one that made him wary. When Madelyn was angelic, she was either blisteringly angry or up to mischief, and he could never tell which until it was too late. "If you interfere in my social life, I'll assume that I have the same freedom with yours," she said sweetly. "In my opinion, you need a little help with your women."

She meant it. She never bluffed, never threatened unless she was prepared to carry through on her threats. Without a word, Robert tugged his white handkerchief out of his pocket and waved it in surrender.

CHAPTER TWO

THE FLIGHT WAS a bit early landing in Billings. Madelyn carefully scrutinized the small group of people waiting to greet those leaving the plane, but she didn't see any lone males who appeared to be looking for her. She took a deep breath, glad of the small reprieve. She was unexpectedly nervous.

She used the time to duck into the ladies' room; when she came out, she heard her name being called in a tinny voice. "Madelyn Patterson, please meet your party at the Information desk. Madelyn Patterson, please meet your party at the Information desk."

Her heart was beating a little fast, but not unpleasantly so. She liked the feeling of excitement. The moment was finally at hand. Anticipation and curiosity were killing her.

She walked with an easy stride that was more of a stroll than anything else, despite her excitement. Her eyes were bright with pleasure. The Billings airport, with its big fountain, was more attractive than the general run of airports, and she let the surroundings begin to soothe her. She was only a little nervous now, and even that small bit wasn't revealed.

That must be him, leaning against the Information desk. He was wearing a hat, so she couldn't see his face all that well, but he was trim and fit. A smile quirked her mouth. This was a truly impossible situation. A real wild-goose chase. They would meet, be polite, spend a polite day together; then tomorrow she would shake his hand and tell him she had enjoyed the visit, and that would be the end of it. It would all be very civil and low-keyed, just the way she liked—

He straightened from his relaxed position against the desk and turned toward her. Madelyn felt his eyes focus on her and grow intent.

She knew the meaning of the word *poleaxed*, but this was the first time she had ever experienced the feeling. Her lazy walk faltered, then stopped altogether. She stood frozen in the middle of the airport, unable to take another step. This had never happened to her before, this total loss of composure, but she was helpless. She felt stunned, as if she'd been kicked in the chest. Her heart was racing now, pounding out a painful rhythm. Her breath came in short, shallow gasps; her carry-on bag slipped out of her fingers and landed on the floor with a soft thud. She felt like a fool, but didn't really care. She couldn't stop staring at him.

It was just old-fashioned lust, that was all. It couldn't be anything else, not at first sight. She felt panic at the very idea that it could be anything else. Just lust.

He wasn't the most handsome man she'd ever seen, because New York was full of gorgeous men, but it didn't matter. In all the ways that did matter, all the primitive, instinctual ways, call it chemistry or electricity or biology or whatever, he was devastating. The man oozed sex. Every move he made was imbued with the sort of sensuality and masculinity that made her think of sweaty skin and twisted sheets. Dear God, why on earth should this man ever have had to advertise for a wife?

He was at least six-three, and muscled with the iron,

layered strength of a man who does hard physical labor every day of his life. He was very tanned, and his hair, what she could see of it under his hat, was dark brown, almost black. His jaw was strongly shaped, his chin square, his mouth clear-cut and bracketed by twin grooves. He hadn't dressed up to meet her, but was wearing a plain white shirt with the cuffs unbuttoned and rolled back, ancient jeans and scuffed boots. She found herself frantically concentrating on the details of his appearance while she tried to deal with the havoc he was wreaking on her senses, all without saying a word.

None of her excited imaginings had prepared her for this. What was a woman supposed to do when she finally met the man who turned her banked coals into a roaring inferno? Madelyn's first thought was to run for her life, but she couldn't move.

Reese's first thought was that he'd like to take her to bed, but there was no way he'd take her to wife.

She was everything he'd been afraid she would be: a chic, sophisticated city woman, who knew absolutely nothing about a ranch. It was obvious from the top of her silky blond head down to the tips of her expensive shoes.

She was wearing white, not the most practical color for travel, but she was immaculate, without even a wrinkle to mar her appearance. Her skirt was pencil-slim and stopped just above her knees, revealing knock-out legs. Reese felt his guts tighten, just looking at her legs. He wrenched his gaze upward with an effort that almost hurt and was struck by her eyes.

Beneath the loose, matching jacket she was wearing a skimpy top in a rich blue color that should have made her eyes look blue, but didn't. Her eyes made him feel as if he were drowning. They were gray, very gray, without a tinge of blue. Soft-looking eyes, even now when they were large with…dismay? He wasn't certain of the expression, but belatedly he realized that she was very pale and still, and that she'd dropped her bag.

He stepped forward, seizing on the excuse to touch her. He curved his hand around her upper arm, which felt cool and slim under his warm palm. "Are you all right? Miss Patterson?"

Madelyn almost shuddered at his touch, her response to it was so strong. How could such a small thing produce such an upheaval? His closeness brought with it the animal heat of his body, the scent of him, and she wanted to simply turn into his arms and bury her face against his neck. Panic welled up in her. She had to get out of here, away from him. She hadn't bargained on this. But instead of running, she called on all her reserves of control and even managed to smile as she held out her hand. "Mr. Duncan."

Her voice had a small rasp to it that tugged at him. He shook her hand, noting the absence of jewelry except for the plain gold hoops in her ears. He didn't like to see a woman's hands weighted down with rings on every finger, especially when the hands were as slim as hers. He didn't release her as he repeated, "Are you all right?"

Madelyn blinked, a slow closing and opening of her eyelids that masked a deep shifting and settling inside. "Yes, thank you," she replied, not bothering to make an excuse for her behavior. What could she say? That she'd been stunned by a sudden surge of lust for him? It was the truth, but one that couldn't be voiced. She knew she should be charming to ease the awkwardness of this meeting, but somehow she couldn't summon up the superficial chatter to gloss things over. She could do nothing but stand there.

They faced each other like gunfighters on a dirt street, oblivious to the eddies of people stepping around their small, immobile island. He was watching her from beneath level brows, taking his time with his survey but keeping his thoughts hidden. Madelyn stood still, very aware of her femaleness as he looked her up and down with acutely masculine appraisal, though he revealed neither appreciation nor disapproval. His thoughts were very much his own, his face that of an intensely private man.

Even shadowed by his hat brim as they were, she could tell that his eyes were a dark green-blue-hazel color, shot through with white striations that made them gleam. They were wrinkled at the outer corners from what must have been years of squinting into the sun, because he sure didn't look as if he'd gotten those lines from laughing. His face was stern and unyielding, making her long to see how he'd look if he smiled, and wonder if he had ever been carefree. This man wasn't a stranger to rough times or hard work.

"Let's go fetch your other luggage," he said, breaking the silent confrontation. It was a long drive back to the ranch, and he was impatient to be on the way. Chores had to be done no matter how late he got back.

His voice was a baritone, a bit gravelly. Madelyn registered the rough texture of it even as she nodded toward the carry-on bag. "That's it."

"All of it?"

"Yes."

If all her clothes were in that one small bag, she sure hadn't made any big plans to impress him with her wardrobe, he thought wryly. Of course, she would impress him most without any wardrobe at all.

He bent down to lift the carry-on, still keeping his hand on her arm. She was pure, walking provocation, totally unsuitable for ranch life, but every male hormone in him was clanging alert signals. She was only going to be here for a day; why shouldn't he enjoy being with her? It would be sort of a last fling before settling down with someone better prepared for the job, and job it would be. Ranching was hard work, and Madelyn Patterson didn't look as if she had ever been exposed to the concept.

Right now, though, he didn't mind, because she was so damn enticing and he was dead tired of the relentless months—years—of sixteen-hour days and backbreaking work. He would take her out to eat tonight, after his chores were done; maybe they'd go to Jasper's for some dancing, and he'd hold her in his arms for a while, feel the softness of her skin, smell her perfume. Who knew, maybe when they went back to the ranch it wouldn't be to separate beds. He'd have to be up front in telling her that she wasn't right for the job, so there wouldn't be any misunderstanding, but maybe it wouldn't make any difference to her. Maybe.

His hand naturally moved from her arm to her back as he led her out of the terminal. Deliberately he set about charming her, something he had once done with women as effortlessly as he had smiled. Those days were far in the past, but the touch remained. She chatted easily, thank God, asking questions about Montana, and he answered them just as easily, letting her relax and get comfortable with him, and all the while he studied her face and expressions.

Strictly speaking, she was merely pretty, but her face

was lit by a liveliness that made her stunningly attractive. Her nose had a slight bump in it and was just a tiny bit crooked. A light dusting of freckles covered the bridge of it and scattered across her cheekbones, which were exquisitely chiseled. World-class cheekbones, just like her legs. Her lips weren't full, but her mouth was wide and mobile, as if she were forever on the verge of smiling. Her eyes were the grayest eyes he'd ever seen. They were calm, sleepy eyes that nevertheless revealed on closer inspection an alert and often amused intelligence, though he didn't see what she found so amusing.

If he'd met her before his rotten marriage and disastrous divorce, he would have gone after her like gangbusters, and gotten her, too, by God. Just the thought of those legs wrapped around his waist brought him to instant, uncomfortable arousal. No way, though, would he let his gonads lead him into another unsuitable marriage. He knew what he wanted in a wife, and Madelyn wasn't it. She didn't look as if she'd ever even seen a steer.

None of that decreased his physical response to her one whit. He'd been attracted to a lot of women at first sight, but not like this, not like a slam in the gut. This wasn't just attraction, a mild word to describe a mild interest; this was strong and wrenching, flooding his body with heat, making him grow hard even though he sure as hell didn't want to here in the middle of the airport. His hands actually hurt from wanting to touch her, to smooth over her breast and hip in a braille investigation of those sleek curves.

He felt a twinge of regret that she was so out of place, so totally unsuitable for his purposes. Walking beside her, he saw the sidelong glances that other men were giving her. Women like her just naturally attracted male speculation, and he wished he could afford to keep her, but she was too expensive for him. Reese was broke now, but at one time he had been accustomed to money; he knew how it looked and smelled and tasted, and how it fit. It fit Madelyn Patterson as perfectly as her silky skin did. She was slim and bright in her Paris-made suit, and the perfume sweetened by her warm flesh cost over two hundred dollars an ounce. He knew because it was one of his favorites. He couldn't even afford to keep her in perfume, much less clothes.

"What sort of work do you do?" he asked as they stepped into the bright sunshine. Those terse little letters she'd written hadn't revealed much.

She made a face, wrinkling her nose. "I work in an office without a window, doing nothing important, in my stepbrother's company. It's one of those jobs made for family." She didn't tell him that she'd turned in her notice, because he might assume she had done it thinking that she would be moving to Montana, and the one had nothing to do with the other. But her racing pulse told her that if he asked, she'd be packed and moved in with him so fast he'd think she owned her own moving company.

"Have you ever been on a ranch?" He asked it even though he already knew the answer.

"No." Madelyn looked up at him, something she still had to do despite her three-inch heels. "But I do know how to ride." She was actually a very good horsewoman, courtesy of her college roommate in Virginia, who had been horse mad.

He dismissed any riding she might have done. Recreational riding was a far cry from riding a workhorse, and that was what his horses were, trained and as valuable in their own way as a racehorse. It was just one more area where she didn't measure up.

They reached his truck, and he watched to see if she turned up her nose at it, as dusty and battered as it was. She didn't blink an eye, just stood to the side while he unlocked the door and placed her bag on the middle of the seat. Then he stepped back for her to get in.

Madelyn tried to seat herself and found that she couldn't. An astonished expression crossed her face; then she began to laugh as she realized her skirt was too tight. She couldn't lift her legs enough to climb up on the seat. "What women won't do for vanity," she said in a voice full of humor at her own expense and began tugging up the hem of the skirt. "I wore this because I wanted to look nice, but it would have been smarter to have worn slacks."

Reese's throat locked as he watched her pull up the skirt, exposing increasing amounts of her slim thighs. Heat exploded through him, making him feel as if his entire body were expanding. The thought flashed through his mind that he wouldn't be able to stand it if she pulled that skirt up one more inch, and in the next split second his hands shot out, catching her around the waist and lifting her onto the seat. She gave a startled little cry at his abrupt movement and grabbed his forearms to brace herself.

His mouth was dry, and sweat beaded on his forehead. "Don't pull up your skirt around me again, unless you want me to do something about it," he said in a guttural tone. His pulse was throbbing through him. She had the best legs he'd ever seen, long and strong, with sleek muscles. She'd be able to lock them around him and hang on, no matter how wild the ride.

Madelyn couldn't speak. Tension stretched between

them, heavy and dark. Fierce, open lust burned in his narrowed eyes, and she couldn't look away, caught in the silent intensity. She was still gripping his forearms, and she felt the heat of his arms, the steely muscles bunched iron-hard under her fingers. Her heart lurched at the sharp realization that he felt some of the turmoil she had been feeling.

She began babbling an apology. "I'm sorry. I didn't intend—that is, I didn't realize—" She stopped, because she couldn't come right out and say that she hadn't meant to arouse him. No matter how she reacted to him, he was still essentially a stranger.

He looked down at her legs, with the skirt still halfway up them, and his hands involuntarily tightened on her waist before he forced himself to release her. "Yeah, I know. It's all right," he muttered. His voice was still hoarse. It wasn't all right. Every muscle in his body was tight. He stepped back before he could give in to the impulse to move forward instead, putting himself between her legs and opening them wider. All he would have to do would be to slide his hands under the skirt to push it up the rest of the way— He crushed the thought, because if he'd let himself finish it, his control would have shattered.

THEY HAD LEFT Billings far behind before he spoke again. "Are you hungry? If you are, there's a café at the crossroads up ahead."

"No, thank you," Madelyn replied a bit dreamily as she stared at the wide vista of countryside around her. She was used to enormous buildings, but suddenly they seemed puny in comparison with this endless expanse of earth and sky. It made her feel both insignificant and fresh, as if her life were just starting now. "How far is it to your ranch?"

"About a hundred and twenty miles. It'll take us almost three hours to get there."

She blinked, astonished at the distance. She hadn't realized how much effort it was for him to come to Billings to meet her. "Do you go to Billings often?"

He glanced at her, wondering if she was trying to find out how much he isolated himself on the ranch. "No," he said briefly.

"So this is a special trip?"

"I did some business this morning, too." He'd stopped by the bank to give his loan officer the newest figures on the ranch's projected income for the coming year. Right now, it looked better than it had in a long time. He was still flat broke, but he could see daylight now. The banker had been pleased.

Madelyn looked at him with concern darkening her gray eyes. "So you've been on the road since about dawn."

"About that."

"You must be tired."

"You get used to early hours on a ranch. I'm up before dawn every day."

She looked around again. "I don't know why anyone would stay in bed and miss dawn out here. It must be wonderful."

Reese thought about it. He could remember how spectacular the dawns were, but it had been a long while since he'd had the time to notice one. "Like everything else, you get used to them. I know for a fact that there are dawns in New York, too."

She chuckled at his dry tone. "I seem to remember

them, but my apartment faces to the west. I see sunsets, not dawns."

It was on the tip of his tongue to say that they would watch a lot of dawns together, but common sense stopped him. The only dawn they would have in common would be the next day. She wasn't the woman he would choose for a wife.

He reached into his shirt pocket and got out the pack of cigarettes that always resided there, shaking one free and drawing it the rest of the way out with his lips. As he dug in his jeans pocket for his lighter he heard her say incredulously, "You *smoke*?"

Swift irritation rose in him. From the tone of her voice you would have thought she had caught him kicking puppies, or something else equally repulsive. He lit the cigarette and blew smoke into the cab. "Yeah," he said. "Do you mind?" He made it plain from *his* tone of voice that, since it was his truck, he was damn well going to smoke in it.

Madelyn faced forward again. "If you mean, does the smoke bother me, the answer is no. I just hate to see anyone smoking. It's like playing Russian roulette with your life."

"Exactly. It's my life."

She bit her lip at his curtness. Great going, she thought. That's a good way to get to know someone, attack his personal habits.

"I'm sorry," she apologized with sincerity. "It's none of my business, and I shouldn't have said anything. It just startled me."

"Why? People smoke. Or don't you associate with anyone who smokes?"

She thought a minute, treating his sarcastic remark seriously. "Not really. Some of our clients smoke, but none of my personal friends do. I spent a lot of time with my grandmother, and she was very old-fashioned about the vices. I was taught never to swear, smoke or drink spirits. I've never smoked," she said righteously.

Despite his irritation, he found himself trying not to laugh. "Does that mean you swear and drink spirits?"

"I've been known to be a bit aggressive in my language in moments of stress," she allowed. Her eyes twinkled at him. "And Grandma Lily thought it was perfectly suitable for a lady to take an occasional glass of wine, medicinally, of course. During my college days, I also swilled beer."

"Swilled?"

"There's no other word to describe a college student's drinking manners."

Remembering his own college days, he had to agree.

"But I don't enjoy spirits," she continued. "So I'd say at least half of Grandma Lily's teachings stuck. Not bad odds."

"Did she have any rules against gambling?"

Madelyn looked at him, her mouth both wry and tender, gray eyes full of a strange acceptance. "Grandma Lily believed that life is a gamble, and everyone has to take their chances. Sometimes you bust, sometimes you break the house." It was an outlook she had passed on to her granddaughter. Otherwise, Madelyn thought, why would she be sitting here in a pickup truck, in the process of falling in love with a stranger?

IT HAD BEEN a long time since Reese had seen his home through the eyes of a stranger, but as he stopped the truck next to the house, he was suddenly, bitterly ashamed. The paint on the house was badly chipped and peeling, and the outbuildings were even worse.

Long ago he'd given up trying to keep the yard neat
and had finally destroyed the flower beds that had once
delineated the house, because they had been overrun
with weeds. In the past seven years nothing new had
been added, and nothing broken had been replaced, except for the absolute necessities. Parts for the truck and
tractor had come before house paint. Taking care of the
herd had been more important than cutting the grass
or weeding the flower beds. Sheer survival hadn't left
time for the niceties of life. He'd done what he'd had
to do, but that didn't mean he had to like the shape his
home was in. He hated for Madelyn to see it like this,
when it had once been, if not a showplace, a house no
woman would have been ashamed of.

Madelyn saw the peeling paint, but dismissed it;
after all, it wasn't anything that a little effort and several gallons of paint wouldn't fix. What caught her attention was the shaded porch, complete with swing,
that wrapped all the way around the two-story house.
Grandma Lily had had a porch like that, and a swing
where they had whiled away many a lazy summer day
to the accompaniment of the slow creak of the chains
as they gently swayed.

"It reminds me of Grandma Lily's house," she said,
her eyes dreamy again.

He opened her door and put his hands on her waist,
lifting her out of the truck before she could slide to the
ground. Startled all over again, she quickly looked up
at him.

"I wasn't taking any chances with that skirt," he
said, almost growling.

Her pulse began thudding again.

He reached inside the truck and hooked her carry-on
bag with one hand, then took her arm with the other.

They entered by the back door, which was unlocked. She was struck by the fact that he felt safe in not locking his door when he was going to be gone all day.

The back door opened into a combination mudroom and laundry. A washer and dryer lined the wall to the left, and the right wall bristled with pegs from which hung an assortment of hats, coats, ponchos and bright yellow rain slickers. A variety of boots, most of them muddy, were lined up on a rubber mat. Straight ahead and across a small hall was a full bathroom, which she realized would be convenient when he came in muddy from head to foot. He could take a bath without tracking mud or dripping water all through the house to the bathroom upstairs.

They turned left and were in the kitchen, a big, open, sunny room with a breakfast nook. Madelyn looked with interest at the enormous appliances, which didn't fit her image of what the kitchen of a small-scale, bachelor rancher should look like. She had expected something smaller and much more old-fashioned than this efficient room with its institutional-sized appliances.

"The house has ten rooms," he said. "Six downstairs, and four bedrooms upstairs."

"It's a big house for just one person," she commented, following him upstairs.

"That's why I want to get married." He made the comment as if explaining why he wanted a drink of water. "My parents built this house when I was a baby. I grew up here. I want to pass it on to my own children."

She felt a little breathless, and not just from climbing the stairs. The thought of having his children weakened her.

He opened a door directly across from the top of the stairs and ushered her into a large, pleasant bedroom with white curtains at the windows and a white bed-spread on the four-poster bed. She made a soft sound of pleasure. An old rocking chair sat before one of the windows, and what was surely a handmade rug covered the smooth, hardwood plank flooring. The flooring itself was worth a small fortune. For all the charm of the room, there was a sense of bareness to it, no soft touches to personalize it in any way. But he lived here alone, she reminded herself; the personal touches would be in the rooms he used, not in the empty bedrooms waiting for his children to fill them.

He stepped past her and put her bag on the bed. "I can't take the whole day off," he said. "The chores have to be done, so I'll have to leave you to entertain yourself for a while. You can rest or do whatever you want. The bathroom is right down the hall if you want to freshen up. My bedroom has a private bath, so you don't have to worry about running into me."

In the space of a heartbeat she knew she didn't want to be left alone to twirl her fingers for the rest of the day. "Can't I go with you?"

"You'll be bored, and it's dirty work."

She shrugged. "I've been dirty before."

He looked at her for a long moment, his face unsmiling and expressionless. "All right," he finally said, wondering if she'd feel the same when her designer shoes were caked with the makings of compost.

Her smile crinkled her eyes. "I'll be changed in three minutes flat."

He doubted it. "I'll be in the barn. Come on out when you're ready."

As soon as he had closed the door behind him, Madelyn stripped out of her clothes, slithered into a pair of jeans and shoved her feet into her oldest pair of loafers, which she had brought along for this very purpose. After all, she couldn't very well explore a ranch in high heels. She pulled a white cotton camisole on over her head and sauntered out the door just as he was starting downstairs after changing shirts himself. He gave her a startled look; then his eyes took on a heavy-lidded expression as his gaze swept her throat and shoulders, left bare by the sleeveless camisole. Madelyn almost faltered as that very male look settled on her breasts, and her body felt suddenly warm and weighed down. She had seen men cast quick furtive glances at her breasts before, but Reese was making no effort to hide his speculation. She felt her nipples tingle and harden, rasping against the cotton covering them.

"I didn't think you'd make it," he said.

"I don't fuss about clothes."

She didn't have to, he thought. The body she put inside them was enough; anything else was superfluous. He was all but salivating just thinking of her breasts and those long, slender legs. The jeans covered them, but now he knew exactly how long and shapely they were, and, as she turned to close the bedroom door, how curved her buttocks were, like an inverted heart. He felt a lot hotter than the weather warranted.

She walked beside him out to the barn, her head swiveling from side to side as she took in all the aspects of the ranch. A three-door garage in the same style as the house stood behind it. She pointed to it. "How many other cars do you have?"

"None," he said curtly.

Three other buildings stood empty, their windows blank. "What are those?"

"Bunkhouses."

There was a well-built chicken coop, with fat white

chickens pecking industriously around the yard. She said, "I see you grow your own eggs."

From the corner of her eye she saw his lips twitch as if he'd almost smiled. "I grow my own milk, too."

"Very efficient. I'm impressed. I haven't had fresh milk since I was about six."

"I didn't think that accent was New York City. Where are you from originally?"

"Virginia. We moved to New York when my mother remarried, but I went back to Virginia for college."

"Your parents were divorced?"

"No. My father died. Mom remarried three years later."

He opened the barn door. "My parents died within a year of each other. I don't think they could exist apart."

The rich, earthy smell of an occupied barn enveloped her, and she took a deep breath. The odors of animals, leather, manure, hay and feed all mixed into that one unmistakable scent. She found it much more pleasant than the smell of exhaust.

The barn was huge. She had noticed a stable beside it, also empty, as well as a machinery shed and a hay shed. Everything about the ranch shouted that this had once been a very prosperous holding, but Reese had evidently fallen on hard times. How that must grate on a man with his obvious pride. She wanted to put her hand in his and tell him that it didn't matter, but she had the feeling he would reject the gesture. The pride that kept him working this huge place alone wouldn't allow him to accept anything he could interpret as pity.

She didn't know what chores needed doing or how to do them, so she tried to stay out of his way and simply watch, noting the meticulous attention he paid to everything he did. He cleaned out stalls and put down fresh hay, his powerful arms and back flowing with muscles. He put feed in the troughs, checked and repaired tack, brought in fresh water. Three horses were in a corral between the barn and stable; he checked and cleaned their hooves, brought them in to feed and water them, then put them in their stalls for the night. He called a ridiculously docile cow to him and put her in a stall, where she munched contentedly while he milked her. With a bucket half full of hot, foaming milk, he went back to the house, and two cats appeared to meow imperiously at him as they scented the milk. "Scat," he said. "Go catch a mouse."

Madelyn knew what to do now. She got the sterilized jugs she had noticed on her first trip through the kitchen and found a straining cloth. He gave her a strange look as she held the straining cloth over the mouth of the jug for him to pour the milk through. "Grandma Lily used to do this," she said in a blissful tone. "I was never strong enough to hold the bucket and pour, but I knew I'd be an adult the day she let me pour out the milk."

"Did you ever get to pour it?"

"No. She sold the cow the summer before I started school. She just had the one cow, for fresh milk, but the area was already building up and becoming less rural, so she got rid of it."

He set the bucket down and took the straining cloth. "Then here's your chance for adulthood. Pour."

A whimsical smile touched her lips as she lifted the bucket and carefully poured the creamy white liquid through the cloth into the jug. The warm, sweet scent filled the kitchen. When the bucket was empty she set it aside and said, "Thank you. As a rite of passage, that beats the socks off of getting my driver's license."

This time it happened. Reese's eyes crinkled, and his lips moved in a little half grin. Madelyn felt more of that inner shifting and settling, and knew that she was lost.

CHAPTER THREE

"THERE ISN'T MUCH nightlife around, but there is a beer joint and café about twenty miles from here if you'd like to go dancing."

Madelyn hesitated. "Would you mind very much if we just stayed here? You must be tired, and I know I am. I'd rather put my feet up and relax."

Reese was silent. He hadn't expected her to refuse, and though he was tired, he'd been looking forward to holding her while they danced. Not only that, having people around them would dilute his focus on her, ease the strain of being alone with her. She wasn't right for him, damn it.

On the other hand, he'd been up since four that morning, and relaxing at home sounded like heaven. The hard part would be relaxing with her anywhere around.

"We could play Monopoly. I saw a game in the bookcase," she said. "Or cards. I know how to play poker, blackjack, spades, hearts, rummy, Shanghai, Spite and Malice, Old Maid and Go Fish."

He gave her a sharp glance at that improbable list. She looked as innocent as an angel. "I lost my Old Maid cards, but we can play rummy."

"Jokers, two-eyed jacks, threes, fives, sevens and Rachel are wild," she said promptly.

"On the other hand, there's a baseball game on television tonight. What the hell is a rachel?"

"It's the queen of diamonds. They have names, you know."

"No, I didn't know. Are you making that up?"

"Nope. Rachel is the queen of diamonds, Palas is the queen of spades, Judith is the queen of hearts, and Argine is the queen of clubs."

"Do the kings and jacks have names?"

"I don't know. That little bit of information has never come my way."

He eyed her again, then leaned back on the couch and propped his boots on the coffee table. She saw a hint of green gleam in his eyes as he said, "The little plastic doohickey on the end of your shoelaces is called an aglet."

She mimicked his position, her lips quirking with suppressed laughter. "The dimple in the bottom of a champagne bottle is called a punt."

"The empty space between the bottle top and the liquid is called ullage."

"A newly formed embryo is called a zygote."

"Bird's nest soup is made from the nests of swiftlets, which make the nests by secreting a glutinous substance from under their tongues."

Madelyn's eyes rounded with fascination, but she rose to the challenge. "Pink flamingos are pink because they eat so many shrimp."

"It takes light from the sun eight minutes and twenty seconds to reach earth."

"The common housefly flies at the speed of five miles an hour."

"An ant can lift fifty times its own weight."

She paused and eyed him consideringly. "Were you lying about the bird nests?"

He shook his head. "Are you giving up?"

"Never use all your ammunition in the opening salvo."

There wouldn't be much opportunity for follow-up salvos, he thought. In about eighteen hours he'd be putting her on a plane back to New York and they would never meet again.

The silence that fell between them was a little awkward. Madelyn got up and smiled at him. "I'll leave you to your baseball game, if you don't mind. I want to sit on the porch swing and listen to the frogs and crickets."

Reese watched her as she left the room, her hips rolling in a lazy sway. After a minute he heard the squeak of the chains as she sat down in the swing; then the creaking as she began pushing it back and forth. He turned on the television and actually watched a little of the ball game, but his mind was on the rhythmic creaking. He turned the television off.

Madelyn had been swinging and dreaming, her eyes closed, but she opened them when she heard the screen door open and close, then his boots on the wooden porch. He stopped a few feet away and leaned his shoulder against one of the posts.

His lighter flared; then the end of the cigarette glowed as it began to burn. Madelyn stared at his dim figure, wishing she had the right to get up and go to him, to slide her arms around his waist and rest her head on his shoulder. When he didn't speak, she closed her eyes again and began drifting in the peaceful darkness. The late spring night was comfortable, and the night creatures were going about their business as usual. This was the type of life she wanted, a life close to the earth, where serenity could be drawn from nature.

"Why did you answer the ad?"

His rough-textured voice was quiet, not disturbing the night. A few seconds passed before Madelyn opened her eyes and answered.

"For much the same reason you placed it, I suppose. Partly out of curiosity, I admit, but I also want to get married and have a family."

"You don't have to come all the way out here to do that."

She said, "Maybe I do," and was completely serious.

"You don't have any boyfriends in New York?"

"I have friends, yes, but no one I'm serious about, no one I'd want to marry. And I don't think I want to live in New York. This place is wonderful."

"You've only seen it at its best. Winter is frozen hell. Every place has its drawbacks."

"And its advantages. If you didn't think the positives outweighed the negatives, you wouldn't be here."

"I grew up here. This is my home. The Eskimos are attached to their homes, too, but I wouldn't live there."

Madelyn turned her head and looked out into the night, sensing what was coming and wishing, praying, that he wouldn't say it. She could tell from the way he'd been throwing up those subtle obstacles and objections what he was going to say.

"Madelyn. You don't fit in out here."

Her right foot kept up the slow, steady rhythm of the swing. "So the visit has been a failure?"

"Yes."

"Even though you're attracted to me?" In the darkness she could be bolder than she would have been otherwise. If faint heart ne'er won fair lady, she was sure that the fair lady ne'er won with a faint heart, either.

"The spark goes both ways." He stubbed out the cigarette on his boot heel and flipped it out into the yard.

"Yes. So why am I unsuitable for your purposes?"

"You're real suitable for the purposes of bed," he said grimly. "I'd like to take you there right now. But out of bed—no. You won't do at all."

"Please explain. I like to understand my rejections."

Suddenly he moved away from the post and sat next to her on the swing, setting it to dipping and swaying with his weight. One firmly planted boot took control of the motion and began the gentle rocking movement again.

"I was married before, for two years. You're like my first wife in a lot of ways. She was a city person. She liked the entertainment and variety of a big city. She'd never been on a ranch before, and thought it was romantic, just like a movie—until she realized that most of a rancher's time is spent working, instead of having a good time. She was already restless before winter came, and that just put the frosting on the cake. Our second year was pure hell."

"Don't judge me by someone else, Reese Duncan. Just because one woman didn't like it, doesn't mean another won't."

"A man who doesn't learn from his mistakes is a damn fool. When I marry again, it'll be to a woman who knows what ranch life is like, who'll be able to work with me. I won't risk the ranch again."

"What do you mean?"

"This ranch was once one of the biggest and best. You can tell by looking around you that it used to be a lot more than what it is now. I had the two best breeding bulls in four states, a good insemination program going, over four thousand head of beef, and fifty people working for me. Then I got divorced." He lifted his arm and rested it along the back of the swing. She could see only his profile, but even in the darkness she could make out the bitter line of his mouth, hear his bitterness in his voice. "April's family had a lot of influence with the judge. He agreed that two years as my wife entitled her to half of my assets, but she sweetly decided that a lump sum settlement would do just fine, thank you. I nearly went bankrupt. I had to liquidate almost everything to buy her off. I sold land that had been in my family for over a hundred years. That was seven years ago. I've been working my ass off since then just trying to keep this place going, and this year it looks like I'll finally make a profit again. I want kids, someone to leave the ranch to, but this time I'll make a better choice of woman."

She was appalled at the cause of his circumstances, but still said tartly, "What about love? How does that fit into your plans?"

"It doesn't," he replied in a flat tone.

"What if your wife wants more?"

"I don't plan to spin her a pretty story. She'll know where I stand from the first. But I'll be a good husband. I don't stray, or mistreat women. All I ask from a wife is loyalty and competence and the same values I have."

"And to be ready to stand as a broodmare."

"That, too," he agreed.

Disappointment so sharp that it felt like a knife stabbed into her midsection. He was going to marry someone else. She looked away from him and reached deep for the control she needed. "Then I wish you luck.

I hope you have a happy marriage this time. Do you have any more applicants?"

"Two more. If either of them is interested in ranch life, I'll probably ask her to marry me."

He had it as cut-and-dried as any business deal, which was all it was to him, even though he would be sleeping with his business partner. Madelyn could have cried at such a waste of passion, but she held on to her control. All she could do now was cut her losses and try to forget him, so she wouldn't measure every man she met against him for the rest of her life.

The darkness hid the desolation in her eyes as she said, "A jackrabbit can run as fast as a racehorse—for a short distance, of course."

He didn't miss a beat. "A group of bears is called a sloth."

"The Pacific Ocean covers almost sixty-four-million square miles."

"The safety pin was invented in 1849."

"No! That long ago? Zippers were invented in 1893, and it's a good thing, because wouldn't you hate to get caught in a safety pin?"

SHE WAS QUIET on the drive back to Billings the next morning. The evening had ended well, with the hilarity of their mutual store of odd facts, but the strain had told on her in the form of a sleepless night. She couldn't bear the thought of never seeing him again, but that was the way it was, and she was determined to keep her pain to herself. Nothing would be gained by weeping all over him, which was exactly what she felt like doing.

He looked tired, too, and it was no wonder when she considered how early he'd had to get up for the past two days, and how much driving he'd done. She said,

"I'm sorry you're having to go to so much trouble to take me back."

He shot her a glance before returning his attention to the road. "You had a wasted trip, too."

So she was categorized under "Wasted Trip." She wondered wryly if her other dates had merely been flattering her all these years.

It was only about half an hour before her flight when they reached the airport. He'd timed it nicely, she thought. She wouldn't have to rush, but on the other hand, there wasn't time for a lengthy goodbye, and she was glad. She didn't know how much she could take. "You don't need to park," she said. "Just let me out."

He gave her another glance, but this one was strangely angry. He didn't speak, just parked and came around to open the door for her. Quickly she jumped out before he could catch her by the waist and lift her out again.

Reese's mouth had a grim set as he put his hand on the small of her back and walked with her into the terminal. At least the skirt she was wearing today was full enough that she could move freely, but the way it swung around her legs was just as maddening, in a different way, as that tight white skirt had been. He kept thinking that this one would be even easier to push up out of the way.

Her flight was just being called when they reached the gate. She turned with a smile that cost more than she could afford and held out her hand. "Goodbye, Reese. I wish you luck."

He took her hand, feeling the smooth texture of her fingers in contrast to his hardened, callused palm. She would be that smooth and silky all over, and that was why he was sending her away. He saw her wide, soft lips part as she started to say something else, and hunger rose up in him like a tidal wave, crashing over barriers and sweeping everything away.

"I have to taste you," he said in a low, harsh tone, carrying her hand upward to tuck it around his neck. "Just once." His other arm circled her waist and pulled her to him as he bent his head.

It wasn't a polite goodbye kiss. It was hard and deep. His mouth was hot and wild, with the taste of tobacco and himself. Madelyn put her other arm around his neck and hung on, because her legs had gone watery. The force of his mouth opened hers, and he took her with his tongue. He held her to him with painful pressure, crushing her breasts against him and cradling her pelvis against the hard, aching ridge of his manhood.

Vaguely she heard other people around them. It didn't matter. He was making love to her with his mouth, arousing her, satisfying her, consuming her. He increased the slant of his head, tucking her head more firmly into his shoulder, and kissed her with all the burning sensuality she had sensed in him on first sight.

Her heart lurched as pleasure overrode shock, swiftly escalating to an almost unbearable tension. She not only welcomed the intrusion of his tongue, she met it with her own, making love to him as surely as he was to her. He shuddered, and for a second his arms tightened so fiercely that she moaned into his mouth. Instantly they loosened, and he lifted his head.

Breathing swiftly, only inches apart, they stared at each other. His expression was hard and sensual, his eyes dilated with arousal, his lips still gleaming from the moisture of their kiss. He was bending back toward her when another call for her flight stopped him, and he slowly released her.

Her entire body ached for him. She waited, hoping he would say the words that would keep her there, but instead he said, "You'd better go. You'll miss your flight."

She couldn't speak. She nodded instead and walked away on shaky legs. She didn't look back. It was bad form for a grown woman to howl like an infant, and that was what she was very much afraid she would do if she gave in to the need to see him for even a split second.

She had gotten off the plane in Billings feeling confident and alive with anticipation. She left twenty-four hours later feeling shattered.

ROBERT MET HER plane in New York, which told Madelyn how worried he'd been. She gave him a parody of a smile and saw his pale eyes sharpen as he immediately read her distress. The smile wobbled and collapsed, and she walked into his arms. She didn't cry; she didn't let herself cry, but her chest heaved with convulsive breaths as she fought for control.

"I'll kill him," Robert said in a very soft, almost gentle tone.

Madelyn shook her head and took one more deep breath so she could talk. "He was a perfect gentleman. He's a hard-working, salt-of-the-earth type, and he said I wasn't suitable for the job."

He rocked her gently back and forth. "And that hurt your ego?"

She raised her head and managed a real smile this time, though it was just as wobbly as the first. "No, I think he managed to break my heart."

Robert gave her a searching look, reading the expression in her bottomless gray eyes. "You don't fall in love in one day."

"Sometimes you don't, sometimes you do. He didn't feel the same way, so it's something I have to live with."

"Maybe it's just as well." Keeping his arm around her shoulders, he guided her toward the entrance. "I investigated him—I know, you told me not to," he added warily as he saw the menacing look she gave him. "But he would be a tough man for any woman to live with. He's understandably bitter about the raw deal he got in his divorce—"

"I know," she said. "He told me about it."

"Then you know that any woman he marries will have a cold marriage. He's still carrying a lot of anger inside him."

"I saw the ranch. He has reason to be angry."

"His ex-wife and her family took him to the cleaners. I've dealt with them—cautiously. You have to be careful when you wade into a pool of barracudas."

"I'd like for you to ruin them financially, if you can, please," she said in the manner of a socialite idly asking for another glass of champagne.

"That won't give him back what he lost."

"No, but I'm vindictive enough that I want to see them get what they deserve."

"You don't have a vindictive bone in your body."

"Yes I do," she said in the same gentle tone he occasionally used, the one that made smart people back away.

He kissed her hair and hugged her closer. "So what are you going to do now?"

"Carry on, I suppose." She shrugged. "There's nothing else I can do."

Robert looked at her, wryly admiring her resilience. Madelyn was a trouper; she always carried on. Sometimes she needed a crutch for a while, but in the end she

stood upright again and continued on her own. Reese
Duncan had to be a lot of man to have gotten to her
this way.

TWO WEEKS LATER, Reese got back into his truck after
seeing his latest visitor, Juliet Johnson, off on the bus.
He cursed and slammed his fist against the steering
wheel, then lit a cigarette and began smoking it with
fast, furious puffs.

This had all been a damn waste of time and money.
The schoolteacher, Dale Quillan, had taken a good hard
look at the isolation of the ranch and politely told him
she wasn't interested. Miss Johnson, on the other hand,
had been willing to take on the job, but he couldn't
bring himself to make the offer. That was the sourest
woman he'd ever met, humorless and disapproving of
almost everything she saw. He'd imagined her as the
family-oriented type, since she had sacrificed her life
to care for her invalid mother, but now he figured she
had been more of a cross than a blessing to the poor
woman. She had informed him tartly that she would be
willing to perform her duties by him once they were
sanctified by marriage, but she hoped he didn't plan on
a lot of foolish shenanigans because she didn't believe
in such. Reese had told her just as sharply that he believed she could rest easy on that score.

Three applicants. One he wouldn't have, one
wouldn't have him, and the other was all wrong for
the job.

Madelyn. Long, beautiful legs. Silky blond hair and
deep gray eyes. A soft mouth and a taste like honey.
What would ranch life do to someone that elegant and
unprepared?

But he'd spent two weeks turning his bed into a

shambles every night because his frustrated body wouldn't let him sleep, and when he did manage to sleep he dreamed about her and woke up in even worse shape than when he'd dozed off. His loins ached, his temper was frayed, and he was smoking twice as much as normal. Damn her for being more than he wanted, or could afford.

She had clung to him and kissed him with such a fiery response that he hadn't been able to sleep at all that night, but she'd walked away from him without a backward glance. If she'd turned around just once, if she'd shown the least reluctance to go, he might have weakened and asked her to stay, but she hadn't. She'd even wished him good luck in finding a wife. It didn't sound as if his rejection had wounded her too badly.

He could have kept her. It drove him half-wild to know that she would have stayed if he'd asked her, that they could have been married by now. She would be lying under him every night, and the bed might get torn up, but it wouldn't be out of frustration.

No. She was too much like April. If he ever let her get her claws into him, she would rip him to shreds even worse than April had done, because even in the beginning he'd never been as hot to have April as he was to have Madelyn. She was used to city life, and though she'd appeared to like Montana and the ranch, the real test was living through a winter here. She'd never make it.

He ground out the cigarette and lit another, feeling the smoke burn his throat and lungs.

Fury and frustration boiled over. He got out of the truck and strode to a pay phone. A call to Information got her number. This was probably another waste of time; at this time of day she'd be at work, but he was driven by an urgency he bitterly resented and was still unable to resist.

He punched in her number, and an operator came on the line to tell him how much money to deposit. He dug in his pocket for change, swearing under his breath when he saw he didn't have enough.

"Sir, please deposit the correct amount."

"Just a minute." He got out his wallet and flipped through the papers until he found his telephone credit card and read off the account number to the operator. He hadn't used the card in seven years, so he hoped it was still good.

Evidently it was, because the operator said, "Thank you," and he heard the electronic beeps as the call went through.

It rang three times; then there was a click as the receiver was picked up and that warm, faintly raspy voice said, "Hello."

"Madelyn."

There was a pause; then she said, "Yes. Reese?"

"Yes." He stopped as a truck roared by, waiting until he could hear again. "You've been out here and seen what it's like. Are you willing to marry me?"

The pause this time was longer, and his fist tightened on the receiver until he thought the plastic might crack under the pressure. Finally she said, "The other two didn't work out?"

"No. What's your answer?"

"Yes," she said calmly.

He closed his eyes as the almost unbearable tension eased. God, he might be making a mistake as bad as the one he'd made with April, but he had to have her. "You'll have to sign a prenuptial agreement giving up all rights to the property I own prior to marriage and waiving any right to alimony or a lump sum settlement in case of divorce."

"All right. That's a mutual agreement, isn't it? What's yours remains yours and what's mine remains mine?"

Irritation lashed at him. "Of course."

"Fine, then."

"I want a certification from a doctor that you're in good health."

"All right. I require a certification from *your* doctor, as well."

The irritation threatened to become rage, but he held it in control. She had as much right to be reassured about his health as he did to be reassured about hers. Sexually transmitted diseases didn't stop at the Montana border, and AIDS wasn't the only concern people should have.

"I want the wedding within two weeks. When can you get out here?"

"How long is the waiting period?"

"Five days, I think. I'll have to check. Can you get here next week?"

"I think so. Give me your number and I'll call you."

He recited his phone number; then silence crackled along the line. He said, "I'll see you next week."

Another pause. Then, "Yes. I'll see you then. 'Bye."

He said goodbye and hung up, then leaned against the booth for a minute, his eyes closed. He'd done it. He'd asked her to marry him against all common sense, but this time he would protect himself and the ranch. He'd have her, but he'd keep her at a distance, and all the legal documents would keep the ranch safe.

He lit another cigarette and coughed as the acrid smoke stung his raw throat. In his mind's eye he saw her incredulous face when she'd looked at him and said, "*You smoke?*" He took the cigarette out of his mouth and looked at it; he'd smoked for years, and usually enjoyed it, but he'd been smoking too much lately.

You smoke?

Swearing again, he put out the cigarette. As he strode angrily back to the truck he passed a trash barrel, and without giving himself time to think he tossed the cigarette pack into it. He was still swearing as he got into the truck and started it. For a few days he was going to be in the mood to wrestle grizzlies, and he didn't look forward to it.

MADELYN SLOWLY REPLACED the receiver, numb with shock. She couldn't believe he'd called. She couldn't believe she'd said she would marry him. She couldn't believe anything about their conversation. It had to be the most unromantic, businesslike, *insulting* proposal on record. And she'd still said yes. Yes! A thousand times *yes*!

She had to be in Montana in a week. She had a million things to do: get packed, get the apartment closed up, say goodbye to all her friends—and have a physical, of course. But all she could do right now was sit, her thoughts whirling.

She had to be practical. It was obvious Reese wasn't giving the marriage much of a chance, even though he was going into it for his own reasons. She wondered why the other two hadn't worked out, because he'd been so adamant that she was wrong for the job. But he wanted her, she knew, remembering that kiss at the airport and the way he'd looked at her. She wanted him, more than she'd ever thought it was possible to want a man, both physically and emotionally, but was that enough to hold together a relationship when they were faced with the day-in, day-out routine that marriage entailed? Would she still love him when he had a cold and was grouchy, or yelled at her for something that wasn't her fault? Would he still want her after he'd seen her without makeup, stumbling around in the morning with uncombed hair, or when she was in a bad mood, too?

Looking at it clearly, she decided that she should ask the doctor about birth control pills while she was there. If everything worked out and they decided to have children, it would be easy to go off the Pill, but what a mess it would be if she got pregnant right away and then the marriage fell apart. It was something she would already have discussed with Reese if their situation had been a normal one, but nothing about this was normal.

She was making a complete change in her life, from urban to rural, from single to marriage, all without really knowing the man she was marrying. She didn't know his favorite foods or colors, his moods, how he would react to any given situation; all she really knew about him was that his store of miscellaneous knowledge rivaled hers, and that she responded more violently to him than anyone she'd ever met before. She was definitely following her heart here, and not her head.

Reese would want the marriage ceremony to be conducted with as little fuss as possible, before a magistrate or a justice of the peace. She didn't mind that, but she made up her mind that Robert would be there, and her friend Christine. They could be the witnesses, rather than two strangers.

Robert was less than thrilled with the news, as she had expected. "I know you fell for him, but shouldn't you give this more time? You've met him once. Or did you get to know him *really* well during that one meeting?"

"I told you, he was a perfect gentleman."

"Ah, but were you a perfect lady?"

"I'm good at whatever I do, but I've never claimed to be perfect."

His eyes twinkled, and he leaned over to pinch her cheek. "You're determined to have this man, aren't you?"

"He gave me this chance, and I'm taking it before he changes his mind. Oh yes, we're getting married now if I have to kidnap him."

"He may be in for a surprise," Robert mused. "Does he know about that bulldog stubbornness you hide behind that lazy walk and talk?"

"Of course not. Give me some credit. He'll learn about that in due time, after we're married." She smiled that sweet smile.

"So, when do I get to meet him?"

"The day of the wedding, probably. No matter what you have scheduled, I expect you to drop everything and fly out when I call you."

"Wouldn't miss it."

Christine was even less encouraging. "What do you know about ranch life?" she asked ominously. "Nothing. There are no movies, no neighbors, not even any television reception to speak of. No plays, no operas or concerts."

"No pollution, no having to put six different locks on my door when I go out, no getting mugged when I go shopping."

"You've never been mugged."

"But there's always the possibility. I know people who've been mugged several times."

"There's the *possibility* of a lot of things. It's *possible* I may even get married some day, but I'm not holding my breath waiting. That isn't the point. You really have no idea what life on a ranch is like. At least I have *some* idea. It's a hard, lonely way to live, and you're not the isolated type."

"*Au contraire,* dear friend. I'm just as content by myself as I am surrounded by people. If I had to live in Outer Mongolia to be with him, I'd do it."

Christine looked amazed. "Ye gods," she blurted. "You're in love!"

Madelyn nodded. "Of course. Why else would I marry him?"

"Well, that explains the sudden madness. Does he feel the same way?"

"Not yet. I'm going to do my best to convince him, though."

"Would it be wasting my breath to point out that that usually comes *before* the part where you say 'I do'? That courtship usually covers this phase?"

Pursing her lips, Madelyn considered it, then said, "No, I think it would come more under 'falling on deaf ears' than 'wasting your breath.' I'm getting married. I'd like you to be there."

"Of course I'll be there! Nothing could keep me away. I have to see this paragon of manly virtues."

"I never said he was virtuous."

In complete understanding, they looked at each other and smiled.

CHAPTER FOUR

THEY WERE MARRIED in Billings twelve days later. Madelyn was exhausted by the time of the wedding, which was performed in the judge's chambers. She had gotten only a few hours of sleep each night since Reese's phone call, because it had taken so much time to pack up a lifetime of belongings, sorting through and discarding what she wasn't taking, and packing what she couldn't bear to do without. She had also gotten the required physical and expressed the results to Reese, and hadn't been surprised when she had received his results by express mail the same day.

She had shipped numerous boxes containing books, albums, tapes, CDs, stereo equipment and winter clothes to the ranch, wondering what Reese would have to say about having his home taken over by the paraphernalia of a stranger. But when she'd spoken to him during two brief telephone calls he hadn't mentioned it. Before she knew it she was flying to Billings again, but this time she wasn't coming back.

Reese didn't kiss her when he met her at the airport, and she was glad. She was tired and on edge, and the first self-doubts were creeping in. From the look on his face, when he started kissing her again he didn't intend to stop, and she wasn't ready for that. But her heart leaped at the sight of him, reassuring her that she was doing the right thing.

She planned to stay at a motel in Billings for the five days until their marriage; Reese scowled at her when she told him her plan.

"There's no point in paying for a motel when you can stay at the ranch."

"Yes, there is. For one thing, most of my New York clothes are useless and will just stay packed up. I have to have Montana clothing—jeans, boots and the like. There's no point in making an extra trip later on to buy it when I'm here already. Moreover, I'm not staying alone with you right now, and you know why."

He put his hands on her waist and pulled her up against him. His narrowed eyes were dark green. "Because I'd have you under me as soon as we got in the house."

She swallowed, her slender hands resting on his chest. She could feel the heavy beat of his heart under her palms, a powerful pumping that revealed the sexual tension he was holding under control. "Yes. I'm not ready to start that part of our relationship. I'm tired, and nervous, and we really don't know each other that well—"

"We're getting married in five days. We won't know each other much better by then, baby, but I don't plan on spending my wedding night alone."

"You won't," she whispered.

"So one of the conditions for getting you in bed is to put a ring on your finger first?" His voice was getting harsher.

He was angry, and she didn't want him to be; she just wanted him to understand. She said steadily, "That isn't it at all. If the wedding were two months away, or even just a month, I'm certain we'd…we'd make love before the ceremony, but it isn't. I'm just asking you for a little time to rest and recuperate first."

He studied her upturned face, seeing the translucent shadows under her eyes and the slight pale cast to her skin. She was resting against him, letting his body support hers, and despite his surging lust he realized that she really was tired. She had uprooted her entire life in just one week, and the emotional strain had to be as exhausting as the physical work.

"Then sleep," he said in a slow, deep voice. "Get a lot of sleep, baby, and rest up. You'll need it. I can wait five days—just barely."

She did get some sleep, but the emotional strain was still telling on her. She was getting married; it was natural to be nervous, she told herself.

The day they signed the prenuptial agreement at the lawyer's office was another day of stress. Reese was in a bad mood when he picked her up at the motel, growling and snapping at everything she said, so she lapsed into silence. She didn't think it was a very good omen for their marriage.

The prenuptial agreement was brief and easily understood. In case of divorce, they both kept the property and assets they had possessed prior to their marriage, and Madelyn gave up all rights to alimony in any form. She balked, however, at the condition that he retain custody of any children that should result from their union.

"No," she said flatly. "I'm not giving up my children."

Reese leaned back in the chair and gave her a look that would have seared metal. "You're not taking my children away from me."

"Calm down," the lawyer soothed. "This is all hypothetical. Both of you are talking as if a divorce is inevitable, and if that's the case, I would suggest that you *not* get married. Statistics say that half of new marriages end in divorce, but that means that half don't. You may well be married to each other for the rest of your lives, and there may not be any children anyway."

Madelyn ignored him. She looked only at Reese. "I don't intend to take our children away from you, but neither do I intend to give them up. I think we should share custody, because children need both parents. Don't try to make me pay for what April did," she warned.

"But you'd want them to live with you."

"Yes, I would, just as you'd want them to live with you. We aren't going to change that by negotation. If we did divorce, I'd never try to turn our children against you, nor would I take them out of the area, but that's something you'll just have to take on trust, because I'm not signing any paper that says I'll give up my children."

There were times, he noted, when those sleepy gray eyes could become sharp and clear. She was all but baring her teeth at him. It seemed there were some things that mattered enough to rouse her from her habitual lazy amusement, and it was oddly reassuring that the subject of their children, hypothetical though they were, was one of them. If he and April had had a child, she would have wanted custody of it only as a way to get back at him, not because she really wanted the child itself. April hadn't wanted to have children at all, a fact for which he was now deeply grateful. Madelyn not only appeared to want children, she was ready to fight for them even before they existed.

"All right," he finally said, and nodded to the lawyer. "Strike that clause from the agreement. If there's ever a divorce, we'll hash that out then."

Madelyn felt drained when they left the lawyer's office. Until then, she hadn't realized the depth of Reese's bitterness. He was so determined not to let another woman get the upper hand on him that it might not be possible for her to reach him at all. The realization that she could be fighting a losing battle settled on her shoulders like a heavy weight.

"When do your stepbrother and best friend get here?" he asked curtly. He hadn't liked the idea of Robert and Christine being at their wedding, and now Madelyn knew why. Having friends and relatives there made it seem more like a real wedding than just a business agreement, and a business agreement, with bed privileges, was all Reese wanted, all he could accept.

"The day before the wedding. They won't be able to stay afterward, so we're going out to a restaurant the night before. You can be here, can't you?"

"No. There's no one at the ranch to put the animals up for the night and do the chores for me. Even if I left immediately afterward, it's almost a three-hour drive, so there's no point in it."

She flushed. She should have thought of the long drive and how hard he had to work. It was a sign of how much she had to learn about ranching. "I'm sorry, I should have thought. I'll call Robert—"

He interrupted her. "There's no reason why you should cancel just because I can't be here. Go out with them and enjoy it. We won't have much chance to eat out after we're married."

If he'd expected her to react with horror at that news, he was disappointed. She'd already figured that out on her own, and she didn't care. She intended to be his partner in rebuilding the ranch; maybe when it was prosperous again he could let go of some of his bitterness. She would gladly forgo restaurant meals to accomplish that.

"If you're certain…"

"I said so, didn't I?" he snapped.

She stopped and put her hands on her hips. "I'd like to know just what your problem is! I've seen men with prostate problems and women with terminal PMS who aren't as ill-tempered as you. Have you been eating gunpowder or something?"

"I'll tell you what's wrong!" he roared. "I'm trying to quit smoking!" Then he strode angrily to the truck, leaving her standing there.

She blinked her eyes, and slowly a smile stretched her lips. She strolled to the truck and got in. "So, are you homicidal or merely as irritable as a wounded water buffalo?"

"About halfway in between," he said through clenched teeth.

"Anything I can do to help?"

His eyes were narrow and intense. "It isn't just the cigarettes. Take off your panties and lock your legs around me, and I'll show you."

She didn't want to refuse him. She loved him, and he needed her, even if it was only in a sexual way. But she didn't want their first time to be a hasty coupling in a motel room, especially when she was still jittery from stress and he was irritable from lack of nicotine. She didn't know if it would be any better by their wedding day, but she hoped she would be calmer.

He saw the answer in her eyes and cursed as he ran his hand around the back of his neck. "It's just two damn days."

"For both of us." She looked out the window. "I admit, I'm trying to put it off. I'm nervous about it."

"Why? I don't abuse women. If I don't have the control I need the first time, I will the second. I won't hurt you, Maddie, and I'll make certain you enjoy it."

"I know," she said softly. "It's just that you're still basically a stranger."

"A lot of women crawl into bed with men they've just met in a bar."

"*I* don't."

"Evidently you don't crawl into bed with the man you're going to marry, either."

She rounded on him. "That's unfair and you know it, because we aren't getting married under the usual circumstances. If you're not going to do anything but snap at me and try to pressure me into bed, maybe we shouldn't see each other until the wedding."

His teeth came together with a snap. "That sounds like a damn fine idea to me."

So she spent the last two days before her wedding alone, at least until Robert and Christine arrived the afternoon before. She hadn't expected Reese to drive to Billings every day, and in fact he hadn't, except to meet her at the airport and to go to the lawyer's office, but it disturbed her that they had already quarreled. If their marriage survived, it looked like it would be a tempestuous one.

When she met Christine and Robert at the airport, Christine looked around impatiently. "Well, where is he?"

"At the ranch, working. He doesn't have anyone to look after the animals, so he isn't coming in tonight."

Christine frowned, but to Madelyn's surprise Robert took it in stride. It only took a moment's thought to realize that if there was anything Robert understood, it was work coming before everything else.

She hooked her arms through theirs and hugged both of them. "I'm so glad you're here. How was the flight?"

"Exciting," Christine said. "I've never traveled with the boss before. He gets red-carpet treatment, did you know?"

"Exasperating," Robert answered smoothly. "She makes smartmouth comments, just like you do. I kept hearing those sotto voce remarks in my ear every time a flight attendant came by."

"They didn't just come by," Christine explained. "They stopped, they lingered, they swooned."

Madelyn nodded. "Typical." She was pleased that Christine wasn't intimidated by Robert, as so many people were. Christine would never have been so familiar in the office, and in fact Madelyn doubted that the two had ever met before, but in this situation he was merely the bride's brother and she was the bride's best friend, and she had treated him as such. It also said something about Robert's urbanity that Christine did feel at ease with him; when he chose, her stepbrother could turn people to stone with his icy manner.

Now if only her two favorite people in the world would like the man she loved. She hoped he'd recovered from his nicotine fit by the morning, or it could be an interesting occasion.

They took a cab to the motel where she was staying, and Robert got a room, but Madelyn insisted that Christine stay in the room with her. On this last night as a single woman, her nerves were frayed, and she wanted someone to talk to, someone she could keep up all night if she couldn't sleep herself. After all, she reasoned, what were friends for if not to share misery?

They shared a pleasant meal and enjoyed themselves, though Madelyn wished Reese could have been there. By ten o'clock Christine was yawning openly and pointed out that it was midnight in New York. Robert signaled for the check; he looked as fresh as he had that morning, but he was used to working long hours and usually only slept four hours a night anyway.

"Will you sleep tonight?" he asked Madelyn when they got back to the motel, having noticed her shadowed eyes.

"Probably not, but I don't think a bride is supposed to sleep the night before she gets married."

"Honey, it's the night she gets married that she isn't supposed to sleep."

She wrinkled her nose at him. "Then either. I'm tired, but I'm too nervous and excited to sleep. It's been that way since he called."

"You aren't having second thoughts?"

"Second, third and fourth thoughts, but it always comes back to the fact that I can't let this chance pass."

"You could always postpone it."

She thought of how impatient Reese was and wryly shook her head. "No, I couldn't, not one more day."

He hugged her close, resting his cheek on her bright head. "Then give it all you've got, honey, and he'll never know what hit him. But if it doesn't work out, don't punish yourself. Come home."

"I've never heard such a bunch of doubting Thomases before," she chided. "But thanks for the concern. I love you, too."

By the time she went inside, Christine was already crawling into bed. Madelyn picked up the pillow and hit her with it. "You can't sleep tonight. You have to hold my hand and keep me calm."

Christine yawned. "Buy some beer, get wasted and go to sleep."

"I'd have a hangover on my wedding day. I need sympathy, not alcohol."

"The most I can offer you is two aspirin. I'm too tired to offer sympathy. Besides, why are you nervous? You want to marry him, don't you?"

"Very much. Just wait until you see him, then you'll know why."

One of Christine's eyes opened a crack. "Intimidating?"

"He's very…male."

"Ah."

"Eloquent comment."

"It covered a lot of ground. What did you expect at—" she stopped to peer at her watch "—one o'clock in the morning? Shakespearean sonnets?"

"It's only eleven o'clock here."

"My body may be here, but my spirit is on Eastern Daylight Time. Good night, or good morning, whichever the case may be."

Laughing, Madelyn let Christine crash in peace. She got ready for bed herself, then lay awake until almost dawn, both mind and body tense.

THE DRESS SHE had bought for the wedding was old-fashioned in design, almost to her ankles, with eyelet lace around the hem and neckline. She pinned up her hair in a modified Gibson girl, and put on white lace hosiery and white shoes. Even though it was just going to be a civil ceremony, she was determined to look like a bride. Now that the day had actually arrived she felt calm, and her hands were steady as she applied her makeup. Maybe she had finally gotten too tired for nervousness.

"You look gorgeous," said Christine, who looked pretty good herself in an ice-blue dress that did wonders for her olive complexion. "Cool and old-fashioned and fragile."

Fragile was a word Madelyn had never used to describe herself, and she turned to Christine in disbelief.

"I didn't say you *were* fragile, I said you *looked* fragile, which is just the way you're supposed to look on your wedding day."

"You have some interesting ideas. I know the something borrowed, something blue routine, but I always thought a bride was supposed to look radiant, not fragile."

"Pooh. Radiance is easy. Just a few whisks with a blusher brush. Fragile is much harder to achieve. I'll bet you stayed up nights perfecting it."

Madelyn sighed and looked at herself in the mirror again. "I didn't think it showed."

"Did you sleep any?"

"An hour or so."

"It shows."

When Reese knocked on the door, Madelyn froze. She knew it was Reese, and not Robert. Her heart began that slow, heavy beat as she crossed the room to open the door.

Reese looked down at her, his expression shadowed by his gray dress Stetson. With his boots on he stood over six-four, closer to six-five, and he filled the doorway. Behind her Madelyn heard Christine gasp, but Reese didn't even glance at her; he kept his eyes on Madelyn. "Are you ready?"

"Yes," she whispered. "I'm completely packed."

"I'll put your suitcases in the car."

He was wearing a charcoal pin-striped suit with a

spotlessly white shirt. Madelyn recognized both the cut
and fabric as being expensive, and knew this must be a
suit he'd had before his divorce. He was breathtaking in
it. She glanced at Christine, who still wasn't breathing.

"Christine, this is Reese Duncan. Reese, my best
friend, Christine Rizzotto."

Reese gave Christine a half smile and touched his
fingers to the brim of his hat. "I'm pleased to meet
you, ma'am."

She was still ogling him, but she managed a weak,
"And you, Mr. Duncan."

He picked up two of Madelyn's suitcases, nodded
to Christine, and carried them out. Christine's breath
escaped her with a whoosh. "That man is…is potent,"
she half gasped. "Now I understand."

Madelyn knew how she felt, and fingered the string
of pearls around her neck. The nervousness was coming back.

Robert's pale eyes were cool when he was introduced
to Reese, which bothered Reese not at all. They were
polite to each other. Madelyn hadn't hoped for anything
more. Their personalities were both too strong to allow
for easy companionship.

It wasn't until everyone had checked out that she
realized what he had said and turned to him in bewil-
derment. "You said you'd put the suitcases in the car.
You don't have a car."

"I do now. You'll need something to drive when I
have the truck out on the range. It isn't new, but it's
dependable."

She was overwhelmed, and her throat tightened. It
was a white Ford station wagon, a useful vehicle on a
working ranch. She'd had a car while she'd been in college in Virginia, but that had been years ago, and she

hadn't had any need for one in the city. With money so tight for Reese, this was a big gesture for him to make. If she had thought about it she would have bought her own car, but she hadn't.

The judge was waiting for them in his chambers. Madelyn opened her purse and got out the ring she'd bought for Reese, slipping it on her finger and closing her hand into a fist to keep it on. The judge saw her do it, and smiled. Christine took her purse from her, and after clearing his throat twice, the judge began.

Her hands were cold. Reese held her left one, folding his hard, warm fingers over hers to share his body heat with her, and when he felt her shaking he put his arm around her waist. He repeated the vows, his dark-textured voice steady. She learned that Gideon was his first name, something she hadn't known before and hadn't gotten around to asking. When it was her turn, she was surprised to hear her own vows repeated just as evenly. He slipped a plain gold band on her finger, and the judge smoothly continued, having seen Madelyn take out Reese's ring. Reese started with surprise when the judge did the ring ceremony again, and Madelyn slid a gold band over his knuckle. It was a plain band, like hers, but he hadn't expected a ring. He hadn't worn one before. The wedding band looked odd on his hand, a thin ring of gold signaling that he was now a married man.

Then he kissed her. It was just a light touch of the lips, lingering only a moment, because he didn't want to start kissing her now. He was under control, and he wanted it to stay that way. It was done. They were married.

Madelyn was quiet as they drove Robert and Christine back to the airport. Their flight was already being called, so they didn't have time to do more than hug her fiercely. Reese shook Robert's hand, and a very male look passed between the two men. Madelyn blinked back tears as both Christine and Robert turned back to wave just before they disappeared from view.

They were alone. Reese kept his arm clamped around her waist as they walked back to the car. "You look like you're about to collapse," he growled.

She felt light-headed. "I may. I've never been married before. It's a nerve-racking business."

He put her in the car. "Have you had anything to eat today?"

She shook her head.

He was cursing when he slid under the steering wheel. "No wonder you're so shaky. We'll stop and get something."

"Not just yet, please. We can stop closer to home. I'm still too nervous right now to eat anything."

In the end, they wound up driving straight to the ranch. Reese carried her suitcases up to his bedroom. "There's a big walk-in closet," he said, opening the door to show her the enormous closet, as big as a small room. "But don't start unpacking now. You need to eat first."

She gestured to her clothes. "I'll have to change before I start cooking."

"I'll do the cooking," he said sharply.

There wasn't much cooking to it, just soup and sandwiches. Madelyn forced herself to eat half a sandwich and a bowl of soup. It all seemed so unreal. She was married. This was her home now.

Reese went upstairs and changed into his work clothes. Wedding day or no, the chores had to be done. Madelyn cleaned up the kitchen, then went upstairs and began hanging up her new clothes. His bedroom was much larger than the one she had slept in before, with a big private bath that included both bathtub and shower. The bed was king-size. She thought of lying in that bed with him and felt herself get dizzy. It was already late afternoon.

She was in the kitchen again, dressed more appropriately this time in jeans and a short-sleeved sweater, when he came in tired and dirty. "Are you hungry again?" she asked. "I can do something fast while you're showering."

"Just more sandwiches tonight," he said. "I'm not much interested in food right now." He was unbuttoning his shirt as he went up the stairs.

She made the sandwiches and sat at the table with him, drinking a glass of milk while he ate. She had never thought about how much a hard-working man needed to eat, but she could see she would have to cook twice the amount she had imagined.

"I have some paperwork to do," he said when he'd finished and carried his plate to the sink. "It won't take me long."

She understood. After she'd washed the few dishes, she went upstairs and took a bath. She had just left the bathroom, her skin flushed from the damp heat, when he entered the bedroom.

She stopped, biting her lip at the searing look he gave her from her tumbled hair down to her bare toes, as if he could see through her white cotton gown. He sat down on the bed and took off his boots, then stood and tugged his shirt free. His eyes never left her as he unbuttoned the shirt and took it off.

His chest was tanned and muscled and covered with curly black hair. The smooth skin of his shoulders gleamed as he unbuckled his belt and began unfastening his jeans.

Madelyn drew a deep breath and lifted her head. "There's something you need to know."

He paused, his eyes narrowing. She was standing ramrod straight, her pale hair swirling around her shoulders and down her back. That loose, sleeveless gown wasn't anything like the sheer silk confection April had worn, but Madelyn didn't need silk to be seductive. The shadow of her nipples pressing against the white cotton was seduction enough. What could she have to tell him that was keeping her strung as tight as fence wire?

He said softly, "Don't tell me you've decided to wait another couple of nights, because I'm not going for it. Why are you so nervous?"

She gestured at the bed. "I've never done this before."

He couldn't have heard right. Stunned, he released his zipper. "You've never had sex before?"

"No, and to be honest, I'm not really looking forward to it. I want you and I want to be intimate with you, but I don't expect to enjoy the first time." Her gaze was very direct.

An odd kind of anger shook him. "Damn it, Maddie, if you're a virgin why didn't you say so, instead of having that damn physical?"

She looked like a haughty queen. "For one thing, we weren't married before. Until you became my husband this morning it wasn't any of your business. For another, you wouldn't have believed me. You believe me now because there's no reason for me to lie when you'll find out the truth for yourself in a few minutes." She spoke with cool dignity, her head high.

"We were planning to get married."

"And it could have been called off."

Reese stared silently at her. Part of him was stunned and elated. No other man had ever had her; she was completely his. He was selfish enough, male enough, primitive enough, to be glad the penetration of her maidenhead would be his right. But part of him was disappointed, because this ruled out the night of hungry lovemaking he'd planned; he would have to be a total bastard to be that insensitive to her. She would be too sore and tender for extended loving.

Maybe this was for the best. He'd take her as gently as possible, but he wouldn't, couldn't, lose his control with her. He wouldn't let himself drown in her; he would simply consummate the marriage as swiftly and easily as he could and preserve the distance between them. He didn't want to give in completely to the fierce desire in him, he just wanted to ease himself and keep her in the slot he'd assigned to her. He wanted her too much; she was a threat to him in every way he'd sworn a woman would never be again. As long as he could keep his passion for her under control she wouldn't be able to breach his defenses, so he would allow himself only a simple mating. He wouldn't linger over her, feast on her, as he wanted to do.

Madelyn forced herself not to tremble when he walked over to her. It had been nothing less than the bald truth when she'd said she wasn't looking forward to this first time. Romantically, she wanted a night of rapture. Realistically, she expected much less. All they had shared was one kiss, and Reese was sexually frustrated, his control stretched to the limit. She was going to open her body to a stranger, and she couldn't help being apprehensive.

He saw the almost imperceptible way she braced herself as he came near, and he slid his hand into her hair. "You don't have to be afraid," he murmured. "I'm not going to jump on you like a bull." He tilted her head up so she had to look at him. His eyes were greener than she'd ever seen them before. "I can make it good for you, baby."

She swallowed. "I'd rather you didn't try, I think, not this time. I'm too nervous, and it might not work, and then I'd be disappointed. Just do it and get it over with."

A faint smile touched his lips. "That's the last thing a woman should ever say to a man." It was also a measure of her fear. "The slower I am, the better it will be for you."

"Unless I have a nervous breakdown in the middle of it."

She wasn't joking. He rubbed his thumb over her bottom lip, feeling the softness of it. It was beginning to make sense. A woman who reached the age of twenty-eight still a virgin had to have a strong sense of reserve about being intimate with a man. The way she'd kissed him had set him on fire, but this final step wasn't one she took easily. She preferred to gradually get used to this powerful new intimacy, rather than throw herself totally into the experience expecting stars and fireworks.

He picked her up and put her on the bed, then turned out all the lights except for one lamp. Madelyn would have preferred total darkness but didn't say anything. She couldn't stop staring when he stripped off his jeans and got into bed with her. She had seen male nudity before: babies and little boys, men in clinical magazines. She knew how the male body functioned. But she had never before seen a fully aroused man, and Reese was definitely that. She lost her hope for nothing worse than discomfort.

He was a big man. He leaned over her, and she felt totally dwarfed by the width of his chest and shoulders, the muscled power of his body. She could barely breathe, her lungs pumping desperately for quick, shallow gasps. By her own will and actions she had brought herself to this, placed herself in bed with a man she didn't know.

He slid his hand under her nightgown and up her thigh, his hard, warm palm shocking on her bare skin. The nightgown was pulled upward by his action, steadily baring more and more of her body until the gown was around her waist and she lay exposed to him. She closed her eyes tightly, wondering if she could go through with this.

He pulled the nightgown completely off. She shivered as she felt him against every inch of her bare body. "It won't be horrible," he murmured as he brushed her lips in a gentle kiss. "I'll make certain of it." Then she felt him close his mouth on her nipple, and the incredible heat and pressure made her moan. She kept her eyes closed as he stroked and fondled her body until gradually the tension eased and she was pliable under his hands.

Her senses couldn't reach fever pitch. She was too tired and nervous. He slid his hand between her legs and she jumped, her body tensing again even though she parted her thighs and allowed him the intimacy. His long fingers gently parted and stroked, probed to find both the degree of her readiness and the strength of her virginity. When his finger slid into her she flinched and turned her head against his shoulder.

"Shh, it's all right," he murmured soothingly. He

stretched to reach the bedside table and opened the top drawer to retrieve the tube of lubricant he had put in there earlier. She flinched again at the cool slickness of it as his finger entered her once more and moved gently back and forth.

Her heart was slamming so hard against her ribs that she thought she might be sick. He mounted her, his muscled thighs spreading hers wide, and her eyes flew open in quick panic. She subdued the fear, forcing herself to relax as much as possible. "I'm sorry," she whispered. "I know you wanted it to be better than this."

He rubbed his lips over hers, and she clung to him, her nails digging into his shoulders as she felt his hips lift and his hardness begin to probe her. "I wish it were better for you," he said in a low, taut voice. "But I'm glad you're a virgin, that this first time is mine." Then he started entering her.

She couldn't prevent the tears that scalded her eyes and ran down her temples. He was as gentle as possible, but she didn't accept him easily. The stretching and penetration of her body was a burning pain, and the rhythmic motions of his body only added to it. The only thing that made it bearable for her was, perversely, the very intimacy of having her body so deeply invaded by the man she loved. She was shattered by how primitively natural it was to give herself to him and let him find pleasure within her. Beyond the pain was a growing warmth that promised much more.

CHAPTER FIVE

THE ALARM WENT off at four-thirty. She felt him stretch beside her and reach out to shut off the insistent buzzing. Then he sat up, yawning, and turned on the lamp. She blinked at the sudden bright light.

Unconcernedly naked, he went into the bathroom. Madelyn used the privacy to bound out of bed and scramble into her clothes. She was just stepping into her jeans when he came out to begin dressing. His eyes lingered on her legs as she pulled the jeans up and snapped them.

Surrounded by the early-morning quiet and darkness, with only the one lamp lighting the room, looking at his naked body seemed as intimate as the night before when he had entered her. Warmth surged in her as she realized that intimacy had many facets. It wasn't just sex, it was being at ease with each other, the daily routine of nakedness and dressing together.

As he dressed, he watched her drag a brush through her hair in several swift strokes, restoring it to casual order. Her slender body bent and swayed with a feminine grace that made it impossible for him to look away. He remembered the way it had felt to be inside her the night before, the tightness and heat, and against his will his loins responded. He couldn't take her now; she would be too tender. She had cried the night before, and every tear had burned him. He could wait.

She put the brush down and began plumping the pillows. He went over to help her make the bed, but when she threw the tumbled covers back to straighten the bottom sheet, she saw the red stains smeared on the linen and went still.

Reese looked at the stains, too, wondering if she had any pleasure to remember as he had, or if they reminded her only of the pain. He bent and tugged the sheet loose and began stripping the bed. "The next time will be better," he said, and she gave him such a solemn look that he wanted to hold her in his arms and rock her. If she had wanted it, he could have brought her to pleasure in other ways, but she had made it plain she wasn't ready for that. He wondered how he would be able to retain his control if she did give him the total freedom of her body. That one, restricted episode of lovemaking hadn't come close to satisfying the surging hunger he felt, and that was the danger of it.

He tossed the sheet to the floor. "I'll do the morning chores while you cook breakfast."

Madelyn nodded. As he went out the door she called, "Wait! Do you like pancakes?"

He paused and looked back. "Yes, and a lot of them."

She remembered from her earlier visit that he liked his coffee strong. She yawned as she went downstairs to the kitchen; then she stood in the middle of the room and looked around. It was difficult to know where to begin when you didn't know where anything was.

Coffee first. At least his coffeemaker was an automatic drip. She found the filters and dipped in enough coffee to make the brew twice as strong as she would have made it for herself.

She had to guess at the amount of bacon and sausage to fry. As hard as he worked, he would need an enormous amount of food to eat, since he would normally burn off four or five thousand calories a day. As the combined smells of brewing coffee and frying breakfast meats began to fill the kitchen, she realized for the first time what an ongoing chore just the cooking would be. She would have to become very familiar with some cookbooks, because her skills tended toward the most basic.

Thank God he had pancake mix. She stirred up the batter, searched out the syrup, then set the table. How long should she give him before she poured the pancakes on the griddle?

A heaping platter of bacon and sausage was browned and on the table before he came back from the barn, carrying a pail of fresh milk. As soon as the door opened, Madelyn poured four circles of batter on the griddle. He put the milk on the countertop and turned on the tap to wash his hands. "How much longer will it be until breakfast is ready?"

"Two minutes. Pancakes don't take long." She flipped them over. "The coffee's ready."

He poured himself a cup and leaned against the cabinet beside her, watching her stand guard over the pancakes. It was only a couple of minutes before she stacked them on a plate and handed it to him. "The butter's on the table. Start on these while I cook some more."

He carried the plate to the table and began eating. He was finished with the first round of pancakes by the time the second was ready. Madelyn poured four more circles on the griddle. This made an even dozen. How many would he eat?

He only ate ten. She got the remaining two from the

last batch and slid onto a chair beside him. "What are you doing today?"

"I have to check fences in the west quarter so I can move the herd there for grazing."

"Will you be back for lunch, or should I pack some sandwiches?"

"Sandwiches."

And that, she thought half an hour later when he'd saddled a horse and ridden out, was that. So much for conversation over breakfast. He hadn't even kissed her this morning. She knew he had a lot of work to do, but a pat on the head wouldn't have taken too much of his time.

Their first full day of marriage didn't appear to be starting out too well.

Then she wondered just what she had expected. She knew how Reese felt, knew he didn't want her to get too close to him. It would take time to break down those barriers. The best thing she could do was learn how to be a rancher's wife. She didn't have time to fret because he hadn't kissed her good morning.

She cleaned the kitchen, which became an entire morning's work. She mopped the floor, scrubbed the oven, cleaned out the big double refrigerator, and re-arranged the pantry so she'd know where everything was. She inventoried the pantry and started a list of things she'd need. She did the laundry and remade the bed with fresh linens. She vacuumed and dusted both upstairs and down, cleaned the three bathrooms, sewed buttons on his shirts and repaired a myriad of small rips in his shirts and jeans. All in all, she felt very domestic.

Marriage was work, after all. It wasn't an endless round of parties and romantic picnics by a river.

Marriage was also night after night in bed with the

same man, opening her arms and thighs to him, easing his passion within her. He'd said it would be better, and she sensed that it would, that she had just been too tired and tense the night before for it to have been pleasurable no matter what he'd done. The whole process had been a bit shocking. No matter how much she had technically known about sex, nothing had prepared her for the reality of penetration, of actually feeling his hardness inside her. Her heartbeat picked up speed as she thought of the coming night.

She started unpacking some of the boxes she had shipped, reassembling the stereo equipment and putting some of her books out. She was so busy that when she noted the time, it was almost dark. Reese would be coming in soon, and she hadn't even started dinner. She stopped what she was doing and raced to the kitchen. She hadn't even planned what they would have, but at least she knew what was in the pantry.

A quick check of the freezer produced some thick steaks and one pack of pork chops and very little else. She made mental additions to the grocery list as she unwrapped the chops and put them in the microwave to defrost. If he hadn't had a microwave she would have been in big trouble. She was peeling a small mountain of potatoes when the back door opened. She heard him scrape his boots, then sigh tiredly as he took them off.

He came into the kitchen and stopped, looking around at the bare table and stove. "Why isn't dinner ready?" he asked in a very quiet, ominous tone.

"I was busy and didn't notice the time—"

"It's your job to notice the time. I'm dead tired and hungry. I've worked twelve hours straight, the least you could do is take the time to cook."

His words stung, but she didn't pause in what she

was doing. "I'm doing it as fast as I can. Go take a shower and relax for a few minutes."

He stomped up the stairs. She bit her lip as she cut up the potatoes and put them in a pan of hot water to stew. If he hadn't looked so exhausted she might have told him a few things, but he'd been slumping with weariness and filthy from head to foot. His day hadn't been an easy one.

She opened a big can of green beans and dumped it into a pan, then added seasonings. The chops were already baking. Bread. She needed bread. There were no canned biscuits in the refrigerator. She couldn't dredge the recipe for biscuits from her memory, no matter how many times she'd watched Grandma Lily make them. She found the cookbooks and began checking the indexes for biscuits.

Once she had the list of ingredients before her it all began to come back. She mixed the dough, then kneaded it and rolled it out as she'd done when she was a little girl. She couldn't find a biscuit cutter, so she used a water glass, pressing it down into the dough and coming up with a perfect circle. A few minutes later, a dozen biscuits were popped into the oven.

Dessert. She'd seen some small, individually wrapped devil's food cakes. She got those out, and a big can of peaches. It would have to do, because she didn't have time to bake. She opened the can of peaches and poured them into a bowl.

By the time she had the table set, Reese had come back downstairs, considerably cleaner but unimproved in mood. He looked pointedly at the empty table and stalked into the living room.

She checked the potatoes; they were tender. She mixed up a small amount of flour and milk and poured it into the potatoes; it instantly began thickening. She let them stew while she checked the chops and green beans.

The biscuits were golden brown, and had risen nicely. Now if only they were edible... Since she'd followed a recipe, they shouldn't be too bad, she hoped. She stacked them on a plate and crossed her fingers for luck.

The chops were done, finally. "Reese! Dinner's ready."

"It's about time."

She hurried to put the food on the table, realizing at the last minute that she had made neither coffee nor tea. Quickly she got two glasses from the cabinet and poured milk. She knew that he liked milk, so perhaps he sometimes drank it at dinner.

The chops weren't the tenderest she'd ever cooked, and the biscuits were a bit heavy, but he ate steadily, without comment. Heavy or not, the dozen biscuits disappeared in short order, and she ate only one. As his third helping of stewed potatoes was disappearing, she got up. "Do you want any dessert?"

His head came up. "Dessert?"

She couldn't help smiling. You could tell the man had lived alone for seven years. "It isn't much, because I didn't get around to baking." She put the small cakes in a bowl and dipped peaches and juice over them. Reese gave them a quizzical look as she set the bowl in front of him.

"Just try it," she said. "I know it's junk food, but it tastes good."

He did, and cleaned the bowl. Some of the fatigue was fading from his face. "The stereo in the living room looks like a good one."

"I've had it for several years. I hope it survived the shipping."

He'd sold his stereo system years ago, deciding that he needed the money more than he needed the music, and he'd never let himself think too much about it. When you were fighting for survival, you quickly learned how to get your priorities in order. But he'd missed music and was looking forward to playing some of his old classics again.

The house was full of signs of what she'd been doing all day, and he felt guilty about yelling at her because dinner hadn't been ready. The floors were cleaner than they'd been in years, and the dust was gone from every surface. The house smelled of household cleaner and furniture polish, and the bathroom had sparkled with cleanliness. The house was ten rooms and over four thousand square feet; his fancy city woman knew how to work.

He helped her clean the table and load the dishwasher. "What's that?" he asked, pointing to her list.

"The shopping list. The pantry has a limited selection."

He shrugged. "I was usually so tired I just ate sandwiches."

"How far is the nearest market? And don't tell me I'm going to have to go to Billings."

"There's a general store about twenty miles from here. It isn't a supermarket, but you can get the basics there. I'll take you there day after tomorrow. I can't do it tomorrow because I've got more fencing to repair before I can move the herd."

"Just give me directions. I don't think the food situation will wait until the day after tomorrow."

"I don't want you out wandering around," he said flatly.

"I won't be wandering. Just give me the directions."

"I'd rather you wait. I don't know how reliable the car is yet."

"Then I can take the truck."

"I said I'll take you day after tomorrow, and that's that."

Fuming, she went upstairs and took a shower. Why on earth was he so intractable? The way he'd acted, she might as well have said she was going to find a bar and spend the day in it. But then, that might have been what his first wife had done. Even if it were true, Madelyn was determined that she wasn't going to spend her life paying for April's sins.

She finished unpacking her clothes, hanging most of her New York clothes in the closet in another bedroom, since she wouldn't have much use for them now. It still made her feel strange to see her clothes in the same closet with a man's; she'd shared room, closet and clothes in college, but that was different. This was serious. This was a lifetime.

One thing about getting up at four-thirty: she was already sleepy, and it was only eight. Of course, she was still feeling the effects of not getting enough sleep for the past two weeks, as well as a very active day, but she could barely hold her eyes open.

She heard Reese come upstairs and go into their bedroom; then he called, "Maddie?" in a rougher voice than usual.

"In here," she called.

He appeared in the doorway, and his eyes sharpened as he took in the clothes piled on the bed. "What're you doing?" There was an oddly tense set to his shoulders.

"I'm hanging the clothes I won't use in here, so they won't clutter up our closet."

Maybe it was only her imagination, but he appeared to relax. "Are you ready to go to bed?"

"Yes, I can finish this tomorrow."

He stood aside to let her get past him, then turned out the light and followed her down the hall. Madelyn was barefoot and in another thin gown much like the one she'd worn the night before, and she got that dwarfed, suffocated feeling again, sensing him so close behind her. The top of her head would just reach his chin, and he had to weigh at least two hundred pounds, all of it muscle. It would be easy to let herself be intimidated by him, especially when she thought of lying beneath him on that big bed. She would be going to bed with him like this for the rest of her life. Maybe he had doubts about the longevity of their marriage, but she didn't.

It was easier this time. She lay in his muscular arms and felt the warmth grow under his stroking hands. But now that she was less nervous she sensed something wrong, as if he were keeping part of himself separate from their lovemaking. He touched her, but only under strict control, as if he were allowing himself only so much enjoyment and not a bit more. She didn't want those measured touches, she wanted his passion. She knew it was there, she sensed it, but he wasn't giving it to her.

It still hurt when he entered her, though not as much as before. He was gentle, but he wasn't loving. This was the way he would have treated either of those other two women he'd been willing to marry, she thought dimly, as a body he'd been given the use of, not as a warm, loving woman who needed more. This was only sex, not making love. He made her feel like a faceless stranger.

This was war. As she went to sleep afterward, she was planning her campaign.

"I WANT to go with you today," she said the next morning over breakfast.

He didn't look up from his eggs and biscuits. "You're not up to it."

"How do you know?" she retorted.

He looked annoyed. "Because a lot of *men* aren't up to it."

"You're repairing fencing today, right? I can help you with the wire and at least keep you company."

That was exactly what Reese didn't want. If he spent a lot of time in her company he'd end up making love to her, and that was something he wanted to limit. If he could hold himself to once a night, he'd be able to keep everything under control.

"It'll only take a couple of hours to finish repairing the fence, then I'll bring the truck home and go back out on horseback to move the herd."

"I told you, I can ride."

He shook his head impatiently. "How long has it been since you've been on a horse? What kind of riding did you do, tame trail riding on a rented hack? This is open country, and my horses are trained to work cattle."

"Granted, it's been almost a year since I've been on a horse, but I know all about liniment. I have to get used to it sometime."

"You'd just be in the way. Stay here and see if you can have dinner done on time tonight."

She narrowed her eyes and put her hands on her hips. "Reese Duncan, I'm going with you and that's final."

He got up from the table. "You'd better learn that this is my ranch, and what I say goes. That includes you. A few words by a judge doesn't give you any say-so in my work. I do the ranch work, you take care of the house. I want fried chicken for dinner, so you can get started on that."

"There isn't any chicken in the freezer," she retorted. "Since you don't want me to go shopping, I guess you'll have to change your request."

He pointed out to the yard. "There are plenty of chickens out there, city slicker. Meat doesn't always come shrink-wrapped."

Madelyn's temper was usually as languorous as her walk, but she'd had enough. "You want me to catch a chicken?" she asked, tight-lipped. "You don't think I can do it, do you? That's why you said it. You want to show me how much I don't know about ranch life. You'll have your damn chicken for dinner, if I have to ram it down your throat feathers and all!"

She turned and stormed up the stairs. Reese stood there, a little taken aback. He hadn't known Madelyn could move that fast.

She was back downstairs before he could get the truck loaded and leave. He heard the back door slam and turned. His eyes widened. She had strapped protective pads on her knees and elbows, with the knee-pads over her jeans. She'd put on athletic shoes. She still looked furious, and she didn't even glance at him. Reese hooked his thumbs in his belt loops and leaned against the truck to watch.

She picked out a hen and eased up to it, scattering a few handfuls of feed to lure the bird. Reese lifted his eyebrows, impressed. But she made her move just a little too soon; the hen squawked and ran for her life with Madelyn in pursuit.

She dove for the bird, sliding along the ground on her

belly and just missing the frantic bird. Reese winced and straightened away from the truck, horrified at the thought of what the dirt and rocks were doing to her soft skin, but she jumped up and took off after the hen. The bird ran in erratic circles around the yard, then darted under the truck. Madelyn swerved to head it off, and another headlong tackle fell an inch short.

"Look, just forget about the chick—" he began, but she was already gone.

The bird managed to take flight enough to land in the lower branches of a tree, but it was still over Madelyn's head. She narrowed her eyes and bent to pick a few rocks up from the ground. She wound up and let fly. The rock went over the chicken's head. The hen pulled her head down, her bright little eyes glittering. The next rock hit the limb next to her and she squawked, shifing position. The third rock hit her on the leg, and she took flight again.

This time Madelyn judged her dive perfectly. She slid along the ground in a flurry of dust and pebbles, and her hand closed over one of the hen's legs. The bird immediately went wild, flapping her wings and trying to peck the imprisoning hand that held her. They grappled in the dust for a minute, but then Madelyn stood up with the hen upside down and firmly held by both feet, its wings spread. Her hands were dotted with blood where the furious hen had pecked her, breaking the skin. "Faster than a speeding pullet," she said with grim triumph.

Reese could only stare at her in silence as she stalked up to him. Her hair was a mess, tangled and hanging in her eyes. Her face was caked with dust, her shirt was filthy and torn, and her jeans were a mess. One knee-pad had come loose and was drooping down her shin.

The look in those gray eyes, however, kept him from laughing. He didn't dare even smile.

The chicken hit him in the chest, and he grabbed for it, just preventing the bird from making a break for freedom.

"There's your damn chicken," she said between her teeth. "I hope you're very happy together." She slammed back into the house.

Reese looked down at the bird and remembered the blood on Madelyn's hands. He wrung the hen's neck with one quick, competent twist. He'd never felt less like laughing.

He carried the dead bird inside and dropped it on the floor. Madelyn was standing at the sink, carefully soaping her hands. "Let me see," he said, coming up behind her and reaching around to take her hands in his, effectively pinning her in place. The hen had drawn blood in several places, painful little puncture wounds that were blue around the edges. He'd had a few of them himself and knew how easily they could become infected.

He reached for a towel to wrap around her hands. "Come upstairs to the bathroom and I'll put disinfectant on them."

She didn't move. "It's my hands, not my back. I can reach them just fine, thank you. I'll do it myself."

His muscled arms were iron bands around her; his hard hands held her easily. Her front was pressed against the sink, and his big body was against her back, hemming her in, holding her. She felt utterly surrounded by him and had the sudden violent thought that she should never have married someone who was almost a foot taller than she was. She was at a woeful disadvantage here.

He bent, hooked his right arm under her kness and

lifted her with insulting ease. Madelyn grabbed for his shoulders to keep her balance. "The hen pecked my hands, not my feet," she said caustically.

He slanted a warning look at her as he started up the stairs.

"Men who use force against women are lower than slugs."

His arms tightened, but he kept a tight rein on his temper. He carried her into the bathroom and put her on her feet. As he opened the medicine cabinet she headed out the door, and he grabbed her with one hand, hauling her back. She tugged violently, trying to free her arm. "I said I'd do it myself!" she said, furious with him.

He put the lid down on the toilet, sat down and pulled her onto his lap. "Be still and let me clean your hands. If you still want to fight after I'm finished, then I'll be glad to oblige you."

Fuming, Madelyn sat on his lap while he dabbed the small wounds with an antiseptic that stung sharply. Then he smoothed antibiotic cream on them and put Band-Aids over the two worst breaks. His arms were still around her; he was holding her as a parent would a child, to soothe it and tend its hurts. She didn't like the comparison, even if it was her own. She shifted restlessly, feeling his hard thighs under her bottom.

His face was very close to hers. She could see all the different colored specks in his eyes, green and blue dominating, but shot through with black and white and a few glittering flecks of gold. Though he had shaved the night before, his beard had already grown enough to roughen his cheeks and chin. The brackets on each side of his mouth framed the beautiful cut of his lips, and suddenly she remembered the way he had closed those lips over her nipple, sucking her tender flesh into his mouth. She quivered, and the rigidity went out of her body.

Reese closed the first-aid box and set it aside, then let his arm rest loosely across her thighs as he gave her a measuring look. "Your face is dirty."

"So let me up and I'll wash it."

He didn't. He washed it himself, slowly drawing a wet washcloth over her features, the fabric almost caressing her skin. He wiped her mouth with a touch so light she could barely feel it and watched the cloth tug slightly at her soft, enticing lower lip. Madelyn's head tilted back, and her eyelids drooped. He drew the cloth down her neck, wiped it across her exposed collarbone, then dipped his hand down inside the loose neck of her top.

She caught her breath at the damp coolness on her breasts. He drew the cloth back and forth, slowly rasping it across her nipples and bringing them to wet attention. Her breasts began to throb, and her back arched involuntarily, offering them for more. She could feel a hard ridge growing, pressing against her hip, and her blood moved heavily through her veins.

He tossed the washcloth into the basin and took his hat off, dropping it onto the floor. The arm behind her back tightened and drew her in to him as he bent his head, and his mouth closed over hers.

It was the same way he'd kissed her in the airport, the way he hadn't kissed her since. His mouth was hard and hot, urgent in his demands. His tongue pushed into her mouth, and she met it with her own, welcoming, enticing, wanting more.

She gave way beneath his onslaught, her head falling back against his shoulder. He pursued the advantage, taking her mouth again, putting his hand beneath her shirt and closing it over her breast. Gently he kneaded the firm mound, rubbing his rough palm over the nipple until she whimpered into his mouth from the exquisite pain of it. She turned toward him, lifting her arms around his neck. Excitement pounded in the pit of her stomach, tightening every muscle in her body and starting an aching tension between her legs.

With a rough sound of passion he bent her back over his arm and shoved her top up, exposing her breasts. His warm breath feathered across them as he bent to her; then he extended the tip of his tongue and circled one pink nipple, making it constrict into a tightly puckered nub and turn reddish. He shifted her body, bringing her other breast closer to his mouth, and gave that nipple identical treatment, watching with pleasure as it, too, tightened.

Madelyn clutched at him. "Reese," she begged in a low, shaking voice. She needed him.

This was the hot magic she had sensed about him from the beginning, the blatant sensuality. This was the warm promise she had felt lying beneath him at night, and she wanted more.

He drew her nipple into his mouth with a strong, sucking pressure, and she arched again, her thighs shifting. She felt like a dessert offered up to him, lying across his lap with her body lifted to his mouth, glorying in the way his lips and teeth and tongue worked at her breast.

"Reese," she said again. It was little more than a moan, heavy with desire. Everything that was male in him responded to that female cry of need, urging him to surge deep within her and ease the empty ache that made her twist in his arms and cry out for him. His loins were throbbing, his body radiating heat. If she needed to be filled, he needed to fill her. The two re-strained matings he'd had with her hadn't been enough, would never satisfy the lust that intensified every time he looked at her.

But if he ever let himself go with her, he'd never be able to get that control back. April had taught him a bitter lesson, one that he relearned every day when he worked on his diminished acres, or saw the paint peeling on his house. Madelyn might never turn on him, but he couldn't take the chance and let his guard down.

With an effort that brought sweat to his brow, he lifted his mouth from her maddeningly sweet flesh and shifted her to her feet. She swayed, her eyes dazed, her top twisted up under her arms and exposing those firm, round breasts. She didn't understand and reached for him, offering a drugging sensuality that he wouldn't let himself take.

He caught her wrists and held her arms to her sides while he stood up, an action that brought their bodies together. He heard her moan softly again, and she let her head fall forward against his chest, where she rubbed her cheek back and forth in a subtle caress that made him curse his shirt for covering his bare skin.

If he didn't get out of here now, he wouldn't go at all.

"I have work to do." His voice was hoarse with strain. She didn't move. She was melting against him, her slim hips starting a drumbeat roll that rocked into his loins and made him feel as if his pants would split under the pressure.

"Madelyn, stop it. I have to go."

"Yes," she whispered, rising on tiptoe to brush her lips against his throat.

His hands closed tightly on her hips, for one convulsive second pulling her into his pelvis as if he would grind himself into her; then he pushed her away. He picked up his hat and strode from the bathroom before she could recover and reach for him again, because he damn sure wouldn't have the strength to stop this time.

Madelyn stared after him, confused by his sudden departure and aching from the loss of contact. She swayed; then realization burst within her, and she gave a hoarse cry of mingled rage and pain, putting her hand out to catch the basin so she wouldn't fall to her knees.

Damn him, damn him, damn him! He'd brought her to fever pitch, then left her empty and aching. She knew he'd wanted her; she had felt his hardness, felt the tension in his corded muscles. He could have carried her to the bed or even had her right there in the bathroom, and she would have gloried in it, but instead he'd pushed her away.

He'd been too close to losing control. Like a flash she knew what had happened, knew that at the last minute he'd had to prove to himself that he could still walk away from her, that he didn't want her so much that he couldn't master it. The sexuality of his nature was so strong that it kept burning through those walls he'd built around himself, but he was still fighting it, and so far he'd won.

Slowly she went downstairs, holding the banister because her knees felt like overcooked noodles. If she were to have any chance with him at all, she would have to find some way to shatter that iron control, but she didn't know if her nerves or self-esteem would hold out.

He was already gone, the truck nowhere in sight. She looked around blankly, unable to think what she should do, and her eyes lit on the dead chicken lying on the floor.

"I'll get back at you for this," she said with grim promise in her voice, and began the loathsome task of getting that blasted hen ready to cook.

CHAPTER SIX

WHEN REESE CAME in that evening, Madelyn didn't look up from the bowl of potatoes she was mashing. The force with which she wielded the potato masher went far beyond what was required and carried a hint of savagery. One look at her averted face told Reese she was probably imagining using that potato masher on him. He looked thoughtful. He'd expected her to be cool, maybe even a little hurt, but he hadn't expected her temper to still be at boiling point; it took a lot of energy to sustain a rage that many hours. Evidently it took her as long to cool off as it did to lose her temper to begin with.

He said, "It'll take me about fifteen minutes to get cleaned up."

She still didn't look up. "Dinner will be ready in ten."

From that he deduced that she wasn't going to wait for him. The thoughtful look deepened as he went upstairs.

He took one of the fastest showers of his life and thought about not shaving, but he didn't like the idea of scraping her soft skin with his beard, so he ran the risk of cutting his own throat due to the speed with which he dragged the razor across his skin. He was barefoot and still buttoning his shirt when he went back down the stairs.

She was just placing the glasses of iced tea on the table, and they sat down together. The platter of fried chicken was sitting right in front of his plate. He'd either have to eat the damn bird or wear it, he decided.

He piled his plate with chicken, mashed potatoes, biscuits and gravy, all the while eying the platter curiously. He continued to examine the contents while he took his first bite and controlled a grunt of pleasure. The chicken was tender, the crust crisp and spicy. Madelyn made a better cook than he'd expected. But the remaining pieces of chicken looked…strange.

"What piece is that?" he asked, pointing at a strangely configured section of chicken.

"I have no idea," she replied without looking at him. "I've never cleaned and butchered my food before."

He bit the inside of his cheek to keep from grinning. If he made the mistake of laughing she would probably dump the bowl of gravy over his head.

The meal was strained and mostly silent. If he made a comment, she replied, but other than that she made no effort to hold a conversation. She ate a small portion of each item, though minuscule was perhaps a better word. As soon as she was finished she carried her plate to the sink and brought back a clean saucer, as well as a cherry cobbler that was still bubbling.

Very little in life had ever interfered with Reese's appetite, and tonight was no exception. He worked too hard to pick at his food. By the time Madelyn had finished dabbling with a small helping of cobbler he had demolished most of the chicken, all the potatoes and gravy, and only two biscuits were left. He was feeling almost contented as Madelyn placed an enormous portion of cobbler onto a clean plate for him. A quick look at her icy face, however, told him that food hadn't worked the same miracle on her.

"How did you learn to cook like this?"

"There are cookbooks in the cabinet. I can read."

So much for that conversational gambit.

She went upstairs immediately after the kitchen was clean. Reese went into his office and took a stab at the paperwork that never ended, but his mind wasn't on it, and by eight o'clock he was glancing at his watch, wondering if Madelyn was ready to go to bed. He'd already heard the shower running, and the image of her standing nude under the steaming water had had him shifting restlessly in his chair. There were times when a man's sexual organs could make him damned uncomfortable, and this was one of them. He'd been hard most of the day, cursing himself for not having made love to her that morning, even though it would have been a huge mistake.

He tossed the pen onto his desk and closed the books, getting to his feet with restrained violence. Damn it, he needed her, and he couldn't wait any longer.

He turned out the lights as he went upstairs, his tread heavy and deliberate. His mind was on that searing, gut-wrenching moment when he first entered her, feeling the small resistance of her tight flesh, the giving, the enveloping, then the wet, clasping heat and his senses exploding. It was all he could do not to keep after her time and again, to try to remember that she was very new to lovemaking and still tender, to stay in control.

The bedroom door was open. He walked in and found her sitting on the bed painting her toenails, her long legs bare and curled in one of those positions that only females seemed able to achieve and males went crazy looking at. His whole body tightened, and he became fully, painfully erect. She was wearing a dark pink satin chemise that ended at the tops of her thighs and revealed matching petal pants. The satin molded to her breasts, revealing their round shape and soft nipples. Her blond hair was pulled to one side, tumbling over her shoulder, and her skin was still delicately flushed from her shower. Her expression was solemn and intent as she concentrated on the strokes of the tiny brush that turned her toenails the same deep pink as the chemise.

"Let's go to bed." His voice was guttural. He was already peeling off his shirt.

She hadn't even glanced at him. "I can't. My toenails are wet."

He didn't much care. He'd keep her legs raised long enough that the polish would be dry when he'd finished.

She capped the polish bottle and set it aside, then bent bonelessly over to blow on her toes. Reese unsnapped and unzipped his jeans. "Come to bed anyway."

She gave him an impatient look and got to her feet. "You go on. I'll go downstairs and read awhile."

He stretched his arm out in front of her when she would have passed, barring her way. His hand closed on her upper arm. "Forget reading," he muttered, pulling her toward him.

Madelyn wrenched away, staring at him in incredulous anger. "I don't believe this! You actually think I could want to make love *now*?"

His eyebrows lowered, and he hooked his thumbs in his belt loops. "Why not?" he asked very softly.

"For one very good reason. I'm angry! What you did stinks, and I'm not even close to forgiving you for it." Just the way he was standing there with his thumbs in his belt loops, his jeans open and his attitude one of incredible male arrogance, made her so angry she almost couldn't talk.

"The best way to make up is in bed."

"That's what men think," she said scornfully. "Let me tell you, no woman wants to make love with a man while she's still thinking how funny it would have been if he'd choked on a chicken bone!" She whirled and stalked barefoot from the bedroom.

Reese began swearing. Frustration boiled up in him, and for a moment he started after her. He reached the door and stopped, then slammed his fist into the door frame. Damn it all to hell!

THE ATMOSPHERE WAS decidedly chilly between them the next morning when he drove her to the small town of Crook to buy groceries. Though she was no longer so furious, she was no less determined. He couldn't reject her one time and the next expect her to accommodate him without question. If that was his idea of what a marriage should be, they were both in for some rocky times.

To call Crook a town was to flatter it. There were a few residences sprawled out in a haphazard manner, a service station, a feed store, the general store, and a small café with the expected assortment of pickup trucks parked in front of it. Madelyn wondered just what sort of dangerous behavior Reese had expected her to get up to in Crook. Maybe he thought she'd run wild and drive on the sidewalks, which looked as if someone had already done so. They were actually wood, and were the only sidewalks she'd ever seen with skid-marks on them.

"Let's get a cup of coffee," Reese suggested as they got out of the station wagon, and Madelyn agreed. It would be nice to have a cup of coffee she didn't have to water down before she could drink it.

The café had five swivel stools, covered in split black imitation leather, in front of the counter. Three round tables were each surrounded by four chairs, and along the left side were three booths. Four of the stools were occupied, evidently by the owners of the four trucks outside. The men had different features but were identical in weathered skin, battered hats, and worn jeans and boots. Reese nodded to all of them, and they nodded back, then returned their attention to their coffee and pie.

He guided her to a booth, and they slid onto the plastic seats. The waitress behind the counter gave them a sour look. "You want something to eat, or just coffee?"

"Coffee," Reese said.

She came out from behind the counter and plunked two coffee cups down in front of them. Then she went back for the coffeepot and returned to pour the coffee, all without changing her expression, which bordered on a glare. "Coffee's fifty cents a cup," she said as if it were their fault, then marched back to her post behind the counter.

Madelyn sighed as she saw how black the coffee was. A tentative sip told her that this, too, was strong enough to strip paint.

One of the men eased down from the stool and went over to the corner jukebox. The waitress looked up. "I'll unplug that thing if you play one of them caterwauling love songs," she said, her voice just as sour as her looks.

"You'll owe me a quarter if you do."

"And don't play none of them god-awful rock songs, neither. I don't like music where the singers sound like they're being gelded."

Madelyn's eyes rounded, and she choked a little on the coffee. Fascinated, she stared at the waitress.

The cowboy was grumbling, "I don't know of nothing you *do* like, Floris, so just shut your ears and don't listen."

"I'll tell you what I like," she snapped. "I like peace and quiet."

"Then find some library to work in." He jammed his quarter into the slot and defiantly punched buttons.

A rollicking country song filled the café. Floris began clattering cups and saucers and silverware. Madelyn wondered what the breakage bill was every month if Floris began abusing the crockery every time someone played the jukebox. The cowboy glared, and Floris banged louder. He stomped back to the jukebox and fed it another quarter, but in the manner of vending machines everywhere, it took the coin but refused his selection. He scowled and beat it with his fist. The arm scratched across the record with a hair-raising screech, then, having reached the end of the groove, lifted automatically as the record was returned to its slot, and silence reigned.

With a triumphant look Floris sailed through the swinging door into the kitchen.

"The waitress from hell," Madelyn breathed in awe, watching the door swing gently back and forth.

Reese choked and had to spit his coffee back into the cup. She didn't want to look at him, but the urge was irresistible. Without turning her head she glanced toward him and found him watching her, his face unnaturally stiff. She looked at him, and he looked at her, and they began snickering. He tried to control it and quickly gulped his coffee, but Madelyn was still giggling as he grabbed for his wallet. He threw a dollar and change on the table, grabbed her hand and pulled her toward the entrance. The door had barely closed behind them when he released her and bent forward, bracing his hands on his knees as a great roar of laughter burst from him. Madelyn collapsed over his back, seeing again the helpless, stunned look on the cowboy's face and the gleeful look on Floris's, and went off into helpless gales.

After her bad temper the laughter felt great. It was even more wonderful to hear Reese laughing, and a pang struck her as she realized that this was the first time she had heard him laugh. He rarely even smiled, but now he was hugging his ribs and wiping tears from his eyes, and still the deep sounds were booming up from his chest. She had an overwhelming urge to cry, but conquered it.

A lot of the tension between them dissolved as they bought groceries. Reese had been right; the general store did carry mostly basics, but Madelyn had carefully studied the cookbooks and knew what she could do with what was available. Thank God Reese wasn't a fussy eater.

A cheerful woman with a truly awesome bosom checked them out while carrying on a casual conversation with Reese. She eyed Madelyn questioningly, then looked down at the ring on her left hand. Reese saw the look and braced himself for the curiosity he knew would come. "Glenna, this is my wife, Madelyn."

Glenna looked startled, and her glance flew down to his own left hand. The gold ring on his tanned finger clearly astounded her. Reese carried on with the introduction, hoping to bridge her reaction. "Maddie, this is Glenna Kinnaird. We went to school together."

Recovering herself, Glenna beamed and held out

her hand. "I can't believe it! Congratulations! You got married, after all this time. Why, just wait until I tell Boomer. We didn't really go to school together," she said chattily to Madelyn. "I'm ten years older than he is, so I graduated when he was in third grade, but I've known him all his life. How on earth did you catch him? I'd have sworn he'd never marry again— Uh, that is…" Her voice trailed off uneasily as she glanced at Reese.

Madelyn smiled. "It's okay. I know about April. As for how I caught him…well, I didn't. He caught me."

Glenna's face regained its cheerful expression. "Took one look and forgot about being a bachelor, huh?"

"Something like that," Reese said. He'd taken one look and gotten hard, but the end result had been the same: the leggy blonde with the lazy, seductive stroll was now his wife.

As they left the store with Glenna waving at them, he realized something that had him frowning thoughtfully as they loaded the groceries into the station wagon: Glenna had disliked April on sight, but had been perfectly comfortable and friendly with Madelyn. Even though, in an indescribable way, Madelyn dressed more fashionably than April, she had an easy, friendly manner to which Glenna had responded. Madelyn didn't dress as expensively as April, but what she wore had a certain style to it, as if she had practiced for hours to get her collar to stand up just so, or her sleeves to roll up that precise amount. She would always draw eyes, but she didn't inspire the sort of hostility from her own sex that April had.

Style. He looked at his wife and thought of how she'd looked the day before, with one kneepad slipping down her shin and her hair hanging in her face. He hadn't dared laugh then, but in retrospect he couldn't help himself and began to chuckle. Even when chasing chickens, Madelyn did it with style.

MADELYN HAD BEEN outside all morning, scraping the peeling paint off the house. Having brought the interior up to snuff, she was working on the exterior, and it was such a beautiful morning that she'd been enjoying herself despite the hard work. It was getting close to noon, though, and the temperature was rising uncomfortably. Sweat was making her clothes stick to her. Deciding that she'd done enough for the day, she climbed down from the ladder and went inside to take a shower.

When she came back downstairs, the first thing she saw was the bag containing Reese's lunch sitting on the cabinet. He was out repairing fencing again and wouldn't be back until dinnertime, but he'd forgotten his lunch and thermos of tea.

She checked the clock. He had to be starving by now. Quickly she emptied the thermos and filled it with fresh ice cubes and tea, then got the keys to the station wagon and hurried outside with his lunch. By chance she knew where he was working, because in the past two weeks he'd shown her around the ranch a little, and he'd mentioned this morning where he'd be. It was actually a safety precaution for someone to know where he was, and she frowned as she thought of the years he'd worked alone, with no one at the house to know where he'd gone or how long he'd been out. If he'd gotten hurt, he could have lain there and died without anyone ever knowing he'd been hurt until it was too late.

Her marriage wasn't even three weeks old yet, and already she could barely remember her previous life. She'd never before been as busy as she was now, though she had to admit she would gladly forgo the housework to ride around the ranch with Reese, but he still refused to hear of it. She was certain that if anyone looked up the word "stubborn" in the dictionary, it would have Reese Duncan's picture beside it. He'd decided where she would fit in his life, and he wouldn't let her get outside that boundary.

She could almost feel the hunger in him at night when he made love to her, but he never let himself go, never released the passion she sensed, and as a result she couldn't let herself go, either. Sex was no longer uncomfortable, and she desperately wanted more from their lovemaking, but the intensity she needed wasn't there. He held back, diminishing the pleasure they both could have had and thereby preserving that damned inner wall of his. She didn't know how much longer she would be able to bear it, how much longer it would be before she began making excuses and turn away from him in the night. The situation was dire, she knew, when she was actually looking forward to having her period!

She drove slowly, preoccupied with her thoughts and with watching for any sign of his truck out on the range somewhere. Like all ranchers, Reese paid no attention to roads; he simply drove across the land. The truck was a tool to him, not a prized and pampered status symbol. If it had been a Rolls he would have treated it the same, because it had no value beyond that of its worth as a working vehicle. So she knew the area where he was working, but that area covered a lot of ground and he could be anywhere in it. She didn't see him anywhere, but fresh tire tracks scored the ground, and she simply followed them, carefully steering around the rougher ground that Reese had driven over without concern, because the station wagon was much lower than the truck and couldn't negotiate such terrain.

It took her almost forty-five minutes to find him. He'd parked the truck under a tree, partially shielding it from view. It was the chance glint off a strand of wire as he pulled it tight that caught her eye, and she eased the car across the range to him.

He glanced up briefly as she approached but didn't pause in his work. Her throat tightened. He'd removed his shirt and hung it over the side of the truck bed, and his muscled torso glistened with sweat. She'd known he was strong, realized from the first that his body made her mouth go dry with almost painful appreciation, but this was the first time she had seen those powerful muscles bunching and flexing like that. He moved with a fluid grace that made his strength that much more noticeable. His biceps and triceps bulged as he hammered a staple into the post, securing the new strand of wire.

When he was finished he tossed the hammer onto the sack of staples and pulled his hat off, wiping the sweat from his face with his forearm. "What are you doing out here?" He didn't sound at all pleased to see her.

Madelyn got out of the car, carrying the thermos and sandwiches with her. "You forgot your lunch."

He walked toward her and took the thermos, twisting the top off and tilting it up to drink directly from the spout. His strong throat worked as he swallowed the cold liquid. He'd been working all morning without anything to drink, she realized. A drop of tea escaped his lips and ran down his throat. She watched it in painful fascination as it slid down his hot skin, and she envied it the path it was taking. So often she had wanted to trail kisses down his body but had held back because he didn't want that sort of intimacy. All he wanted was the release of sex, not the love expressed in slow, sensual feasting.

He set the thermos down on the lowered tailgate and reached for his shirt, using it to wipe the sweat from his face, shoulders, arms and chest. Tossing the garment back across the side, he eased one hip onto the tailgate and took the sandwiches from her. "The station wagon isn't meant for driving across the range," he said as he unwrapped a sandwich.

Madelyn's lips tightened. "I didn't want you to go all day without anything to eat or drink, and I was careful."

"How did you find me?"

"I followed your tire tracks."

He grunted and applied himself to the sandwich. It and another disappeared without another word being said between them. Madelyn lifted her hair off her neck, letting a slight breeze cool her heated skin. She usually braided her hair away from her face during the day, but she'd taken it down when she showered and hadn't put it back up again before she'd started searching for Reese.

Reese watched her graceful gesture, and his heartbeat speeded up. She was wearing a gathered white cotton skirt with one of her favorite white camisole tops, and a pair of sandals that were little more than thin soles with a few delicate straps. She looked cool and fragrant, while he was hot and sweaty, a result of the difference in the way they'd spent the day. Now that the house was clean and polished it probably didn't take much to keep it that way.

The breeze caught a strand of hair and blew it across her face. She shook it back, tilting her head to make all of her hair swing down her back.

Every movement she made was naturally seductive. He felt the response in his groin and in his veins, as his blood heated and began racing. It was becoming more and more difficult to keep his hands off her during the day, to keep from turning to her time and again during the night. He grew angry at himself for wanting her so much, and at her for doing everything she could to make it worse.

"Why did you really come out here?" he asked harshly. "I would've finished with this and gotten back to the house in another hour or so. I've gone without eating or drinking all day before, and I'll do it again. So why did you really come parading out here?"

Madelyn's eyes narrowed as she slowly turned her head to look at him. She didn't say anything, and the combined anger and sexual frustration built up even more pressure in him.

"Do you want me to stop work and play with you? Can't you go a whole day without a man's attention? Maybe you thought we'd have a sexy little picnic out here and you'd get your skirt tossed."

She turned to fully face him, her eyes locked with his. Her words were slow and precise. "Why would I care? From what I can tell, sex isn't worth a walk across the yard, let alone chasing it down on the range. I've got better things to do with my time."

He took the verbal jab square on the ego, and suddenly it was too much. It was all too much, the wanting and not having, the needing and not taking. A red mist swam before his eyes, and his whole body seemed to expand as he blindly reached for her, catching her by the arm and swinging her up against him.

Madelyn was unprepared for the blurring speed with which he moved. She didn't even have time to take a step back. Suddenly he had her arm in a painful grip and with one motion brought her colliding with his hard body, almost knocking the breath from her. His mouth came down, hot and ravaging, not waiting for her compliance but taking it. His teeth raked across her bottom lip, and when she made a shaky sound of…response? protest? he used the opportunity to enter her mouth with his tongue.

Her heart lunged wildly in her chest as she realized he was out of control. His arms had tightened around her, lifting her off her feet, and his mouth took hers with bruising force. Elation swirled in her, and she wound her arms tightly around his neck as she kissed him back.

He hefted her onto the tailgate of the truck and reached for his shirt, tossing it down on the truck bed. With a motion so smooth it seemed like one movement he slid her backward and leaped to a crouching position on the tailgate; then he was pushing her down onto the shirt and lowering himself on top of her.

Dimly she realized that once you had unleashed a tiger, it wasn't so easy to get him back under control again. Of course, she wasn't sure she wanted to. The sunlight sifted down through the leaves, dappling his gleaming skin, and his eyes were fiercely primitive as he kneed her thighs apart. He looked wild and magnificent, and she made a soft whimpering sound of need as she reached for him.

He tore her clothes, and she didn't care. The seam of her chemise gave way beneath his twisting fingers, and the taut rise of her breasts thrust nakedly up at him. He sucked strongly at her while he shoved her skirt to her waist and hooked his fingers in the waistband of her underpants. She lifted her hips to aid him, but heard the rip of lace, and then he threw the shreds to one side. He transferred his lips to her other breast and sucked the nipple into his mouth while he worked at the fastening of his jeans. He grunted as the zipper parted, releasing his throbbing length, and he shoved both underwear and jeans downward with one movement.

His entry was hard and fast. Her body shuddered under the impact of it, and her hips lifted. He groaned aloud as the exquisite feminine sheath enveloped him, immediately changing his unbearable ache into unbearable pleasure.

Madelyn sank her nails into his back as she arched up, driven by an explosion of heat. Coiling tension tightened her body until she thought she would go mad, and she struggled with both him and the tension, crying out a little as her heaving body strained to throw him off even as her legs tightened around him to pull him deeper. If he was wild, so was she. He pounded into her, and she took him. Her hips hammered back at him and he rode her, wrapping his arms under her buttocks to pull her up tighter, to shove himself in deeper.

A great rolling surge exploded her senses without warning, and she gave a primal scream that sliced across the clear air. He kept thrusting heavily into her, and it happened again, the second time following the first so closely that she hadn't had time to regain her breath, and the second time was more powerful, tossing her even higher. She bit his shoulder, sobbing from the force of it, and suddenly she could feel him grow even harder and bigger inside her, and his entire body began shuddering and heaving. He threw back his head with a guttural cry that ripped up from his chest as his hips jerked in the spasms of completion.

The quiet afterward had a drifting, dreamy quality to it. She could feel the sunlight filtering down on her skin, the heat of the metal truck bed beneath her, his shirt pillowing her head. A bird sang, and a breeze rustled the leaves and grass. She could hear the faint buzzing of a bee somewhere, and the slowing sound of his breathing.

They lay beside each other, his heavy arm across her stomach. She might have dozed. The breeze dried the sweat on her body with a gentle, cooling touch. After a long, long time that might have been only minutes, she turned into his arms and pressed her mouth to his.

He got his boots and jeans off this time. As rawly frenzied as the first time had been, this one wasn't much less. The force of his restrained hunger had built up until, like a flooding river overwhelming a dam, it had broken through and could no longer be controlled. He undid her skirt and stripped it down her legs; then she parted her thighs and reached for him again, and he couldn't wait a minute longer. The sight of those sleek legs opening for him was an image that had haunted his dreams. He'd intended to be easier with her this time, but as soon as he penetrated she made a wild sound in her throat and her hips rolled, and he went mad again.

This time when it was over he didn't withdraw, but lay on her in continued possession. "Reese," she whispered, her fingers sliding into his damp hair. He slid his thumbs under her chin and tilted her face up, slanting his head so he could drink from her in the long, deep kisses he'd been craving. He began to grow hard again, but he was still inside her and there was no urgency, only steadily increasing pleasure.

They were both drugged with it. He fondled her breasts, caressing them with both hands and mouth. Her slim hands moved over him like silk, sleeking over his broad shoulders and down the taut muscles of his back, finally cupping and kneading his buttocks. Lifting himself on his arms, he began a slow, steady thrusting. She surged upward, too, kissing his throat and chest and licking at his little nipples, half-hidden in the curls of hair on his chest. When her time was close, she writhed on the twisted bed of clothing, and he watched enthralled as her torso flushed and her nipples tightened. He caught her hips and lifted them, sliding her up and down on his impaling flesh, and the sight of her convulsive satisfaction brought him to the peak before she had finished.

The hot midday hours slipped away as they sated themselves on each other's bodies. Nothing else existed but sensual exploration and hot satisfaction. He kissed her from head to toe, tasting the sweetness of her flesh, delighting in the way she responded to his slightest touch. When her back became tender from rubbing on the hard bed he pulled her on top of him, watching her pleasure at the freedom it gave her to take him at her own pace.

He thought he had to be completely empty, yet he couldn't stop. He didn't know if he'd ever be able to stop. The peaks were no longer shattering, but were slow, strong swells that seemed to last forever.

Madelyn clung to him, not thinking, never wanting to think. This was the magic she had wanted, the burning sensuality she had sensed in him. No part of her body was untouched, unloved. Exhaustion crept in and entwined with pleasure, and at some point they went to sleep.

The sun was low when they woke, and the air was getting cooler. Reese pulled her into the heat of his body and smoothed her hair back from her face. "Are you all right?" he murmured, concerned when he remembered the violent intensity of their lovemaking.

She nuzzled her face against his throat, lifting one

slender arm to curl it around his neck. "Umm," she said and closed her eyes again. She didn't feel like moving.

He sleeked his hand over her hip and up her side, then cupped her breast. "Wake up, honey."

"I am awake." The words were slow and muffled against his throat.

"It's almost sunset. We need to go."

"We can sleep here." She moved as if trying to sink into his skin, and her own hand strayed downward. He closed his eyes as her fingers closed gently around him. Her lips opened against his throat, then slid upward to his jaw. "Make love to me again, Reese. Please."

"Don't worry about that," he said beneath his breath. There was no way he could restrain himself now that he'd tasted her passion, no way she would let him, now that she knew. With a mixture of anger and despair he knew he'd never be able to keep his hands off her now. But the temperature was getting cooler by the second as the sun began dipping below the horizon; even though he was tempted to lie there with her, he didn't want her to get chilled.

He sat up and drew her with him. "Home," he said, his voice roughening. "My knees have had about all they can take. I want to be in bed the next time."

Her eyes were slumberous, her lips swollen from his kisses. "As long as it's soon," she whispered, and thought she would cry, she loved him so much.

CHAPTER SEVEN

HER SPIRIT WAS willing but her body went to sleep. She slept in his arms that night, her head on his shoulder and one leg thrown over his hip. Reese let her sleep, feeling the contentment of his own body as well as a certain wryness. If Madelyn had been seductive before, she was doubly so now. It was as if she had been holding back, too. That night, she hadn't walked past him without reaching out to touch him somewhere: a lingering hand sliding along his ribs, a gentle touch on his hand or arm, or a light ruffling of his hair, a tickle of his ear, a quick kiss on his chin, an appreciative pat on his butt, even a bold caress of his crotch. After denying himself for so long, he couldn't keep his hands off her, either. By the time he'd showered, eaten dinner and rested for an hour, the accumulated effect of all those caresses, both given and received, had had him hard and aching again. She had gone sweetly into his arms in bed, he'd made love to her, this time with lingering gentleness, and then she had gone to sleep before he'd withdrawn from her.

He'd stayed inside her for a long time, dozing himself and luxuriating in the intimacy. When he tried to move she muttered a protest and turned with him, burrowing against him and retaining the connection. So he hooked his arm around her bottom and kept her locked to him all night, and he slept better than he had since the day he'd met her.

He was on his back and she was sprawled on top of him when the alarm went off the next morning. He stretched to shut it off while she wiggled sleepily on his chest like a cat. He rubbed his hand down her back. "Time to get up."

His early-morning voice was dark and rough. Madelyn settled her head in the hollow of his shoulder again. "Did you know," she said sleepily, "that more words in the English language start with S than with any other letter?"

"Ah, God, not now," he groaned. "Not before coffee."

"Chicken."

"I don't want to talk about any damn chickens, either." He struggled to wake up. "Canada is over two hundred thousand square miles larger than the United States."

"A pound of feathers weighs more than a pound of gold because of the different weighing systems used."

"Catgut comes from sheep guts, not cat guts."

She jerked upright, frowning at him, and he used the opportunity to turn on the lamp. "No gross stuff," she ordered, then settled back down on his chest. "A blue whale's heart beats just nine times a minute."

"Robert E. Lee's family home is now Arlington National Cemetery."

"*Mona Lisa* doesn't have any eyebrows, and the real name of the painting is *La Gioconda*."

"Quicksand is more buoyant that water. Contrary to Hollywood, you'd really have to work at it to go completely under in quicksand."

She yawned and was silent, listening to his heartbeat, a strong, steady drumming in her ear. As she listened it began beating faster, and she raised her head to look at him. His eyes were narrowed and intent. He locked his arms around her and rolled until she was beneath him, his legs between hers and spreading them wide. Madelyn clung to him and gave herself up to the now-familiar rise of ecstasy as he began making love to her.

"WHAT ARE you doing today?" she asked over breakfast.

"Moving a portion of the herd to another section so they won't overgraze."

"I'm going with you."

He automatically started to refuse, and she gave him a hard look. "Don't say no," she warned. "I've already got steaks marinating in the refrigerator, and the baked potatoes are almost done, so they'll finish baking while the steaks are grilling. There's no reason for me to sit here every day when I can be with you."

"What I wonder," he muttered, "is if I'll get any work done at all. All right, I'll saddle a horse for you. But I'm warning you, Maddie, if you can't ride well enough to keep up, you won't go out with me again."

She showed up at the barn half an hour later wearing jeans, boots and one of his denim workshirts with the sleeves rolled up and the tails tied in a knot at her waist. Her hair was French-braided in one long braid down the center of her back, she wore a new pair of wrist-length gloves, and she looked as chic as if she were modeling clothes rather than heading out for a day of herding cattle. She carried a western straw hat and settled it on her head before she approached the horse Reese had saddled for her.

He watched as she gave the animal time to get acquainted with her, letting it snuffle at her arms, scratching it behind its ears. She wasn't afraid of horses, at least. April had never been around them, and as a result had been jumpy in their vicinity, which in turn made the horses skittish. Madelyn petted the horse and crooned to it, then untied the reins, put her boot in the stirrup and competently swung into the saddle. Reese eyed the stirrups and decided he had judged the length correctly, then mounted his own horse.

He watched her carefully as they cantered across a field. She had a good seat and nice steady hands, though she lacked the easy posture he possessed, but he'd been riding since he was a toddler. The smile she gave him was so full of pleasure he felt guilty at not taking her with him before.

He set an easy pace, not wanting to push her too hard. When they reached the herd he explained how he worked. The herd was already divided into three smaller groups grazing different sections; the entire herd was too big for him to move by himself. He spent a lot of time moving them to fresh grazing and making certain they didn't destroy the plant cycle by overgrazing. He pointed out the bunch they would be moving and gave her a coiled section of rope. "Just wave it alongside the horse's shoulder in a shooing motion, and let the horse do the work if a cow decides to go in a different direction. All you have to do is sit deep in the saddle and hang on."

Sitting deep in the saddle was no problem; the big western rig felt like a cradle after the small eastern saddle she was familiar with. She took the coil of rope and practiced a few waves with it, just to be certain it didn't startle the horse. He treated it as commonplace, which, of course, to him it was.

She enjoyed the work. She liked being outside, and

there was a sort of peace to riding alongside the cattle and waving a coil of rope at them occasionally, listening to the deep-throated bawls and learning the joy of riding a well-trained cutting horse. She liked watching Reese most of all. He had been born to do this, and it was obvious in every movement and sound he made. He rode as if he were a part of the horse, anticipating every change of direction, encouraging the cattle with whistles and calls that seemed to reassure them at the same time.

She felt almost dazed with pleasure, her senses overloaded. She had felt that way since the afternoon before, when his self-control had broken and he had taken her like a man possessed. Her body was sated, her emotions freed to reach out to him and shower him with the love that had been dammed up inside her. She had no illusions that the battle was won, but the first skirmish was hers; until yesterday, he would never have allowed her to pet him as she had been doing, nor would he have lingered in bed that morning to make love again. His face was still set in those stern, unsmiling lines, but he was subtly more relaxed. Judging from the past twenty-four hours, he must have had a difficult time controlling his sex drive. The thought made her smile.

They stopped for lunch and to let the cattle and horses drink from a small natural pond. When the horses had been seen to, Reese tethered them nearby and sat down next to her on the small rise she'd chosen for the site of their meal. He took off his hat and put it on the grass beside him. "How do you like it so far?"

"A lot." Her lips curved softly as she handed him a sandwich. "It's so peaceful out here, no cars, no telephones, no smog. You may have to help me out of bed in the morning, but it'll be worth it."

"I'll rub you down with liniment tonight." His eyes glinted at her. "Afterward."

That statement earned him a kiss. Then she straightened and unwrapped her own sandwich. "How am I doing? Have I done anything totally amateurish?"

"You're doing fine. The only problem is that I keep worrying you're going to get tossed and stepped on. You're the first female cowhand I've ever had."

He was very western in his attitude toward women, but she didn't mind him coddling her as long as he didn't also try to stop her from doing what she wanted. Since he was bound to do that, their lives together should never become too complacent.

He propped himself on one elbow and stretched his long legs out as he ate his second sandwich. She began to feel warm as she watched him; though he was simply dressed in brown jeans, a white shirt and those disreputably scuffed boots, he outshone male models she'd seen in tuxedos. His first wife had to be president of a Stupid Club somewhere, but the wretched woman shouldn't be allowed to get away with what she'd done to him. Madelyn had never before thought of herself as vindictive, but she felt that way about anyone who had ever harmed Reese. If she ever met April, she would snatch her bald-headed.

He found the cookies she'd packed and washed them down with the last of the tea. Feeding this man could be a full-time job, she thought fondly. If his children inherited his appetite, she'd never get out of the kitchen.

Thinking of having his children made her feel even warmer, but reminded her of something she'd meant to discuss with him. She turned to face him, sitting with her legs folded in front of her.

"There's something we have to talk about."

"What's that?" he asked, stretching out on his back and settling his hat over his eyes.

"Children."

One eye opened and peered at her; then he removed the hat and gave her his full attention. "Ye gods, are you already pregnant?"

"No, and even if I were, I wouldn't know yet, because it isn't time for my period. We didn't talk about it before we got married, so I didn't know if you wanted to wait before we had children or if you wanted to have them right away. When you called, it was almost time for my period, so when I went to the doctor for the physical I got a prescription for birth control pills."

He sat up, his face darkening. "You're on the Pill?"

"Yes. I've only taken it for this month. If you want to start trying to have children right away, I can stop."

"You should have discussed it with me before, or was that another one of those subjects, like your virginity, that you didn't think were any of my business?"

She gave him one of those sidelong glances. "Something like that. I didn't know you, and I didn't feel very comfortable with you."

He watched her for a minute, then reached out to take her hand, rubbing his rough thumb over her soft palm. "How do you feel about getting pregnant right away?"

"I wouldn't mind. I want your children. If you want to wait, that's okay with me, too, but I don't want to wait more than a year. I'm twenty-eight. I don't want to be in my mid-thirties when we get started."

He thought about it while he studied the contrast of her delicate hand in his big, rough one. Now that he'd given in to the powerful physical attraction between them, he didn't want to give it up too soon. He wanted to fully enjoy her for a while before pregnancy put necessary limits on the wildness of their lovemaking. He carried her hand to his mouth and licked her palm. "Take the Pill for a few months," he said. "We'll talk about it again in the fall."

She shivered, a dazed expression coming into her eyes at the stroke of his tongue on her palm. As he pulled her down on the grass she asked, "Do you think you'll get your boots off this time?"

And he replied, "I doubt it."

He didn't, but she didn't care.

SHE WENT WITH him often after that. She helped him move cattle, inoculate them, and staple tags in their ears. After he'd cut and baled the hay, she drove the truck pulling the hay trailer around while he swung the heavy bales onto it. It was work that really required a third person, to stack the bales, but it was easier than when Reese had had to do it by himself. When she didn't go out with him, she continued with the project of scraping the house.

He finally noticed the difference in the house and investigated. The dusting of white paint chips on the ground told him all he needed to know.

He leaned against the kitchen cabinet and crossed his arms. "Are you scraping the house?"

"Yep."

"Don't pull the Gary Cooper routine on me. I want it stopped right now."

"The routine or the scraping?"

"Both."

"The house can't be painted until the old paint is scraped off," she said reasonably.

"I can't afford the paint, so it doesn't make any difference. And I don't want you climbing around on a fourteen-foot ladder. What if you fell while I'm out on the range?"

"What if you got hurt out on the range by yourself?" she retorted. "I'm careful, and I haven't had any trouble so far. It shouldn't take too much longer."

"No," he said, enunciating carefully. "I can't afford the paint, and even if I could I wouldn't let you do the scraping."

"*You* don't have time for it, so who else is going to do it?"

"For the third time," he yelled, "*I can't afford the paint!* What does it take to make you understand that?"

"That's something else we've never talked about. What makes you think *we* can't afford the paint? I supported myself before I married you, you know." She put her hands on her hips and faced off with him. "I have both a checking and a savings account, which I transferred to a bank in Billings. I also have a trust fund that I inherited from Grandma Lily. It isn't a fortune by any means, but we can certainly afford a few gallons of paint!"

Reese's face was like granite. "No. Remember our prenuptial agreement? What's yours is yours and what's mine is mine. If you spent your money on the ranch it would go a long way toward negating that agreement, giving you a claim to it on the basis of upkeep."

She poked him in the chest, her jaw jutting forward. "For one thing, G. Reese Duncan, *I'm* not planning on getting a divorce, so I don't give a flip what's in your precious agreement. For another, how much would it cost to paint the house? A hundred dollars? Two hundred?"

"Closer to two hundred, and no, by God, you're not buying the paint!"

"I'm not only going to buy it, I'm going to paint it! If you're so set on protecting the ranch from my scheming, then we'll draw up a contract where you agree to repay me for the paint—and my time, too, if you insist—and that will take care of any claim I could make against you. But I live here, too, you know, and I want the outside to look as nice as the inside. Next spring I'm planting flowers in the flower beds, so if you object to that we might as well fight it out now. The only choice you have right now is the color you want the house painted, and your choices are white and white." She was yelling by the time she finished, her face flushed.

He was more furious than she'd ever seen him before. "Do whatever the hell you want," he snapped and slammed out of the kitchen.

She did. The next time they went into town she bought the paint and brushes and paid for them with one of her own checks, glaring at him and daring him to start again. He carried the paint out to the truck with ill grace. The high point of that day was when they stopped at the café for coffee and listened to Floris berating her customers.

She had the house painted by the middle of August, and had developed a healthy respect for people who painted houses for a living. It was some of the hardest work she'd ever done, leaving her shoulders and arms aching by the end of the day. The most aggravating part was painting the hundreds of thin porch railings; the most nerve-racking was doing the second floor, because she had to anchor herself to something. But when it was finished and the house gleamed like a jewel, and the shutters wore a new coat of black all-weather enamel, she was prouder of her efforts than she had ever been before of anything she'd done.

Even Reese grudgingly admitted that the house looked nice and she'd done a good job, but he still resented the fact that she'd done it. Maybe it was only male pride, but he didn't want his wife paying for something when he couldn't afford it himself.

His wife. By the time they had been married two months, she had insinuated herself so completely into his life that there wasn't a portion of it she hadn't touched. She had even rearranged his underwear drawer. Sometimes he wondered how she managed to accomplish as much as she did when her pace seldom exceeded a stroll, but it was a fact that she got things done. In her own way she worked as hard as he did.

One hot morning at the end of August she discovered that she didn't have enough flour to do the day's cooking. Reese had already left for the day and wouldn't be coming back for lunch, so she ran upstairs and got ready. It was almost time they replenished their supplies anyway, so she carried the grocery list with her. It would save an extra trip if she did all the shopping while she was in town.

She loved listening to Floris, so she stopped by the café and had coffee and pie. After Floris had sent her only other customer stomping out in anger, she came over to Madelyn's booth and sat down.

"Where's that man of yours today?"

"Out on the range. I ran out of flour and came in to stock up."

Floris nodded approvingly, though her sour face never lightened. "That first wife of his never bought no groceries. Don't guess she knew nothing about cooking, though of course Reese had a cook hired back then. It's a shame what happened to that ranch. It used to be a fine operation."

"It will be again," Madelyn said with confidence. "Reese is working hard to build it back up."

"One thing about him, he's never been afraid of work. Not like some men around here." Floris glared at the door as if she could still see the cowboy who had just left.

After talking with Floris, Glenna's cheerfulness was almost culture shock. They chatted for a while; then Madelyn loaded the groceries into the station wagon and drove back to the ranch. It wasn't quite noon, so she would have plenty of time to cook the cake she'd planned.

To her surprise, Reese's truck was in the yard when she drove up. He was coming around from the back of the house carrying a bucket of water, but when he saw her, he changed direction and stalked over, his face dark with temper and his eyes shooting green sparks. "Where in hell have you been?" he roared.

She didn't like his manner, but she answered his question in a reasonable tone. "I didn't have enough flour to do the cooking today, so I drove to Crook and bought groceries."

"Damn it, don't you ever go off without telling me where you're going!"

She retained her reasonableness, but it was becoming a strain. "How could I tell you when you weren't here?"

"You could have left a note."

"Why would I leave a note when you weren't supposed to be back for lunch, and I'd be back long before you? Why *are* you back?"

"One of the hoses sprang a leak. I came back to put a new hose on." For whatever reason, he wasn't in a mood to let it go. "If I hadn't, I wouldn't have found out you've started running around the country on your own, would I? How long has this been going on?"

"Buying food? Several centuries, I'd say."

Very carefully he put the bucket down. As he straightened, Madelyn saw his eyes; he wasn't just angry or aggravated, he was in a rage. He hadn't been this angry before, even over painting the house. With his teeth clenched he said, "You dressed like that to buy groceries?"

She looked down at her clothes. She wore a slim pink skirt that ended just above her knees and a white silk blouse with the sleeves rolled up. Her legs were bare, and she had on sandals. "Yes, I dressed like this to buy groceries! It's hot, in case you haven't noticed. I didn't want to wear jeans, I wanted to wear a skirt, because it's cooler."

"Did you get a kick out of men looking at your legs?"

"As far as I noticed, no one looked at my legs. I told you once that I won't pay for April's sins, and I meant it. Now, if you don't mind, I need to get the groceries into the house."

He caught her arm as she turned away and whirled her back around to face him. "Don't walk away when I'm talking to you."

"Well excuse me, Your Majesty!"

He grabbed her other arm and held her in front of him. "If you want to go to town, I'll take you," he said in an iron-hard voice. "Otherwise, you keep your little butt here on the ranch, and don't you ever, *ever,* leave the house without letting me know where you are."

She went up on tiptoe, so angry she was shaking. "Let me tell you a few things, and you'd better listen. I'm your wife, not your prisoner of war. I won't ask your permission to buy groceries, and I won't be kept locked up here like some criminal. If you take the keys to the car or do something to it so it won't run, then I'll walk wherever I want to go, and you can bet the farm on that. I'm not April, do you understand? *I'm not April.*"

He released her arms, and they stood frozen, neither of them giving an inch. Very deliberately Madelyn bent down and lifted the bucket of water, then upended it over him. The water splashed on his head and shoulders and ran down his torso, to finally end up pooling around his boots.

"If that isn't enough to cool you off, I can get another one," she offered in an icily polite tone.

His movements were just as deliberate as hers as he removed his hat and slapped it against his leg to rid it of excess water, then dropped it to the ground. She saw his teeth clench; then he moved like a snake striking, his hands darting out to grasp her around the waist. With one swift movement he lifted her and plonked her down on the front fender of the car.

His hands were flexing on her waist; his forearms were trembling with the force it took to restrain his temper. His dark hair was plastered to his skull; water still dripped down his face, and his eyes were pure green fire.

His dilemma nearly tore him apart. He was trembling with rage, but there wasn't a damn thing he could do about it. His wife didn't back down from anyone, not even him, and he'd cut off his own hands before he would do anything to hurt her. All he could do was stand there and try to get his temper back under control.

They faced each other in silence for nearly a minute, with him still holding her on the fender of the car. She tilted her chin, her eyes daring him to start the fight again. He looked down at her legs, and a shudder ran through him. When he looked back up at her, it wasn't rage in his eyes.

Green eyes locked with gray. He hooked his fingers in the hem of her skirt and jerked it upward, at the same time spreading her legs and moving forward between them. She sank her hands into his wet hair and held his head while her mouth attacked his with a fierce kiss that held mingled anger and desire. He said, "Maddie," in a rough tone as he tore her underpants out of the way, then jerked at his belt and the fastening of his jeans.

It was just as it had been in the back of the truck. The rush of passion was hard and fast and overwhelming. With one hand he guided himself, while the other propelled her hips forward onto him. She moaned and wrapped her legs around him, then held his head so that their eyes met again. "I love you," she said fiercely. "I love you, damn it."

The words hit him like a thunderbolt, but her eyes were clear and direct, and he was losing himself in her depths. What had begun wild suddenly turned slow and hot and tender. He put his hand in her hair and tugged her head back to expose the graceful arch of her throat to his searching mouth. He began moving within her, probing deep and slow, and he said, "Maddie," again, this time in a voice that shook.

She was like fire, and she was all his. She burned for him and with him, her intense sensuality matching his. They clung together, savoring the hot rise of passion and the erotic strokes that fed it and would eventually extinguish it, but not now. Not right now.

He unbuttoned her blouse while she performed the same service for his shirt. When he had unclipped her bra he slowly brought their bare torsos together, turning her slightly from side to side so that her breasts rubbed his chest and his curly hair rasped against her nipples, making her arch in his arms.

"God, I can't get enough of you," he muttered.

"I don't want you to." Passion had glazed her eyes, making them heavy and slumberous. He took her mouth again, and he was still kissing her when she cried out and convulsed in a crest of pleasure. He held himself deep within her, feeling the hot, gentle tightening of her inner caresses around him. He would never find this kind of overwhelming passion with any other woman, he thought dimly. Only with Maddie.

Release left her weak, pliable. She lay back across the hood of the car, breathing hard, her eyes closed. Reese gripped her hips and began thrusting hard and fast, wanting that sweet weakness for himself. Her eyes slowly opened as he drove into her, and she closed her hands around his wrists. "I love you," she said again.

Until he heard the words once more he hadn't realized how badly he'd needed them, wanted them. She was his, and had been from the moment she'd walked through the airport toward him. He groaned, and his hips jerked; then the pleasure hit him, and he couldn't think for a long time. All he could do was feel, and sink forward onto her soft body and into her arms.

In bed that night, he gently traced his fingertips over the curve of her shoulder. "I'm sorry," he murmured. "I was out of line today, way out."

She kissed him drowsily on the jaw. "I think I understand more than before. Did April…?"

"Have other men? Yeah."

"The fool," she muttered, sliding her hand down to intimately caress him.

He tilted her head up. "I wasn't a saint, Maddie. I can be hard to live with."

She widened her eyes mockingly and made a disbelieving sound. He chuckled and then sighed, spreading his legs. What her hand was doing to him felt so good it was almost criminal. She was all woman, and this was going to end up only one way, but he wanted to put it off for a few minutes.

"You're right, I've been trying to keep you a prisoner on the ranch. It won't happen again."

"I'm not going to run off," she assured him in a whisper. "I've got what I want right here. And you were right about one thing."

"What?"

"Making love is one of the best ways to make up."

CHAPTER EIGHT

REESE SOLD THE beef herd for more than he had anticipated, or even hoped. With cholesterol-consciousness
at such a high level he had been working to breed and
raise cattle with leaner meat that still remained tender,
and all his research was paying off. He made his mortgage payments with grim satisfaction, because he had
enough left over to expand the herd come spring and
bring in some new blood strains he'd been wanting to
try. He'd be able to repair equipment when it needed
it, instead of scraping and saving and doing without.
He'd even be able to take Madelyn out to eat once in a
while. It galled him that the limit of their outside entertainment was an occasional cup of coffee or slice of pie
at Floris's café. He wanted to be able to take Madelyn
places and spoil her, buy her new clothes and jewelry,
all the things he had once taken for granted in his life.
The ranch was a long way from being as rich as it had
once been, but he was clawing his way back. He'd made
a profit, by God! He was in the black.

Madelyn had gone into Billings with him when he
conferred with his banker. He'd expected her to want
to go shopping; though he realized more every day
how different Maddie was from April, he also wryly
accepted that his wife was a clotheshorse. The fact that
she loved clothes was evident in the way she dressed
even while working at the ranch. It might be just jeans

and a shirt, but the jeans would fit her in a way guaranteed to send his blood pressure up, and the shirt would look as stylish as if it had come straight from Paris. What really got to him was the way she would put on one of his white dress shirts, not button *any* of the buttons, and knot the tails at her waist. She wouldn't have a bra on under it, either. It was a style and a provocation that he couldn't resist, and she knew it. First his hand would be inside the shirt; then the shirt would be off; then they would be making love wherever they happened to be.

She did shop, but again she surprised him. She bought underwear and jeans for him; then she was ready to go home. "I don't know how I ever stood a city as large as New York," she said absently, looking around at the traffic. "This is too noisy." He was astonished; Billings had less than seventy thousand inhabitants, and barroom brawls were far more the norm than any gang- or drug-related violence. No, Maddie wasn't like April, who had considered Billings nothing more than a backwater crossroads. To April, only cities like New York, London, Paris, Los Angeles and Hong Kong had been sophisticated enough for her enjoyment.

Madelyn was indeed glad to get back to the ranch. She was happiest there, she realized. It was quiet, with the peace that came only from being close to earth and nature. And it was her home now.

It was the middle of the afternoon when they got back, and Reese changed clothes to begin his chores. It was too early to start dinner, so Madelyn went out on the porch and sat in the swing. It was early autumn, and already the heat was leaving the day. Reese said it wasn't unusual to have snow in October, so the days when she would be able to sit out on the porch were limited. Still, she was looking forward to the winter, hard as it might be. The days would be short and the nights long, and she smiled as she thought of those long nights.

Reese came back downstairs from changing his clothes and found her there. The chores would wait a little while, he thought, and joined her on the swing. He put his arm around her and brought her closer, so that her head was nestled in the hollow of his shoulder.

"I was just thinking," she said, "it'll be winter soon."

"Sooner than you think."

"Christmas isn't that far away now. Could I invite Robert?"

"Of course. He's your family."

She smiled. "I know, but the warmth between you at our wedding wasn't exactly overwhelming."

"What did you expect, given the circumstances? Men are territorial. He didn't want to give you up, and I was determined to have you come hell or high water." He nudged her chin up with his thumb and gave her a slow kiss. "And I was a stranger who was going to be taking his sister to bed that night."

For a moment there was only the creaking of the swing. He kissed her again, then just held her. He hadn't known marriage could be like this, he thought with vague surprise. Both passion and contentment.

He said quietly, "Let's have a baby."

After a pause she said, "I'll stop taking the Pill." Then she reached for his hand and cradled it to her face.

The tenderness of the gesture was almost painful. He lifted her up and settled her astride his lap so he could see her expression. "Is that what you want?"

Her face looked as if it had been lit from within. "You know it is." She leaned forward and brushed his lips with hers, then suddenly laughed and threw her arms around his neck, fiercely hugging him. "Are there any twins in your family?"

"No!" he said explosively, then drew back and gave her a suspicious look. "Are there in yours?"

"Actually, yes. Grandma Lily was a twin."

Even the thought of twins was too much. He shook his head, denying the possibility. "Just one at a time, gal. No doubling up." He rubbed his hands up her thighs and under her skirt, then slid them inside her underpants to cup her bare buttocks. "You might be pregnant by Christmas."

"Umm, I'd like that."

His eyes glinted at her. "I'll do my best."

"But it'll probably take longer than that."

"Then I'll just have to try harder."

Her lips quirked. "I can't lose," she said in contentment.

THE FIRST SNOW did come in October, three inches of fine, dry powder. She learned that snow didn't stop a rancher's work, it only intensified it, though three inches was nothing to worry about. In the dead of winter Reese would have to carry hay to the cattle and break the ice in the stock ponds so they could drink. He'd have to find lost calves before they froze to death and move the herd to more sheltered areas during the worst weather.

For the first time, winter began to worry her. "What if there are blizzard conditions?" she asked him one night.

"Then I hope for the best," he said flatly. "I'll lose some calves during any bad snowstorm, but if it doesn't last too long the biggest part of the herd will weather it. The danger is if blizzard conditions or extreme cold last for several days. Then the cattle start freezing to death, and during a blizzard I can't get feed out to them. I have hooks attached to the barn and the house. When it looks like a bad storm, I run a static line between them and hook myself to it so I can get back and forth to the barn."

She stared at him, appalled at the years he'd coped by himself and the danger he'd been in. It was testimony to his strength and intelligence that he was still alive, and characteristic of his stubbornness that he'd even tried.

The preparations for winter were ongoing and not to be taken lightly. He moved the herd to the closer pastures where they would winter. Cords of firewood were stacked close to the back door, and the pantry was well stocked with candles and batteries, while he cleaned and tested two big kerosene heaters in case they were needed. The truck and car were both filled with new antifreeze and given new batteries, and he began parking them in the garage to keep them out of the wind. During October the temperature steadily slipped lower, until the only time it was above freezing was at high noon.

"Does it stay below freezing for six months?" she asked, and he laughed.

"No. We'll have cold spells and warm spells. It may be sixty degrees or higher in January, but if we get blizzard conditions or a deep freeze the temperatures can go way below zero. We prepare for a blizzard and hope for the sixty degrees."

As if to bear him out, the weather then showed a warming trend and inched the temperatures upward into the fifties during the day. Madelyn felt more confident, because he'd been making preparations as if they were going into six months of darkness. That was how he'd made it by himself for seven years, by being cautious and prepared for anything. Still, by his own admission the winters could be hell. She would just have to make certain he didn't take any chances with his own safety.

Robert flew in the day before Christmas and spent three days with them. When he first saw Madelyn he gave her a hard, searching look, but whatever he saw must have reassured him, because he relaxed then and was an affable guest. She was amused at the way Reese and Robert related to each other, since they were so much alike, both very private and strong men. Their conversation consisted of sentence fragments, as if they were just throwing out random comments, but they both seemed comfortable with it. She was amazed at how much alike they were in manner, too. Robert was smoothly cosmopolitan, yet Reese's mannerisms were much like his, illustrating how prosperous the ranch had been before the divorce. They differed only in that she had never seen Robert lose his temper, while Reese's temper was like a volcano.

Robert was surprisingly interested in the working of the ranch and rode out with Reese every day he was there. They spent a lot of time talking about futures and stock options, the ratio of feed to pound of beef, interest rates, inflation and government subsidies. Robert looked thoughtful a lot, as if he were weighing everything Reese said.

The day before he left, Robert approached Madelyn. She was sprawled bonelessly across a big armchair, listening to the stereo with her eyes closed and one foot keeping time to the music. He said in amusement, "Never run if you can walk, never walk if you can stand, never stand if you can sit, and never sit if you can lie."

"Never talk if you can listen," Madelyn added without opening her eyes.

"Then you listen, and I'll talk."

"This sounds serious. Are you going to tell me you're in love with someone and are thinking of marriage?"

"Good God, no," he said, his amusement deepening.

"Is there a new woman on the horizon?"

"A bit closer than that."

"Why didn't you bring her? Is it anyone I know?"

"This is a family Christmas," he replied, telling her with that one short sentence that his new lover hadn't touched him any deeper than any of the others. "Her name is Natalie VanWein."

"Nope. I don't know her."

"You're supposed to listen while I talk, not ask questions about my love life." He drew up a hassock and sat down on it, smiling a little as he noticed that she hadn't even opened her eyes during their conversation.

"So talk."

"I've never met anyone with a clearer head for business than Reese—excepting myself, of course," he said mockingly.

"Oh, of course."

"Listen, don't talk. He sees what has to be done and he does it, without regard to obstacles. He has the kind of determination that won't give up, no matter what the odds. He'll make a go of this ranch. He'll fight like hell until he has it the way it used to be."

Madelyn opened one eye. "And the point of this is?"

"I'm a businessman. He strikes me as a better risk than a lot of ventures I've bet on. He doesn't have to wait to build this place up. He could accept an investor and start right now."

"The investor, of course, being yurself."

He nodded. "I look for a profit. He'd make one. I want to invest in it personally, without involving Cannon Companies."

"Have you already talked to him about it?"

"I wanted to talk to you first. You're his wife, you know him better than I do. Would he go for it, or would I be wasting my time?"

"Well, I won't give you an opinion either way. You're on your own. Like you said, he knows the business, so let him make up his own mind without having to consider anything I might have said either pro or con."

"It's your home, too."

"I'm still learning to help, but I don't know enough about the business of ranching to even begin to make an educated decision. And when it comes down to it, my home is based on my marriage, not where we live. We could live anywhere and I'd be content."

He looked down at her, and a strangely tender look entered his pale eyes. "You're really in love with him, aren't you?"

"I have been from the beginning. I never would have married him otherwise."

He examined her face closely, in much the same way he'd looked at her when he had first arrived, as if satisfying himself of the truth of her answer. Then he gave a brusque nod and got to his feet. "Then I'll put the proposition to Reese and see what he thinks."

Reese turned it down, as Madelyn had expected he would. The ranch was his; it might take longer and be a harder fight to do it on his own, but every tree and every speck of dirt on the ranch belonged to him, and he refused to risk even one square inch of it with an outside investor. Robert took the refusal in good humor, because business was business, and his emotions were never involved any more than they were with women.

Reese talked to her about it that night, lying in the darkness with her head pillowed on his shoulder. "Robert made me an offer today. If I took him as an investor, I could double the ranch's operation, hire enough hands to work it and probably get back most of the former acreage within five years."

"I know. He talked to me about it, too."

He stiffened. "What did you tell him?"

"To talk to you. It's your ranch, and you know more about running it than anyone else."

"Would you rather I took his offer?"

"Why should I care?"

"Money," he said succinctly.

"I'm not doing without anything." Her voice had a warm, amused tone to it.

"You could have a lot more."

"I could have a lot less, too. I'm happy, Reese. If you took the offer I'd still be happy, and I'll still be happy if you don't take it."

"He said you wouldn't take sides."

"That's right, I won't. It would be a no-win situation for me, and I don't waste my energy."

He lay awake long after she was sleeping quietly in his arms. It was a way to instant financial security, but it would require that he do something he'd sworn never to do: risk ownership of the ranch. He already had a mortgage, but he was managing to make the payments. If he took an investor he would be paying off the bank but taking on another debtor, at a price he might not be able to meet. The big lure of it was that, perversely, he wanted to give Madelyn all the luxuries he would have been able to provide before.

To take care of his wife as he wanted, he'd have to risk his ranch. He didn't miss the irony of it.

THE DAY AFTER Robert left, a big weather system swept in from Canada and it began snowing. At first it was just snow, but it didn't stop. The temperature began dropping like a rock, and the wind picked up. Reese watched the weather build into something nasty, and the weather reports said it would get worse. While he still could, he herded the cattle into the most sheltered area and put out as much hay as possible, but he wasn't certain he'd had enough time to get out as much as would be needed.

On the way back to the barn it started snowing so heavily that visibility dropped to about ten feet, and the wind began piling up drifts that masked the shape of the land. His own ranch became an alien landscape to him, without any familiar landmarks to guide him. All he could go on was his own sense of direction, and he had to fight to ignore the disorienting swirl of snow. His horse picked its way carefully, trying to avoid the snow-covered holes and indentations that could easily cause it to fall and perhaps break a leg. Icicles began to form on the horse's nose as the warm vapor of its breath froze. Reese put a gloved hand to his own face and found it coated with ice crystals.

A ride that normally took twenty minutes stretched into an hour. He began to wonder if he had missed the barn entirely when it materialized out of the blowing snow, and even then he would have missed it if the door hadn't been open revealing the gleam of yellow light. A brief frown creased his face; he knew he'd closed the door, and he certainly hadn't left a light on. But it had been too close a call for him to be anything but grate-ful; another half hour and he wouldn't have made it.

He ducked his head and rode straight into the barn. It wasn't until he caught movement out of the corner of his eye that he realized Madelyn had come out to the barn and was waiting for him, literally with a light in the window. She struggled against the wind to close the big doors, her slender body leaning into the teeth of the gale. The cow bawled restlessly, and the cats leaped for the loft. Reese slid out of the saddle and added his weight to Madelyn's, closing the doors and dropping the big two-by-eight bar into the brackets.

"What the hell are you doing out here?" he asked in a raspy voice as he grabbed her to him. "Damn it, Maddie, you can get lost going from the house to the barn in a blow like this!"

"I hooked up to the tension line," she said, clinging to him. Her voice was thin. "How did you get back? You can't see out there."

He felt the panic in her, because he'd begun feeling some of it himself. If he'd been five feet farther away, he wouldn't have seen the light. "Sheer blind luck," he said grimly.

She looked up at his ice-crusted face. "You have to get warm before frostbite starts."

"The horse first."

"I'll do it." She pointed toward the tack room, where he kept a small space heater. "I turned on the heater so it would be warm in there. Now, go on."

Actually, the barn felt warm to him after being out-side; the animals gave off enough heat that the tempera-ture inside the barn was above freezing, which was all that he required right now. Still, he went into the tack room and felt the heat envelop him almost unbearably.

He didn't try to brush the ice from his face; he let it melt, so it wouldn't damage his skin. It had actually insulated his face from the wind, but too much longer would have resulted in frostbite. He'd had mild cases before, and it was painful enough that he'd rather not go through it again.

Madelyn unsaddled the horse and rubbed it down. The big animal sighed with pleasure in a way that was almost human. Then she threw a warm blanket over it and gave it feed and water, patting the muscled neck in appreciation. The animal had earned it.

She hurried to Reese and found him knocking chunks of snow off his heavy shearling coat. That shocking white layer of ice and snow was gone from his face; what was almost as shocking was that he already seemed to have recovered his strength, as if the ordeal had been nothing out of the ordinary. She had been in torment since the howling wind had started, pacing the house and trying not to weep uncontrollably, and finally fighting her way out to the barn so she would be there to help him if—no, *when*—he made it back. Her heart was still pounding. She didn't have to be told how easily he might not have made it back, even though she couldn't bear to let the thought form.

"It won't be easy getting back to the house," he said grimly. "The wind is probably gusting up to sixty miles an hour. We'll both hook on to the line, but I'm going to tie you to me as a safeguard."

He knotted a rope around his waist, then looped and knotted it around her, with no more than four feet of slack between them. "I want you within reach. I'm going to try to hold on to you, but I damn sure don't want you getting any farther away from me than this."

He put his coat back on and settled his hat firmly on

his head. He eyed Madelyn sternly. "Don't you have a hat?"

She produced a thick woolen scarf from her pocket and draped it over her head, then wound the ends around her neck. They each got a length of nylon cord with heavy metal clips on each end and attached one end to their belts, leaving the other end free to clip to the line. They left the barn by the small side door; though the line was anchored right beside it, Reese had to grab Madelyn by the waist to keep the wind from tumbling her head over heels. Still holding her, he grabbed her line and hooked it overhead, then secured his own.

It was almost impossible to make headway. For every yard they progressed, stumbling and fighting, the wind would knock them back two feet. It tore her out of his grasp and knocked her feet out from under her, hanging her in the air from the line at her waist. Reese lunged for her, yelling something that she couldn't understand, and hauled her against him. It was obvious she wasn't going to be able to stay on her feet. He locked her against his side with a grip that compressed her ribs, almost shutting off her breath. She gasped for air, but couldn't manage more than a painful wheeze. She couldn't have yelled to make him understand, even if she'd had the breath, because the howling wind drowned out everything else. She dangled in his grip like a rag doll, her sight fading and her struggles becoming weaker.

Reese stumbled against the back steps, then up onto the porch. The house blocked some of the wind, and he managed to open the back door, then reach up and unhook both their lines. He staggered into the house and fell to the floor of the utility room with Madelyn still in his arms, but managed to turn so that he took most of the shock. "Are you all right?" He gasped the question, breathing hard from exertion. The wind had gotten worse just since he'd made it back to the barn.

She didn't answer, and sudden fear brought him up on his knees beside her. Her eyes were closed, her lips blue. He grabbed her shoulder, shouting at her. "Maddie! Madelyn, damn it, what's wrong? Are you hurt—wake up and answer me!"

She coughed, then moaned a little and tried to curl on her side, her arms coming up to hug herself. She coughed again, then went into a paroxysm of convulsive coughing and gagging, writhing from the force of it. Reese pulled her up into his arms and held her, his face white.

Finally she managed to wheeze, "Shut the door," and he lashed out with his boot, kicking the door shut with a force that rattled it on its frame.

He unwound the scarf from her head and began opening her coat. The rope around their waists still tied them together and he hastily pulled the knots out. "Are you hurt?" he asked again, his face a grim mask.

Coughing had brought color to her face, but it was quickly fading, leaving her deathly pale. "I'm all right," she said, her voice so hoarse she could barely make a sound. "I just couldn't breathe."

Realization hit him like a kick by a mule. He'd almost smothered her with the force of his grip. His face grim, vicious curses coming from between his tightly clenched teeth, he laid her back on the floor as gently as possible and stretched out his leg so he could get his knife out of his pocket. Her eyes widened as he snapped the blade open and began slicing through the pullover sweater she wore under the coat. Beneath the sweater was a shirt, but it buttoned down the front and therefore escaped being cut off. When her torso was bare he bagan carefully feeling her ribs, his face intent as he searched for any sign of give, his eyes locked on her face to see the least hint of discomfort. She flinched several times, but the ribs felt all right. Her pale skin was already becoming discolored with bruises.

"I almost killed you," he said harshly as he lifted her in his arms and got to his feet.

"It wasn't that bad," she managed to say.

He gave her a violent look. "You were unconscious." He carried her up the stairs and to their bedroom, where he laid her on the bed. He shrugged out of his own coat and let it fall to the floor; then he very gently but implacably stripped her of every stitch and examined her from head to toe. Except for the bruising across her ribs, she was fine. He bent his head and brushed his lips across the dark band as if he would absorb the pain.

Madelyn put her hand on his hair, threading her fingers through the dark strands. "Reese, I'm okay, I promise."

He got to his feet. "I'll put a cold compress on it to stop the bruising from getting any worse."

She made a disbelieving sound. "Trust me, I can't just lie here and let you put an ice bag on my side! You know how ice down your shirt feels, and besides, I'm cold. I'd rather have a cup of hot chocolate, or coffee."

The strength of her tone reassured him, and another critical look told him that the color was coming back into her face. She sat up, rather gingerly holding her side but without any real pain, and gave him a wifely survey. "You're soaking wet from riding in that blizzard. You need to get out of those clothes, and then we'll both have something hot to drink."

She got dry clothes out for both Reese and herself

and began dressing while he stripped and toweled off. She looked at her ruined sweater with disbelief, then tossed it into the trash. Reese saw her expression and smiled faintly. "I didn't want to move you any more than I had to until I knew what was wrong," he explained, rubbing a towel over his shoulders.

"Actually, I was a little relieved when the sweater was all you cut. For a split second I was afraid you were going to do a tracheotomy."

"You were talking and breathing, so I ruled that out. I've done one before, though."

"You've actually taken your pocketknife and cut someone's throat open?" she demanded incredulously, her voice rising.

"I had to. One of the hands got kicked in the throat, and he was choking to death. I slit his trachea and held it open with my finger until someone brought a drinking straw to insert for him to breathe through. We got him to a hospital, they put in a regular trach tube until the swelling went down enough for him to breathe again, and he did just fine."

"How did you know what to do?"

"Every rancher absorbs a lot of medical knowledge just in the ordinary workday. I've set broken bones, sewn up cuts, given injections. It's a rough life, sweetheart." His face darkened as he said it. It had almost been too rough for her. He could so easily have crushed her ribs.

He pulled on the dry underwear and jeans she had put out for him, watching as she brushed her hair and swung it back over her shoulder with a practiced toss of her head, every movement as graceful as a ballet. How could she still look elegant after what she'd been through? How could she be so casual about it? He was still shaking.

When she started past him on the way downstairs, he caught her and wrapped his arms around her, holding her to him for a long minute with his cheek resting on top of her pale hair. Madelyn circled his waist with her arms and let herself revel in his closeness; he was home, and he was all right. Nothing was said, because nothing needed saying. It was enough just to hold each other.

Reese paced the house that day like a restless cougar, periodically looking out the window to monitor the weather. He tried a radio station, but nothing came through the static. Around dusk the electricity went off, and he built a roaring fire in the fireplace, then put one of the kerosene heaters in the kitchen. Madelyn lit candles and lamps, and thanked the stars that the water heater and stove were gas-operated.

They ate soup and sandwiches by candlelight, then brought down quilts and blankets and pillows to sleep in front of the fireplace. They sat on their bed of quilts with their backs resting against the front of the couch and their legs stretched toward the fire. Madelyn's head was on his shoulder. He could almost hear her mind working as she stared at the fire, and he decided he might as well get it started before she did. "A flag with a swallow-tail end is called a burgee."

She gave him a quick look of delight. "The small flag carried in front or to the right of marchers to guide them is called a guidon."

"You want to do flags? Okay, we'll do flags. The study of flags is called vexillology."

"The United States flag has seven red stripes and six white."

"That one's so easy it's cheating."

"A fact is a fact. Carry on."

"Bamboo is the fastest growing plant in the world."

"Cleopatra was Macedonian, not Egyptian."

They played the game for several more minutes, laughing at the more ridiculous items they pulled out. Then they got a deck of cards and played strip poker, which wasn't much of a challenge, since she was wearing only his shirt and a pair of socks, and he was wearing only jeans. Once she had him naked, she lost interest in playing cards and moved on to a more rewarding occupation. With flame-burnished skin they moved together and for a long while forgot about the swirling white storm that enveloped them.

The blizzard conditions had subsided by the next morning, though deep drifts had been piled up by the wind. The electricity came back on, and the weather report predicted slowly moderating temperatures. Reese checked on the herd and found that the cattle had withstood the storm in good condition; he lost only one calf, which had gotten lost from its mother. He found the little animal lying in a snowbank, while its mother bawled mournfully, calling it.

They had been lucky this time. He looked up at the gray sky, where patches of blue were just starting to show through. All he needed was a mild winter, or at least one where the bad spells didn't last long enough to endanger the herd.

He was pulling his way out of the morass of debt, but one year of profit was a long way from being home free. He needed the mortgage paid off, he needed an expanded herd and the money to hire cowhands to work that herd. When he could expand his capital into other areas so he wasn't entirely dependent on the weather and the market for beef, then he would feel more secure about their future.

The next few years wouldn't be easy. Madelyn wasn't pregnant yet, but as soon as she was they would have medical bills to consider, as well as the cost of providing for a growing baby. Maybe he should take Robert's offer despite his disinclination to allow anyone else any authority over the ranch. It would give him a financial cushion, the means of putting his plans into operation sooner, as well as taking care of Madelyn and their child, or children.

But he had been through too much, fought too hard and too long, to change his mind now. The ranch was his, as much a part of him as bone and blood.

He could easier lose his own life than the ranch. He loved every foot of it with the same fierce, independent possessiveness that had kept his ancestors there despite Indian attacks, weather and disease. Reese had grown up with the sun on his face and the scent of cattle in his nostrils, as much a part of this land as the purple-tinged mountains and enormous sky.

"I'll make it yet," he said aloud to the white, silent land. It wasn't in him to give up, but the land had required men like him from the beginning. It had broken weaker men, and the ones who had survived were tougher and stronger than most. The land had needed strong women, too, and if Madelyn wasn't quite what he'd planned on, he was too satisfied to care.

CHAPTER NINE

AT THE END of January another big weather system began moving in from the Arctic, and this one looked bad. They had a couple of days' warning, and they worked together to do everything they could to safeguard the herd. The cold front moved in during the night, and they woke the next morning to steady snow and a temperature that was ten below zero, but at least the wind wasn't as bad as it had been before.

Reese made a couple of forays out to break the ice in the troughs and stock ponds so the cattle could drink, and Madelyn was terrified every time he went out. This kind of cold was the killing kind, and the weather reports said it would get worse.

It did. The temperature dropped all that day, and by nightfall it was twenty-three below zero.

When morning came it was forty-one degrees below zero, and the wind was blowing.

If Reese had been restless before, he was like a caged animal now. They wore layers of clothing even in the house, and he kept a fire in the fireplace even though the electricity was still on. They constantly drank hot coffee or chocolate to keep their temperatures up, and they moved down to the living room to sleep before the fire.

The third day he just sat, his eyes black with inner rage. His cattle were dying out there, and he was helpless to do a damn thing about it; the blowing snow kept him from getting to them. The killing temperatures would kill him even faster than they would the cattle. The wind chill was seventy below zero.

Lying before the fire that night, Madelyn put her hand on his chest and felt the tautness of his body. His eyes were open, and he was staring at the ceiling. She rose up on her elbow. "No matter what happens," she said quietly, "we'll make it."

His voice was harsh. "We can't make it without the cattle."

"Then you're just giving up?"

The look he gave her was violent. He didn't know how to give up; the words were obscene to him.

"We'll work harder," she said. "Last spring you didn't have me here to help you. We'll be able to do more."

His face softened, and he lifted her hand in his, holding it up in the firelight and studying it, slim and femininely graceful. She was willing to turn her hands to any job, no matter how rough or dirty, so he didn't have the heart to tell her that whenever she was with him, he was so concerned for her safety that he spent most of his time watching after her. She wouldn't understand it; they had been married for seven months, and she hadn't backed down from anything that had been thrown at her. She certainly hadn't backed down from him. Remembering some of their fights made him smile, and remembering others made him get hard. It hadn't been a dull seven months.

"You're right," he said, holding her hand to his face. "We'll just work harder."

It was the fourth day before they could get out. The wind had died, and the sky was a clear blue bowl, making a mockery of the bitter cold. They had to wrap their faces to even breathe, it was so cold, and it taxed their endurance just to get to the barn to care for the animals there. The cow was in abject misery, her udder so swollen and sore she kicked every time Reese tried to milk her. It took over an hour of starts and stops before she would stand still and let him finish the job. Madelyn took care of the horses while he attended to the milking, carrying water and feed, and then shoveling out the stalls and putting down fresh straw.

The animals seemed nervous and glad to see them; tears stung her eyes as she rubbed Reese's favorite mount on the forehead. These animals had had the protection of the barn; she couldn't bear to even think about the cattle.

Reese got the truck started and loaded it and a small trailer with hay. Madelyn climbed into the cab and gave him a steady look when he frowned at her. There was no way she would let him go out on the range by himself in such bitter cold; if anything happened to him, if he fell and couldn't get back to the truck or lost consciousness, he would die in a short while.

He drove carefully to the protected area where he had herded the cattle and stopped, his face bleak. There was nothing there, just a blank white landscape. The sun glittered on the snow, and he reached for his sunglasses. Without a word Madelyn followed suit.

He began driving, looking for any sign of the herd, if indeed any of them had survived. That white blanket could be covering their frozen carcasses.

Finally it was the pitiful bawling that led them to some of the cattle. They had gone in search of food, or perhaps more shelter, but they were in a stand of trees where the snow had blown an enormous snowbank up against the tree trunks, blocking some of the wind and perhaps saving them.

Reese's face was still shuttered as he got out to toss some bales of hay down from the trailer, and Madelyn knew how he felt. He was afraid to hope, afraid that only a few head had survived. He cut the twine on the bales and loosened the hay, then took a shovel and dug an opening in the snowbank. The anxious cattle crowded out of what had become a pen to them and headed for the hay. Reese counted them, and his face tightened. Madelyn could tell that this was only a fraction of the number there should have been.

He got back into the truck and sat with his gloved hands clenched on the steering wheel.

"If these survived, there could be more," Madelyn said. "We have to keep looking."

By a frozen pond they found more, but these were lying on their sides in pathetic, snow-covered humps. Reese counted again. Thirty-six were dead, and there could be calves too small to find under all the snow.

One cow had become trapped in a tangle of brush and wire, and her calf was lying on the snow beside her, watching with innocent brown eyes as its mother weakly struggled. Reese cut her free, and she scrambled to her feet, but then was too weak to do anything else. The calf got up, too, stumbling on shaky legs to seek her milk. Reese put out hay for her to eat and continued the search for more.

They found seven survivors in a gully, and ten more carcasses not five hundred feet away. That was how it went for the rest of the day: as many as they found alive, they found that many dead. He put out hay, used an axe to chop holes in the ice-covered ponds, and kept a tally of both his losses and the ones that had survived. Half of the herd was dead, and more could die. The grimness of the situation weighed down on him. He'd been so close—and now this!

The next day they rounded up the strays, trying to get the herd together. Reese rode, and Madelyn drove the truck, pulling another trailer of hay. The temperature was moderating, if you could call ten below zero moderate, but it was too late.

One yearling objected to rejoining the herd and darted to the left, with the horse immediately following suit and getting in front of the impetuous young animal, herding it back the way it had come. The young bull stubbornly stopped, its head swinging back and forth, looking for all the world like a recalcitrant teenager. Then it made another break for freedom and bolted across a pond, but it was a pond where Reese had chopped holes in the ice near the bank, and it hadn't refrozen solid enough to hold the yearling's weight, which was already considerable. Its rear feet broke through, and it fell backward, great eyes rolling while it bawled in terror.

Cussing a blue streak, Reese got his rope and approached the bank. Madelyn pulled the truck up and got out. "Don't go out on the ice," she warned.

"Don't worry, I'm not as stupid as he is," he muttered, shaking loose a loop and twirling it a few times. He missed the first throw because the young bull was struggling frantically, and its struggles were breaking off more ice; it slipped backward and went completely under the icy water just as Reese made his throw. Still swearing, he quickly recoiled the rope as Madelyn joined him.

The second throw settled neatly around the tossing head, and Reese quickly wound the rope around the saddle horn. The horse began backing up under his quiet instructions and the pressure of his hand, dragging the yearling from the water.

As soon as the yearling was free of the water the horse stopped and Reese kept his hand on the rope as he worked to loosen the loop around the bull's neck. As soon as it was free, the animal gave a panicked bawl and bolted into Reese, its muscled shoulder knocking him sideways into the water.

Madelyn bit back a scream as she ran forward, waiting for him to surface. He did, only about ten feet out, but they were ten feet he couldn't negotiate. The numbing cold of the water was almost immediately paralyzing. All he could do was drape his arms over the edge of the broken ice and hang on.

She grabbed the rope and urged the horse forward, but she couldn't swing a loop and in any case wouldn't drag him out by his neck. "Can you catch the rope?" she called urgently, and one gloved hand moved in what she hoped was an affirmative answer. She slung the rope across the water toward him, and he made an effort to raise his arm and catch it, but his movement was slow and clumsy, and the rope fell into the water.

She had to get him out of there *now*. Two minutes from now might be too late. Her heart was slamming against her rib cage, and her face was paper-white. There was no help for him except herself, and no time for indecision. She pulled the rope back to her and ran to the pond, edging out on the ice herself.

He raised his head, his eyes filling with horror as he saw her inching toward him. "No!" he said hoarsely.

She went down on her belly and began snaking toward him, distributing her weight over as much of the ice as she could, but even so she felt it cracking beneath her. Ten feet. Just ten feet. It sounded so close in theory, and in practice it was forever.

The edge of the ice he'd been holding crumbled, and he went under. She scrambled forward, forsaking safety for speed. Just as he broke the surface again she grabbed the collar of his coat and pulled him upward; the combined pressure of their weight caused more ice to fracture and she almost fell in with him but she scrambled back just enough.

"I have the rope," she said, her teeth chattering in terror. "I'm going to slip it over your head and under your arms. Then the horse will drag you out. Okay?"

He nodded. His lips were blue, but he managed to raise one arm at a time so she could get the rope on him. She leaned forward to tighten the slip knot, and the ice beneath her gave with a sharp crack, dropping her straight downward.

Cold. She had never known such cold. It took her breath, and her limbs immediately went numb. Her eyes were open, and she saw her hair float in front of her face. She was under the water. Odd that it didn't matter. Up above she could see a white blanket with dark spots in it, and a strange disturbance. Reese...maybe it was Reese.

The thought of Reese was what focused her splintered thoughts. Somehow she managed to begin flailing her arms and legs, fighting her way to the surface, aiming for one of those dark spots that represented breaks in the ice.

Her face broke the surface just as the horse, working on its own, hauled Reese up on the bank. It was trained to pull when it felt weight on the end of the rope, so it had. She reached for the edge of the ice as Reese struggled to his hands and knees.

"Maddie!" His voice was a hoarse cry as he fought to free himself of the rope, his coordination almost gone.

Hold on. All she had to do was hold on. It was what she had been praying he would be able to do, and now it was what she had to do. She tried, but she didn't have his strength. Her weight began dragging her down, and she couldn't stop it. The water closed over her head again.

She had to fight upward, had to swim. Her thoughts were sluggish, but they directed her movements enough so that just when she thought her tortured lungs would give out and she would have to inhale, she broke through to the surface again.

"Grab the ice. Maddie, grab the ice!" He barked out the command in a tone of voice that made her reach outward in a blind motion, one that by chance laid her arm across the ice.

The wet rope was freezing, making it stiff. Reese fought the cold, fought his own clumsiness as he swung the loop. "Hold your other arm up so I can get the loop over it. Maddie, hold—your—other—arm—*up!*"

She couldn't. She had already been in the water too long. All she could do was lift the arm that had been holding on to the ice and hope that he could snare it before she went completely under.

He swung the loop out as her face disappeared under the water. It settled around her outstretched arm, and with a frantic jerk he tightened it, the loop shrinking to almost nothing as it closed around her slender wrist. "Back, back!" he yelled at the horse, which was already bracing itself against the weight it could feel.

She was dragged underwater toward the bank, and finally up on it. Reese fell to his knees beside her, screaming hell in his eyes until she began choking and retching. "We'll be all right," he said fiercely as he fumbled with the slip knot around her wrist, trying to free her. "All we have to do is get to the house and we'll be all right." He didn't even let himself think that they might not make it. Even though they weren't that far, it would take all his strength.

He was too cold to lift her, so he dragged her to the truck. Her eyes kept closing. "Don't go to sleep," he said harshly. "Open your eyes. Fight, damn it! Fight!"

Her gray eyes opened, but there was no real comprehension in them. To his astonishment, her fist doubled, and she tried to swing at him as she obeyed his rough command.

He got the truck door open and half boosted, half pushed her up onto the seat. She sprawled across it, dripping water.

The horse nudged him. If the animal hadn't been so close he would have left it behind, but a lifetime of taking care of his livestock prompted him to tie the reins to the rear bumper. He wouldn't be able to drive so fast that the horse couldn't easily keep pace, even though every instinct screamed that he had to get to the house and get both of them warm.

He pulled himself onto the seat behind the steering wheel and turned on the ignition, then struggled to slide the knob that turned the heater on high. Hot air poured out of the vents, but he was too numb to feel it.

They had to get out of their clothes. The icy wetness was just leaching more heat away from their bodies. He began fighting out of his coat as he barked orders at Madelyn to do the same.

She managed to sit up somehow, but she had almost no coordination. She had been in the water even longer than he had. He didn't have an easy time of it, but by the time he was naked she was weakly pushing her heavy shearling coat onto the floorboard. Ice crystals had already caked it.

He reached for her buttons. "Come on, sweetheart, we have to get you naked. The clothes will just make you that much colder. Can you talk to me? Say something, Maddie. Talk to me."

She slowly lifted one hand, with all the fingers folded down except the middle one. He looked at the obscene, or suggestive, gesture—it all depended on how he took it—and despite the gravity of the situation a rough laugh burst from his throat. "I'll take you up on that, sweetheart, just as soon as we get warm." A sparkle came into her eyes, giving him hope.

His teeth began chattering, and convulsive shudders racked him. Maddie wasn't shivering, and that was a bad sign. There were always a blanket and a thermos of coffee in the truck when he went out in the winter, and he pulled the blanket out from behind the seat. Even the simplest movement was a battle requiring all his strength, but he finally got it out and roughly dried them with it as best he could, then wrapped it around her.

With shaking hands he opened the thermos and poured a small amount of steaming coffee into the top, then held it to her lips. "Drink, baby. It's nice and hot."

She managed to swallow a little of it, and he drank the rest himself, then poured more into the cup. He could feel it burning down into his stomach. If he didn't get himself into shape to drive to the ranch, neither one of them would make it. He fought the shaking of his hands until he had downed the entire cup, then poured more and coaxed Madelyn into taking it. That was all he could do for now. He focused his attention and put the truck in gear.

It was slow going. He was shaking so hard that his body wouldn't obey. He was a little disoriented, sometimes unable to tell where they were. Beside him, Madelyn finally began shivering as the heat blasting from the vents combined with the coffee to revive her a little.

The house had never looked so good to him as it did when it finally came into view and he nursed the truck across the rough ground toward it. He parked as close to the back door as possible and walked naked around the truck to haul Madelyn out the passenger door. He couldn't feel the snow under his bare feet.

She could walk a little now, and that helped. With their arms around each other they half crawled up the steps to the porch, then into the utility room. The downstairs bathroom was directly across from the utility room; he dragged Madelyn into it and propped her against the wall while he turned on the water in the tub to let it get hot. When steam began rising he turned the cold water tap and hoped he adjusted it right, or they would be scalded. His hands were so cold he simply couldn't tell.

"Come on, into the tub."

She struggled to her knees, and Reese pulled her up the rest of the way, but in the end it was simpler for both of them to literally crawl over the edge of the tub into the rising water. She sat in front of him and between his legs, lying back against his chest. Tears ran down her face as the warm water lapped against her cold flesh, bringing it painfully back to life. Reese let his head tilt back until it rested on the wall, his teeth gritted. They had to endure it because it was necessary; they didn't have anyone else here to take care of them. This was the fastest way to get warm, but it wasn't pleasant.

Slowly the pain in their extremities eased. When the

water was so high that it was lapping out the overflow drain, he turned off the tap and sank deeper until his shoulders were covered. Madelyn's hair floated on the surface like wet gold.

He tightened his arms around her, trying to absorb her shivering into him.

"Better?"

"Yes." Her voice was low and even huskier than usual. "That was close."

He turned her in his arms and hugged her to him with barely controlled desperation. "I was planning to keep that bull for breeding," he said tightly, "but the sonofabitch is going to be a steer now—if he lives through this."

She managed a laugh, her lips moving against his throat. The water lapped her chin. "Don't ever get rid of that horse. He saved our bacon."

"I'll give him the biggest stall for the rest of his life."

They lay in the water until it began to cool; then he pulled the plug and urged her to her feet. She was still looking sleepy, so he held her to him while he closed the shower curtain and turned on the shower, letting the water beat down on their heads. She just stood in his arms with her head on his chest, the way she had stood so many times, but this time was infinitely precious. This time they had cheated death.

The water rained over them. He turned her face up and took her mouth, needing her taste, her touch, to reassure himself that they were really okay. He had come incredibly close to losing her, even closer than he had come to dying himself.

When the hot water began to go he snapped off the tap and reached for towels, wrapping one around her dripping hair and using another to dry her. Though her

lips and nails had color now, she was still shivering a little, and he supported her as she stepped carefully from
the tub. He took another towel and began rubbing his
own head, all the while watching every move she made.

Madelyn felt warm, but incredibly lethargic. She
had no more energy than if she had been recovering
from a monster case of the flu. More than anything she
wanted to lie down in front of the fire and sleep for a
week, but she knew enough about hypothermia to be
afraid to. She sat on the toilet seat and watched him
towel dry, focusing on the magnificent strength made
more evident by his nakedness. He gave her a reason
to fight her lethargy now, just as he had when she had
been on the bottom of the pond.

He cupped her face, making certain she was paying attention. "Don't go to sleep," he warned. "Stay
in here where it's hot while I go upstairs to get your
robe. Okay?"

She nodded. "Okay."

"I won't be but a minute."

She managed a smile, just to reassure him. "Bring
my brush and comb, too."

It took several minutes, but he came back with her
robe toasty warm from the clothes dryer, and she shuddered with pleasure as he wrapped it around her. He had
taken the time to almost dress, too; he had on socks,
unsnapped jeans and a flannel shirt left unbuttoned.
He had brought socks for her, and he knelt to slip them
on her feet.

He kept his arm around her waist as they went into
the kitchen. He pulled out a chair and placed her in it.
"Open your mouth," he said, and when she did he slid
the thermometer, which he'd brought from the upstairs

bathroom, under her tongue. "Now sit there and be still while I make a pot of coffee."

That wasn't hard to do. The only thing she wanted to do more than sit still was to lie down.

When the digital thermometer twittered its alarm, he pulled it out of her mouth and frowned at it. "Ninety six point four. I want it up at least another degree."

"What about you?"

"I'm more alert than you are. I'm bigger, and I wasn't in the water as long." He could still feel a deep inner chill, but nothing like the bone-numbing cold he had felt before. The first cup of coffee almost completely dispelled the rest of the coldness, as both the heat and the caffeine did their work. He made Madelyn drink three cups of coffee, even though she had revived enough to caustically point out that, as usual, he'd made it so strong she was likely to go into caffeine overdose. He watered it down for her, his mouth wry.

When he felt safer about leaving her, he deposited her on the quilts in front of the fire. "I have to go back out," he said, and he saw panic flare in her eyes. "Not to the range," he added quickly. "I have to put the horse back in the barn and take care of him. I'll be back as soon as I'm finished."

"I'm not going anywhere," she reassured him.

She was still afraid to lie down and go to sleep, even though so much caffeine was humming through her system that she wasn't certain she would be able to go to sleep that night. She pulled the towel off her head and began combing the tangles out of her hair.

By the time he got back, her hair was dry and she was brushing it into order. He stopped in the doorway, struck as always by the intensely female beauty of the ritual. Her sleeves dropped away from her arms as she lifted them, revealing pale, slender forearms. Her neck was gracefully bent, like a flower nodding in the breeze. His throat tightened, and blood rushed to his loins as he watched her; seven months of marriage and he was still reacting to her like a stallion scenting a mare.

"How are you feeling?" The words were raspy. He had to force them out.

She looked up, her slow smile heating his blood even more. "Better. Warm and awake. How are *you* after going back out into the cold?"

"I'm okay." More than okay. They were both alive, and there wasn't a cell in his body that was cold.

He insisted on taking her temperature again and waited impatiently until the thermometer twittered. "Ninety-seven point six. Good."

"My normal temperature isn't much more than that. It usually hovers in the low ninety-eights."

"Mine is usually around ninety-nine or a little higher."

"I'm not surprised. Sleeping with you is like sleeping with a furnace."

"Complaining?"

She shook her head. "Bragging." Her smile faded, and her gray eyes darkened to charcoal as she reached out to touch his face. "I almost lost you." He saw the flash of sheer terror in her eyes just before she closed them, and he grabbed her to him with almost desperate relief.

"Baby, I came a lot closer to losing you than you did to losing me," he said roughly, moving his lips against her hair.

Madelyn wound her arms around his neck. She didn't often cry; her moods were too even and generally upbeat. The two times she had cried since their marriage had both been the result of pain, once on their wedding night and again just an hour before when the warm water in the tub had begun bringing life back into her frozen skin. But suddenly the enormity and strain of what they had been through swept over her, and her chest tightened. She tried to fight it, tried to keep her composure, but it was a losing battle. With a wrenching sob she buried her face against his throat and clung to him while her body shook with the force of her weeping.

He was more than surprised by her sudden tears, he was astounded. His Maddie was a fighter, one who met his strength with her own and didn't flinch even from his worst tempers. But now she was sobbing as if she would never stop, and the depth of her distress punched him in the chest. He crooned to her and rubbed her back, whispering reassurances as he lowered her to the quilts.

It took a long time for her sobs to quiet. He didn't try to get her to stop, sensing that she needed the release, just as he had needed the release of savagely kicking a feed bucket the length of the barn after he had taken care of his horse. He just held her until the storm was over, then gave her his handkerchief for mopping up.

Her eyelids were swollen, and she looked exhausted, but there was no more tightly wound tension in her eyes as she lay quietly in the aftermath. Reese propped himself up on an elbow and tugged at the belt of her robe, pulling it loose and then spreading the lapels to expose her nude body.

He trailed his fingers across the hollow of her throat, then over to her slender collarbone. "Have I ever told you," he asked musingly, "that just looking at you gets me so hard it hurts?"

Her voice was husky. "No, but you've demonstrated it a few times."

"It does hurt. I feel like I'm going to explode. Then, when I get inside you, the hurt changes to pleasure." He stroked his hand down to her breast, covering it with the warmth of his palm and feeling her nipple softly pushing at him. Gently he caressed her, circling the nipple with his thumb until it stood upright and darkened in color; then he bent over her to kiss the enticing little nub. Her breathing had changed, getting deeper, and a delicate flush was warming her skin. When he looked up he saw how heavy-lidded her eyes had become, and he was flooded with fiercely masculine satisfaction that he could make her look like that.

Once he had tried to deny himself the sensual pleasure of feasting on her, but no longer. He let himself be absorbed as he stroked his hand down her body, savoring the silky texture of her skin, shaping his hand to the curves and indentations that flowed from one to the other, the swell of her breast to the flat of her stomach, the flare of her hips, the notch between her legs. He watched his tanned, powerful fingers slide through the little triangle of curls and then probe between her soft folds, fascinated by the contrast between his hand and her pale feminine body.

And the taste of her. There was the heated sweetness of her mouth; he sampled it, then tasted again more deeply, making love to her with his tongue. Then there was the warm, fragrant hollow of her throat, and the rose-and-milk taste of her breasts. He lingered there for a long time, until her hands were knotting and twisting in the quilt, and her hips were lifting against him.

Her belly was cool against his lips, and silky smooth. Her tight little navel invited exploration, and he circled it with his tongue. Her hands moved into his hair and tightly pressed against his skull as he moved downward, parting her thighs and draping them over his shoulders.

She was breathing hard, her body twisting and straining. He held her hips and loved her, not stopping until she heaved upward and cried out as the waves of completion overtook her.

She felt drained, more exhausted than before. She lay limply as he knelt between her legs and tore at his clothes, throwing them aside. She could barely open her eyes as he positioned himself and then invaded her with a slow, heavy thrust that carried him into her to the hilt. As always, she was faintly startled by the overwhelming sense of fullness as she adjusted to him.

His full weight was on her, crushing her downward. There was nothing gentlemanly about him now, only the need to enter her as deeply as possible, to carry the embrace to the fullest so that there was no part of her that didn't feel his possession. His lovemaking was often dominant, but she could usually meet it with her own strength. She couldn't now; there was a savagery in him that had to be appeased, a hunger that had to be fed. Even though he restrained himself so that he never hurt her, she was helpless to do anything but lie there and accept him, and feel her passion rising within her again with a beating rhythm.

He paused when his tension reached the critical level, not wanting it to end just yet. His green eyes glittered as he framed her face in his hands and measured the strength of her arousal.

He brushed his mouth against her ear. "Did you know that a man normally has…"

She listened to the words rustling in her ear, her hands tightening on his back as she struggled for control. Though she loved their trivia game, she wasn't in the mood for it now. Finally she gasped, "I wonder why there are so many, when one will do."

In his best big-bad-wolf voice, admittedly ragged, he said, "The better to get you pregnant, my dear," and he began moving again, hard and fast. And, sometime within the next hour, he did.

CHAPTER TEN

REESE WENT OVER the figures again, but the totals didn't change. He got to his feet and looked out the window, his hands knotted into fists and his jaw set. All those years of work. All those *damn* years of work, for nothing.

He had done everything he could think of, cut down on every expense until there was nothing left that could be cut, and still those figures spelled it out in black and white: he had lost. The January blizzard that had killed half of his herd had pushed him so far under that the bank couldn't carry him any longer. He couldn't make the mortgage, and there would be no more extensions.

He had three options: one, he could let the bank foreclose, and they would lose everything; two, he could file chapter eleven bankruptcy and keep the ranch but ruin his credit; and three, he could accept Robert's offer to be an investor. He smiled grimly. Number three was an option only if Robert's offer was still open, considering that he had made it when the ranch was profitable and now it was going under fast.

He had been so close to making it. He thought that was what made the final defeat so bitter, that he had been close enough to see the end of debt. What April had started almost eight years before was finally coming to fruition: the destruction of his ranch. Who knew what her reasoning had been? Maybe she had done it because he had loved the ranch so much, more than he had ever even thought he loved her. It was his life-blood, and he was losing it, unless Robert Cannon still wanted to invest. Reese went over the options again, but Robert was his only chance, and a slim one at that, because when Robert saw the figures he would have to be a hell of a gambler to go through with the deal. Reese didn't hold out much hope, but he would make the effort, because he couldn't do otherwise. He didn't have just himself to consider now; he had Madelyn, and he would do what he could to keep her home for her. She hadn't married him expecting bankruptcy or foreclosure.

It was March; snow was still on the ground, but the throbbing promise of spring was in the air. In another week or so buds would begin to swell on the trees and bushes; the land was alive, but the taste of ashes was in his mouth, because this might be the last spring he would ever see on his ranch.

He could hear Maddie in the kitchen, humming along with the radio as she gathered the ingredients for baking a cake. She'd gotten good at baking, so good that his mouth began watering every time those warm smells drifted his way. She was happy here. He hadn't married her expecting anything more than a work part-ner, but instead he'd gotten a warm, intelligent, amus-ing and sexy woman who loved him. She never seemed embarrassed about it, never tried to pressure him into giving her more than he could; she simply loved him and didn't try to hide it.

He didn't know how he would tell her, but she had a right to know.

She was licking cake batter from a wooden spoon

when he walked in, and she gave him a wink as she held the spoon out. "Wanna lick?"

The batter was on her fingers, too. He started at her fingers and worked his way up the handle of the spoon, his tongue scooping up the sweet batter. When the spoon was clean he turned to her fingers to make certain he'd gotten it all. "Any more?"

She produced the bowl and swiped her finger around the edge, then popped it in her mouth laden with batter. "Your turn."

They cleaned the bowl like two children. That was probably Maddie's most endearing trait, the ease with which she found enjoyment in life, and she had taught him how to have fun again. It was just simple things, like their trivia game or licking a bowl, but he had lost the knack for having fun until she had entered his life and taken over.

He hated having to tell her that they might lose their home. A man was supposed to take care of his wife. Maybe that was old-fashioned and chauvinistic, but that was the way he felt. It ate at his pride like acid not to be able to provide for her.

He sighed and put his hands on her waist, his face grim. "We have to talk."

She eyed him cautiously. "I've never liked conversations that begin with that phrase."

"You won't like this one, either. It's serious."

She searched his face, her eyes becoming somber as she read his expression. "What is it?"

"When we lost half the herd, it put us under. I can't make the mortgage." That was it in a nutshell, as succinct and bald as he could make it.

"Can we get an extension—"

"No. If I had the full herd as collateral, then it would

be possible, but I don't have enough beef on the hoof to cover the outstanding debt."

"Robert said you have the best head for business he's ever seen. What do we have to do, and what can we do?"

He outlined the three things that could happen, and she listened to him with an intent expression. When he had finished she asked, "Why don't you think Robert's offer would still stand?"

"Because the ranch is a losing proposition now."

"You're still here, and it was you he was willing to bet on, not X number of cows." Then she said, "There's another option you haven't mentioned."

"What's that?"

"I told you before, I have some money—"

He dropped his hands. "No. I've told *you* before."

"Why not?" she asked calmly.

"I've told you that before, too. It hasn't changed."

"Do you mean you'd actually give up the ranch before you would let me put my money in it?"

His eyes looked like flint. "Yes, that's exactly what I mean." Maddie had changed a lot of his attitudes, but that one was still intact and as strong as ever. A business partner was one thing, because rights were limited by contract. A marriage was something else, subject to the whims of a judge with little regard to fairness. April had proved that to him.

Madelyn turned away before her expression betrayed her. Not for anything would she let him see how that hurt her. With perfect control she said, "It's your ranch, your decision."

"Exactly, and it will stay my ranch, my decision, until the day I get thrown off."

Her mind was busy as she cooked dinner, and determination grew in her. If he thought she would stand by and see the ranch go under when she had the means to save it, he would learn differently. She didn't know how much the mortgage was, and she had told him the truth when she'd said that her trust fund was far from being a fortune, but surely it was enough to buy them some time until the ranch was on a firmer footing.

He'd never said he loved her. Maybe he didn't, but Madelyn thought he was at least fond of her. He certainly desired her, though it was true that a man could physically desire a woman without caring for her as a person. If he had lived with her for nine months and still thought she was capable of doing the sort of thing April had done, then perhaps he didn't care for her as much as she'd thought. She had been happy, but now her balloon was fast going flat.

Now wasn't the time to tell him she was pregnant. Or maybe it was. Maybe knowing about the baby would bring him to his senses, reassure him that she wasn't going anywhere, and that they had to use whatever means were at their disposal to save their child's inheritance.

But she didn't tell him. His mood varied from taciturn to biting sarcasm, the way it did when he was angry, and she didn't feel like prodding him into a full-scale blowup. Though she was only two months along, she was already beginning to feel the effects of pregnancy in lower energy levels and a slightly upset stomach—not the best time to battle with her husband.

He was still in a bad mood when he left the next morning, and he took a lunch with him, which meant he wouldn't be back until it was time for dinner. Madelyn hesitated for maybe five minutes.

She didn't like going behind his back, but if that was the way it had to be, then she would face the music later. It was a long drive to Billings; she might not make it back before he did, but that was another bridge she would cross when she came to it. While she was there she would also phone around for an obstetrician, because there wasn't any sort of doctor in Crook, and she didn't know of one any closer than Billings. It could get interesting around her delivery time, she thought, with her doctor a three-hour drive away.

She hastily dressed, got her checkbook and the necessary documents, and ran out to the car. It had snow tires on it if she needed them, but the highways were clear, so she hoped she would make good time.

She drove quickly but carefully, thankful that there wasn't much traffic to contend with, and reached the bank at eleven-thirty. She knew who Reese dealt with, having accompanied him before, and she only had to wait about fifteen minutes before the man could see her.

He was smiling the way bankers do, his hand outstretched. "Good morning, Mrs. Duncan. What can we do for you?"

"Good morning, Mr. VanRoden. I'd like to know the amount of our outstanding mortgage."

He stroked his upper lip as if he had a mustache, which he didn't, and looked thoughtful. "Well, I'm not certain I can tell you. You see, the mortgage is only in your husband's name."

She didn't bother trying to argue with bureaucracy or banking rules and went straight to the point. "If it's under two hundred thousand dollars, I want to pay it off."

There was nothing that got a banker's attention like money. He chewed his lip, studying her. She sat very calmly and let him try to pick up what clues he could from her appearance, though she had deliberately dressed that morning in one of her New York suits and twisted her hair up. If he could read anything in a charcoal suit with a pink silk blouse under it and an iridescent peacock pinned to the lapel, he was welcome to draw any conclusions he could.

He made up his mind with a minimum of dithering. "Let me check the file," he said. "I'll be right back."

She waited, certain of the outcome. No bank would refuse the repayment of a loan, regardless of who was doing the paying. She supposed a rank stranger could walk in off the street and pay off any loan he chose, as long as he had the means to do it.

VanRoden was back in less than five minutes with a sheaf of papers in his hand. "I believe we're ready to talk business, Mrs. Duncan. Mr. Duncan doesn't have enough in his checking account to cover the loan, so how were you proposing to pay it?"

"I have a trust fund, Mr. VanRoden. I transferred it from New York to another bank here in Billings. First, is the outstanding debt on the mortgage less than two hundred thousand?"

He coughed. "Yes, it is."

"Then I'll be back. I'm going to my bank now to have the trust fund transferred into my checking account. I've had full access to it since I was twenty-five, so there's no problem."

He pushed the telephone toward her. "Call them, so they'll let you in. They'll be closing for lunch shortly."

She smiled at him as she reached for the phone. "By the way, do you know a good obstetrician?"

A phone call later, it had been arranged for her to enter the other bank by a side door. An hour later she was back at the first bank, cashier's check in hand for the amount VanRoden had given her before she left.

She signed the necessary papers and walked out of the bank with the deed to the ranch and the papers that said the debt had been paid in full. She also had an appointment the following week with the obstetrician VanRoden's wife had used. She grinned as she got into the car. Contacts had their uses, even unlikely ones. Poor Mr. VanRoden had looked startled at being asked to recommend an obstetrician, then had offered his congratulations.

She had no illusions that everything was going to be fine now just because she had paid the mortgage. She hadn't done it lightly; she had done it with the full knowledge that Reese would be furious, but she was willing to fight for their future, their child's future. She had to deal with the scars left by Reese's first marriage, and this was far more serious than painting the house. As a matter of fact, he *had* drawn up a note stating that he would repay her for the cost of the paint and estimated labor, which she thought was ridiculous, but was a fair measure of how determined he was in the matter.

But knowing she had to tell him and knowing how to tell him were two different things. She couldn't just say, "I went into Billings today to make an appointment with an obstetrician because I'm pregnant, and by the way, while I was there I paid off the mortgage." On the other hand, that was certainly a good example of killing two birds with one stone.

She was still worrying it over in her mind when she got home at about four-thirty. There was no sign of Reese's truck, so perhaps she had made it without him even knowing she'd been gone. If he had come back to the house for any reason during the day, he'd ask questions as soon as he got back, and one thing she wouldn't do was lie to him. Delaying telling him about the mortgage was different from lying to him about it.

It was amazing how tired she was, and equally amazing how she could feel so exhausted but still feel well.

She would be having his baby sometime late in October or early in November, if she had figured correctly. The knowledge of it was like a great inner warmth, and she had never wanted anything more than to share it with him. Only the worry he had been enduring over the ranch had kept her from telling him, because she didn't want to give him something else to worry about. The stern lines in his face were deeper, and his eyes were habitually grim these days, as he faced losing everything he had worked so hard for, for so long. How could she burden him with the knowledge that now they had medical bills to consider, as well?

How could she *not* tell him?

As she changed clothes, her fatigue suddenly became overwhelming. She fought it, knowing that it was time to begin cooking dinner, but the thought of all that preparation made the fatigue even worse, and her stomach suddenly rolled. She broke out in a sweat and sank weakly onto the bed. What a great time for morning sickness to hit—late in the afternoon on a day when she needed all her wits about her. She sat there for a minute, and the nausea faded, but the fatigue was worse. There was no way she could summon the energy even to go downstairs; exhaustion pulled on her limbs and eyelids, dragging both down. With a sigh she stretched out on the bed, her eyes already closing. Just a short nap; that was all she needed.

Reese found her there. He had noticed that the kitchen light wasn't on when he got home, but he had taken care of the evening chores before going into the house. The kitchen was empty, with no sign of meal preparations in progress, and the house was strangely silent. "Maddie?" When there was no answer, a worried frown creased his forehead, and he searched the downstairs, then started up the stairs. "Maddie?"

He turned on the light in the bedroom, and there she was, curled on her side on the bed. She didn't stir even when the light came on. He'd never known her to nap during the day, and he was instantly alarmed. Was she sick? She had seemed okay that morning. He was dirty from the day's work, but he didn't care about that as he sat down on the side of the bed and turned her onto her back. She felt warm under his hands, but not unusually so. He shook her, and worry sharpened his tone. "Maddie, wake up!"

Slowly her lids drifted upward, and she sighed. "Reese," she murmured, but she couldn't keep her eyes open.

He shook her again. "Are you all right? Wake up."

Reluctantly she roused, lifting one hand to rub her eyes. "What time is it?" Then she looked at him again as realization sank in and said, "Oh my God, dinner!"

"Dinner can wait. Are you all right?"

Her heart lurched as she stared up at him. His face was lined and grayish with fatigue, but there was worry in his eyes, not irritation. Automatically she reached up to touch his cheek, stroking her fingers over the high ridge of his cheekbone. She loved everything about this man, even his stubborn temper. She took his hand and placed it on her belly. "I'm pregnant," she whispered. "We're having a baby."

His pupils dilated, and he looked down at his hand on her slender body. From the time she had stopped taking the birth control pills, every time he had made love to her he had been aware that he might impregnate her, but the reality of having her say she was pregnant was still almost a physical shock. His baby was growing under his hand, utterly protected in her flat little belly.

He slid off the bed onto his knees beside it, still dazed. "When?" he asked in a strained tone.

"The last week in October, or the first week in November."

He unsnapped her jeans and slid the zipper down, then spread the fly open so he could touch her skin. He pushed her sweatshirt up out of the way and slowly leaned forward, first pressing a light kiss to her belly, then resting his cheek against it. Madelyn stroked his hair and wondered if the baby would have dark coloring like him or her fairness. It was such a new, wonderful consideration, their child, created from the raw passion that still burned between them. Seven more months suddenly seemed too long to wait to hold it, to see Reese's powerful hands turn gentle as he cradled his child. "Do you want a boy or a girl?" she asked, still whispering, as if normal speech might spoil the sweetness of this moment.

"Does it matter?" He rubbed his rough cheek against her belly, his eyes closing as he luxuriated in the caress.

"Not to me."

"Or to me." Silence grew in the room as he fully absorbed the news; then finally he lifted his head. "Are you feeling sick?"

"I was a little nauseated, but mostly I was incredibly tired. I tried, but I just couldn't keep my eyes open," she said apologetically.

"Are you all right now?"

She thought about it, mentally taking stock of herself, then nodded. "All systems are go."

He moved back and let her get to her feet, then caught her to him and tilted her mouth up. The expression in his eyes was intense as he gave her a hard, brief kiss. "Are you certain?"

"I'm certain." She smiled and looped her arms around his neck, letting her weight swing from them. "You'll know if I'm feeling sick. I'll turn green and keel over."

He cupped her bottom and held her against him as he kissed her again, and this time there was nothing brief about it. Madelyn held him tightly, her eyes closing as his familiar nearness sent warmth through her. She loved him so much it sometimes frightened her; she hoped he would remember that.

His lovemaking that night was achingly tender and incredibly prolonged. He couldn't seem to get enough of her, taking her again and again, staying inside her for a long time afterward. They finally went to sleep like that, with her leg thrown over his hip, and she thought it had never been more perfect than it was then, with Reese in her arms and his child in her womb.

A WEEK LATER Reese walked back to the house from the barn with a defeated expression on his face. Madelyn watched him from the kitchen window and knew she couldn't put it off any longer. She simply couldn't let him worry any longer; better to enrage him than watch the lines settle deeper in his face every day. He would sit in his office for hours every night, going over and over the books, pacing and running his hands through his hair, then trying it again, only to come up with the same figures and no hope.

She heard him come in and take off his muddy boots;

then he came into the kitchen in his sock feet. "The truck needs a new oil pump," he said tiredly.

She twisted the hand towel she was holding. "Then buy one." Tension was tightening her muscles, and she swallowed the faint rise of nausea.

His mouth was bitter. "Why bother? We won't be here another month anyway."

Slowly she hung up the towel then turned to face him, leaning back against the cabinet for support. "Yes, we will."

He thought he knew what she meant. He could call Robert—but Robert would have to be a fool to invest in the ranch now. He had put it off as long as he could, and now he didn't see anything else he could do. Madelyn was pregnant; she had her first doctor's appointment the next day, and money would be required up front. Then they were facing bills from the hospital, and he didn't have medical insurance. That had been one of the first things to go.

"I'll call Robert," he said gently. "But don't hope too much."

She put her shoulders back and took a deep breath. "Call Robert if you want, after I tell you what I have to tell you. You'll be in a different situation then and—" She stopped, looking at him helplessly, and began again. "I paid off the mortgage with my trust fund."

For a moment he didn't react at all, just watched her silently, and she started to hope. Then his eyes began to chill, and she braced herself.

"What?" he asked very softly.

"I paid off the mortgage. The papers are in my underwear drawer."

Without a word he turned and went upstairs. Madelyn followed, her heart pounding. She had faced his anger before without turning a hair, but this was different. This was striking at the very basis of his feelings.

He jerked her underwear drawer open just as she entered the bedroom. She hadn't stuffed the papers in the bottom; they were lying right there in plain sight. He picked them up and flipped through them, noting the amount and date on the documents.

He didn't look up. "How did you arrange it?"

"I went to Billings last week, the day you told me about the mortgage. Banks don't care who pays off loans so long as they get their money, and since I'm your wife they didn't question it."

"Did you think presenting me with a fait accompli would change my mind?"

She wished that he would stop using that soft voice. When Reese was angry he roared, and she could handle that, but this was something new.

His head came up, and she flinched. His eyes were like green ice. "Answer me."

She stood very still. "No, I didn't think anything would change your mind, and that's why I did it behind your back."

"You were right. Nothing would change my mind. I'll see you in hell before you get any part of this ranch."

"I don't want to take the ranch away from you. I've never wanted that."

"You've played your part well, Maddie, I'll give you that. You haven't complained, you've acted like a perfect wife. You even carried it so far as to pretend you love me."

"I do love you." She took a step toward him, her hands outstretched. "Listen—"

Suddenly the rage in him erupted, and he threw the sheaf of papers at her. They separated and swirled around her, then drifted to the floor. "That's what I think of your so-called 'love,'" he said with gritted teeth. "If you think doing something you knew I couldn't bear is an expression of 'love,' then you don't have any idea what the real thing is."

"I didn't want you to lose the ranch—"

"So you just took care of the mortgage. Any divorce court now would consider you a co-owner, wouldn't they? They'd figure I talked you into investing your inheritance and the prenuptial agreement wouldn't mean a damn. Hell, why should you get less than April? This isn't the operation it once was, but the land is worth a hell of a lot."

"I don't want a divorce, I haven't even thought of divorce," she said desperately. "I wanted to keep the ranch for you. At least this way you have a chance to rebuild it, if you'll just take it!"

He said sarcastically, "Yeah, if it's worth more, you'll get more."

"For the last time, I don't want a divorce!"

He reached out and pinched her chin, the gesture savagely playful. "You just might get one anyway, dollface, because I sure as hell don't want a wife who'd knife me in the back like that. You weren't my first choice, and I should have listened to my instincts, but you had me as hot as a sixteen-year-old after my first piece in the backseat. April was a bitch, but you're worse, Maddie, because you played along and pretended this was just what you wanted. Then you slipped the blade between my ribs so slick I never even saw it coming."

"This *is* what I want." She was pale, her eyes darkening.

"Well, you're not what I want. You're hot between

the sheets, but you don't have what it takes to be a ranch wife," he said cruelly.

"Reese Duncan, if you're trying to run me off, you're doing a good job of it," she warned shakily.

He raised his eyebrows. His tone was icily polite. "Where would you like to go? I'll give you a ride."

"If you'll climb down off that mountain of pride you'll see how wrong you are! I don't want to take the ranch away. I want to live here and raise our children here. You and I aren't the only ones involved in this. I'm carrying your baby, and it's his heritage, too!"

His eyes went black as he remembered the baby, and his gaze swept down her slender figure. "On second thought, you aren't going anywhere. You're staying right here until that baby's born. Then I don't care what the hell *you* do, but my kid is staying with me."

Coldness settled inside her, pushing away the hurt and anger that had been building with every word he said. Understanding could go only so far. Sympathy held out only so long. He didn't love her, and he didn't believe in her love for him, so exactly how much of a marriage did they have? One made of mirrors and moonshine, and held together by sex. She stared at him, her eyes going blank. Later there would be pain, but not now.

She said very carefully, "When you calm down you'll regret saying this."

"The only thing I regret is marrying you." He took her purse from the top of the dresser and opened it.

"What are you looking for?" She made no effort to grab it from him. In any test of strength against him she would be humiliated.

He held up the car keys. "These." He dropped her purse and shoved the keys into his pocket. "Like I said, you're not going anywhere with my kid inside you. The only moving you're doing is out of my bed. There are three other bedrooms. Pick one, and keep your butt in it."

He stalked from the room, being very careful not to touch her. Madelyn sank down on the bed, her legs folding under her like spaghetti. She could barely breathe, and dark spots swam in front of her eyes. Cold chills made her shake.

She didn't know how long it was before her mind began to function again, but finally it did, slowly at first, then with gathering speed. She began to get angry, a calm, deep, slow-burning anger that grew until it had destroyed all the numbness.

She got up and began methodically moving her things out of Reese's bedroom and into the room where she had slept the night she had visited him. She didn't move a few token things in the hope that he would get over his temper, reconsider and tell her to stay put; she purged the bedroom of all signs of her presence. She left the mortgage papers lying where they were in the middle of the room. Let him walk over them if he didn't want to pick them up.

If he wanted war, she'd give him war.

Pride prompted her to stay in her bedroom and not speak to him; pregnancy insisted that she eat. She went downstairs and cooked a full meal in an effort to rub a little salt in his wounds. If he didn't want to eat what she had prepared, then he could either do it himself or do without.

But he came to the table when she called him and ate his usual hearty meal. As she was clearing the dishes away she said, "Don't forget the doctor's appointment in the morning."

He didn't look at her. "I'll drive you. You aren't getting the keys back."

"Fine."

Then she went upstairs, showered and went to bed.

The next morning they didn't speak a word all the way to Billings. When her name was called in the doctor's office, which was filled with women in various stages of pregnancy, she got up and walked past him to follow the nurse. He turned his head, watching the graceful sway of her retreating figure. In a few months she would lose her grace and the sway would become a waddle. His hand tightened into a fist, and it was all he could do to keep from swearing aloud. *How could she have done that to him?*

Madelyn was questioned, stuck, checked, probed and measured. When she had dressed she was directed into the doctor's office, and in a moment Reese joined her, followed shortly by the doctor.

"Well, everything looks normal," the doctor said, consulting his charts. "You're in good physical shape, Mrs. Duncan. Your uterus is enlarged more like thirteen or fourteen weeks than the nine or ten you think it should be, so you may be off on your conception date. We'll do an ultrasound when you're further along to get a better idea of the baby's maturity. It could just be a large baby, or twins. I see that your maternal grandmother was a twin, and multiple births usually follow the female line."

Reese sat up straight, his eyes sharpening. "Is there any danger in having twins?"

"Not much. They usually come a little early, and we have to be careful about that. At this stage of the game, I'm more worried about a large baby than I am twins. Your wife should be able to have twins without a problem, as their birth weight is usually lower than that of a single baby. The total is more, but the individual weights are less. How much did you weigh when you were born, Mr. Duncan?"

"Ten pounds, two ounces." His mouth was grim.

"I'll want to keep a very close eye on your wife if this baby approaches a birth weight of anything over eight pounds. She has a narrow pelvis, not drastically so, but a ten-pound baby would probably require a C-section."

That said, he began talking to Madelyn about her diet, vitamins and rest, and he gave her several booklets about prenatal care. When they left half an hour later, Madelyn was weighted down with prescriptions and reading material. Reese drove to a pharmacy, where he had the prescriptions filled, then headed home again. Madelyn sat straight and silent beside him. When they got home, he realized that she hadn't looked at him once all day.

CHAPTER ELEVEN

THE NEXT MORNING as he started to leave she asked coolly, "Can you hear the car horn blow from anywhere on the ranch?"

He looked startled. "Of course not." He eyed her questioningly, but she still wasn't looking at him.

"Then how am I supposed to find you or contact you?"

"Why would you want to?" he asked sarcastically.

"I'm pregnant. I could fall, or start to miscarry. Any number of things."

It was an argument he couldn't refute. He set his jaw, faced with the choice between giving her the means to leave or endangering both her life and that of his baby. When it came down to it, he didn't have a choice. He took the keys from his pocket and slammed them down on the cabinet, but he kept his hand on them.

"Do I have your word you won't run?"

She looked at him finally, but her eyes were cool and blank. "No. Why should I waste my breath making promises when you wouldn't believe me anyway?"

"Just what is it you want me to believe? That you haven't worked it so you have just as much claim to the ranch as I have? A woman made a fool of me once and walked away with half of everything I owned, but it won't happen again, even if I have to burn this house to the ground and sell the land for a loss, is that clear?"

He was shouting by the time he finished, and he looked at her as if he hated the sight of her.

Madelyn didn't show any expression or move. "If that was all I'd wanted, I could have paid off the mortgage at any time."

Her point scored; she saw it in his eyes. She could have followed it up, but she held her peace. She had given him something to think about. She would give him a lot more to think about before this was over.

He banged out of the house, leaving the car keys on the cabinet. She picked them up, tossing them in her hand as she went upstairs to the bedroom, where she already had some clothes packed. In the two nights she had spent alone in this room, she had thought through what she was going to do and where she was going to go. Reese would expect her to go running back to New York now that she had a claim on the ranch, but she had never even considered that. To teach him the lesson he needed, she had to be close by.

It would be just like him to deliberately work close by in case she tried to leave, so she didn't, and felt fierce satisfaction when he came home for lunch after telling her that he would be out all day. Since she hadn't cooked anything, she made a plate of sandwiches and put it in front of him, then continued with what she had been doing before, which was cleaning the oven.

He asked, "Aren't you going to eat?"

"I've already eaten."

A few minutes later he asked, "Should you be doing work like that?"

"It isn't hard."

Her cool tone discouraged any more conversational overtures. She wasn't letting him off that easy. She had told him twice that she wasn't going to pay for April's sins, but it evidently hadn't sunk in; now she was going to show him.

When he left again she waited half an hour, then carried her suitcase out to the car. She didn't have far to go, and it wouldn't take him long to find her, a few days at the most. Then he could take the car back if he wanted, so she didn't feel guilty about it. Besides, she didn't need it. She fully expected to be back at the ranch before her next doctor's appointment, but if she wasn't, then she would inform Reese that he had to take her. Her plan had nothing to do with staying away from him.

There was a room above Floris's café that was always for rent, because there was never anyone in Crook who needed to rent it. It would do for her for as long as she needed it. She drove to Crook and parked the car in front of the café. The idea wasn't to hide from Reese; she wanted him to know exactly where she was.

She went into the café, but there wasn't anyone behind the counter. "Floris? Is anyone here?"

"Hold your water," came Floris's unmistakable sour voice from the kitchen. A few minutes later she came through the door. "You want coffee, or something to eat?"

"I want to rent the room upstairs."

Floris stopped and narrowed her eyes at Madelyn. "What do you want to do that for?"

"Because I need a place to stay."

"You've got a big house back on that ranch, and a big man to keep you warm at night, if that's all you need."

"What I have," Madelyn said very clearly, "is a pigheaded husband who needs to be taught a lesson."

"Hmmph. Never seen a man yet wasn't pigheaded."

"I'm pregnant, too."

"Does he know?"

"He does."

"He knows where you are?"

"He will soon. I'm not hiding from him. He'll probably come through the door breathing fire and raising hell, but I'm not going back until he understands a few things."

"Such as?"

"Such as I'm not his first wife. He got a dirty deal, but I'm not the one who gave it to him, and I'm tired of paying for someone else's dirt."

Floris looked her up and down, then nodded, and a pleased expression for once lit her sour face. "All right, the room's yours. I always did like to see a man get his comeuppance," she muttered as she turned to go back into the kitchen. Then she stopped and looked back at Madelyn. "You got any experience as a short-order cook?"

"No. Do you need one?"

"Wouldn't have asked if I didn't. I'm doing the cooking and waitressing, too. That sorry Lundy got mad because I told him his eggs were like rubber and quit on me last week."

Madelyn considered the situation and found she liked it. "I could wait on tables."

"You ever done that before?"

"No, but I've taken care of Reese for nine months."

Floris grunted. "I guess that qualifies you. He don't strike me as an easy man to satisfy. Well, you in good health? I don't want you on your feet if you're having trouble keeping that baby."

"Perfect health. I saw a doctor yesterday."

"Then the job's yours. I'll show you the room. It's nothing fancy, but it's warm during the winter."

The room was clean and snug, and that was about

the limit of its virtues, but Madelyn didn't mind. There was a single bed, a couch, a card table with two chairs, a hot plate and a minuscule bathroom with cracking tile. Floris turned on the heat so it would get warm and returned to the kitchen while Madelyn carried her suitcases in. After hanging up her clothes in the small closet, she went downstairs to the café, tied an apron around her and took up her duties as waitress.

WHEN REESE GOT home that night he was dead tired; he'd been kicked, stepped on and had a rope burn on his arm. The cows would begin dropping their spring calves any time, and that would be even more work, especially if a cold front moved in.

When he saw that the car was gone and the house was dark, it was like taking a kick in the chest, punching the air out of him. He stared at the dark windows, filled with a paralyzing mixture of pain and rage. He hadn't really thought she would leave. Deep down, he had expected her to stay and fight it out, toe-to-toe and chin to chin, the way she'd done so many times. Instead she'd left, and he closed his eyes at the piercing realization that she was exactly what he'd most feared: a grasping, shallow woman who wasn't able to take the hard times. She'd run back to the city and her cushy life-style, the stylish clothes.

And she'd taken his baby with her.

It was a betrayal ten times worse than anything April had done to him. He had begun to trust Maddie, begun to let himself think of their future in terms of years rather than just an unknown number of months. She had lain beneath him and willingly let him get her pregnant; for most of a year she had lived with him, cooked for him, washed his clothes, laughed and teased and worked alongside him, slept in his arms.

Then she had stabbed him in the back. It was a living nightmare, and he was living it for the second time.

He walked slowly into the house, his steps dragging. There were no warm, welcoming smells in the kitchen, no sound except for the hum of the refrigerator and the ticking of the clock. Despite everything, he had a desperate, useless hope that she'd had to go somewhere, that there was a note of explanation somewhere in the house. He searched all the rooms, but there was no note. He went into the bedroom where she had spent the past two nights and found the dresser drawers empty, the bathroom swept clean of the fragrant female paraphernalia. He was still trying to get used to not seeing her clothes in the closet beside his; to find them nowhere in the house was staggering.

It was like pouring salt into an open wound, but he went into the other bedroom where she had stored her "New York" clothes. It was as if he had to check every missing sign of her inhabitance to verify her absence, a wounded and bewildered animal sniffing around for his mate before he sat down and howled his anger and loss at the world.

But when he opened the closet door he stared at the row of silk blouses, hung on satin-padded hangers and protected by plastic covers, the chic suits and lounging pajamas, the high-heeled shoes in a dozen colors and styles. A faint hint of her perfume wafted from the clothes, and he broke out in a sweat, staring at them.

Swiftly he went downstairs. Her books were still here, and her stereo system. She might be gone now, but she had left a lot of her things here, and that meant she would be back. She would probably come back during the day, when she would expect him to be gone, so she could pack the rest and leave without ever seeing him.

But if she were going back to New York, as she almost certainly had been planning, why had she taken her ranch clothes and left the city clothes?

Who knew why Madelyn did anything? he thought wearily. Why had she paid off the mortgage with her trust fund when she knew that was the one thing, given his past, that he would be unable to bear?

He'd never in his life been angrier, not even when he had sat in a courtroom and heard a judge hand over half his ranch to April. He hadn't expected anything better from April, who had given him ample demonstration of just how vindictive and callous she could be. But when Maddie had blindsided him like that, she had really hit him hard and low, and he was still reeling. Every time he tried to think about it, the pain and anger were so great that they crowded out everything else.

Well, she was gone, so he'd have plenty of time to think about it now. But she would have a hell of a time getting back in to get her things while he was gone, because the first chance he got he was going to change the locks on the house.

For now, however, he was going to do something he hadn't done even when April had done such a good job of wrecking his life. He was going to get the bottle of whiskey that had been in the cupboard for so many years and get dead drunk. Maybe then he would be able to sleep without Maddie beside him.

He felt like hell the next day, with a pounding head and a heaving stomach, but he dragged himself up and took care of the animals; it wasn't their fault he was a damn fool. By the time his headache began to fade and he began to feel halfway human again, it was too late to go to the general store to buy new locks.

The next day the cows began dropping their calves. It was the same every time: when the first one went into labor and drifted away to find a quiet place to calve, the others one by one followed suit. And they could pick some of the damnedest places to have their calves. It was an almost impossible task for one man to track down the cows in their hiding places, make certain the little newborns were all right, help the cows who were in difficulty and take care of the calves who were born dead or sickly. Instinct always went wrong with at least one cow, and she would refuse to have anything to do with her new baby, meaning Reese had to either get another cow to adopt it or take it to the barn for hand-feeding.

It was three days before he had a minute to rest, and when he did he dropped down on the couch in an exhausted stupor and slept for sixteen hours.

It was almost a week after Madelyn had left before he finally got time to drive to Crook. The pain and anger had become an empty, numb feeling in his chest.

The first thing he saw as he passed Floris's café was the white Ford station wagon parked out front.

His heart lurched wildly, and the bottom dropped out of his stomach. She was back, probably on her way to get the rest of her things. He parked next door in front of the general store and stared at the car, his fingers drumming on the steering wheel. The familiar anger exploded into the numb vacuum, and something became immediately, blindingly clear to him.

He wasn't going to let her go. If he had to fight her in every court in the country, he was going to keep his ranch intact and she was going to stay his wife. He'd been glad to see the last of April, but there was no way he was going to let Maddie just walk out. She was carrying his baby, a baby that was going to grow up in his house if he had to tie Maddie to the bed every day when he left.

He got out of the truck and strode toward the café, his boot heels thudding on the wooden sidewalk, his face set.

He pushed open the door and walked inside, standing in the middle of the room as he surveyed the booths and tables. There was no long-legged blonde with a lazy smile at any of them, though two lean and bandy-legged cowboys straddled stools at the counter.

Then the kitchen door opened and his long-legged blonde came through it, wrapped in an apron and carrying two plates covered with enormous hamburgers and mounds of steaming French fries. She flicked a glance at him and neither changed expression or missed a beat as she set the plates in front of the cowboys. "Here you go. Let me know if you want any pie. Floris baked an apple cobbler this morning that'll make you cry, it tastes so good."

Then she looked at him with those blank, cool eyes and said, "What can I get for you?"

The cowboys looked around, and one coughed when he saw who Madelyn was talking to; Reese pretty well knew everybody in a hundred-mile range, and they knew him, too, by sight if not personally. Everyone also knew Madelyn; a woman with her looks and style didn't go unnoticed, so it was damn certain those two cowboys realized it was her husband standing behind them looking like a thunderstorm about to spit lightning and hail all over them.

In a calm, deadly voice Reese said, "Bring me a cup

of coffee," and went over to fold his long length into one of the booths.

She brought it immediately, sliding the coffee and a glass of water in front of him. Then she gave him an impersonal smile that didn't reach her eyes and said, "Anything else?" She was already turning to go as she said it.

He snapped his hand out, catching her wrist and pulling her to a halt. He felt the slenderness of her bones under his fingers and was suddenly, shockingly aware of how physically overmatched she was with him, yet she had never backed away from him. Even in bed, when he had held her slim hips in his hands and thrust heavily into her, she had wrapped those legs around him and taken everything he could give her. Maddie wasn't the type to run, unless leaving was something she had planned from the beginning. But if that were so, why was she here? Why hadn't she gone back to New York, out of his reach?

"Sit down," he said in a low, dangerous voice.

"I have work to do."

"I said to sit down." Using his grip on her wrist, he pulled her down into the booth. She was still watching him with those cool, distant eyes.

"What are you doing here?" he snapped, ignoring the looks the two cowboys were giving him.

"I work here."

"That's what I meant. What the *hell* are you doing working here?"

"Supporting myself. What did you expect me to do?"

"I expected you to keep your little butt on the ranch like I told you to."

"Why should I stay where I'm not wanted? By the

way, if you can figure out a way to get the car home, feel free to take it. I don't need it."

With an effort he controlled the anger and impatience building in him. It might be just what she wanted, for him to lose his temper in a public place.

"Where are you staying?" he asked in a voice that showed the strain he was under.

"Upstairs."

"Get your clothes. You're going home with me."

"No."

"What did you say?"

"I said no. N-O. It's a two-letter word signifying refusal."

He flattened his hands on the table to keep himself from grabbing her and giving her a good shaking, or from pulling her onto his lap and kissing her senseless. Right at the moment, he wasn't certain which it would be. "I'm not putting up with this, Maddie. Get upstairs and get your clothes." Despite himself, he couldn't keep his voice down, and the two cowboys were openly staring at him.

She slid out of the booth and was on her feet before he could grab her, and he was reminded that, when she chose, Maddie could move like the wind. "Give me one good reason why I should!" she fired back at him, the chill in her eyes beginning to heat now.

"Because you're carrying my baby!" he roared, surging to his own feet.

"You're the one who said, quote, that you didn't care what the hell I did and that you regret marrying me, unquote. I was carrying the baby then, too, so what's different now?"

"I changed my mind."

"Well, bully for you! You also told me that I'm not

what you want and I don't have what it takes to be a ranch wife. That's another quote."

One of the cowboys cleared his throat. "You sure look like you've got what it takes to me, Miss Maddie."

Reese rounded on the cowboy with death in his eyes and his fist clenched. "Do you want to wear your teeth or carry them?" he asked in an almost soundless voice.

The cowboy still seemed to be having trouble with his throat. He cleared it again, but it took him two tries before he managed to say, "Just making a comment."

"Then make it outside. This is between me and my wife."

In the West, a man broke his own horses and killed his own snakes, and everybody else kept their nose the hell out of his business. The cowboy fumbled in his pocket for a couple of bills and laid them on the counter. "Let's go," he said to his friend.

"You go on." The other cowboy forked up a fry covered in ketchup. "I'm not through eating." *Or watching the show, either.*

Floris came through the kitchen door, her sour expression intact and a spatula in her hand. "Who's making all the noise out here?" she demanded; then her gaze fell on Reese. "Oh, it's you." She made it sound as if he were about as welcome as the plague.

"I've come to take Maddie home," he said.

"Don't see why she'd want to go, you being so sweet-tempered and all."

"She's my wife."

"She can wait on men here and get paid for it." She shook the spatula at him. "What have you got to offer her besides that log in your pants?"

Reese's jaw was like granite. He could toss Madelyn over his shoulder and carry her home, but even though he was willing to bully her, he didn't want to physically force her. For one thing, she was pregnant, but more important, he wanted her to go home with him because she wanted to. One look at her face told him that she wasn't going to willingly take a step toward the ranch.

Well, he knew where she was now. She hadn't gone back to New York. She was within reach, and he wasn't giving up. With one last violent look at her, he threw his money on the table and stomped out.

Madelyn slowly let out the breath she'd been holding. That had been close. He was evidently as determined to take her back to the ranch as he was to believe she was a clone of his first wife. And if she knew one thing about Reese Duncan, it was that he was as stubborn as any mule, and he didn't give up. He'd be back.

She picked up his untouched coffee and carried it back to the counter. Floris looked at the door that was still quivering from the force with which Reese had slammed it, then turned to Madelyn with the most incredible expression on her face. It was like watching the desert floor crack as her leathered skin moved and rearranged itself, and a look of unholy glee came into her eyes. The two cowboys watched in shock as Floris actually smiled.

The older woman held out her hand, palm up and fingers stiffly extended. Madelyn slapped her own hand down on it in victory, then reversed the position for Floris's slap as they gave each other a congratulatory low five.

"Wife one, husband zero," Floris said with immense satisfaction.

HE WAS BACK the next day, sliding into a booth and watching her with hooded eyes as she took care of the customers. The little café was unusually busy today, and he wondered with a sourness that would have done credit to Floris if it was because word of their confrontation the day before had spread. There was nothing like a free floor show to draw people in.

She looked tired today, and he wondered if she'd been sick. She'd had a few bouts of nausea before she'd left, but her morning sickness hadn't been full-blown. From the way she looked now, it was getting there. It made him even angrier, because if she'd been at home where she belonged she would have been able to lie down and rest.

Without asking, she brought a cup of coffee to him and turned to go. Like a replay of the day before, his hand shot out and caught her. He could almost feel everyone's attention fastening on them like magnets. "Have you been sick?" he asked roughly.

"This morning. It passed when Floris fed me some dry toast. Excuse me, I have other customers."

He let her go because he didn't want another scene like yesterday's. He sipped the coffee and watched her as she moved among the customers, dispensing a smile here and a teasing word there, drawing laughter and making faces light up. That was a talent of hers, finding amusement in little things and inviting others to share it with her, almost enticing them. She had done the same thing to him, he realized. The nine months she'd spent with him had been the most contented of his life, emotionally and physically.

He wanted her back. He wanted to watch the lazy way she strolled around the house and accomplished miracles without seeming to put forth much effort at all. He wanted her teasing him, waking him up with some outlandish bit of trivia and expecting him to match it.

He wanted to pull her beneath him, spread her legs and penetrate her body with his, make her admit that she still loved him and would rather be with him than anywhere else.

He didn't understand why she wasn't in New York, why she had only come as far as Crook and stopped, knowing he would soon find her. Hell, running to Crook wasn't running away at all, it was simply moving a little piece down the road.

The only answer was that she had never intended to go back to New York. She hadn't wanted the big city; she had just wanted to get away from him.

The memory of all he'd said to her played in his mind, and he almost flinched. She remembered every word of it, too; she had even quoted some of them back to him. She'd told him at the time that he would regret saying them, but he'd been too enraged, feeling too betrayed, to pay any attention to her. He should have remembered that Maddie gave as good as she got.

She could so easily have gone to New York; she had the money in her checking account to do whatever she wanted, and Robert would welcome her back without question. So if she had stayed it had to be because she liked living in Montana. Even the question of revenge could just as easily have been played out from New York as from Crook, because it was her absence from his house that was punishing him. The emptiness of it was driving him crazy.

Eventually she came back by with the coffeepot to refill his cup and ask, "Do you want some pie with that? It's fresh coconut today."

"Sure." It would give him an excuse to stay longer.

The café eventually had to clear out some. The customers had other things they had to do, and Reese hadn't done anything interesting enough to make them stay. When Madelyn coasted by to pick up his empty dessert saucer and refill his cup she asked, "Don't you have any work to do?"

"Plenty. The cows dropped their spring calves."

Just for a second her eyes lit; then she shrugged and turned away. He said, "Wait. Sit down a minute and rest. You haven't been off your feet since I got here and that's been—" he stopped to check his watch "—two hours ago."

"It's been busy this morning. You don't stop working a herd just because you want to rest, do you?"

Despite himself, he couldn't help grinning at her comparison between a herd of cattle and her customers. "Sit down anyway. I'm not going to yell at you."

"Well, that's a change," she muttered, but she sat down across from him and propped her feet on the seat beside him, stretching her legs out. He lifted her feet and placed them on his knee, rubbing the calves of her legs under the table and holding her firmly in place when she automatically tried to pull away.

"Just relax," he said quietly. "Should you be on your feet this much?"

"I'd be on my feet if I were still at the ranch. I didn't cook sitting down, you know. I feel fine. I'm just pregnant, not incapacitated." But she closed her eyes as his kneading fingers worked at her tired muscles; he had a good touch, one learned from years of working with animals.

He had a good touch in bed, too. Every woman should have a lover like Reese, wild and hungry, as generous with his own body as he was demanding of hers. The memories pooled in her stomach like lava, raising her temperature, and her eyes popped open. If she let herself think about it too much, she would be in his lap before she knew what she was doing.

Reese said, "I want you to come home with me."

If he had been angrily demanding she could have met him with her own anger, but his quiet tone invited instead of demanded. She sighed and leaned her elbows on the table. "My answer is still the same. Give me one good reason why I should."

"And my answer is still the same. You're carrying my baby. It deserves to have its heritage, to grow up on the ranch. You even told me that was one of the reasons you paid the mortgage, to preserve the ranch for our children."

"I haven't taken the baby away from Montana," she pointed out. "I haven't even gone far from the ranch. The baby will have you and the ranch, but I don't have to live there for that to be possible."

"Miss Maddie, you got any more of that coffee?" a customer called, and she pulled her feet down from his lap without another word, going about her business with a smile.

Reese finally gave up and went home, but he tossed in the big bed all night, thinking of her breasts and the way she tasted, the way it felt to slide into her and feel her tight inner clinging, hear the soft sounds she made as he brought her to pleasure.

He had to mend fences the next day, and he worked automatically, his mind still on Maddie, trying to figure out how to get her back.

She'd made a telling point when she had asked him why she hadn't paid the mortgage before, if all she'd wanted had been a legal interest in the ranch that would override any prenuptial agreement, and now he had to ask himself the same thing. If that was all she'd wanted, why had she waited nine months? Why had she chased chickens and cows, fought blizzards and risked her own life to save his if she'd been planning on getting out? Even more telling, why had she gone off her birth control pills and let him get her pregnant? That baby she carried was a planned baby, one they had talked about and agreed to have. A woman didn't deliberately get pregnant if she'd been planning to spend only a few months and then get out. The land was worth a fortune; if money had been all she wanted, paying off the mortgage had entitled her to a great deal without the added, admittedly powerful, asset of a pregnancy. No, she had gotten pregnant only because she'd wanted this baby, and she had paid off the mortgage for one reason: to save the ranch for him, Reese Duncan. She might say she was saving her child's heritage, but the baby was still an abstract, an unknown person, however powerful her budding maternal instincts were. She had saved the ranch for her husband, not her child.

Beyond that, Maddie didn't need money. With Robert Cannon for a stepbrother, she could have anything she wanted just by asking. Robert Cannon had money that made April's family look like two-bit pikers.

It all kept coming back to the same thing, the same question. Why had she paid the mortgage, knowing how dead set he was against it, if she hadn't been planning to file for divorce? The answer was always the same, and she had given it to him. She had never tried to hide it. She loved him.

The realization staggered him anew, and he had to stop to wipe the sweat from his face, even though the temperature was only in the thirties. Maddie loved him. She had tried to tell him when he'd been yelling all those insults at her, and he hadn't listened.

Savagely he jerked the wire tight and hammered in the staple to hold it. Crow had a bitter taste to it, but he was going to have to eat a lot of it if he wanted Maddie to come back to him. He'd gone off the deep end and acted as if she were just like April, even though he knew better. April had never enjoyed living in Montana, while Maddie had wallowed in it like a delighted child. This was the life she wanted.

She loved him enough to take the chance on paying off the mortgage, knowing how angry he would be but doing it anyway because it would save the ranch for him. She had put him before herself, and that was the true measure of love, but he'd been too much of a blind, stubborn ass to admit it.

His temper had gotten him into a hell of a mess, and he didn't have anyone to blame but himself. He had to stop letting April's greed blight his life; he had to stop seeing other people through April-embittered eyes. That was the worst thing she had done to him, not ruining him financially, but ruining the way he had seen other people. He'd even admitted it to himself the day he had met Maddie; if he had run across her before marrying April, he would have been after her with every means at his disposal, and he would have gotten her, too. He would have chased her across every state in the country if necessary, and put her in his bed before she could get away. As it was, he hadn't been able to resist her for long. Even if the schoolteacher—he couldn't even remember her name—had said yes, he would have found some way of getting out of it. Maddie had been the only one he'd wanted wearing his name from the minute he'd seen her.

Damn. If only foresight were as clear as hindsight, he could have saved himself a big helping of crow.

CHAPTER TWELVE

HE WALKED INTO the café and immediately every eye turned toward him. He was beginning to feel like a damn outcast, the way everyone stopped talking and stared at him whenever he showed his face in town. Floris had come out of the kitchen and was arguing with one of the customers, who had ordered something she thought was stupid, from what he could hear, but she stopped yammering and stared at him, too. Then she abruptly turned and went back into the kitchen, probably to get her spatula.

Madelyn didn't acknowledge him, but no more than a minute had passed before a cup of hot coffee was steaming in front of him. She looked so good it was all he could do to keep from grabbing her. Her hair was in a loose French braid down her back, she wore those loose, chic, pleated jeans and a pair of deck shoes, and an oversize khaki shirt with the shirttails knotted at her waist, the collar turned up and the sleeves rolled, an outfit that looked impossibly stylish even under the apron she wore. He took a closer look at the shirt and scowled. It was *his* shirt! Damn it, when she'd left him she'd taken some of his clothes!

No doubt about it. He had to get that woman back, if only for the sake of his wardrobe.

A few minutes later she put a slice of chocolate pie on the table, and he picked up his fork with a hidden smile. They might be separated, but she was still trying to feed him. He'd always been a little startled by the way she had fussed over him and seen to his comfort, as if she had to protect him. Since he was a great deal bigger than she, it had always seemed incongruous to him. His own protective instincts worked overtime where she was concerned, too, so he supposed it evened out.

Finally he caught her eye and indicated the seat across from him with a jerk of his chin. Her eyebrows lifted at the arrogant summons, and she ignored him. He sighed. Well, what had he expected? He should have learned by now that Maddie didn't respond well to orders—unless she wanted to, for her own reasons.

There was evidently a rush hour in Crook now, at least judging by the number of customers who found it necessary to stop by the café. He wondered dourly if there was an alert system to signal everyone in the county when his truck was parked out front. It was over an hour before the place began to empty, but he waited patiently. The next time she came over with a refill of coffee he said, "Talk to me, Maddie. Please."

Perhaps it was the "please" that got to her, because she gave him a startled look and sat down. Floris came out of the kitchen and surveyed Reese with her hands on her hips, as if wondering why he was still there. He winked at her, the first time he'd ever done anything that playful, and her face filled with outrage just before she whirled to go back to the kitchen.

Maddie laughed softly, having seen the byplay. "You're in her bad books now, listed under 'Sorry Low-Down Husbands Who Play Around.'"

He grunted. "What was I listed under before, 'Sorry Low-Down Husbands Who Don't Play Around'?"

"'Yet,'" she added. "Floris doesn't have a high opinion of men."

"I've noticed." He looked her over closely, examining her face. "How do you feel today?"

"Fine. That's the first thing everyone asks me every day. Being pregnant is a fairly common occurrence, you know, but you'd think no other woman in this county had ever had a baby."

"No one's ever had *my* baby before, so I'm entitled to be interested." He reached across the table and took her hand, gently folding her fingers over his. She was still wearing her wedding ring. For that matter, he was still wearing his. It was the only jewelry he'd ever worn in his life, but he'd liked the looks of that thin gold band on his hand almost as much as he had liked the way his ring looked on Maddie. He played with the ring, twisting it on her finger, reminding her of its presence. "Come home with me, Maddie."

Same tune, same lyrics. She smiled sadly as she repeated her line. "Give me one good reason why I should."

"Because you love me." He said it gently, his fingers tightening on hers. That was the most powerful argument he could think of, the one she couldn't deny.

"I've always loved you. That isn't new. I loved you when I packed my clothes and walked out the door. If it wasn't reason enough to stay, why should it be reason enough to go back?"

Her gray, gray eyes were calm as she looked at him. His chest tightened as he realized it wasn't going to work. She wasn't going to come back to him no matter what argument he used. He'd been on a roller coaster of hope since the day he had seen the station wagon parked out front, but suddenly he was plunging down a deep drop that didn't have an end. Dear God, had he ruined the best thing that had ever happened to him because he hadn't been able to accept it?

There was a thick knot in his throat; he had to swallow before he could speak again. "Do you...do you mind if I check up on you every day or so? Just to make sure you're feeling okay. And I'd like to go with you when you have a doctor's appointment, if you don't mind."

Now Maddie had to swallow at her sudden impulse to cry. She had never seen Reese diffident before, and she didn't like it. He was bold and arrogant and quick-tempered, and that was just the way she wanted him, as long as he realized a few important facts about their marriage. "This is your baby, too, Reese. I'd never try to cut you out."

He sighed, still playing with her fingers. "I was wrong, sweetheart. I have a phobia about the ranch after what April did to me—I know, you're not April, and I shouldn't take it out on you for what she did eight years ago. You told me, but I didn't listen. So tell me now what I can do to make it up to you."

"Oh, Reese, it isn't a matter of making anything up to me," she cried softly. "I don't have a scorecard with points on it, and after you tally up so many I'll move back to the ranch. It's about us, our relationship, and whether we have any future together."

"Then tell me what you're still worried about. Baby, I can't fix it if I don't know what it is."

"If you don't know what it is, then nothing *can* fix it."

"Are we down to riddles now? I'm not any good at mind reading," he warned. "Whatever you want, just say it right out. I can deal with reality, but guessing games aren't my strong suit."

"I'm not jerking you around. I'm not happy with this situation, either, but I'm not going back until I know for certain we have a future. That's the way it is, and I won't change my mind."

Slowly he stood up and pulled some bills out of his pocket. Maddie held up her hand dismissively. "Never mind, this one's on me. I get good tips," she said with a crooked smile.

He looked down at her with a surge of hunger that almost took him apart, and he didn't try to resist it. He leaned down and covered her mouth with his, tilting her head back so he could slant his lips more firmly over hers, his tongue sliding between her automatically parted lips. They had made love too often, their senses were too attuned to each other, for it to be anything but overwhelmingly right. She made one of her soft little sounds, and her tongue played with his, her mouth responding. If they had been alone the kiss would have ended in lovemaking; it was that simple, that powerful. No other woman in his life had ever gotten to him the way Maddie did.

The café was totally silent as the few customers still there watched with bated breath. The situation between Reese Duncan and his spirited wife was the best entertainment the county had seen in years.

"Harrummph!"

Reese lifted his head, his lips still shiny from the kiss. The loud interruption had come from Floris, who had left the sanctuary of the kitchen to protect her waitress. At least that was what Reese thought, since she had bypassed the spatula in favor of a butcher knife.

"I don't hold with none of that carrying-on in my place," she said, scowling at him.

He straightened and said softly but very clearly, "Floris, what you need is a good man to give you some loving and cure that sour disposition."

The smile she gave him was truly evil in intent. She gestured with the butcher knife. "The last fool that tried drew back a nub."

It always happened. Some people just didn't know when to keep out of something. The cowboy who had gotten in the argument with her the first time Reese had brought Maddie in just had to stick his oar in now. "Yeah, when was that, Floris?" he asked. "Before or after the Civil War?"

She turned on him like a she-bear on fresh meat. "Hell, boy, it was your daddy, and you're the best he could do with what he had left!"

IT WAS THE end of April. Spring was coming on fast, but Reese couldn't take the pleasure in the rebirth of the land that he usually did. He rattled around in the house, more acutely aware of its emptiness now than he had ever been before. He was busy, but he wasn't content. Maddie still wasn't home.

She had given him financial security with her legacy from her grandmother. Without the remaining payments of the huge mortgage hanging over him, he could use the money from the sale of last year's beef to expand, just as he had originally planned. For that matter, he could take out another loan with the ranch as collateral and start large-scale ranching again, with enough cowhands to help him do it right. Because of Maddie, he could now put the ranch back on a par with what it used to be, even with the reduced acreage. She had never seen it as it had been, probably couldn't imagine the bustle and life in a large, profitable cattle ranch.

He needed to make some sort of decision and make it soon. If he were going to expand, he needed to get working on it right now.

But his heart wasn't in it. As much as he had always loved ranching, as deeply as his soul was planted in this majestically beautiful range, he didn't have the enthusiasm for it that he'd always had before. Without Maddie, he didn't much care.

But she was right; it was their baby's heritage. For that reason he had to take care of it to the best of his ability.

Life was always a fluid series of options. The circumstances and options might change from day to day, but there was always a set of choices to be made, and now he had to make a very important one.

If he expanded on his own it would take all his capital and leave him without anything in reserve if another killing blizzard nearly wiped him out. If he went to the bank for another loan, using the ranch as collateral, he would be putting himself back in the same position Maddie had just gotten him out of. He had no doubt he could make it, given that he would be able to reinvest all of the money in the ranch instead of paying it out to a grasping ex-wife, but he'd had enough of bank loans.

That left an investor. Robert Cannon was brilliant; he'd make one hell of a partner. And Reese did have a very clear business mind, so he could see all the advantages of a partnership. Not only would it broaden his financial base, he would be able to diversify, so the survival of the ranch wouldn't come down to a matter of how severe the winter was. The land was his own legacy to his child.

He picked up the telephone and punched the numbers on the card Robert had given him at Christmas.

When he put the receiver down half an hour later, it was all over except the paperwork. He and Robert dealt very well together, two astute men who were able to hammer out a satisfactory deal with a minimum of words. He felt strange, a little light-headed, and it took him a while to realize what had happened. He had voluntarily put his trust in someone else, surrendering his totalitarian control of the ranch; moreover, his new partner was a member of his wife's family, something he never could have imagined a year before. It was as if he had finally pulled free of the morass of hatred and resentment that had been dragging on him for years. April, finally, was in the past. He had made a mistake in his first choice of a wife; smart people learned from their mistakes and went on with their lives. He had learned, all right, but he hadn't gotten on with living until Maddie had taught him how. Even then he had clung to his bitter preconceptions until he had ruined his marriage.

God, he'd crawl on his hands and knees if it would convince her to come back.

As the days passed he slowly became desperate enough to do just that, but before the need inside him became uncontrollable, he received a phone call that knocked the wind out of him. The call was from April's sister, Erica. April was dead, and he was the main beneficiary in her will; would he please come?

Erica met him at JFK. She was a tall, lean, reserved woman, only two years older than April, but she had always seemed more like an aunt than a sister. Already there was a startling streak of gray in the dark hair waving back from her forehead, one she made no attempt to hide. She held out her hand to him in a cool, distant manner. "Thank you for coming, Reese. Given the circumstances, it's more than I expected and certainly more than we deserve."

He shrugged as he shook her hand. "A year ago I would have agreed with you."

"What's happened in the past year?" Her gaze was direct.

"I remarried. I got back on my feet financially."

Her eyes darkened. She had gray eyes, too, he noticed, though not that soft, slumberous dove gray of Maddie's eyes. "I'm sorry about what happened in the divorce. April was, too, after it was over, but there didn't seem to be any way to make amends. And I'm glad you remarried. I hope you're very happy with your wife."

He would be, he thought, if he could only get her to live with him, but he didn't say that to Erica. "Thank you. We're expecting a baby around the end of October."

"Congratulations." Her severe face lightened for a moment, and she actually smiled, but when the smile faded he saw the tiredness of her soul. She was grieving for her sister, and it couldn't have been easy for her to call him.

"What happened to April?" he asked. "Was she ill?"

"No, not unless you want to call it an illness of the spirit. She remarried, too, you know, less than a year after your divorce, but she was never happy and divorced him a couple of years ago."

It was on the tip of his tongue to ask if she'd taken Number Two to the cleaners, too, but he bit it back. It would be petty of him in the face of Erica's grief. Once he would have said it, once he had been bitter enough that he wouldn't have cared who he wounded. Maddie had changed that.

"She had started drinking heavily," Erica continued. "We tried to convince her to get therapy, to control it, and for a while she tried to stop on her own. But she was sad, Reese, so sad. You could see it in her eyes. She was tired of living."

He drew in a sharp breath. "Suicide?"

"Not technically. Not intentionally. At least, I don't think so. I can't let myself think it was. But she couldn't stop drinking, because it was the only solace she had. The night she died, she'd been drinking heavily and was driving back from Cape Cod. She went to sleep, or at least they think that's what happened, and she became one more statistic on drunk driving." Erica's voice was calm and unemotional, but the pain was in her eyes. She reached out and awkwardly touched his arm, a woman who found it as difficult to receive comfort as she did to give it.

On the taxi ride into the city he asked, "Why did she make me her main beneficiary?"

"Guilt, I think. Maybe love. She was so wild about you in the beginning, and so bitter after the divorce. She was jealous of the ranch, you know. After the divorce, she told me she would rather you'd had a mistress than own that ranch, because she could fight another woman, but that chunk of ground had a hold on you that no woman could equal. That's why she went after the ranch in the divorce, to punish you." She gave him a wry smile. "God, how vindictive people can be. She couldn't see that she simply wasn't the type of wife you needed. You didn't like the same things, didn't want the same things out of life. When you didn't love her as much as you loved the ranch, she thought it was a flaw in her rather than accepting it as the difference between two very different people."

Reese had never thought of April in that light, never seen their marriage and subsequent divorce through her eyes. The only thing he had seen in her had been the bitterness, and that was what he had allowed to color his life. It was a blow to learn the color had been false, as if he had been wearing tinted lenses that had distorted everything.

He spent the night in a hotel, the sort of hotel he had once taken for granted. It felt strange to be back on firm financial ground again, and he wondered if he had ever truly missed the trappings of wealth. It was nice to be able to afford the posh minisuite, but he wouldn't have minded a plain motel. The years without money had rearranged his priorities.

The reading of the will the next day didn't take much time. April's family, too caught up in their grief to be hostile, was subdued. So was her father. April had thoroughly thought out the disposal of her possessions, as if she had anticipated her death. She divided her jewelry and personal possessions among family members, likewise the small fortune in stocks and bonds she had owned. It was her bequest to him that left him stunned.

"To Gideon Reese Duncan, my former husband, I leave the amount of his divorce settlement to me. Should he precede me in death, the same amount shall be given to his heirs in a gesture of fairness too long delayed."

The lawyer droned on, but Reese didn't hear any of it. He couldn't take it in. He was in shock. He leaned forward and braced his elbows on his knees, staring at the Oriental rug under his feet. She had given it all back, and in doing so had shown him the stark futility of the years of hatred.

The most ironic thing was that he had already let go of it. The inner darkness hadn't been able to withstand Maddie's determination. Even if he had never been able to rebuild the ranch to its former size, he would have been happy as long as he had Maddie. He had laughed with her and made love with her, and somewhere along the way his obsession had changed into a love so powerful that now he couldn't live without her, he could only exist.

His heart suddenly squeezed so painfully that he almost grabbed his chest. Hell! How could he have been so stupid?

Come home with me.

Give me one good reason why I should.

That was all she'd asked for, one good reason, but he hadn't given it to her. He'd thrown out reasons, all right, but not the one she'd been asking for, the one she needed. She'd all but told him what it was, but he'd been so caught up in what he needed that he hadn't paid any attention to what *she* needed. How simple it was, and now he knew what to say.

Give me one good reason why I should.

Because I love you.

HE STRODE THROUGH the door of Floris's café and stood in the middle of the room. The increase in customers was still going strong, maybe because Floris was safely isolated in the kitchen and Maddie was out on the floor charming everyone with her lazy drawl and sexy walk.

As usual, silence fell when he entered and everyone turned to look at him. Maddie was behind the counter, wiping up a coffee spill while she exchanged some good-natured quips with Glenna Kinnaird. She looked up, saw him and went still, her eyes locked on him.

He hooked his thumbs in his belt and winked at her. "Riddle me this, sweetheart. What has two legs, a hard head and acts like a jackass?"

"That's easy," she scoffed. "Reese Duncan."

There was a muffled explosion of suppressed snickers all around them. He could see the amusement in her eyes and had to grin. "How are you feeling?" he asked, his voice dropping to a low, intimate tone that excluded everyone else in the café and made several women draw in their breath.

Her mouth quirked in that self-amusement that made him want to grab her to him. "This isn't one of my good days. The only thing holding me together is static cling."

"Come home with me, and I'll take care of you."

She looked him in the eye and said quietly, "Give me one good reason why I should."

Right there in front of God and most of Crook, Montana, he drew in a deep breath and took the gamble of a lifetime, his words plain and heard by all, because no one was making even the pretense of not listening.

"Because I love you."

Maddie blinked, and to his surprise he saw her eyes glitter with tears. Before he could start forward, however, her smile broke through like sunshine through a cloud bank. She didn't take the time to go around the counter; she climbed on top of it and slid off on the other side. "It's about time," she said as she went into his arms.

The customers broke into applause, and Floris came out of the kitchen. She sniffed and looked displeased when she saw Madelyn hanging in Reese's arms with her feet off the floor. "I suppose this means I've got to get another waitress," she muttered.

Someone muttered back, "Hell, Floris, if you'll just stay in the kitchen we'll find you another waitress."

"It's a deal," she said, and startled everyone in the café by actually smiling.

He didn't wait to get back to the house before he made love to her; as soon as they were on Duncan land he stopped the truck and pulled her astride him. Madelyn thought her heart would burst as she listened to his roughly muttered words of love and lust and need. She couldn't get enough of touching him; she wanted to sink into his skin, and she tried to.

When they finally got to the house he carried her inside and up the stairs to their bedroom, where he placed her on the big bed and began stripping her. She laughed, a drugged, wanton sound, as she stretched languidly. "Again?"

"I want to see you," he said, his voice strained. When she was naked he was silent, struck dumb and enchanted by the changes in her body. They were still slight, but obvious to him because he knew every inch of her. There was just beginning to be a faint curve to her belly, and her breasts were a little rounder, even firmer than before, her nipples darkened to a lush reddish brown. He leaned forward and circled one with his tongue, and her entire body quivered. "God, I love you," he said, and laid his head on her belly, his arms locked around her hips.

Madelyn slid her fingers into his hair. "It took you long enough," she said gently.

"What I lack in quickness, I make up in staying power."

"Meaning?"

"That I'll still be telling you that fifty years from now." He paused and turned his head to kiss her stomach. "I have something else to tell you."

"Is it good?"

"I think so. Things are going to be changing around here pretty soon."

"How?" She looked suspicious. "I'm not sure I want things to change."

"I have a new partner. I called Robert a week or so ago, and he bought in. We'll be expanding in a big way as soon as I can get started on it. This is now the Duncan and Cannon ranch."

Madelyn burst into laughter, startling him into lifting his head from her stomach. "Whatever you do," she said, "don't call it the D and C. I don't think I could live on a ranch named after a surgical procedure!"

He grinned, feeling everything in him come alive under the magic spell of her laughter. "It'll keep the same name," he said.

"Good." Slowly her laughter faded, and she gave him a somber look. "Why did you call him?"

"Because I trust you," he said simply. "Through you, I can trust him. Because it was a good business decision. Because I wanted to show you how a really good ranch operates. Because we're having a baby. Because, damn it, I'm too damn proud to be satisfied with a second-rate operation. Is that enough reasons?"

"The first one was good enough." She put her hands on his face and stared at him, her heart in his eyes. It rattled him, even while it made him feel as if he could conquer the world, to see how much Maddie loved him. He started to lean down to kiss her when she said seriously, "Did you know that a ten-gallon hat will really only hold about three quarts?"

ON THE THIRD of November, Madelyn lay in a labor room in Billings, holding Reese's hand and trying to concentrate on her breathing. She had been there over twenty-four hours and she was exhausted, but the nurses kept telling her everything was fine. Reese was unshaven and had dark circles under his eyes. Robert was somewhere outside, wearing a rut in the tile of the hall.

"Give me another one," she said. Reese was looking desperate, but she needed something to get her mind off herself.

"India ink really comes from China."

"You're really scraping the bottom of the barrel, aren't you? Let's see." A contraction interrupted her, and she squeezed his hand as it surged and peaked, then fell off. When she could speak again she said, "The sounds of stomach growling are called borborygmus." She gave him a triumphant look.

He cradled her hand against his cheek. "You've been reading the dictionary again, and that's cheating. I've got a good one. The San Diego Chargers got their name because the original owner also owned the Carte Blanche credit card company. 'Charge' is what he wanted the cardholders to say."

She laughed, but the sound was abruptly cut off as another contraction seized her. This one was a little different in intensity, and in the way it made her feel. She panted her way through it, staring at the monitor with blurring eyes so she could see the mechanical confirmation of what she felt. She lay back against his arm and said weakly, "I don't think it's going to be much longer."

"Thank God." He didn't know if he could hold out

much longer. Watching her in pain was the hardest thing he had ever done, and he was seriously considering limiting the number of their children to one. He kissed her sweaty temple. "I love you, sweetheart."

That earned him one of her slow smiles. "I love you, too." Another contraction.

The nurse checked her and smiled. "You're right, Mrs. Duncan, it won't be much longer. We'd better get you into delivery."

He was with her during delivery. The doctor had kept careful watch on the growing baby and didn't think she'd have any trouble delivering it. Reese wondered violently if the doctor's idea of trouble differed from his. It was thirty-six hours since her labor had begun. Less than half an hour after he'd told her about the San Diego Chargers, Reese was holding his red, squalling son in his hands.

Madelyn watched him through tear-blurred eyes, smiling giddily. The expression on Reese's face was so intense and tender and possessive that she could barely stand it. "Eight pounds, two ounces," he murmured to the infant. "You just barely made it under the wire."

Madelyn laughed and reached for both husband and son. Reese settled the baby in her arms and cradled her in his, unable to take his eyes from the both of them. He'd never seen anything so beautiful in his life, even if her hair was matted with sweat and coming loose from her braid. God, he felt good! Exhausted but good.

She yawned and rested her head against his shoulder. "I think we did a good job," she announced, examining the baby's tiny fingers and damp dark hair. "I also think I'm going to sleep for a week."

When she was in her room, just before she did go to sleep, she heard Reese say it again. "I love you, sweetheart." She was too sleepy to answer, but she reached out and felt him take her hand. Those were three words she never got tired of hearing, though she'd heard them often during the past months.

Reese sat and watched her as she slept, a smile in his eyes. Slowly his eyelids drooped as he succumbed to his weariness, but not once during his sleep did he turn loose of her hand.

* * * * *